SPOOF!

The diaries of the late
Curly Cradock

DISCLAIMER

For information regarding permission, please write to:
info@barringerpublishing.com
Barringer Publishing, Naples, Florida
www.barringerpublishing.com

Cover, graphics, and layout by Linda S. Duider
Cape Coral, Florida

ISBN: 978-1-954396-91-3

Printed in the UK

To Genghis, the kindest person you'll never meet

Prologue

Tim Berners-Lee invented the worldwide web in 1989 and the first news-related website was the University of Florida's journalism site, which launched in October 1993

SPOOF! is set during the last years of the twentieth century. It's based on the diaries of the late Curly Cradock, a convicted Tasmanian banknote forger with a fondness for alcohol, who becomes an early pioneer of the Internet and an unexpected media sensation.

From a forgotten broom cupboard in the City of London, Curly persuades thousands of journalists from around the world to write and to broadcast complete cobblers that will, at no cost to himself, provide him with the necessary means to make his new business a global brand.

Typifying his tactics of concocting false but dramatically eye-catching stories is the occasion when Curly issues a press release about a football fan so concerned about the risk of England's failure to win the World Cup that he insures himself against emotional trauma. The story is initially picked up by two dozen British newspapers and is then broadcast by terrestrial and satellite channels in the UK. Within a week it's appeared in 160 countries across six continents and is translated into more than 200 languages.

Readers get to know and love a close-knit group of characters. They include Tracey, an Essex girl with a heart of gold; Genghis, Curly's younger brother, who has Down syndrome; Araminta, a beautiful, sophisticated and highly intelligent hooker; Ralph, a promiscuous gay banker; Doug, a well-endowed but under-paid journalist; Mavis, a sex-mad Jewish refugee; and Rod, the famous TV comedian and entertainer.

The book is shamelessly non-woke and is unburdened by the constraints of political correctness. It notably contains periodic, vintage, timeless, artisanal humour that may upset gingers, hairdressers, liberals, the British Royal Family and members of Alcoholics Anonymous.

Monday 1 April 1996
BBC Panorama first broadcast the Swiss spaghetti tree harvest spoof in 1957

At just a few minutes to 9am, I arrive at the global headquarters of my new company, NOB. It's situated in a forgotten broom cupboard in a Lime Street office complex, in the heart of the City of London's insurance district.

It's just over a week now since I was released from a three-year stretch at HMP Belmarsh for forgery. I must have been completely bonkers to think it was a good idea to repay the huge losses I made as a Lloyd's Name with forged banknotes. Nevertheless, there's no point dwelling on the past. The best way to atone for my sins is for me to make NOB a success and to expose a mis-selling scandal of epic proportions that both the media and financial regulators have chosen to ignore. My probation officer, Fred, has asked if I can provide work experience for his niece, Tracey. I could do with a bit of low-cost help. I certainly can't afford to pay for a PA.

I carefully push my desk around 45 degrees to make room for the two of us. There are no seats in the tiny room, just two discarded Armitage Shanks lavatory units. They're jolly comfortable and I wonder if I should have them plumbed in.

There's a knock at the door. It's Tracey, an Essex girl through-and-through, with white stilettos and a skirt so short it looks more like a generous cummerbund. She's a few minutes late, but all credit to her for finding NOB's hidden HQ.

I introduce myself and ask Tracey to tell me about herself and her work experience. She says she's from Braintree, that she can type and that she knows how to use a fax machine. She even claims she can unblock a paper jam in a photocopier.

"Any questions?" I ask her.

"Yeah," she says. "I recognise you from TV. Are you in Coronation Street?"

"Sadly not," I say. "I'm just the doppelgänger of global superstar Curly Watts. My real name's Johnnie, but everyone calls me Curly because they think I look like him. Any other questions?"

"Yeah," she says. "What does NOB stand for?"

"It stands for Norris Owen Brown," I reply.

This was my second attempt at choosing an acronym from names picked at random from the phone book. It's a bit of a feeble set of names, I admit, but better than the first lot, Foster Underwood King.

"And what does NOB *do*?" Tracey asks.

"Good question!" I reply. "We're going to sell ethical PPI."

"Okay. And what does PPI mean?"

"Another good question," I reply. "It stands for payment protection insurance." I explain to her that it's a type of insurance that people buy to pay their bills if they lose their jobs or become disabled. Then I ask, "Any more questions?"

"Yes," says Tracey. "You've got a strange accent. Where are you from?"

"I've lived in England since 1965, but I'm originally from Hobart in Tasmania."

"No, where do you *really* come from?" she says.

"Straight up, I'm from Tasmania," I reply. "Now I live in Pimlico, as the commute from Tasmania takes too long."

"Is that where Count Dracula comes from?" asks Tracey.

"Tasmania? Yes, I could see his castle from my bedroom window," I reply.

I offer her the job of executive assistant and ask her to arrange a series of appointments for me with my business contacts from the time I was a Lloyd's underwriter.

Tracey transmits her loud, excited voice and coarse laughter down the phone. As she puts down the receiver, I ask her as politely as I can, "Can you take it down a notch?"

She immediately starts to unbutton her blouse.

I raise my eyebrows and say, "I meant the volume."

"Oh!" she says. Picking up the phone again to arrange a meeting for me, she lowers her voice to a husky whisper. That's much better. If she can keep this up, she'll definitely be an asset to NOB.

After a successful series of calls, she hangs up and I ask her to type up a page of documentation from my notes. She does so, then shakes a bottle of Tippex with which to correct her typos. The corrections appear to apply to about one word in three.

No matter. She's a cheap hire.

At 12.30pm and not a moment too soon, I invite her for a quick lunchtime welcome drink. The two of us take the lift to the ground floor and cross the road to the Grapes.

We don't make it back to the broom cupboard.

Midnight. Home, without my credit card.

Tuesday 2 April 1996
The Hobart Mercury was first published in 1854

I'm yet to get a key cut for Tracey. I ring to advise her not to show up until after lunch, as I've a 10am meeting with her uncle Fred in an unoccupied office on the other side of the corridor that today I'm pretending is my own.

I take the lift to the ground floor at 10am, just as Fred turns up. He greets me stoically.

"Good morning, Fred!" I reply. "You didn't mention to me that Tracey's extensive telephone experience actually comes from her time working for a Braintree adult chat line."

"You f*cked up and trusted me!" he replies.

After an hour, the meeting's over. I insincerely bid Fred farewell and return to the broom cupboard, where I find myself able to get down to an uninterrupted couple of hours of business before I cross the road, gasping for a pint, to the Grapes.

An hour later, back at work, I excitedly scribble down a draft of NOB's first-ever press release. It details PAYMENTSAFE, our new ethical PPI policy, which is the first of its kind to have all the unfair exclusions removed and which will pay out for cancer, heart disease, diabetes, AIDS and all other chronic conditions. Furthermore, it will not penalise smokers, gay men, women who become pregnant or anyone who's injured in a terrorist attack.

I ask Tracey to type up the press release for me, before discovering that the fax machine has broken down.

Determined not to allow the fax to get in the way of a good story, I send my new assistant to Staples, the stationers in Leadenhall Market, to get the press release photocopied 50 times, before we pop them into envelopes, then set out to deliver them by hand to newspaper headquarters across London.

In order to impress Fred by keeping Tracey in some form of employment, I appoint her to the additional role of media executive, so she's now the first point of contact for journalists when they call with press enquiries. I ask her to use her posh accent when speaking to them – the one she tells me she picked up at a young offenders' institution in Cheltenham.

Wednesday 3 April 1996
The Scotsman was first published in 1817

To the broom cupboard early, carrying a bag full of today's newspapers, for an appointment with Alan, the fax repair man.

Just before he leaves, Alan hits a button on the machine. Suddenly, dozens of messages stored in the machine's memory begin to whir out in one long roll. NOB's back in business!

However, as I sit down to read the papers, I experience a slow-motion, sinking feeling. Tracey and I spent hours yesterday hand-delivering copies of the PAYMENTSAFE press release, yet every national newspaper editor appears to have ignored it. I understand the story may be too dry and not sensational enough for the main news pages, but I expected it at least to make it into one or two of the business pages.

Nada! Not a single mention in any of them.

At just after 9am, Tracey bursts into the broom cupboard. "Sorry I'm late!" she cries. As she hangs up her coat, I ask her to call up a few printers to ask for quotes to have NOB's insurance application forms printed.

Excitedly, she turns to me and exclaims, "Del my boyfriend's a printer!" She reaches into her handbag and passes me one of his business cards. With a two-tone grey design on thick card, it looks and feels very professional. "I'm sure he'll do you a good rate!" she says.

Straightaway she picks up the receiver and calls him. She explains to him why she's ringing, then holds the phone to her chest and says, "Del wants to know what typeface you prefer."

"What about the one used by the Big Bristols Channel?" I suggest. Tracey looks puzzled as she listens to his reply, then simply hands me the receiver.

"Hello?" I say.

I hear Del's voice for the first time. "Curly," he says, "I wouldn't go with the Big Bristols Channel typeface. It was designed by Eric Gill, who used to f*ck just about anything, including his children, sister, mother, pet..."

"Okay, can we just go with Helvetica?"

He agrees. I hang up and head out to a meeting with my friend, Jeff, a legal expenses underwriter, in the nearby Lloyd's building.

Just as I reach the edge of Leadenhall Market, I pass Radio Rentals, where my attention's caught by a TV screen in the window displaying the image of agriculture minister John Gummer. He's smiling as he force-feeds a burger to his four-year-old daughter. It's accompanied by a caption revealing that scientists claim to have proved that mad cow disease can now pass from cattle to humans.

When I meet Jeff, I tell him about John Gummer and he tells me that he reckons there's zero chance that CJD will be a catastrophe for humanity, but he predicts that the press will blow the risk out of all proportion, using scaremongering tactics designed to frighten readers into buying more of their newspapers.

I duly concoct a news story that ticks every box. I'll announce the recent launch of the world's first PPI policy to cover CJD. We'll see if *that* gets any news coverage. However, still smarting at having been spurned by the media this week, I decide against going straight to the national press. I resolve instead to use guerrilla-style tactics. I call up *Insurance Now!* – the trade press equivalent of ship hull manufacturers' favourite, *Rivet Monthly*.

One of the reporters, Doug, takes my call. I introduce myself, before telling him that I've an exclusive news story for him. With his full attention grabbed, I inform him that NOB is the world's first insurance company to offer cover against contracting CJD. He asks me if I've actually insured anyone yet.

"John Gummer and a major burger chain," I reply, making it up as I go along. Doug sounds excited and he asks me which burger chain I've insured.

Thinking on the hoof again, I say, "I'm unfortunately bound by client confidentiality."

I choose this moment to make a pivotal move and suggest he might make a quid or two by selling the story to the national press. After all, if they won't listen to me, they might at least pay some attention to the story coming from another journalist.

Thursday 4 April 1996
The British Broadcasting Corporation (BBC) was founded in 1922

I call Doug to find out whether he's written the story. He has, he tells me, proudly informing me that he threw in some of the details I'd given him about the projected pace at which CJD could spread and destroy the lives of meat-eaters, despite the otherwise fantastic opportunity that burger outlets provide to eat a healthy and well-balanced diet (sick).

He then tells me that he called national Sunday broadsheet *Missionary Impossible* and, in return for £50, faxed the story over to Mark, the paper's news editor.

To thank me, Doug gives me some free advice, recommending that in future I should write press releases and send them exclusively to the UK Press Distribution Network. If they like a story, he tells me, they'll distribute it, at no cost to NOB, to newspapers, TV and radio stations all over the world.

I hope he's right. It'd be handy for raising NOB's profile.

As soon as I return to the broom cupboard, with the help of Directory Enquiries I call the news agency that Doug mentioned. I'm eventually put through to the personal finance editor, Jeremy, who explains the approach his organisation takes to distributing stories to the global media. Encouraged by what he tells me, I arrange to buy him a few beers next week.

A minute or two later Tracey, hanging up from a call, asks me what I'm doing after work. I'm not sure, but it'll involve drink, I tell her.

"Wanna meet Del?" she asks.

"I'd love to!" I reply.

We settle for the Grapes. It's unusually quiet as we wander in from across the road and the two of us sit at my favourite table near the bar. I give the barman my credit card for us to run a tab, then order a couple of pints for me and Tracey and a rum for Del.

Five minutes later, in walks a tall, fit-looking West Indian who spots Tracey immediately across the bar and comes straight over to our table. He leans down to give his girlfriend a kiss, then turns to me and we warmly shake hands before discussing business.

"So, I gather you do business cards, brochures, corporate..." He stops me mid-flow. "I do the lot, Curly," he says. "Design, printing, laminating – you name it."

"Banknotes?" I ask.

Del takes a drag on his roll-up. "Too risky," he says, exhaling thoughtfully. I concur, briefly telling him about my own misadventures, my time in Belmarsh and my subsequent tussles with Fred.

"Like I say, too risky," he says, nodding sagely and stubbing out his cigarette.

Friday 5 April 1996
The American Broadcasting Company (ABC) was founded in 1943

Today's Good Friday and I wake up at dawn, fretting over my failure to get NOB into the media. I've managed to make inroads with Doug's help, but that's just one-off good fortune. I need to come up with a more focused, long-term strategy. For this, I must seek serious advice.

I decide to pay a visit to Belmarsh to see my friend and former cellmate Samuel, or Sambo as he's known to his closest friends. He's a former emeritus professor of computer science who's serving a ten-year prison sentence for manslaughter.

I patiently make my way through security to the visitors' room. On the way I recognise a few faces, including one or two of the prison warders. Eventually, Sambo's led in to see me. He's in good form and he seems flattered to be asked for help.

I explain to him my predicament. When I finish, he asks me, "Have you heard of the worldwide web?"

"No," I reply. "What is it?"

"Well, it was invented by this guy I know called Tim and it's commonly abbreviated to the web."

I frown, puzzled.

Patiently, Sambo continues. "It's an information system where documents and other resources are identified by uniform resource locators."

"What the f*ck's one of those?" I ask.

He pauses to think. "In the same way that flats, houses and offices have a street address, web pages have unique addresses to help people to locate them," he says. "That's a uniform resource locator. You need to get one."

He continues to explain patiently about this information system. Slowly grasping what he's telling me, I ask if he can make any suggestions for my own uniform resource locator. He suggests that www.nob.co.uk is the obvious choice and he advises me to look to see if it's available.

"How do I do that?" I ask.

"Try looking in Yellow Pages," he suggests. "When you've got one, come back and see me."

We chat until visiting time is over. My head brimming with things I need to do, I bid Sambo a fond farewell.

Driving away from my former abode, I'm reminded how great it is to be a free man.

Sunday 7 April 1996
The Sunday Times was first published in 1821

I'm enjoying a leisurely breakfast when I see that *Missionary Impossible* has taken the bait from Doug. The lead story of the paper's *Cash!* section informs readers that CJD insurance cover has been launched by NOB to protect worried meat-eaters, including John Gummer and the employees of an international burger chain. Okay, this may not be true, but anyone who purchases PAYMENTSAFE will automatically be covered for CJD and every other medical condition known to the NHS.

To celebrate my media triumph, I decide to pay a visit to Floyd's, my favourite coffee shop in Clerkenwell, to treat myself to a cappuccino while I finish the *Churchgoers Gazette* crossword.

As Edward, the manager, hands me my coffee, I listen to a conversation from the adjacent table. A boy of perhaps eight years old asks his mother, "Why did you call my sister Teresa?"

She looks at him and explains, "Well, I love Easter and Teresa is an anagram of Easter."

He smiles and says, "Thanks, Mum."

His mother nods at her son and says, "No worries, Alan."

Chuckling into my coffee's froth, I look down at the crossword and notice the clue for two across is, "What Jesus was nailed to."

Tuesday 9 April 1996
Independent Television News (ITN) was founded in 1955

As I make my way back to work after an uneventful Easter, I spot a pile of Yellow Pages in the reception area. I pick one of them up and, when I'm back at my desk, I excitedly remove the plastic wrapper, open the directory and look inside for uniform resource locators. There's nothing there! What else did Sambo call them? Got it! Web addresses. But there's no listing for them either.

I keep searching through the flimsy pages before I eventually find a single entry, for a company called Parminder's Web Design in East Ham. I pick up the phone to give the business a call and Parminder himself answers. He seems to possess a very sound understanding of uniform resource locators, so we agree to meet tomorrow. He tells me where to find his studio which, he says, is located behind a shop called Pen Island. I assume it sells stationery.

Meanwhile, NOB's first client for PAYMENTSAFE is confirmed today. It's my old, gay friend Ralph, who works at the Bank of England. He's a dead ringer for Ted Heath who, as we know, was certainly not gay. It's funny to think that NOB's first pound is going to be a pink one.

Wednesday 10 April 1996
The Newham Recorder was first published in 1968

To East Ham. Walking from the Tube station, I see ahead of me the shop that Parminder mentioned. As I approach it, I observe that it's not like any stationery store I've ever seen before. The windows are blacked-out and everyone I see entering or leaving seems to be keen to conceal his identity.

I soon find my way to the studio itself, which I'm quietly amused to note is even more decrepit than the broom cupboard. Getting down to business, I explain to Parminder, "Basically what I need is a uniform resource locator."

"You mean a URL," he says.

"Do I?" I reply. He proceeds to give me a highly detailed description that I vaguely understand, then he tells me the cost of the URL is twenty-five quid.

A few minutes later he beckons me round to look at his computer screen, where I see that www.nob.co.uk is officially registered online.

"So, that's my URL?" I ask.

"Yes," says Parminder. "If you'd like me to build you a website, that'll be £2,000."

Blimey! That's much more than I'd expected to pay. I think for a moment then reach for the secret compartment in my briefcase and hand him a hefty bunch of £20 notes, without mentioning they're from my leftover stash of forgeries.

Parminder's delighted. "However," he says, "before I get started, I need NOB's logo and the four Fs."

What the f*ck are the four Fs, I wonder. We're in East London, so perhaps he means a fahsend fevvers on a frush's froat, but he soon puts me right.

"The four Fs? Simple," he says. "They're who the f*ck, what the f*ck, where the f*ck and, most importantly of all, why the f*ck. In other words, who you are, what you do, where you operate from and why people should choose you."

Reminded of how much more intelligent so many Asians are than most of the rest of us, I make a note to provide Parminder with this information before we arrange to meet again next week.

Succumbing to an obsession I have with anniversaries, on arriving back in the broom cupboard, I mention to Tracey that a hundred years ago today, the modern Olympic Games began.

Thursday 11 April 1996
The Press Association was founded in 1868 and sent its first press telegram in 1870

I make a trip over the Thames today to meet Jeremy from the UK Press Distribution Network in The Old Thameside Inn, a pub right on edge of the river. I go up to the bar and order a glass of wine for Jeremy and a pint of Pride for myself. When Denzil, the barman, brings the drinks, I notice my pint glass isn't filled up to the top.

"Can you fit a double whisky in there?" I ask him.

"Sure," he says.

"Then can you fill it up with beer?" I ask.

That old chestnut.

"Piss off Curly!" Denzil replies with a smile as he tops up the glass.

Sitting down opposite Jeremy at a table in a corner of the bar, I explain to him that my objective is to raise NOB's profile. To my dismay, he tells me that no one in the media is ever likely to be interested in ethical PPI, nor in the fact that banks are massively ripping off their customers. "What the media are looking for are stories so outlandish that they verge on the ridiculous," he says.

I put my glass down, open my briefcase and pull out the notes I've written about NOB providing CJD insurance to burger-chain workers. "Like this, you mean?" I ask, passing them to him.

Jeremy scans my scribble and nods enthusiastically. "Absolutely perfect!" he says. "Can I keep this?"

"Of course," I say.

We agree that in future NOB will exclusively provide him with all news stories that are outlandish and ridiculous. In return, Jeremy kindly agrees to distribute the PAYMENTSAFE press release, warning me not to expect much media interest, if any at all.

Friday 12 April 1996
The Times was first published in 1785

I head East this morning to Parminder's studio, where I pass him the four Fs information he requested, along with NOB's logo.

He scans the page. "Yeah, this'll do," he says, before giving me a long lecture on website optimisation. I've very little idea what he's talking about, but I'm taken by the words 'metadata', 'keywords', 'funnel' and 'rankings'. Meanwhile Parminder mentions Yahoo! so many times that I think he must be a f*cking cowboy, before I remind myself he is, of course, an Indian.

"How long will it take you to build NOB's website?" I ask him.

"About a week," he replies.

I'm beyond excited. I'm about to make NOB the first company in the UK to sell insurance on the web.

I must buy a computer over the weekend.

Saturday 13 April 1996
The Times published the first newspaper weather forecast in 1861

Bloody April showers. I'm as wet as an otter's pocket this morning as I make my way to the Slippery Slope in Westminster for a weekend pint with Ralph. Just as I'm buying the first round in anticipation of his arrival, he bursts in from the rain and exclaims, "Can you believe it? Yesterday one of my colleagues at the bank called me pretentious! I nearly dropped my honey-cardamom latte!"

Before I can respond, we're interrupted by a Japanese tour guide, who brashly demands to know what direction he can find the 'North of England'.

"My pleasure," I reply. "Follow the signs for the Isle of Wight. When you get off the ferry, turn 180 degrees and seek further directions."

He leaves without a word of thanks. Ralph and I finish our drinks before we head off to Captain Morgan Computers on New Oxford Street for me to buy NOB a reasonably priced computer.

Monday 15 April 1996
The Barking & Dagenham Post was first published in 1923

Taking the District Line east this morning to Dagenham for an early breakfast with Ted, a reporter from the *Dagenham Handshake*, I notice a man opposite me reading the early edition of The *Barking Bash Out*. He's engrossed in the paper as he holds it open before him, which enables me to read the front-page headline: *Newham flooded with fake banknotes!*

I do hope Parminder doesn't find out they were mine.

Back at the broom cupboard, the phone rings. It's Ralph. He wants to know if I can meet him for lunch today at Spongles, a posh bar-restaurant just a ten-minute stroll from the broom cupboard. I hesitate, before he explains, "The client I was due to meet has just cancelled, so this is on expenses."

"On expenses!" I exclaim. "Are you sure that's okay?"

"Of course!" says Ralph. "Rachel my line manager at the bank told me that a cavalier attitude to expenses doesn't constitute impropriety."

Just after midday, I set out to meet him. By the time I arrive, he already has four pints of Black Velvet waiting on our table in solid silver tankards. We each down a gallon of the stuff, before staggering to our table. We spend the next couple of hours eating, talking bollocks and getting pissed.

After the tenth round Ralph stands to visit the lavatory. He turns to me and says, "I refused to believe I was both gay and dyslexic." As I sit looking up at him, trying to work out his point, he exclaims, "I was in Daniel!" He shakes with laughter as he turns and staggers off in the direction of the loo.

At about 5pm I make my way back to Lime Street. Tracey has gone home and I fall asleep at my desk, before I'm woken up by Mavis, the building's buxom, sex-mad cleaning lady who's vacuuming the corridor outside the broom cupboard.

Thursday 18 April 1996
The BBC Home Service first broadcast the Greenwich Time Signal in 1924

My workday begins with a call from Liz, a journalist on the *Mansfield Silly Season*. She's seeking more information about PAYMENTSAFE. After a long chat I hang up, feeling much more confident about selling ethical PPI.

At noon, I make my way to the Elephant, a subterranean bar in Fenchurch Street. There I see that NOB's featured in the early edition of London daily tabloid the *Wheelie Bint!* I can hardly believe that one of the largest circulation newspapers in the UK advises readers to shop around for PPI and actually recommends NOB!

On leaving the pub just before 4pm, I check my mobile for messages. There's a voicemail from my friend, Mike, the chief executive of the English Insurance Agents Association, calling to say he can't make it for drinks. He tells me he'd forgotten that he's been invited to the Ritz this evening for a dinner being hosted by NOB's nemesis, Le Rhinoceros Assurance S.A. – better known in the UK as Rhino Insurance. He apologises for the late notice and says he'd like to meet up next week instead.

Rhino's chief executive, Imelda, is a bully, with an atrocious record of unethical work practices. I heard she laughed when I was sent to Belmarsh, so this might be an appropriate opportunity for me to let her know that I'm now a free man. The Rhino event doesn't start until 8pm, so I reach for my phone again and call Tracey's cousin Lance, son of Fred, who's agreed to help NOB out with marketing. I suggest we meet for a drink this afternoon at Browns, a strippers' pub off the beaten track in Fulham that I've frequented for as long as I've lived in London.

Lance knows immediately which pub I mean and tells me he often meets Tracey there at the weekend. We agree to meet at 5pm. I stop by the broom cupboard to let Tracey know where I'm off to and I tell her she's free to join us if she'd like to see Lance for a quick beer.

"Browns in Fulham? I know it well!" she says.

I walk to Bank station and take the Tube to Fulham Broadway. From there, I saunter on to the pub, where I spot Lance straight away. For some unknown reason he's brought along Fred, who looks distinctly unimpressed.

We take a table at the far end of the bar by the pool table. Fred sits down facing us, with his back to most of the stripping action.

While Lance buys a round, I mention to Fred that NOB's had a good bit of coverage in *Wheelie Bint*.

He screws up his eyes. "F*ckin' odd title!" he exclaims.

"Yeah," I say. "The publisher named it after his wife, Sadie, who's so ugly he only takes her out once a week after dark."

Lance returns from the bar with a tray of drinks, just as a woman whom I vaguely recognise approaches me with a Presto carrier bag, which she drops on the table. "Hoped I'd see you here," she says, before nodding fleetingly to Fred and Lance.

Turning back to me, she says, "Tracey left her coke here last week." Startled, I look down at the bag on the table. Not a great omen.

"I tried a bit," she says. "It's really not good. Tell her she should have a word with her dealer. That shit's not cheap!"

With that, she turns to walk away from the table, just as a new dance song starts to make the walls of the building shake. The woman herself then struts onto the dance floor, where she rhythmically disrobes.

I glance across at Fred, who's looking straight at me, sternly. I plead, "The important thing here is the use of the words 'Tracey', 'she' and 'her'," forgetting for a moment that Fred's her uncle. At this moment, he lifts up one side of the top of the carrier bag to take a look at its contents, in the process revealing a few dozen lottery tickets, each torn into squares and folded like origami.

Fred shakes his head. He looks at me with a blend of anger and disappointment, before standing and putting on his coat. Without a word, he turns and heads straight for the exit.

I stuff Tracey's stash into my briefcase while Lance crosses the floor to the cigarette machine. He returns a couple of minutes later and, brandishing a box of 16 Marlboro, exclaims, "Two quid fifty that cost me! *Bloody* Ken Clarke!"

At this moment, a pretty, young stripper comes over and introduces herself to me as Sophie, before asking me if I'd like to take a private room.

"Do you do role play?" I enquire.

She smiles. "It depends. What are you suggesting?"

"Would you play the chief executive of Rhino Insurance and f*ck the consumer?"

She laughs politely and moves to the next table.

Tracey arrives just as Lance is grabbing his coat. He apologises to Tracey for having to leave early and says he'll see her for a pint at the weekend. The two of us stay for another round and, as I pass her the Presto carrier bag, I ask if she'd like to join me on a trip to the Ritz. "Free booze," I add.

She's in.

It's tipping down with rain as we step out of the pub, where I try to hail a black cab. This takes about half an hour, but eventually we arrive in Piccadilly, soaking wet.

"Shit, it's black tie!" says Tracey, as we approach the function room.

"Leave it to me," I utter quietly. "Good evening, sir!" I say, greeting the maître d'hôtel. "My colleague and I are here for the Rhino Insurance event. Unfortunately, my car was stolen earlier this afternoon and our evening dress went with it, along with our invitations."

"Oh, I'm terribly sorry to hear that. I'm sure they won't mind, sir. Please," he says with a smile, waving us in.

I tell Tracey that we'll only be able to stay for the free pre-dinner booze because of course, as gate crashers, we won't have any formal table-setting.

I take a careful look at the seating plan to get an idea who's going to be there. At that moment, a waiter approaches with a silver tray of Champagne flutes. Tracey and I relieve him of four glasses, before walking through to the central alcohol supply area: an unguarded surface where waiters place bottles of both wine and fizz that are in transit. I grab a couple of bottles, then I fill one of my empty glasses with New World red, before passing the other bottle to Tracey, who does the same.

We stand drinking as hard as we can before dinner, our scheduled time of departure.

With five minutes to go, we're clocked by the unmistakable figure of Imelda.

She strides over to us and asks me, "Who the f*ck invited you, Curly?"

"Hi Imelda," I say. "I like your new hairstyle. It certainly makes your nose look smaller."

"Both of you f*ck off!" she snaps.

As we turn to leave, I pretend to slip. In doing so, I deftly flip over my two flutes of shiraz. The effect this has on Imelda's fawn gown is satisfyingly dramatic.

"Sorry about that!" I call out, as we hurry to the exit.

Terrible waste of wine, but it had to be done.

We jump into a black cab. I tell the driver to take us to Liverpool Street station.

It's 10.50pm. "Just time for a pint," I tell Tracey and I lead her across the road for last orders at one of my favourite pubs, Filthy Fannies.

Friday 19 April 1996
BBC Radio 1, 2, 3 & 4 were all founded in 1967

As promised and right on time, www.nob.co.uk can now be seen on the Web!

Parminder swiftly bursts my bubble. "Just because you've a website doesn't mean that anyone can find it," he warns me. After a further flourish on his computer keyboard he adds, "I've optimised yours for the Yahoo! robot, but you need to get NOB some backlinks."

I'm now completely baffled. I ask him what he means. Looking impatient, Parminder tells me, "The robot is an algorithm that can be manipulated by getting other websites to link back to yours."

"What the f*ck does that mean? I mean, how do I do that?" I ask.

He shakes his head in a mild show of despair, before explaining, "The best backlinks come from press and media organisations."

I screw my eyes up in confusion.

"Look," he says, "whenever you can, you should send out press releases that include your URL. When the stories are published online, they may well include a link back to NOB's website. These are called backlinks."

As I write all this down, he continues. "The more of these backlinks you get, the higher you'll be ranked in Yahoo!" he explains.

Meeting finally over and my head somewhat hurting, I thank Parminder for his free advice. As I leave, I see on his desk an unopened copy of the *Lower Swell Cockfest*. Its lead headline reads: *Mad cow cover at crazy prices!*

I'm due to see Sambo again tomorrow. Perhaps he'll be able to help clarify what Parminder's just told me. With that thought in mind, I cross town to the West End to meet Ralph for a much-needed drink at Foreskinzola.

As I exit the Tube station I buy a copy of the *Psychedelic Yodeller*. The front-page headline screams: *CJD scare!*

Saturday 20 April 1996
The Dundee Courier was first published in 1801

I find Sambo in good form. He seems very pleased to see me. He looks even happier when I explain that I've followed his advice and I tell him about the work Parminder has done.

"He certainly knows what he's doing," says Sambo thoughtfully. "The Yahoo! robot is still pretty unsophisticated and this will seriously work to your advantage."

"I'll take your word for it," I say, before telling him about my recent meeting with Jeremy.

"If Jeremy is looking for sensational stories that verge on the ridiculous, then give him what he wants," he says. "If you do that then NOB will get all the backlinks you need."

Short and sweet. Sambo gives me a laconic smile as I thank him and I say goodbye, knowing now that what I need to do is to spoof the media with plausible, yet eye-catching bullshit.

On my way home, I buy a copy of the one million-selling national daily tabloid *Sword Swallower*. Victoria the reporter quotes my suggestions that, for a tenner, "NOB's insurance policy is the price of a beef dinner," and that such a policy "becomes a gimmick" if it's sold for less.

NOB is also featured in a story on page three of today's *Dundee Sloppy Seconds*. I assume this is down to the fact that Dundee is the home of Desperate Dan.

Tuesday 23 April 1996
The Banbury Cake was first published in 1965

I left London yesterday afternoon for a series of press and business meetings in Oxfordshire. This morning, I'm barely awake in my B&B when at 8.45am my mobile rings. It's Fred. I wonder what the f*ck he wants.

Not wishing to upset my parole officer, I answer as promptly and as brightly as I can. "Hi Fred," I say. "How may I help you?"

"What's the matter, Curly?" he asks. "You seem really down at the moment."

"I'm sorry, Fred," I say. "I'm in a really shit place at the moment."

Fred sounds concerned.

"Don't worry, I don't mean mentally," I stress. "I'm in Banbury, the birthplace of Gary f*cking Glitter."

Fred just wants to check that I'm still behaving. It doesn't take much for me to persuade him that I am.

As I hang up, through the bedroom window I see what appears to be the first English Superhero: a man running down the road wearing a cape.

Lunchtime. The word on the streets of Banbury suggests the f*cker hadn't paid for his haircut.

When I get back to the broom cupboard, Tracey greets me with, "Curly! Your ex, Vicky, called. She asked me to tell you that she'd love to get back together with you again."

As I hang up my coat, I tell Tracey, "If she rings back, tell her I was only joking when I told her I'd won the Lottery jackpot." Then I pause to think. "She once described me as a sex machine, you know."

"Really?" asks Tracey.

"Oh yes," I reply. "I think her exact words were, 'Curly, you're a f*cking tool.'"

Wednesday 24 April 1996
The International Press Cuttings Bureau was founded in 1920

There's a report in the highly respected North American publication the *Las Vegas Bankrupt*. It quotes my claim that there's been a "very positive response" to NOB's CJD insurance from several major fast-food outlets eager to protect their employees, among them an international burger chain.

Reading this, I worry that I may have gone a bit far with my burger-chain claim, which is completely untrue, but then again, I'm also fairly sure that no one is ever likely to find out.

I signed NOB up last week to the Global Press Cuttings Agency and the results are already beginning to appear. I've paid Roberto, the manager, an extra fee for the premium translation service. This means that if I ever get any coverage in France or further afield, I'll get an English transcript as well as the original foreign article.

The first cuttings to arrive today include several from mainland Europe. I'm excited to notice that monthly German business magazine *Deutschland Heute* has run a story explaining that, for an annual premium of 70 Deutschmarks, burger-chain workers can now buy insurance that pays up to 285,000 Deutschmarks if they contract CJD.

In the same batch of cuttings, French daily tabloid *La Planète Quotidienne* goes to town with a half-page story ripping the piss out of the English and their gullibility for buying CJD cover. The gist of the story is that the English should be kept away from agriculture and that they deserve all they have coming their way by eating English beef.

I've arranged a 2pm interview about PAYMENTSAFE with a sceptical-sounding news editor at the *Gentleman's Relish* named Errol. I take the Tube to Blackfriars, from where I walk across the Thames to their offices. I check my phone. Lucky I did! A voicemail, presumably left while I was underground, informs me that the meeting's been pushed back by two hours to 4pm – assuming, Errol adds, that I can still make it. Sure I can. I pop into the Red Lion, a pub across the road, where I order a bottle of red and three large Scotches. Then the same again.

At about 4.20pm, I stagger back over the road and into the pale, monochrome reception area, where I announce my arrival to the receptionist.

Errol soon steps out of the lift, clocks my condition immediately and refuses to see me. "You're completely drunk! Now piss off Curly!" he exclaims in disgust, turning straight back to the lift.

I stagger across the road again, where I order myself one more bottle of Bulgarian cabernet sauvignon for the road.

Thursday 25 April 1996
The Public Broadcasting Service (PBS) was founded in 1969

Despite yesterday's mishap with Errol, NOB's name is splashed across yet more UK national newspapers today. Also, I suddenly seem to be a rent-a-quote source for journalists! However, this new status as a media commentator is also turning out to be a bit hit-and-miss. A junior reporter on the *Fannyfield Bargain Bucket* named Youssef calls me just as I'm about to go to the pub, to ask whether I can help him out with a feature he's writing about saving money on motor insurance.

"Of course!" I say. I then proceed to tell him that the best way is to drive uninsured.

"Really?" asks Youssef.

Honestly. Some mothers.

At lunchtime, I get the chance to read today's press cuttings. CJD insurance stories are now appearing in even greater numbers, from all over the world. The *Aberdeen Filthy Thirds*, the *Bletchley Enigma*, the *Denver Hand Solo*, the *Cleveland Rear Admiral* and the *San José Colonic Irrigation* each run a light-hearted story today about NOB's CJD insurance, all of them implying that insurers are mad.

The *Atlanta Skull Buggery* goes deeper into the story, reporting that NOB also conducted market research purportedly showing 100% of people polled in Leadenhall Market in London, England, were of the view that NOB's deal gives excellent value for money.

That last one tickles me. I conducted the imaginary survey while I was walking the last hundred or so yards back to work after a liquid lunch. The news story is true insofar as it includes the words 'Leadenhall' and 'Market'.

This evening, I'm meeting Jacob, an old friend of mine whom I last saw before I was sent to Belmarsh. We're going for a few beers in his local, the Romford Face Lift.

We arrive together and head straight to the bar, where I buy the first round.

Jacob's not his usual jovial self. He frowns at me and says, "I'm becoming a little concerned about my eight-year-old daughter, Esther. She's terrible at reading social clues, she can't make eye contact and she doesn't pick up on sarcasm."

"Is Esther good at anything else?" I ask.

"Well, she's really good at drawing."

I look at him knowingly and advise him, "You've nothing to worry about. I think she's just artistic."

Friday 26 April 1996
The Barrier Daily Truth was first published in 1897

Apart from some lively news stories, it's been a quiet week in the broom cupboard as far as work's concerned. At noon I set off with Tracey to meet Mark, the *Missionary Impossible* news editor to whom Doug sold the story about CJD insurance. Mark says he'd like an update. I take Tracey into the Grapes for a swift pint before we walk to Bank to catch the Docklands Light Railway.

The two of us walk the last stretch of the journey from Shadwell station. Stepping out onto the street, I observe how the whole area's been badly neglected. The crisp and corporate building at Canary Wharf, a mile or two to our east, looks ridiculously out of place, set as it is against the real-life squalor of Docklands.

Tracey snaps me out of my socio-geographical observations, crying out, "F*ck!"

"What?" I ask, startled.

"I've trodden in dog shit!"

I look down to my right. Sure enough, her left stiletto has a sizeable turd dangling from its side. I manoeuvre myself to ensure that I'm walking in front of her with no danger of any associated contamination.

When we reach *Missionary Impossible's* elegant offices, Tracey wipes her shoe on the edge of the revolving door, just as Mark emerges from the lift.

We walk back out of the building and Mark asks Tracey, "Are you from London?"

"No, I'm from Braintree in Essex," she replies.

"Pleased to meet you," he says, before turning to me. "What's the difference between Oliver Twist and a girl from Braintree?" he asks. I look at him expectantly. "Oliver eventually found out who his father was!" he dramatically replies, looking very pleased with himself.

As we walk to the nearby Dickens Inn, I update Mark on NOB's new CJD insurance clients. Mainly burger chains, I say – well, lie.

Mark and Tracey both take a seat while I go to the bar, where I buy a bottle of wine for the three of us, as well as a large vodka that I swiftly neck before paying and taking the wine and three empty wine glasses to the table.

Half an hour later as I step up back to the bar to buy a second round, Tracey takes Mark outside. I'm still waiting to be served and the two of them can't have been gone for more than a few minutes before a slightly dishevelled-looking Tracey bursts through the doorway with a filthy grin on her face.

I certainly can't complain. It's in her contract of employment: £120 per week and as much as she can eat.

Monday 29 April 1996
Reuters was founded in 1851

This morning the phone company has finally fitted a second line. NOB's phone bill is probably going to go up, but with our new computer, we'll be able to email press releases to Jeremy at the push of a button.

"We're on our way to having a paperless office!" Tracey exclaims.

"I'm not sure I like the sound of that," I tell her.

"Oh, the whole insurance industry will be paperless one day," she says, airily.

Unimpressed, I retort, "Great, then we'll all be utterly dependent upon the national grid!"

"What's wrong with that?" she asks.

I look at her in despair. "Have you never heard of power cuts?"

For months, I've had growing concerns about my neighbour Ruth and the way she treats her kids. She's always unpleasant towards them and shouts at them constantly. This evening, on my return from work, it's happening again. Once indoors, I decide to follow my conscience and I call the local child abuse hotline. The phone rings half a dozen times before Ruth's son Tyler answers, calls me a c*nt and hangs up.

Thursday 2 May 1996

The Times published the first newspaper editorial leader column in 1851

A momentous day. Tracey excitedly lets me know our first email has arrived. It's from Mia, a junior producer at Big Bristols Radio, inviting me for an interview on His and Hers, to discuss why burger-chain employees need CJD insurance. I email her back to confirm my acceptance.

An hour later, Mia calls and puts me through to the show's presenter, Lionel, for a live interview.

This media spoofing seems to be working a treat. As I understand it, an advert on a national commercial radio station costs several grand for 30 seconds. A five-minute, full-on advertisement has cost NOB nothing. And they've even given NOB a backlink on the Big Bristols website. Bingo!

Tracey dutifully heads downstairs to collect the post and returns with the latest press cuttings. The media excitement just keeps growing. Yesterday's story on the website of the *Glasgow Soundbite* suggests that if your missus is a mad cow then you should contact NOB. I sit down to read the article as Tracey reaches over to hand me a fax that has just come in from Japanese TV company Fuji News, requesting a televised interview about CJD insurance. At last, the NOB brand is truly out there and we're seeing a noticeable growth in sales of PAYMENTSAFE.

Just as I'm marvelling at the results of cheap marketing in action, the latest issue of insurance trade weekly *Lunchbox Lancer* arrives. Its editorial leader column reports that NOB is offering protection against the risk of contracting CJD. However, the headline condemns our initiative as being "in poor taste". This smarts a bit, but then I remind myself of the old saying: there's no such thing as bad publicity.

I decide to win back trust from that particular organ with a bit of corporate hospitality. A phone call to the senior reporter, Benito, reveals he's off deadline and hungry for news. And thirsty, too, by all accounts. At noon, we meet at the Amazing Dancing Bare, a seedy East End pub, for an afternoon of strippers.

Friday 3 May 1996
Nippon Hōsō Kyōkai (NHK) was founded in 1926

Benito rings to thank me for yesterday's drinks and to tell me that at 5pm he breezed back into the office, where he says Len his boss snapped, "Where have you been?"

"I told him, 'Staring at tits and fannies, sir!'"

At lunchtime, I'm meeting with Jeff in the Grapes and tell him that I can't have more than a couple of pints because a Japanese TV crew is due to come to interview me at 1pm about CJD insurance.

I stagger back to the broom cupboard at 1.30pm, only to find the guys from Fuji News waiting anxiously in reception downstairs. When I take them upstairs, they don't look happy as they try to set up the lighting in NOB's tiny broom cupboard.

Still, at least their Japanese audience won't notice me slurring my words.

I've sobered up in time for an important meeting this evening with Fred at the police station in Hackney. I'm not sure how I'm going to get there, but Tracey says she'll help. She leaves the broom cupboard and then, just five minutes later, she calls, ordering me to get down sharpish to a yellow A-reg Golf that she's hot-wired on Gracechurch Street. I grab my bag and dash out to get my lift.

About 20 minutes later, Tracey pulls up alongside the police station. Conscious that I'm late, I hurry inside.

Fred frowns and looks back at his notes. Basically, he wants me to persuade him that I'm rehabilitated and not doing anything antisocial or illegal.

"Absolutely nothing," I assure him, deliberately omitting to mention that I'd come to today's meeting in a stolen car.

Fred waves me out of the meeting.

I'm chuffed at that result. Tracey drops the car back just where she found it and we both go for a pint in Filthy Fannies.

BASICALLY, HE WANTS TO KNOW
I AM KEEPING OUT OF TROUBLE

Wednesday 8 May 1996
Bild was first published in 1952

Hooray! Three big-selling daily papers – the *Naples Nipples*, the *Vatican Roulette* and the *Berlin Fudgebox* – report on their respective websites that NOB is offering PAYMENTSAFE, an insurance policy to protect workers who fall ill, have an accident, or lose their job. The three papers' corresponding websites also report the story and provide NOB with a backlink. (Thank you, Jeremy!)

After a lunchtime pint with Jeff, I return to the broom cupboard sooner than expected, only to clock Del surreptitiously passing Tracey a familiar-looking Presto carrier bag. As her employer I'm gutted, but what if I turn out to be wrong and they aren't drugs at all? I decide to let sleeping dogs lie.

I spend most of the afternoon taking calls mainly from the US and Canadian press about CJD insurance. Lucky North America. Links from such titles as the *Indiana Cock Chomper*, the *New York Bum Bandit* and the *Dallas Cockalorum* are bound to help NOB's Yahoo! search rankings. Also, it really is fun. For me, anyway.

I'm beginning to recognise some of the techniques that enable original news stories to spread and grow. The UK Press Distribution Network is invaluable, but so too is the specialist insurance press such as Doug's paper, *Insurance Now!* From time to time, it breaks sensational stories which, when they're not tipped off or flogged by the papers themselves, are often read by diligent national press reporters as part of their own quest for comprehensive news coverage. In turn, the international media helpfully pick up and cover many of these stories themselves, under somewhat less pressure to stand them up than the domestic press.

I accept the offer of drinks after work with Lance at the Zest Fest in Camden. The whole area is a flea-infested, rundown shithole. Lance and I chat for an hour or so before I make my way back to the Tube station, dodging muggers, beggars and other social miscreants. Luckily, I have a bottle of Scotch in my briefcase.

A guard wakes me up in Morden, the last stop on the last train of the evening. I open my eyes to see dribble down my tie. I then observe that my whisky bottle is empty, before realising my wallet and shoes have gone too.

I've no choice but to walk about ten miles home in just my socks.

It's daylight long before I reach my front door. My battle-weary feet are broken.

Friday 10 May 1996
Independent Television (ITV) was founded in 1955

Tracey tells me her friend, Chris, is having a house-warming party tonight in Bethnal Green and that she's kindly invited me to join her.

A tedious few hours of urgent paperwork follow, with no time for a pint.

F*ck it! At 3pm, I suggest we leave the broom cupboard for the day. We lock up and take a number 8 bus to the Marquis of Cornwallis, the nearest pub to Chris' house.

Many rounds later, Tracey and I are finding it hard to walk straight as we leave for the party, which is being held in a nearby side street. As we turn the corner, ahead I see a cluster of guests being welcomed into a Victorian end-terrace house. Led by my companion, the two of us bundle in behind them and slowly shuffle through the crowd of happy partygoers into the kitchen.

Suddenly a tall chap wearing a purple shirt, a moustache and a face painted with makeup pushes his way through the throng towards us. "Who the f*ck are you?" he asks, abruptly.

"Who are *you*?" I ask.

"I'm Gordon," he replies. "I didn't invite you!"

"F*ck! We've got the wrong house!" cries Tracey.

"Terribly sorry!" I say to the Liberace lookalike, before Tracey and I both push our way back to the front door and out onto the street. On the pavement, she fumbles in her pocket for the scrap of paper with the right address. "It's number 25 we need, not 5!" she cries. We make it to our intended destination, where Chris opens the door and greets Tracey with a warm hug. It turns out Chris is a girl.

"Chris, this is my boss, Curly!" Tracey says, stepping into the hallway and turning to face me.

"Hi Curly. Nice to meet you," says Chris.

For the second time in less than ten minutes, I make my way with Tracey through a crowded hallway to a Bethnal Green kitchen. I find a pint glass in the cupboard, fill it with vodka and promptly down it. Thus fortified, I set off to find the loo.

There's a queue. Bollocks to that. I return to the kitchen, unzip my trousers and take a piss in the sink. The loud and animated voices and laughter behind me quickly fade to near silence. After a few seconds, all I can hear, above the muffled conversation and tinny music from a cheap stereo next door in the sitting room, is the sound of piss hitting metal.

I finish, shake, zip up my flies and turn round, just as Chris pushes her way through the hallway and into the kitchen. She's non-plussed and she yells at me to leave.

I'm led back out of the house by two of Chris's butch female friends and wander off back down the road to Threshers, where I pick up half a dozen cans of lager before taking the Tube home to Pimlico.

Wednesday 15 May 1996
The Grand River Sachem was first published in 1853

Doug calls, asking to meet for a drink. It's raining, so I hail a cab to the Globe, which is situated on the edge of an almost permanently deserted car park off a side road that runs between Borough Market and Southwark Cathedral.

The pub's a traditional spit-and-sawdust affair, with a plain, unvarnished bar. Its walls don't appear to have seen a lick of paint in decades. I buy a round and we get down to business.

I attempt to explain to Doug the serious issue that UK banks and French insurers are mis-selling PPI to British consumers on a scandalous level. That's a far bigger story than the CJD nonsense. But Doug's still chasing my burger-chain claim, so I decide to come clean when he asks me, "How many burger chains does NOB now have as clients?"

I pause for effect, then say, "None."

I can almost see the cogs whirring in his brain. The penny having dropped, smiling, he says, "Cool! So, you just made it up!" He clearly relishes the idea of having presented bullshit as sensationalist fact to a national newspaper.

A couple of rounds later we stagger off in opposite directions.

I seem to remember dropping by the broom cupboard to look for my house keys.

Thursday 16 May 1996
British Sky Broadcasting (BSKYB) was founded in 1990

I wake up with my head on my briefcase, on the ground in my front porch. I brush myself down, take a crap under my neighbour's tree, wipe my arse with yesterday's *Colchester Condom* – no way to treat one of the world's oldest daily newspapers – and head back to the station.

I push open the broom cupboard door and straightaway I notice my bunch of keys on the floor beneath my desk. I spend the next few hours taking calls from the press, before making my way to the Grapes for a well-deserved pint.

I eventually arrive home at the same time as my neighbour, Finbar, who calls out to me, "Curly! Someone's taken a shit in my front garden!"

"It's those f*cking badgers!" I tell him.

"Really? I thought it was human shit!" he says. "Badgers, you say."

"Yeah, they're always doing that. They're terrible!"

"Well, thanks. Now I know," he says, turning for the front door.

I bid him farewell, open my own door and drop my briefcase on the living room floor. I put on a record (Black Sabbath, since you ask) and settle down to reflect on the day.

Badgers! What a clueless c*nt.

Monday 20 May 1996
Agence France-Presse was founded in 1835

Postman's late today. He finally arrives at 10am The first letter I open is from the telephone company. I stare at it, perplexed. My phone bill has gone up by about 400 per cent! I examine it more closely, before realising most of the cost relates to dial-up web charges. The fiends!

At midday I take a call from Ralph, inviting me for a lunchtime drink at the Cock & Bull.

"I'm up for cock anytime!" he says, predictably.

I turn up half an hour later at the Smithfield pub. Ralph arrives as I'm drinking my second pint and finishing a call with Fidel, a reporter on the *Santiago de Cuba Bacardi Geezer.*

"Bring your drink with you through to the restaurant. I've booked us a table," Ralph says, before uttering the magical words, "Lunch is on me."

We take our seats. "Have you ever drunk Kummel?" he asks.

I look up from the menu and shake my head.

"It's the dog's bollocks," he says. The waiter approaches us, and Ralph calls out to order us each two double Kummel's for starters.

I look at the waiter and correct my companion. "Just leave the bottle," I say, before turning off my phone so we can enjoy a leisurely lunch without it ringing every two minutes. Then I ask Ralph, "Why *are* gay men so promiscuous?"

He looks at me indignantly, as if he's about to condemn me for sexually stereotyping gay men, when his own mobile phone rings.

After a brief conversation, Ralph puts down the phone and I ask him, "Who was that?"

"A guy I f*cked last night behind the pub," Ralph replies. "I just can't remember if it was the guy at the Golden Lion, the Rose and Crown, the Green Man, the White Hart or the Queen's Head."

I splutter with laughter then wipe my chin. "The Kummel's brilliant!" I say to Ralph.

At around 4pm, Ralph pays the bill. I turn my phone back on and it soon begins to beep repeatedly, alerting me to unanswered calls and voicemail messages, as we stagger along High Holborn to the Five Knuckle Shuffle.

The pub is situated in a quiet Georgian alley scattered with half a dozen tall, upturned wooden beer barrels, allowing for al fresco drinking. Ralph bags one of these, while I go indoors for a slash and to buy a round.

Six pints later, he tells me that he's got to leave the pub to meet work colleagues in the Cheshire Cat and he invites me along. I duly follow him. Both of us are swaying.

Tuesday 21 May 1996
BBC One was founded in 1936

The sound of crows wakes me from my slumbers on a bench in St Paul's churchyard. It's 6.30am. I stand up, brush myself down, then walk the half a mile or so to the Honourable Member in Smithfield, where I enjoy six pints of Bass before sauntering happily to work in the bright spring sunshine.

Biology lesson for Tracey when I arrive at the broom cupboard today. "I've got a man on the phone who wants to know if our PPI policies cover prostate problems," she says.

"Of course they do!" I say. "NOB's policies offer the widest cover on the market."

When she finishes the call, Tracey hangs up and asks me, "What's a prostate?"

"The prostate is a small gland found only in men and trans-women," I reply. "It surrounds the tube that carries urine out of the body."

I pause and reflect. During my own recent prostate examination, my doctor told me it's perfectly normal to become aroused and even ejaculate. That said, I wish she hadn't.

I hate shopping, particularly in the evening, when I could be in the pub, but needs must. I've an important meeting coming up in Knightsbridge next week and I really don't want to turn up wearing a vomit-encrusted suit with a scent to match.

I take the Tube to Oxford Circus, then wander through the crowds to Marks & Spencer. I head straight to the men's department, where I thumb through a few rails, before finding just the kind of garment I'm after: dark, charcoal and single-breasted. I take it across the shop floor to the changing rooms, where I'm greeted by a well-endowed, pretty, young lady called Lillian. Holding up the suit in my left hand, I say, "May I try it on?"

"Certainly sir," she says.

"In that case, you've terrific boobs."

"Piss off Curly!" she replies with a smile.

Monday 27 May 1996
The Croydon Advertiser was first published in 1869

The phone rings just as I arrive at the broom cupboard. Tracey takes the call. "Good morning, NOB. How may I help you?" she asks brightly.

She listens for a couple of minutes, then puts the caller on hold and says to me, "Curly, I've got an elderly lady on the phone called Mrs Mainwaring who'd like to know if NOB's PPI will cover her against losing her job as a volunteer at the Cat Protection shop in Croydon. She says she saw that NOB was recommended in her local paper, the *Croydon Pignoramus*."

I instinctively know that any elderly woman who's working as a volunteer isn't going to be eligible to make a claim under a PPI policy on account of both her age and the fact that her employment is voluntary.

"She says she's had a PPI policy with her bank for the past five years," says Tracey.

"It sounds as though they've been taking her money without any intention of paying out," I tell her. "Please, let me have a word with her." Tracey passes me the phone.

"Good morning, Mrs Mainwaring," I say. "I regret to inform you that you'll never be able to make a claim under any PPI policy and that you'll be much better off simply saving your money than paying for an insurance policy you'll never be able to claim on."

But she continues, "You see, some years ago I took this call from a delightful young man at my bank who said it'd only cost £200 per month and would pay out if all sorts of things went wrong," she explains.

"This simply isn't true, I'm afraid," I tell her. "Your PPI policy has been mis-sold and you should contact your bank and ask for a full refund of all the premiums that you've paid."

"Are you really sure?" she asks.

"I most certainly am!" I reply. "If they put up any resistance, I'll take over your complaint to ensure you get back every penny."

Mrs Mainwaring's overcome with gratitude. When I put the phone down, Tracey smiles at me and simply says, "Thank you, Curly. She was *such* a nice old lady!"

Tuesday 28 May 1996
The Wall Street Journal was first published in 1889

To Knightsbridge this morning, to discuss the PPI requirements of a group of wealthy new clients.

I leave the meeting in high spirits, confident that I've sealed a big deal. So confident, in fact, that I reckon I deserve a bit of decent-quality booze. I'm just a stone's throw from Harrod's. As I approach the famous department store, I wonder whether it provides trolleys.

I find my way to the fine wines and spirits department, where I gaze in awe at the fantastic premium beverages and their equally fantastic prices. I'm in a world of my own when I suddenly hear the tinny sound of a Walkman behind me. I glance over my shoulder to see a familiar, tall figure. It's my old friend and Princess Di-lookalike, Genevieve, another one of my numerous friends whom I've not seen since I was convicted and sent to Belmarsh. She notices me turning around, then throws her arms around me.

"Big hugs!" she cries.

"Fancy a pint?" I ask, catching my breath. It's nearly noon, after all.

"A pint? No! Come for lunch!" she pleads before taking me by cab to Goblin Mode, a nearby restaurant. There she tells me she's now editing a niche magazine for wealthy individuals called *Megabucks*, which is published by Marlon, her multi-millionaire godfather.

Just as we finish our main course, my phone rings. It's Tracey, who tells me I'm late for a meeting with Fred.

"I'm so sorry. I have to go," I say, embarrassed. "Let me leave you some money."

"Not a bit of it!" Genevieve insists, clicking her right hand in the air to order herself one more glass of red for the road. As I head for the door I turn and call out to her, "The next one's on me!"

As I walk into the broom cupboard, Tracey informs me that Vicky has been on the phone again.

"She told me to tell you that you've got a small penis," says Tracey.

I think for a moment then reply, "If she calls again, tell her from me that she's got a big mouth and besides, that's not what her sister Heidi said."

Wednesday 29 May 1996
The Press Gazette was first published in 1965

I'm early into work today and as soon as I'm sitting down, the phone rings.

I lift the receiver. "My dear!" exclaims Genevieve. "That was such fun yesterday! An absolute hoot!"

"Indeed it was!" I reply. "Many thanks! I was going to ask you when I could return the favour."

"A return match? How jolly nice of you!"

"Not at all," I say. "How about dinner at the Frog & Snail this evening?"

"Sounds delightful!" Then she suddenly pauses. "Oh bugger," she says.

"What?" I ask.

"Well, I'm supposed to be going to press with the March edition."

"It's *May*," I tell her.

"Oh, is it? Jolly good," she says. "Then let's meet around seven."

"See you there!" I say and I hang up. A moment later I take a call from Gabrielle at the *Horsham F*ckme Doris*, asking me about PAYMENTSAFE. I answer her question and thank her for her call before ringing to book a table for two at my West End restaurant of choice.

A few hours later, I take a Number 15 bus to Park Lane and wander down to the restaurant. When I'm shown to our table, I'm puzzled for a moment, seeing an unfamiliar figure sitting there. It then dawns on me that this is in fact Genevieve as I've rarely seen her before: without her Princess Di wig and with her natural, brown crow's-nest of hair.

She smiles up at me as I take my seat and I apologise awkwardly for my tardiness.

"Not a bit of it, dear thing!" she says. "Nice here, isn't it?"

"Yes, it's rather nice," I say, looking around the expansive room.

Three bottles of Bordeaux later, I pay for the dinner and we head for the Tube – Genevieve southwest to Chelsea, me back eastwards on the Central Line to Bank to sleep off dinner on the broom cupboard floor.

Saturday 1 June 1996
The Stoke Sentinel was first published in 1854

I take the train back to London from the Potteries after a day out with my teenage brother, Genghis, who suffers from Down syndrome. Or mongolism, as my parents call it. I take my reserved seat, place my briefcase on the table and walk through several crowded carriages to buy myself a couple of bottles of wine.

The return journey to my seat seems to take even longer. As I sit down, a regal-looking woman opposite me smiles to acknowledge my frustration at the effort I've just endured making it back. She's a dead ringer for Her Majesty the Queen. We get chatting and I pour us each a plastic beaker of French red. It tastes like stale vinegar.

My new companion reveals that her name's Elizabeth and that she really is a professional Queen-lookalike. In the surreal conversation that follows, she confides in me that the real Queen Elizabeth has enormous tits and that, in order to embody the full character of Her Royal Highness, she relies on substantial bust-enhancers for a convincing impersonation.

We exchange business cards and Elizabeth gives me one of her glossy promotional photographs. I promise to keep in touch, before nicking the rest of the revolting wine and dozing off.

Sunday 2 June 1996
The Sunday Post was first published in 1914

Elizabeth, my new Queen-lookalike friend, has given me an idea. I look for her photo before making a quick call to ask whether she'd be happy to pretend that Her Majesty has purchased PPI cover from NOB. She tells me she'd be delighted to help in any way she can.

In the afternoon, I take an unexpected call from Dad. My parents need me to look after Genghis this week. This is going to take some serious strategic planning. I drive to the supermarket to stock up on provisions for the week. Booze, mainly. Then I call Tracey.

"Hi Tracey, it's Curly," I say. "I'm sorry to be ringing you on a Sunday, only I've a bit of a problem."

"Oh no, Curly! What's wrong?" she asks.

"Nothing serious," I say. "It's just I've to look after my brother Genghis this week."

"That's no problem, is it?" she asks.

"Well, it sort of is," I reply. "He's disabled and he needs a lot of looking after."

"Like nursing?" she asks.

"Nothing really like that," I say. "He takes lots of medication and he often needs a wheelchair, which is hard to take around central London. Public transport is usually off limits." I pause again. "Basically, everything I'd planned needs to change. I was rather hoping you'd be able to help me look after him."

"Are you bringing him to the broom cupboard?" Tracey asks.

"Oh yes," I say. "He's mobile. He just needs care and attention."

"When's he arriving?" she asks. I tell her I'm picking him up from the station on Tuesday morning.

"We'll manage!" she says, brightly. I thank her, before reminding her that I'm not in work tomorrow. I then hang up overwhelmed.

Monday 3 June 1996
The Emu Bay Times was first published in 1890

I wake up in an armchair with an uncomfortably twisted neck, with no idea where I am. Raising my head, I see Genevieve lying asleep on a sofa, her wig half-off, spread-eagle, in a crumpled yellow frock that's decorated with a dark red stain and flecks of carrot. More of the same is on the floor beside her.

I stand up to go to make myself a drink. As I do so, I knock over an open bottle of whisky. I rescue it just as a slick of golden liquid colours the pale carpet, then I wander through the property to find out where there may be some coffee. I stumble into the kitchen, fumbling in semi-darkness, until I find a light switch. I make myself a mug and take it with me back to the armchair where, exercising constraint, I spike it with just a double measure of whisky.

I sit down on a chaise longue and look across the room. Through the window I can make out dawn breaking over the cobbles of a mews. It looks uncannily like that of Stephen Ward's Marylebone bolthole in the film Scandal. This must be Genevieve's Chelsea flat. I wonder how on Earth I ended up here.

As I stir my coffee, Genevieve sits up with a start. I wander off to make her a cup of tea, which she takes with her to dress in her bedroom.

A few minutes later she appears back in the hallway in jeans and a flowery blouse and without her Princess Di wig. I remember now why I'm here. I'm accompanying Genevieve to a press conference today in Cambridgeshire.

Half an hour later, we're on our way. The sun is fully up as we emerge from Kings Cross Tube station, a scary place at any time of day. Stepping over pools of drug-addict piss and skirting hypodermic needles, we make it inside the station to queue for tickets. I buy us both a day-return to Peterborough. It's a bit of a hike, but Genevieve assures me the insurance company staging the event has a reputation for serving booze of outstanding quality.

Our train is already waiting at the platform. I pull open the door and board, turning to help my companion up, taking care to prevent her frock from catching on either the handle or the latch. A guard slams the door closed behind us.

"Bar's this way," I say, pointing to the front of the carriage.

"Don't you want to find a seat first?" she asks.

Across the aisle is a group of four vacant, high-backed blue seats. I drop my coat and bag on one of them. Genevieve takes the seat opposite next to the window as I hurry off to the buffet carriage. There, supported by a bloke with a pint in his hand, is the familiar face of a bird I recognise immediately.

"Emu!" I cry in amazement.

"Curly Watts!" Rod Hull replies.

"Hi Rod," I say. "I'm actually Curly Cradock from NOB, but I'm always being mistaken for global superstar Curly Watts."

Rod nods. We get talking and within a minute or two I find myself addressing Emu rather than Rod, to the apparent amusement of the barman. After a short while, we're joined by Genevieve, who's now wearing her Princess Di wig. She looks quite the part.

As we're leaving the buffet carriage to return to our seats, the ticket collector wipes his brow and says to the barman, "Give me a whisky, Sean. I've just seen Princess Di, Emu and Curly f*cking Watts!"

Tuesday 4 June 1996
The Financial Times was first published in 1888

I drop some documents off at the broom cupboard and make a couple of calls, before taking the Tube to Euston to collect Genghis from the train. A black cab obligingly takes me, my brother and his wheelchair to Lime Street, where we meet Tracey for a swift pint in the Grapes.

"Meet Genghis!" I exclaim. Tracey smiles warmly and greets him. Then I look at her, lower my voice and warn her, "He's a bit like PPI from a bank."

"What do you mean?" she asks.

"He's riddled with appalling conditions," I reply.

Tracey thinks for a few moments, then says, "You mean conditions that wouldn't be covered under their PPI policy, right?"

I look down at Genghis in his wheelchair and say to him, "F*ck me! She's not the airhead I thought she was!"

Ignoring the insult, Tracey lowers herself to Genghis' level. Looking at him with a broad smile, she reaches out to shake his hand and says, "Nice to meet you, Handsome!"

"Look like a Cabbage Patch Kid, don't I?" says Genghis.

Tracey smiles and shakes her head. As she stands up again, I tell her, "I know he's my brother, so I'm biased, but when you get to know him, I think you'll find him to be one of the kindest people you'll ever meet."

"I can believe that," says Tracey, smiling.

HI NATALIE, THIS IS GHENGIS.
UNFORTUNATELY, JUST LIKE P.P.I.
FROM A BANK, HE'S GOT LOTS OF
APPALLING CONDITIONS

Wednesday 5 June 1996
United News of Bangladesh was founded in 1988

Delighted to receive a call from Elizabeth this morning. She tells me she has an appointment tonight at the nearby Royal Exchange and says she wonders if I'd fancy a drink beforehand. I explain to her that I have my teenage brother, Genghis, with me.

"Well, I'd love to meet him too!" she says.

I hold the phone to my chest and ask Genghis if he'd like to meet the Queen.

"At Buckingham Palace?" he asks excitedly. "I want to see the corgis!"

"No, at the Royal Exchange in the City," I tell him.

Genghis is excited as we leave work this evening. Navigating kerbs and traffic lights, I push the wheelchair down Cornhill. As we approach our destination, we can see Elizabeth ahead of us stepping out of a black cab onto the street outside the Bank of England. She looks most regal and she waits as we approach her.

"Good evening, your Majesty," says Genghis, bowled over with excitement. "Did you bring your corgis?"

"Dogs are not allowed here, unfortunately. But I did bring this," she says as she presents him with a box wrapped in fine crimson paper and tied with a ribbon. "This is for you," she says.

Genghis' eyes light up and he eagerly tears open the wrapping to reveal the original James Bond Aston Martin DB5 by Corgi Toys, complete with ejector-seat and all its other amazing gadgets.

"Thank you!" he exclaims. "Did your corgis make these?"

"Yes," she replies with a smile. "Just for you."

I'm compelled to take a photograph and I quickly reach in my pocket for my Kodak Instamatic. Genghis has a determined look on his face as he proudly poses with Elizabeth, certain that she's the Queen herself.

We choose a watering hole called the Devil's Doorbell. We find a table and Genghis promptly takes a nap.

Elizabeth remarks, "Your brother's absolutely charming. He's quite a lot younger than you."

"Yes, he was a late-in-life gift for my parents," I say. "And thank you so much for your lovely gift," I add. "Genghis really loves it."

Saturday 8 June 1996
Deutsche Presse-Agentur was founded in 1949

I pay a visit this morning to Waterstones in Old Brompton Road, my favourite bookshop. Here I spot a lovely book of German fairytales entitled Rumpledforeskin, an ideal gift for Genghis.

Ahead of me in the queue, a short man in a filthy donkey jacket asks the assistant, "Do you have the sex manual I ordered for men with small penises?"

She looks down at her computer screen, moves her mouse a few times and replies, "I don't know if it's in yet."

"Yeah, that's the one," he says.

"No, we haven't," she replies. Shoulders hunched, the man turns and leaves.

My turn. With an apology I hand her the book for Genghis. As she types into her cash register, I ask her "Do you have any books on paranoia?"

She looks up at me for a moment, then says, "*Behind* you!"

From the bookshop, I take a cab to the Broadcasting Wank Hut for my live interview on the Big Bristols personal finance show Piggy Bank. Nathaniel, the interviewer, wants to discuss NOB's new campaign featuring Elizabeth, with the slogan, 'I don't need PPI cover, but you might. So don't ring the Royal, ring NOB instead!'

He's most impressed that Her Royal Highness has actually agreed to do this for NOB and Bingo! Another backlink on the broadcaster's website.

Monday 10 June 1996
BBC World at One was first broadcast in 1965

I'm reading today's *Two Nuns on a Bike* when the post arrives, bringing with it a letter of complaint from Alfred, the chief finance director at Royal Protection plc, objecting to NOB's plagiarisation of his company's slogan, 'If you need to make a claim, don't ring the Royal.'

He really should have taken it in good spirit. There was no malice intended, but Alfred didn't get the joke. With an honorary PhD in sarcasm from Harvard College of Further Education, I fire back an email saying:

Email: alfred@royalprotection.com
Subject: My sincere apologies
Message: Dear Alfred,

Thank you so much for kindly taking the trouble to write such a lovely letter. May I please apologise unreservedly for the obvious distress I've caused you. I'll write to Buckingham Palace immediately.

With all good wishes,
Curly

Alfred's reply is swift:

Email: curly@nob.co.uk
Subject: For the attention of Curly Cradock
Message: Piss off Curly!

Out for an evening pint with Finbar. Our two elderly neighbours are chatting at the next table.

"Did you come on the bus, Doris?" asks Gladys.

Doris replies, "Yes, but I made it look like an asthma attack."

Tuesday 11 June 1996
The Washington Post was first published in 1877

I call Ralph and then Lance, to invite them both to meet me for a drink at the Lamb.

"The wrong side of Bishopsgate!" protests Ralph, a banker somewhat unhappy at the thought of mixing with the insurance fraternity.

Just as we're walking in, my phone rings. It's Genevieve. She's finally sent the latest issue of her magazine to press and now she says she really needs a drink, so I invite her along to join us.

Some 20 minutes later she arrives, elegantly dressed and in her Princess Di wig. She steps from a black cab, before a gentleman in a dark suit, white shirt and pink tie steps up to hold the pub door open for her. She smiles and nods in gratitude, crosses the bar and parks herself on a low stool opposite me at the table I've chosen. The noise of rowdy conversation around us dims.

Behind the bar is a picture of the Queen Mother pulling a pint of bitter. The landlord, Sid, crosses over to our table. He bows and politely asks if our companion, whom he mistakenly believes to be Princess Di, would kindly be photographed doing the same, in return for some free drinks. Straight away she stands up, walks behind the bar and pulls a pint, while Sid takes pictures with a large, professional-looking camera.

True to his word, he serves several free rounds. After her second bottle of red wine, Genevieve asks for a bottle of cava. Concerned for her welfare, I give her a look that says, "Are you *sure?*"

A worried-looking Sid comes reluctantly to the table with the bottle of fizz and a glass on a tray. Genevieve fills her glass and downs it in one. Seconds later, out gushes a stinking, high-pressure jet of vomit.

Lance and Ralph hurry out without saying goodbye. My concern is now for Genevieve more than it is about the mess. With her leaning against me, I manoeuvre her out onto the street, where I try to hail a black cab to take her home.

The first three or so black cabs to approach clock Genevieve's condition and drive off immediately. Eventually one stops and allows her to board. I bid her farewell, before stumbling off back towards Lime Street, making a mental note to drop by the pub tomorrow to apologise to Sid and give a tip to his cleaner.

Friday 14 June 1996
Lloyd's List was first published in 1734

I'm about to head out to the Grapes for a lunchtime drink when the phone rings. Tracey answers. "It's Genevieve," she tells me. "She wants to know if you'd like to get mouse-bummed with her this evening."

"No idea what she means," I say, taking the receiver from her. "*Mouse-bummed?*" I ask.

"Sorry, I mean rat-arsed," Genevieve replies. "It's my convent school education, I'm afraid."

"In that case, most definitely!" I say, before informing her that Ralph and I are planning to gatecrash one of the Lloyd's Summer press parties, which is taking place this evening.

At 5pm I wander down Lime Street with Ralph, who's already pissed from lunch. We wait for Genevieve at the foot of the western steps to the Lloyd's building.

After a few minutes, I see her approaching us from the bottom end of Leadenhall Street. She's not wearing her wig. With her natural, wayward, spiky hair and with two pens sticking out of her jacket pocket, she looks every bit the journalist.

Gaining entrance to the press party is a breeze for all three of us. We're taken up in the lift with a couple of other members of the press including Kelly, a tall, elegant, blonde American woman, London correspondent for the *Austin Metro*, to be led into the conference room.

We take our seats before Sir David, the chairman, spells out what a great job Lloyd's is doing - with the help of a few rocket scientists - to balance the books after years of huge losses. Then I sit through the tedium of questions from the press, which go on for nearly an hour - from Genevieve, mainly, who's once again doing the work of her colleagues on the other titles present. At least they stand an outside chance of publishing the stories she uncovers.

Finally, we can have a drink. Reporter's notebook still in hand, Genevieve's the first to the table of booze, in its traditional spot at the back of the conference room.

For some reason, Ralph heads straight for Sir David, while Genevieve wanders towards a group of hacks.

Ralph is talking to Sir David, who's looking non-plussed.

"Okay, how's this for an insurance joke?" he slurs, keenly. "What's the difference between a hurricane and a woman?"

"I've absolutely *no* idea," the chairman replies despairingly, looking around for an escape.

"Well, I'll tell you, sweetie," he slurs, taking a swig from a bottle of red wine that he swiped from the table. "They both start out with a little blow - and end up taking your house!" he exclaims, before bursting into fits of uncontrollable giggles and dropping the wine bottle, which falls at Sir David's feet and splashes down one side of his trousers.

Sir David is understandably underwhelmed but, ever the diplomat, he realises there's nothing he can do: this is a press party and this is just how some journalists behave.

I walk over to Genevieve and ask, "Want to cause some mischief?"

"Yes!" she says, beaming all of a sudden. "Show me where and how!"

I wave to Ralph, then I shepherd the two of them in the direction of the loos to enable Genevieve to put on her Princess Di wig, before deftly ushering them into a lift, which we take to the ground floor.

Walking ahead of them, I sneak us all into the huge underwriting room, an area of the building normally off limits to the public.

Standing tall and elegant in her blonde wig, Genevieve looks around in awe at the huge space around her. "What's that?" she asks, pointing at a gilded bell suspended within an elegant, circular structure of dark pillars.

"It's called the Lutine bell," I say. "It's rung if there's been a massive loss for the Lloyd's Names underwriting a risk."

Still staring at it, she asks why it's thus named.

"It came from the frigate HMS Lutine that Lloyd's insured, before it was wrecked in 1799," I venture. Ralph nods to confirm this.

While dispensing historical information, I add, "Tracey told me that her flatmate Natalie's great-grandmother went down on the Titanic."

"Is Natalie the one with the huge bazookas?" asks Ralph.

Genevieve ignores him. "Really? How sad!" she says.

"Not really!" I say. "She was rescued and lived to the age of 103."

Ralph and Genevieve both gaze up at the bell.

"I dare one of you to ring it!" I say.

Ralph looks horrified and steps back, but Genevieve jumps forward in a flash. A deafening double-chime rings out.

"*Run!*" I shout. In hysterics, we leg it back out, unchallenged, through the Old Library, before making our escape out into the night, still laughing.

WE SHOULD COMMEMORATE NATALIE'S GREAT GRANDMOTHER GOING DOWN ON THE TITANIC IN THE TRADITIONAL MANNER

Monday 17 June 1996
The Hendon & Finchley Times was first published in 1878

Off to an early-morning meeting with Abraham, a journalist at the *North London Topspin & Grout*. As I exit the Tube at Hendon, I pass a group of disabled people protesting with banners and placards.

I stop to ask what they're doing. Xavier their spokesman replies, "There's a vast amount of discrimination against paraplegic people these days. We're here to send the message that we're not going to stand for it."

I drop a quid coin in their collection box and saunter on to my meeting.

After lunch, Lance swings by the broom cupboard to tell me that he's excited by the UEFA European football tournament. "England will definitely win it!" he assures me. "By the way, what do Terry Venables and a girl from Braintree have in common?" he asks.

"I've *no* idea," I say, knowing neither anything about football nor the identity of Mr Venables.

"Both prefer Seaman to Flowers," he says, before bursting out laughing.

I've no choice now but to respond with the only football-related joke I know. "What did the girl from Braintree say when she became a goalkeeper?" I ask. Without giving him time to reply, I say, "'I was wondering why the ball kept getting bigger and bigger, then it hit me.'"

More press pranks. Last week, Doug let me into one of those secrets that journalists tend to know: he told me that the Pope is a Lloyd's name, with unlimited liability on some very risky syndicates. So, the following morning, posing as His Holiness, I penned a spoof letter to *Insurance Now!* And, hey presto, it's published today.

To a readership of perhaps 30,000, His Holiness allegedly suggests that Curly Cradock has one of the finest minds in the insurance industry, has an excellent sense of humour and is one of the most ethical people that he knows.

It's been on the paper's website since yesterday, from where I'm happy to see it's been picked up (that is, plagiarised) by some of the UK regional press, including the *Rhondda Evergreen*, the *Wirral Off The Record* and, in Yorkshire, by both the *Wakefield Clitty Litter* and the *Leeds Chocolate Starfish*.

Cheers, Doug!

Wednesday 19 June 1996
The Los Angeles Times was first published in 1881

Over the past three months, NOB has appeared in newspapers all over the world and I've given countless TV and radio interviews. Bollocks though it may all be, it's certainly turned out to be great fun spoofing the media with my bogus burger-chain claim.

Parminder assures me that all the backlinks NOB's getting are having a very positive impact and that we'll soon be number one in Yahoo!

To the Grapes at noon with *Tehran Missile Herald* news correspondent Aadam. He flew over to London yesterday after I mentioned to him on Monday that the Pope's a Lloyd's Name and that, what's more, I could show him the evidence.

However, when I take him along to the heavily guarded Lloyd's library to confirm this, it transpires that Doug was wrong – or joking. John Paul II's name is nowhere to be seen in the directories of wealthy Names. A few people with the surname Pope do appear, but Aadam is obviously not impressed and he storms off alone. Presumably to face some stern words from his editor, Abdullah.

Never mind. I've brought my tux in with me for another Lloyd's Summer press party this evening. Tracey's even wiped clean her stilettos. By mid-afternoon we've got a vast amount of work done, so I suggest we lock up and head to the Grapes. Tracey carries a smart holdall containing our smart evening attire and we each get changed in the pub's loos. They're a bit more spacious than the broom cupboard.

Dolled up, at the entrance to the Lloyd's building we're greeted by a gentleman wearing a distinct red liveried uniform. In the 17th century, Lloyd's first started out as a coffee house owned by Edward Lloyd and to this day all its doormen are called waiters. They're the Beefeaters of the City of London.

I lie to the smartly dressed chap that we're guests of the Lloyd's marketing team and we're waved through. I set out to find contacts from my days as an underwriter, while Tracey skips gaily off to do her own thing.

I blank out after my third bottle of red and after only about two hours I'm led forcibly to the exit. Tracey kindly joins me as I'm jettisoned from the premises.

"Where've you been?" I slur as I stagger down the steps.

"Enjoying excellent waiter service!" she replies.

Monday 24 June 1996
BBC Two was founded in 1964

I arrive early at work and as I head to the lift to the broom cupboard, I bump into Mavis.

"How're you doing?" I ask.

"I'm a bit pissed off, to tell you the truth," Mavis replies. "I took a taxi last night and the driver agreed to have sex in lieu of the fare."

"Lucky you!" I say.

"Well no, actually," she replies. "The cheeky tw*t asked me if I'd got anything smaller."

At noon, after a financially productive morning, I step into the sunshine and cross the road to the Grapes, just as it's filling up with some of London's thirstiest insurance practitioners. As I sit at the last free table, a smartly dressed, blonde woman approaches and asks if she can take the seat opposite me. I smile and nod, shifting my papers to make room.

"You here for a job interview?" I ask her.

"Good lord no!" she exclaims. "I've just signed up as a Lloyd's Name!"

"Have you *really*?" I ask.

"Yes!" she says excitedly. "My financial adviser recommended that I go to Lloyd's because of the huge profits that Names make."

I splutter in disbelief and wish her the best of luck.

As I return to the broom cupboard, I ponder the calamity that in recent years has befallen myself and so many other Lloyd's Names: wealthy individuals who naïvely put up their capital as collateral against large-scale insurance claims and who have unfortunately ended up, as the saying goes, down to their last cufflinks.

Before I leave work, I quickly flick through the business pages of the regional press. The *Heathrow Aeroplane Blond*, the *Gatwick Black Box* and the *Grimsby Whitewater Wrister* all have the same headline: *Lloyd's Names go down with huge losses!*

Thursday 27 June 1996
The Trump of Fame was first published in 1812

I set off for a lunchtime meeting in the Elephant with Lance. I need to pick his brains. He's in good form and he kindly suggests to me that since NOB's policies don't contain the neurological or spinal injury exclusion clause common to the rest of the PPI market, I should publicise the fact that NOB is now providing hookers with insurance cover against headache and backache.

"Genius! We'll call it HOOKERSAFE!" I exclaim. "Being a receiver of swollen goods is definitely a risky business and this'll make a page-turner of a news story."

This campaign is going to need careful planning. Back in the broom cupboard, I make a note to be sure to offer the story to Jeremy as an exclusive, but I also set Tracey to work organising NOB's first-ever press conference. I task her with booking a room at the Lamb for the event in early August. While she's getting on with that, I put together a list of journalists for her to invite from the broadsheets, the tabloids and the insurance press.

By the time I've finished, Tracey's booked the venue for lunchtime on 5 August. I hand her my list of a dozen or so reporters and editors for her to invite, along with my friend and industry figure, Mike, who I'm sure will help me out on the day.

Friday 28 June 1996
The Daily Mail was first published in 1896

No RSVPs yet for NOB's landmark press conference. I decide it might be helpful to send Tracey on a tour to butter up the media. I call Doug to ask to borrow his press card, so that Del can forge one for Tracey.

Doug stops me in my tracks. "That'd be a complete bloody waste of time," he says.

"What do you mean?" I ask.

"Press card!" he exclaims derisively. "In three years as a journalist, I've not once been asked to show one."

I'm a little disappointed by this. "So how do we get Tracey into press conferences?" I ask him.

"Just print her some fake business cards," Doug suggests. "Give her the title of insurance reporter at some made-up trade newspaper and add NOB's phone number."

"Is that really all we need to do?" I ask.

"Yes," he says. "She won't be challenged. Generally, the more bums on seats they get at these events the better as it makes the PR people look as though they're doing a good job."

Tracey, I decide, is going to masquerade as the insurance reporter for *Prison Gazette*. I call Del to ask him to print some fake business cards for her to collect this evening. I then call Doug, who tells me that Royal Protection plc is holding a press conference tonight, where Tracey can press the flesh with the media ahead of NOB's own event in August.

I carefully explain to Tracey what she should do at the press conference this evening, stressing that if there are any bottles of wine there, they're for journalists to drink only *after* the formalities of the conference are over. That's what Doug tells me, anyway.

Thursday 1 July 1996
Teletext was founded in 1974

A dental appointment means I'm late this morning into the broom cupboard. Tracey's at her desk when I arrive.

I hang my jacket on my chair before asking her how the press conference went yesterday. She promptly produces the business cards of a couple of dozen journalists. Some of them I know already, but there are quite a few others, including several business correspondents that I'm yet to meet from papers including the *Peckham Disco*, the *Dalston Diamonds*, the *Camberwell Carrot*, the *Newham Bunting*, the *Whitechapel Jetlag*, the *Enfield Pint* and the news editor of the *Putney Ginger Stepchild*. They've all agreed to turn up next month to NOB's press conference.

I'm most impressed and I thank Tracey for her sterling work.

This evening the weather's uncomfortably warm. The broom cupboard could do with air-conditioning. It's therefore a great relief to be outdoors today. After a pint in the Grapes, I walk up the road for the summer party being staged tonight by Syndicate 305, the company where I used to work.

I show my invitation to the waiter before approaching the ground-floor lifts. Standing there is the newly recruited Lloyd's Name I saw a week ago. She looks severely depressed.

A pair of lift doors slide open and I follow her in.

"Are you going down, Madam?" I ask.

"Piss off Curly!" she snaps.

ARE YOU GOING DOWN,
MADAM?

Thursday 4 July 1996
The Chicago Tribune was first published in 1847

I've been trying for about a week to persuade at least one of my female friends to be photographed posing as a hooker touting for business. Unsurprisingly, none of them seem interested. I'm about to leave work when Doug calls to invite me to a media event this evening that's being staged in Soho by *Erotica Fantasia* magazine. I hope I'll have more luck there.

After closing up the broom cupboard, I make my way to the West End. Standing outside the door waiting for Doug to arrive, I notice a group of ladies in short skirts and high heels heading straight towards me.

"Excuse me," says a tall, young woman dressed in brightly striped tights and a crop top.

"My apologies!" I exclaim, quickly moving out onto the street to let them file in through the door. I'm not even inside the event yet and already it's shaping up to be highly promising.

Doug arrives and I follow him inside. A waiter in baggy, colourful clothing stands at the entrance to the event, holding a silver tray of Champagne flutes for guests to help themselves. Through the doorway I see an elegant dining hall, quite incongruous in this seedy Soho setting, with a long table decked with premium drinks and hors d'oeuvres. I neck my Champagne then pour myself a glass of red, before taking a look around at the other guests. Immediately, I identify the host of the event, *Erotica Fantasia* editor Rouen, wearing a glamorous dress and an infectious smile.

I cross the room to introduce myself to her and find myself immediately relaxing: she's really easy to talk to. Soon conscious of others now hovering for her attention, I skip to the business at hand.

"I insure hookers against headache and backache," I tell her. "I'm looking for someone who's prepared to be a case study for the press conference I'm organising in August." Rouen's smile immediately broadens and she gestures to the far corner of the hall where the girls I'd made way for at the building's entrance are gathered.

I walk straight over to them and hand them each my business card.

"Bloody hell! An insurance salesman!" exclaims Destiny, a lovely brunette, in a tone of mock despair, and she and her entourage laugh.

Unperturbed, I explain, "I specialise in insuring hookers against backache and headache."

"Who says we're hookers?" asks Destiny indignantly, just as Rouen walks by.

"Trust me. They are," she says.

Turning back to the girls, I ask if any of them would be up for a modelling job. A cute-looking girl with piercing blue eyes whom I hadn't noticed before steps forward. Her name is Bella. I explain to her that I'd simply like to take a few shots of her in high heels leaning in through a car window as though she's soliciting business which I can give to the press. Bella gives me an enchanting smile and kindly agrees to help me out for free. We arrange to meet up in the Family Jewels near Spitalfields Market the Tuesday after next.

"I INSURE PROSTITUTES
AGAINST LOSS OF INCOME,"
I EXPLAIN

Friday 5 July 1996
The Columbia Broadcasting System (CBS) was founded in 1927

As I arrive at work, Mavis appears at the broom cupboard door and says to Tracey, "I've just bought some condoms from Woolworths and the cheesy tw*t who served me asked if I needed a paper bag. I told him I wasn't *that* f*cking ugly!"

Moments later a courier arrives with a huge bouquet of flowers. "Have a look who they're from, would you?" I say to Tracey.

She places them on the desk and fumbles for a few moments with cellophane, ribbons and paper, before exclaiming, "They're from Mrs Mainwaring!" She proceeds to read the thank-you note aloud. "'Thank you so much for your very kind help with my PPI. With lots of love from Mrs Mainwaring.' How sweet!"

The phone rings again just as I'm taking my jacket off, so Tracey puts it on loudspeaker. It turns out that it's Mrs Mainwaring herself.

"Thank you so much for the lovely flowers!" Tracey cries. "That was most thoughtful of you, they're lovely!"

"My pleasure!" says Mrs Mainwaring. "I contacted my bank as Curly kindly suggested and they've just refunded me every penny of the £12,000 that I've paid in premiums over the past five years."

"That's brilliant news!" says Tracey. "It's always our pleasure to help you in any way that we can."

"Thank you, dear, I know that. Now, would it be possible please to have one of those CJD policies I heard that you offered on Croydon Late Night Radio the other evening?"

"Are you a big meat-eater?" asks Tracey.

"No dear, I'm a vegetarian," she replies.

"In that case you'd really be wasting your money, Mrs Mainwaring. CJD insurance is really not for you."

"Thank you, dear," she replies. She even tells Tracey that she'll recommend NOB to visitors to the Cat Protection shop, where she works as a volunteer every Tuesday and Thursday.

Tracey bids her farewell, thanking her once again for the flowers. Then she hangs up, smiles, looks across at me and says, "She's *such* a nice old lady!"

Wednesday 11 July 1996
Einkommende Zeitungen became the world's first daily newspaper in 1650

I've never knowingly met a wizard, but today I'm having lunchtime drinks with Merlin, the openly gay editor of *The Joy of Hex* magazine. A backlink from there should be powerful magic indeed.

Merlin comes across as a very polite but highly unusual gentleman. He tells me, "I may be a wizard, but I sexually self-identify as a witch doctor."

"Really?" I say, urging him to explain.

"I'll take a little head from anyone," he says with a lecherous grin.

When I return to the broom cupboard, Tracey's on the phone. When she finishes, she says, "I'm afraid that we've got another claim, Curly."

I'm all ears.

She continues, "The guy who just rang says he was recently made redundant from his job as a greengrocer." She pretends to consult her notes then looks up and says, "The poor sod was only given a month's celery and four leeks in lieu of notice."

I look at her for a second before she bursts out laughing.

Tuesday 16 July 1996
The Press Trust of India was founded in 1947

Tracey arrives at the broom cupboard just before 9am She hangs up her coat and asks, "Is it true that most people from Braintree have a speech impediment?"

"Nah! It'zer myff," I reply.

After a long and pretty unproductive day, I ask Tracey if she'd care to join me for a drink in the East End and to meet Bella. I could have guessed the answer would be yes.

As we reach the Family Jewels, a few ladies are already plying their trade on the street outside. We see Bella sitting alone at a table near the bar. I greet her and introduce her to Tracey, before buying a round of drinks. I return from the bar and explain to Bella just what I'd like her to do.

A few minutes later she steps out of the pub and walks slowly along the kerb, just as instructed. As she does so, I draw from my pocket my Kodak Instamatic with a new 24-exposure film loaded at the ready. In a matter of seconds, presumably to the envy of the local competition, Bella is waved to by a driver in a BMW. He pulls over and, as Bella approaches the car, I raise the camera and shoot. I immediately wind on the film and repeat this a few times. Bella starts to lean in closer to the driver, with her head almost through the car window as I take a seventh, then an eighth shot.

I'm still winding on the camera when she opens the passenger door and climbs in. As the car turns around, she waves to us, before disappearing into the warm summer night.

Tracey and I return to the pub and I make a note to have a few dozen copies of the film processed tomorrow, for us to hand out to journalists along with the HOOKERSAFE press release.

OKAY, BUT NOTHING TOO RISKY!
I DON'T WANT TO LOSE MY
NO-CLAIMS-BONUS

Monday 29 July 1996
National Public Radio (NPR) was founded in 1970

Approaching the Lloyd's building this morning, I see what appears to be a crowd of tramps. I say hello and comment on the remarkably high proportion of them reading formidable financial newspaper the *Wembley No Score Drawers*.

"Yes. Well, of course, finance is merely of academic interest these days," says Milo, a chap in an extraordinarily posh voice wearing a grubby, navy-coloured velvet suit. A tall, elegant, white-haired woman stands beside him slowly nodding.

It suddenly dawns on me that today is the Lloyd's AGM. These poor, down-on-their-luck individuals must all in fact be Lloyd's Names. I pass on my best wishes as I make my way to the broom cupboard.

"Orright?" says Tracey when I walk in.

"Yes, thanks," I reply. "I've just bumped into Snow White and the Seven Lloyd's Names."

"*Who?*" she asks, looking puzzled.

I reply, "Broke, Skint, Penniless, Boracic, Bereft, Hard-Up and Bankrupt."

My day improves when Tracey tells me, "Vicky called to say that she'll kill herself if you don't take her back."

"Isn't it great when problems just solve themselves?" I ask, rhetorically.

"What's Vicky actually like?" asks Tracey.

"She's a bit like the Mona Lisa," I reply. "Not quite as pretty, but I'd be over the moon if I got home and found her hanging in the living room."

"Curly, that's really cruel!" Tracey exclaims.

"I'm only joking," I say reassuringly. "When Vicky and I first went out together, we got on okay. She used to give me nicknames when we made love."

"That's sweet!" says Tracey.

I nod. "It was," I say. "'Impaler' was my favourite, until I realised she was asthmatic."

NAME DROPPING AT LLOYD'S

Monday 5 August 1996
The People's Daily was first published in 1948

Big day today, preparing for NOB's first press conference. One important thing I must do this morning is write the HOOKERSAFE press release and email it to Jeremy. I'll add a spoof comment from Kimmy Head of the British Sex Workers Association, who I'll claim told me that her members can now swing from chandeliers without worrying about losing their no-claims bonus. Tracey can then print out 50 copies for journalists at the event, along with the photos of Bella.

It's raining. From her desk drawer, she pulls a Presto carrier bag in which to keep the press releases and photos dry during our walk to the venue.

To save having an argument about the use of illegal drugs in the workplace, I empty my briefcase and pass it to her to use instead of the crumpled polythene bag. "Looks more professional," I assure her.

The format of the press conference is simple: free booze for all journalists as they arrive. Then I'll stand to tell them that, basically, all the info they need is in the press release. Next, Mike has kindly agreed to speak for about five minutes, in his capacity as chief executive of the English Insurance Agents Association, about the significance of NOB's breakthrough in offering hookers headache and backache cover. Then I'll answer a couple of questions, before – bingo! – It's time for more drinks. Piece of piss.

As soon as we arrive at the Lamb, I go for a slash. As I pee at one of the urinals, I hear the sound of muffled choking to my left. There's a kerfuffle, then a cubicle door opens and out comes Louis from the *Gateshead Spike* in corduroys and a smoking jacket, doing up his flies and looking rather pleased with himself, in the mirror.

Tracey emerges soon behind him. "All done!" she says, wiping her chin. "Off to mingle!"

And mingle she does. She chats away and exchanges business cards with every hack there.

A few journalists hang around for another hour or so to enjoy the free booze. By 3.30pm, they've all left. I'm about to leave myself, when Sid the landlord waves a bar bill of £510.94 in front of me.

"For your attention, Curly!" he says, politely but firmly.

"Send it to Accounts Payable at the Big Bristols Channel," I say, handing him a spoof business card that Del has kindly printed for me as the channel's insurance correspondent.

Sid looks at it puzzled as I make a hasty exit.

As I make my way to the Tube, I buy a copy of the late edition of the *Jaywick Verminillionaire*. Sure enough, it has the story, which reveals that, for the first time in history, Lloyd's is underwriting cover on behalf of "professional ladies".

Trust me. If you're looking for fun, spoof the press.

Tuesday 6 August 1996
L'Illustration published the first newspaper photograph in 1848

At yesterday's press conference, Tracey amazed me when she offered to be photographed naked on the steps of the Lloyd's building to help publicise NOB. I really didn't think she meant it, but at dawn this morning I find myself driving her, Doug and his flatmate, Alison, to the imposing Richard Rodgers creation, situated a hundred or so yards from the broom cupboard.

I park nearby on yellow lines in a side street off Leadenhall Market. Tracey walks up the steps to the edifice, where she removes her light, minimalist dress – all she happens to be wearing apart from her sandals. Alison takes a series of photographs of Tracey, tits out and holding a placard with the slogan I LOVE NOB over her fanny.

As Tracey's going through various poses, some deliberately more revealing than others, the sounds of running footsteps and voices broadcast by CB radio burst into the air. I look round to see Derek, Lloyd's head of security and a convoy of other security guards that I recognise emerging from the Lloyd's building. I watch them jog, single file, not straight towards us, but instead across the road to the smaller, older Lloyd's building opposite, presumably to get a chance to see what its CCTV cameras have caught.

After a few more shots, Tracey whips her summer dress back on before I drive the four of us to the Loop the Loop pub, conveniently open early for Smithfield market traders.

Tracey seems anxious as I approach the bar. I suspect it's delayed stage-fright after her magnificent naked performance. But it's not. Standing next to me as I wait to be served, she asks, "Curly, if you've to pay out to burger-chain employees, will you still be able to afford to pay my wages?"

With that, I address the barman. "I'll have a double whisky and a Tracey of lager, please."

"A pint, sir?" he asks.

"No," I reply, "a bottle. Empty from the neck up."

After half a dozen rounds, I take the roll of film from Alison. I drop it off at Boots, where Freda the assistant assures me that the pictures will be ready for collection first thing tomorrow.

Wednesday 7 August 1996
Granada Television was founded in 1956

Doug drops by the broom cupboard to collect the developed pictures, before leaving to doorstep Derek for a comment on the naked truth.

Mid-morning, I take a call from Sir David. The Lloyd's chairman wishes me to know that he thinks I'm a wanker.

"Sticks and stones may break my bones, but Lloyd's Names will never hurt me!" I reply before putting the phone down.

The silly season is truly upon us. The photo of Bella has now been published in several national UK newspapers. A few regional papers, among them the *Belfast Hatchetjob*, the *Felixstowe Dockers Omelette* and the *Penistone Bone of Contention*, have the headline: *Man from the Pro!* The *Spam Javelin* reports that insurers are offering cover to hookers "hurt in the line of duty" and today's *Bootle Divergent Thinker* reports my claim – false, of course – that if HOOKERSAFE doesn't make me rich then I'll open a massage parlour.

Down Under, the *Melbourne Morning Commode*, the *Wagga Wagga False Dichotomy* and the *Cook Islands Ring Ripper* report that business is "hotting up" for hookers, while in New Zealand, the *Christchurch Balearics* informs its readers in a front-page splash that hookers *insure their assets!* Finally, the *Auckland Brown Admiral* leads on page three with *Insurers prostitute themselves*. It *nearly* works.

Evening drinks with Ralph. The evening's going swimmingly, right up until the point when I tell him that Tracey thinks she knows who's been stealing her underwear. At this, Ralph's complexion changes and he nearly craps her pants.

Thursday 8 August 1996
The Roswell Daily Record was first published in 1891

Walking down Lime Street, I bump into my friend and former colleague, Joe. Italian by birth, he's a complete UFO fanatic. I cajole him into accepting a pint in the Grapes, where I quiz him about alien abductions. He reels off accounts of recorded sightings of unidentified flying objects in places like Roswell and Bonnybridge before he tells me he was once nearly arrested by the military police at a base near Swindon while he was out UFO-spotting.

I tell him that NOB's thinking about launching ETSAFE, an alien abduction insurance policy. We're onto our third round before Joe poses a question. "Have you got anyone who's interested in being a case study?"

"Funny you should ask that," I reply. "I have. And I'm looking at him right now."

"Me?" he says, sounding surprised.

"Fancy being in the papers?

"Do I!" he exclaims. I think by this he means yes.

"We can give you a false name," I suggest. "How about Joseph Carpenter?"

Suddenly Joe looks at his watch and dashes off late back to work.

Meanwhile, I owe Mike a drink for his help at the press conference. He's arriving back in London by train at 6pm, so after work I head to the Cottage Cheese Pasty in Kings Cross, one of my favourite strippers' pubs. We wander into the unassuming-looking bar where, every few minutes, a scantily clad young lady invites patrons to drop money into a pint jug, while another waltzes around naked for the pleasure of the overwhelmingly male punters.

I look around at the pub's wasted clientèle. Beneath the iron staircase at the rear of the bar, I spot a party of gentlemen from Rhino Insurance. Beside them is a vacant table. I stride over and jump up in one go onto the unoccupied table. I drop my trousers and moon them, to show them a Made-in-Staffordshire tattoo on my arse. Although I was born in Tasmania, I was conceived in the Potteries, when my parents spent their honeymoon there. The trip was a wedding present from my mum's sister Auntie Phyllis, which she bought using Green Shield stamps.

I jump back down from the table, taking a quick look at their horrified faces. Suddenly it turns out I was wrong. I've actually no idea who they are.

It's approaching 10pm and Mike and I are thrown out of the pub. The sun's gone down as we head off in different directions for our respective trains home.

Friday 9 August 1996
The Southport Visiter (sic) was first published in 1844

I'm in work early this morning, catching up on paperwork, when I notice an invitation to visit Southport to meet Clare, the editor of the *Southport Gossipor*, who's promised me that if she runs the story, she'll give NOB a backlink from her paper's website. I do hope that she can spell 'NOB', for she clearly has some difficulty with the word 'Gossiper'.

Southport. It's one of those resorts that was elegant in the 19th century but which, for decades, has become the go-to destination for immigrants who enjoy living in seaside hotels at the expense of the British taxpayer. As long ago as the mid-1970s, not only had the tourists f*cked off, but so too had the sea.

Listening to Ophelia Balls on Das Kapital Radio, the only news seems to concern the imminent release of Independence Day, a film about an alien attack on Earth. I'm hugely impressed. Quite how they've managed to time the film's release to coincide with scientists' discovery this week of evidence of life on Mars is beyond me.

Time for some low-budget spoofing. I send an ETSAFE press release to Jeremy, with details of the £1 million policy NOB has issued to Joseph Carpenter in the event that he's abducted, eaten or impregnated by aliens.

Saturday 10 August 1996
The Bullfrog Miner was first published in 1905

On my way to meet Doug and Alison for a lunchtime drink at the Mutton Musket in the theatre district of the West End, I pop into the broom cupboard to read the latest press cuttings.

The French just can't help themselves. A story in *Nouvelles du monde* has the headline *Hookers Under the Protection of Lloyd's!* The story begins, "From the coveted legs of Marilyn Monroe to the breasts of Ingrid Bergman, Lloyd's is an insurance market for the most exceptional risks. The launch of the first insurance contract for hookers gives a big shakeup to this esteemed institution...Even the positions described in the Kamasutra are insured!"

I'm still chuckling about this faithful interpretation of my off-the-cuff bollocks, when Mavis suddenly walks into the broom cupboard. She looks distraught.

"What's the matter, Mavis?" I ask. "You look awful!"

"Oh Curly, I've just had a terrible shock," she says.

"Oh no! What happened?" I ask.

"I'd left the launderette and was coming into work when I was knocked down at a zebra crossing outside the East London Hospital," she says.

"Oh no! Are you okay?"

"Yes, I am, thank goodness" she says. "Fortunately, a doctor was at hand to check for concussion. He said to me slowly, 'Now listen carefully – how many fingers am I putting up?' I suddenly thought, 'Oh f*ck! I must be paralysed from the waist down!'"

Monday 12 August 1996
Yahoo! News is founded today

Not a day passes without some or other news story or TV show dedicated to the approaching "new millennium". I'm certainly looking forward to it myself, for that's when my professional association with Fred will mercifully come to an end. But it occurs to me that the so-called Y2K bug is getting far more publicity than it truly deserves. It's obviously time for NOB to inform the media that we're now offering women protection against virgin birth.

For good measure, I'll also mention that for girls called Mary, there's an obvious extra level of concern and that we're going to step in to give these Marys some much-needed peace of mind for the same premium as everyone else. With any luck, this will generate decent worldwide coverage, along with the backlinks needed to boost NOB's search rankings.

I unlock the broom cupboard and turn on my computer to draft a VIRGINSAFE press release to send by email to Jeremy. I add a spoof comment from Fonda Cox of the Catholic Media Office about immaculate conceptions being quite rare and that she could only think of one. I suppose the church will object to the idea of virgin birth insurance, but hey, it's love thy neighbour, not thy choirboy.

That's three press releases in a week. I cross the road for a self-congratulatory pint at the Grapes.

" ALTHOUGH WOMEN NAMED MARY ARE
DEEMED BY UNDERWRITERS TO BE AT
HIGHER RISK, THE POLICY DOES NOT
DISCRIMINATE AGAINST THEM IN PRICE "

Tuesday 13 August 1996
The Thai News Agency was founded in 1977

I'm in the broom cupboard early when Tracey passes me the phone. It's a call from Li, a reporter from the *Bangkok Fudge Nudger*, whom I'm able to inform – untruthfully, of course – that a couple of her paper's readers have indeed bought VIRGINSAFE. I *love* making up complete bollocks on the spot.

It's approaching lunchtime when Tracey takes a call from Mrs Mainwaring. After she hangs up, Tracey says, "Don't worry, Curly. I was able to put her off buying VIRGINSAFE. When I asked her if her name was Mary, she said, 'No, it's Betsy,' so I told her that she'd be better off saving her money."

"Thank you," I say. "It's just a pity that UK banks don't do the same and instead keep selling the kind of shit cover that their customers will never be able to claim on."

Doug's story about Tracey stripping on the steps of Lloyd's is now out in print and includes a made-up quote from Derek describing Tracey as an elegant young woman who was posing naked apart from a strategically placed advertisement for NOB.

His paper's story quotes me praising the security staff for their alertness – being at the scene within seconds of the 27th shot taken. It concludes with another rather dubious quote from Derek: "This job is normally quite boring. I couldn't believe my eyes when I saw the security camera's TV screens. But by the time we arrived, the bird had got her kit back on."

Meanwhile a photo of the naked Tracey also appears in the *Quimlich Manoeuvre*, the *Phoenix Firestarter*, the *El Paso Three-Wheeler* and my old favourite, the *Wilmslow Boss-Eyed Bimbo*.

At lunchtime I head out for drinks with Brian, an old colleague of mine who now works for Aardvark Insurance, a neighbouring underwriting firm in Lime Street. Net result: NOB, in a strategic shift to concentrate exclusively on PPI, has sold its entire portfolio of travel insurance to Aardvark.

NOB has of course never sold travel insurance but Brian is happy to play ball. In exchange for a few pints, he hands me a cheque made out for the sum of Six Pounds Only. That to me is a six-figure sum.

I write a quick press release and email it to Jeremy.

Thursday 15 August 1996
The Coventry Telegraph was first published in 1891

A string of calls from various broadcasters today.

I'm just coming back to my desk from the lavatory when Tracey passes me the receiver. It's Francesco from Christian Radio, asking for an interview. I'm happy to oblige, I say, provided it doesn't take long. Straight away Francesco asks me, "Are you a Christian, Mr Cradock?"

Somewhat baffled, I reply, "I was baptised into the Church of England, but I had little choice in the matter." I then proceed to tell him that I believe that Jesus was a wise and decent human, adding, "I also believe that charlatans have subverted his teachings. If he'd come back 500 years ago, he'd have been burned at the stake as a heretic."

Francesco stops me and demands, "Explain why you hold this extreme view!"

"I shall!" I say. "Let me give you an example. While the new Coventry Cathedral was being built after the original 14th century building was bombed by the Nazis, many senior figures in the church didn't want the sculpture of Saint Michael to be made by Jacob Epstein simply because he was a Jew. Can you believe it? Now I'd like to ask you a question," I say.

"Go ahead," replies Francesco.

"Do you know of a decent carpenter?"

CLICK-CLICK-BRRRRRR.

With big grin on my face I open the post.

At the top of the pile is a formal-looking envelope with a Vatican City postmark. I open it excitedly, hoping that His Holiness the Pope has decided to make me a Knight of the Holy See. But no. It merely says:

Dear Mr Cradock,

Please be aware that His Holiness the Pope is both the Bishop of Rome and Sovereign of the Vatican City State. Immediately desist from referring to His Holiness as the head of the world's largest paedophile gang. If you do so again you will be excommunicated without further notice. This means you will go definitely go to Hell provided that you don't repent at the last minute,

Yours Faithfully,
Father Ted Harden-Thicke
Child Abuse Denial Department
The Roman Catholic Church

Friday 16 August 1996
The New York Tribune published the first newspaper editorial in 1841

Business reporters from the *Münich Felchmeister*, the *Tijuana Cha-Cha*, the *Manhattan Marmalade Madam* and the *Mexico Liquid Bookmark* all call one after the other today to ask me the same question: just how much did NOB receive from the sale of its travel insurance business? I apologise for being vague, saying I'm under contractual non-disclosure obligations, but I tell each of them, off the record, that the undisclosed six-figure sum is closer to £100,000 than it is to £1 million.

Well, I can't lie to the press, can I?

I'm having lunch today with Verity, the editor of the *Blackpool Dead Donkey* to thank her for the editorial she wrote about NOB's sale of its portfolio of travel insurance. After I've paid the bill and we're about to leave the restaurant, Verity becomes abusive when I tell her the truth about the six-figure sum. I'm puzzled for a moment, until it transpires that she simply doesn't like being spoofed into writing a false editorial. With a bit of luck, she won't remove the backlink from her website.

Just as I arrive in the broom cupboard after a successful client lunch, Tracey says, "You just missed a call from Vicky."

"Not again!" I reply. "What does she want this time?"

"She asked me to let you know you're a contrarian," says Tracey.

"Well, if she calls back, tell her I disagree."

Joe calls at noon to ask me if I saw Hi-V TV news yesterday. I confess to him that I didn't, so he tells me that he said, to camera, that when Oprah the presenter said that a million quid pay-out would be no use to him on Mars, he told her that 97% of all alien abductees come back to Earth.

A diamond geezer!

Tuesday 27 August 1996
The Azerbaijan TV and Radio Programme Society was founded in 1956

A juvenile idea – my favourite kind – crosses my mind while I'm skimming through the *North Dakota Bender*. It features an article on professional indemnity specialist Mike Hunt Underwriting Inc. in its business pages. The Lloyd's building uses a Tannoy public address system, which is operated by a panel of strait-laced ladies of late middle-age. The idea I find myself struggling to resist is that of walking into the huge building and requesting that one of them page the US insurer in question.

It's getting too much of a temptation. Mid-morning, leaving Tracey in charge of the broom cupboard, I walk to the end of Lime Street, up the stairs and into Lloyd's. There I cross to the bank of Tannoy ladies. The first of them looks up. "May I help you sir?" she asks.

"Yes, please," I reply. "I'm dreadfully sorry to trouble you, but I have an appointment with a chap called Mike Hunt, and I fear he may be lost somewhere in the building. I don't suppose you could ask if anyone has seen him."

"No problem at all, sir," says the Mrs Slocombe-lookalike as she turns on the microphone, clearing her throat. "Has anyone seen Mike Hunt?" she says to the entire building of around 8,500 staff. Deadpan and without smiling.

"Thank you very much," I say, before slipping back out via one of the revolving doors and down the steps – by this time laughing uncontrollably.

My phone's been buzzing intermittently this afternoon with messages that I've had no time to listen to. At 3pm I dial in to hear two dozen voicemails. Half of them are from a newspaper reporter called Khalil in Baku. He starts by telling me that as well as writing for the *Beetle Bonnet*, Azerbaijan's best-selling newspaper, he freelances for the *Minsk Love Truncheon*, the *Khartoum Pant Stripper* and the *Kandahar Iced Fingers*. He seems to be after details on the global availability of hooker insurance policies. In broken but largely comprehensible English, he informs me in the message that the Azerbaijani hooker market has expanded massively since the fall of the Soviet Union a few years ago. I hang up, wondering what the Azerbaijani word is for backlink, before dealing with a grim couple of hours of administration.

Tracey finally cheers me up as she opens the door to leave the broom cupboard. "Do you know what I like best about press conferences?" she asks.

"No. Tell me," I reply.

"The all-you-can-eat press releases!" she replies, laughing raucously as she shuts the door behind her.

HAS ANYONE SEEN MIKE HUNT?

Thursday 29 August 1996
The Kingston Whig Standard was first published in 1926

The broom cupboard's unusually peaceful this morning as I read through this week's disparate array of cuttings. The *Redditch Ragman's Trumpet*, the *Bradwell Bricky's Crack* and the *Bristol Cliterati* all quote English Insurance Agents Association director of communications, Sally, saying, "We've looked closely at the ETSAFE policy offered by NOB and, given the increasing number of claims related to alien abductions, we'd advise consumers to contact NOB without delay." I hope Sally will forgive me for falsely using her name when she returns to work from her maternity leave.

I delve deeper into the pile, where I'm delighted to see the same quote from Sally featured in the *Ghana Yellow Banana*, the *Belgrade Balkans*, the *Hanoi Afterburner* and the *Caracas Maracas*.

Tracey finally comes into work nearly 90 minutes late but in an unusually excited mood. She tells me that it's two years to the day since Rolf Harris broadcast the first episode of Animal Hospital from the Billabong Veterinary Hospital.

"It was absolutely brilliant!" she cries. "Rolf met 12 Great Dane puppies as well as their parents, Digger and Brandy. Rolf's such a lovely man!"

"If you say so," I reply.

With that, I make my fourth visit of the week to the Tannoy ladies at Lloyd's. When I get back to the broom cupboard, Tracey is talking to Mavis about how fantastic Rolf is. Mavis then tells Tracey that at Easter she took her niece Sharon to meet him and the animals while they were filming in London.

"Rolf was absolutely fantastic!" says Mavis. "He gave Sharon a lovely plastic kangaroo and a sore pussy."

ROLF GAVE ME A LOVELY
PLASTIC KANGAROO AND
A SORE PUSSY

Friday 30 August 1996
The Sarajevo Oslobođenje was first published in 1943

Fifth visit of the week to the ladies of Lloyd's. I begin my preamble to the last of them, but on this occasion the woman next to her hears me. Looking across, she recognises me and snaps, "Piss off Curly!"

Rumbled, I stagger out, pissing myself with laughter.

Oh well. Fun while it lasted.

At noon, I get a call from Sir David, this time to complain about my misuse of the Lloyd's Tannoy system and to let me know that he still thinks that I'm a wanker.

"Is that a Lloyd's Name?" I ask.

"Sarcasm is the lowest form of wit," he replies.

"The phrase you're looking for is, 'Sarcasm is the lowest form of wit, but the highest form of intelligence,'" I reply. Tempting further sarcasm, I say, "So, F*ck wit?"

I resist the temptation to ask him whether *he's* ever seen Mike Hunt, but I'm still fairly sure that's me off the Lloyd's Christmas card list.

I hang up and Tracey asks me, "Do you really not like Lloyd's?"

"On the contrary!" I reply.

She looks confused. "But I just thought they took people's money to make themselves rich," she says.

"Not at all!" I reply. "Lloyd's is the world's pre-eminent insurance market."

"You really think so?" asks Tracey.

"Absolutely! Listen to this," I say. "Four years ago, before I was sent to Belmarsh, my family ran a large haulage company. The United Nations asked us to get the first humanitarian aid to the citizens of Sarajevo during the war in Bosnia. This initially consisted of 90 truckloads of potatoes."

Tracey's already absorbed in the story. I continue, "As you can imagine, this was a lousy risk that no sensible insurer would want to cover. Lloyd's, on the other hand, kindly agreed to underwrite it when one else would touch it. As far as they were concerned, starving people trumped profits."

"Did the hungry people get their spuds?" Tracey asks.

"Indeed they did!" I reply. "In fact, owing to the bravery and professionalism of the drivers and the British Army who provided them with protection, the potatoes were delivered without loss of either life or property. And it ended up costing Lloyd's nothing."

Tracey's spellbound, but I haven't finished. "Some days later I was called to Lloyd's, where I was informed that every single underwriter had voluntarily given a 100% refund of the premium. The result was that the United Nations was charged nothing." I pause before adding, "That's why Lloyd's is still around after 300 years."

Monday 2 September 1996
Associated Press was founded in 1846

Raising NOB's profile and, more importantly, giving NOB another backlink, the *Canterbury Anal Delight* reports that insurance for virgins is 'no joke' and that the Church of England is unimpressed. The paper loyally uses verbatim my fabricated quote, attributed to a spokesman for the General Synod: "Parishioners are advised to do better things with their money, such as paying to have their loved ones released from purgatory."

Today, Tracey's quoted for the first time under her media name in the *Baghdad Ball Buster*. The article reports that Mary Kelly, 28, is NOB's first-ever virgin birth insurance policyholder. She says that if she were to be impregnated by God then she'd want to ensure she could afford the school fees and to bring up his Son in a lifestyle commensurate with his status. The story even features my made-up quote from the Catholic Media Office: "Immaculate conceptions are rare. I can only think of one."

A column in this morning's *Bolton Bit of Rough* details how much light-hearted fun journalists are having with NOB's stories, suggesting virgin birth is a useful alibi for a young lady to have. Also, Margaret, a researcher from WCTV's The End of the Week Show, invites me to appear on Friday's programme to discuss immaculate conception insurance. She writes,

> "The pre-millennial aspects of your insurance policies are especially intriguing. We'd dearly love to have you and one of your policyholders to appear on our programme to discuss those anxieties that have necessitated the creation of such a policy."

Keen not to disappoint Margaret, I send her Tracey's mobile number.

At 4pm I ask Tracey if she has any plans for the evening.

"A night in with the BBC," she replies.

"You've got to be kidding!" I exclaim. "The Big Bristols Channel hasn't broadcast anything worth watching since The Rise of Woman. These days, it's all quizzes, reality TV and other such crap for retards."

Tracey interrupts me impatiently. "I *know* that," she says. "But Del's coming round to give me his own BBC."

"His BBC? What on Earth are you talking about?"

"His big black cock," she says, rolling her eyes.

I'm embarrassingly slow on the uptake. But it makes me think. I'm becoming increasingly annoyed by the lowbrow garbage that's almost exclusively broadcast by the Big Bristols Channel. I'd always understood that it was their job to inform, to educate and to entertain. How wrong I was!

Tuesday 3 September 1996
BBC News Quiz was first broadcast in 1977

Today, NOB's treated to coverage that money can't buy. Researching a story on HOOKERSAFE, a reporter for the *Three-Nob Gob* named Leonard has done his job and taken the trouble to ring Nina, the manager of a South London massage parlour, who told him that all the girls there have BUPA, so none of them will be buying HOOKERSAFE.

Now the first stories about ETSAFE are fast appearing in the increasingly fat envelopes of press cuttings arriving from the agency. The headline, *Close Encounters of the Third Party!* appears across a dozen or so UK newspapers as well as the *Wollongong Aussie Kiss* and the *Colombo Deadline*. Meanwhile, an editorial in the *Luxor Inverted Pyramid* accuses Britain's insurers of resorting to desperate measures. It reports that NOB is the first company in the world to offer insurance against alien impregnation regardless of its sex appeal.

The *Kinshasa Chum Bucket* runs the story in style, revealing that NOB has alien insurance policies to give away to four lucky readers. And its front-page headline screams: NOB *is offering Cover for Uranus!*

I head out to lunch at the Grapes with Tracey just before 1pm to beat the rush. I buy us each a drink and sit down opposite her. "Is it the 3rd today?" I ask.

She glances down at her copy of today's *Islington Reverse Ferret*. "It is," she replies.

"Then today's the birthday of William Wilberforce."

"Who?" she asks.

I'm amazed that she doesn't know. "Mr Wilberforce helped abolish slavery in the early 19th century. Great Britain was the first country in the world to do so," I tell her.

"Do you know what else Mr Wilberforce wanted to do?" I ask her.

"No. What?" she asks.

"He wanted to abolish the National Lottery."

"Oh, that's not fair!" she says. "I *love* the Lottery!"

"Well, personally I can't abide gambling," I retort. "It's more damaging than porn. Entire families are f*cked with gambling! I used to insure the directors of Jack Potts, the UK's largest bookmakers, but I'd never play the Lottery."

"Really?" she asks.

"Really!" I reply. "Statistically, I still have the same chance of winning the jackpot as anyone who spends £10 a week on it: virtually nil! They don't advertise *that* on TV."

"Blimey!" says Tracey.

Wednesday 4 September 1996
Thames Television was founded in 1968

It's stiflingly warm in the unventilated broom cupboard this morning when the phone rings. Tracey answers, then puts her hand over the mouthpiece and tells me across the desk, "It's someone called Carl Sagan for you."

Excitedly, I reach out and take the phone from her. In a distinguished American accent, the astronomer tells me, "Curly, I just wanted to give you a call to thank you for raising awareness of extra-terrestrial intelligence."

I'm flattered and deeply honoured at the opportunity to speak to such a distinguished figure. We chat for the best part of half an hour and he suggests that any future extra-terrestrial life that visits Earth will be synthetic and not natural. "There won't be anything artificial about it, that's for sure!" he says. I promise him I'll pass this insight on to my underwriters.

At the end of the call, I agree to send him a complimentary ETSAFE policy to hang on the wall of – as he puts it – his restroom. He doesn't sound well, but he promises in return to send me a signed first edition copy of Cosmos. What a gent!

I hang up, exhilarated by the call. "Tracey," I say, "What's the difference between Braintree and Mars?"

She looks at me blankly.

"There might be intelligent life on Mars."

"Sometimes you can be really cutting!" she snaps.

"Please forgive me," I say. "Sarcasm is the brain's natural defence against the less intelligent. As an outsider, what's your perspective on intelligence?"

"Cheeky tw*t!" she says.

"I know you think that I'm sarcastic," I say, "but you should watch me pretend to care."

She looks at me, frowning. "I don't get it," she says as we set off for the pub.

"Don't worry," I say, "I've neither the time nor the crayons to explain it to you."

Thursday 5 September 1996
The Amityville Record was first published in 1904

NOB is the first insurance company in the UK to remove pregnancy as an exclusion in a PPI policy. However, I know from my experience with PAYMENTSAFE that nobody in the media will be interested. We're therefore upping the ante with the launch of SPOOKSAFE, a policy to protect housewives against having the willies put up them. I'm sure this'll get NOB plenty of media coverage and some much-needed backlinks.

I've made up a lovely spoof comment from Colchester housewife, Annie Position, who allegedly told me that the thought of her home having been built over a plague-pit really gave her the willies. I'll include this in my email to Jeremy.

Tracey and I take 50 printed copies of the press release with us to tonight's hastily organised press conference venue, the famously haunted Blue-Veined Blunderbuss in Spitalfields. I haven't bothered to reserve a room. The 50 or so journalists that Tracey emailed this morning will be able to soak up the atmosphere, get plastered and then leave, to provide NOB with some much-needed backlinks.

The pub is worryingly full of regular punters as we arrive ahead of the event, but the crowd soon thins as members of the press start to arrive just before 7pm To my relief there's easily enough space for us all to stand together at one end of the bar.

I choose my moment, clear my throat and announce, "Ladies and gentlemen of the press, good evening."

Nobody pays any attention. I stand on a bar stool and repeat my words more slowly, loudly and clearly. Still hardly any response. So I try, "Help yourself to spirits!"

That works. Tracey hands out a copy of the press release to the hacks present, then places the remaining pile on the bar.

Just before 10pm, I reward myself with one more pint before thanking everyone for their support and leaving myself. I make my way along Commercial Street, past Spitalfields Market and the distinctive Christ Church by Nicholas Hawksmoor. There I see the familiar Tower Hamlets sight of a small group of Asian hookers touting for business. I suppose this gives the term "Just popping out for an Indian" a whole new meaning. I must tell Parminder.

Monday 9 September 1996
The International Herald Tribune was first published in 1967

By lunchtime, I'm already enjoying a lucrative start to the week. Since early summer, PAYMENTSAFE has really been taking off. It's horrifying to think of all those customers having a gun put to their head by banks to make them sign up for their worthless PPI when they could buy far cheaper and infinitely more legitimate cover from NOB.

I expect SPOOKSAFE will take a day or two to work through the editorial news desks. In the meantime, I open the latest batch of cuttings that arrive in a fat A4 envelope. Top of the pile is a front-page report in the *Elgin Marble*, which runs the headline: *Knocked Up by Aliens!* With this alien abduction insurance, the story says, you could be a million quid better off if a Cyberman has his way with you, now that a "top insurer" – think NOB and its broom cupboard – is offering insurance against MEN being raped by aliens.

This paper certainly knows how to report a story in style.

Mid-afternoon, Tracey finds herself in another phone conversation with Mrs Mainwaring, who's obviously read somewhere in the press that NOB's insuring housewives against having the willies put up them.

"Don't panic, Mrs Mainwaring," says Tracey. "It's quite natural when you live alone to feel nervous or frightened sometimes. If you make sure that you lock your doors and windows when you go to bed, you should be fine."

She finishes the call and hangs up. "Mrs Mainwaring's absolutely terrified of that man they call the Minstead Rapist," she says.

"I've heard about that f*cker!" I say. "Police say he's a Jamaican who's raping pensioners in South London. He should be publicly hanged, but he won't be. I doubt he'll even be convicted of a hate crime." I think for a moment, before angrily exclaiming, "To do so he'll have needed to have demonstrated hostility based on race, religion, disability, sexual orientation or transgender identity!" I'm fuming as I conclude, "Blacks raping white pensioners or murdering white children isn't classed as a hate crime, according to the *wankers* in the Home Office!"

Tuesday 10 September 1996
The Sun was first published in 1964

Newspaper coverage of SPOOKSAFE starts to materialise in the press cuttings. A news analysis piece in *The Broadmoor Broadsheet* wittily suggests that the policy could be just the thing to offer peace of mind after an episode of The X-Files. Meanwhile a report in the *Oslo Splash* reveals that I admit NOB's customers would need to look beyond just the *spirit* of the policy – geddit?

Wednesday 11 September 1996
The Daily Record was first published in 1895

SPOOKSAFE coverage continues apace. Hungover, I receive a call this morning from Gideon, an independent radio news broadcaster from Alcopoop FM, requesting an interview on insurance cover for "people who fear they may be attacked by evil spirits."

The only evil spirit I can think of now is the bottle of whisky I drank yesterday evening. But I valiantly struggle through his questions.

Before hanging up, Gideon tells me the interview is set for broadcast on more than 20 independent local radio stations "from Land's End to John O'Groats". That cheers me up: I reckon it'll generate a fair few backlinks.

It's mid-morning. Tracey brings me a mug of coffee. Irish, two sugars. Just how I like it. As she places it on my desk, she says, "Nearly time for Johnnie Walker."

I look up and point at the mug. "It's Johnnie Walker?"

"No!" she snaps. "Your call with him is any moment now." Right then my phone rings and I find myself interrogated at length by the very same radio DJ that I remember having had the pleasure of listening to in the mid-1970s when he presented Top Hits on national radio.

Johnnie asks me why NOB launched SPOOKSAFE in the first place. I explain to the broadcast legend that many housewives are concerned about having the willies put up them and that NOB is simply rising to the challenge.

However, to my dismay he scoffs, telling me SPOOKSAFE doesn't sound credible. He continues to challenge me relentlessly, before eventually I ask, "Tell me, Johnnie, what's hung like a donkey and hangs up?"

CLICK-CLICK-BRRRRRR.

I don't think that last bit was ever broadcast.

Thursday 12 September 1996
The Unterrified Democrat was first published in 1866

I meet up with Jeff for a liquid lunch in the Chocolate Shark. Six pints in, just as Jeff goes for a slash, my phone rings. It's Shawn from Pocket Billiards TV. He wants me to come to his studio to appear on their flagship 6pm show to talk about NOB's unusual insurance policies.

"Thank you so much for the call," I say. "The problem is that I've already had six pints, with a seventh on its way. I'm truly in no state to be interviewed today."

Shawn asks me if there's anyone else from NOB who can attend. I think for a second. "Yes. Jeff, my senior underwriter," I say, before giving him Jeff's mobile number, whose phone starts to ring just as he returns from the loo. He answers and I listen, amused, as he speaks. He kindly doesn't divulge to Shawn that he doesn't actually work for NOB and he fails in his attempts not to appear on the show. The TV channel promptly sends a car to collect him.

I skip going back to the broom cupboard and instead stagger off to take the Tube home.

At around 9pm I'm awoken from a drunken slumber on the sofa by a call from Jeff, ringing to tell me about his TV interview. He clearly has a gift when it comes to spoofing, for he explains that after he was given several strong espressos in the studio to sober him up ahead of filming, he was asked to run through his unusual insurance products.

"I rambled on a bit about legal expenses insurance," he says. "But the presenter said it sounded dull and he asked if I have anything more exciting. So, I claimed to offer alien abduction insurance. That made him sit up," he tells me. "He asked me for more information, so I made up a load of crap about the actuarial assessment of abductions, until he stopped me and asked how a policyholder can actually make a claim."

"Great!" I say.

"Yeah, but when I explained that the alien had to sign the claim form, he did a quick segue into the weather forecast."

What a man!

Friday 13 September 1996
ITV Evening News was first broadcast in 1955

Journalists have been regularly asking for a while now to speak to clients of NOB's various non-existent insurance policies. On each occasion, I've been able to fob them off with the excuse that client confidentiality clauses mean that I can't name any individual policyholders. Now, bombarded with requests from the media to speak to an ETSAFE policyholder, I can give them Joe's contact details. It helps at least that he actually *believes* in the existence of space aliens.

I forgot my credit card today, so I leave straight for home without calling in at the pub. For once, I'm back in time to see myself on telly. I watch myself explain sincerely to Katie, a reporter on STD TV's After Four programme, that SPOOKSAFE offers peace of mind to housewives across the UK who live in haunted properties and are fearful about having the willies put up them.

As I never tire of pointing out, when it comes to insurance, peace of mind is a piece of piss. I might trademark that slogan.

Tuesday 17 September 1996
The Saskatoon Star Phoenix was first published in 1902

It's back-to-school time after the quiet news days of summer that helped NOB's stories proliferate in the global media. I've been expecting things to slow down now, as hacks return in sufficient numbers to guard the gates and to see off all but news of the highest quality.

How wrong I was! The regional press leads the charge today, with stories about the Church of England being upset by VIRGINSAFE. This makes the front page in a couple of dozen regional papers from Cumbria to Kent, including my first appearance in the *Longton Sub-Editor* and the *St. Albans Spoiler*. If I carry on upsetting religious establishments at this rate, I may find myself on the sects' offenders register. But the backlinks that NOB's getting from all this are astoundingly useful, for actual PPI sales are growing by the day.

In the foreign press, the *Singapore Leg-Pull*, the *Mostar Itchy Crotch*, as well as the *Slovenian Ankle Spanker*, all seemingly part of the same media conglomerate, have as their lead front page story the same headline: *Virgin on the Ridiculous!* They go on to report that virgins are at a premium – geddit?

Over in the US, *The Kansas Curtain Call* lead headline on page 3 exclaims: *Good Lord!* while in Ireland, the *Dublin Tradesman's Entrance* describes virgin insurance as "no joke".

Just before I leave the broom cupboard for a boozy evening at the Bronx Cheer in Soho with Morag, the editor of the *Blonde Bombshell*, Tracey takes a call from Ava, publicist Max Clifford's PA. Max, she says, would like to buy us lunch and to pick our brains on quite how NOB is so successful in generating foreign media coverage.

Wednesday 18 September 1996
Corriere della Sera was first published in 1876

I awaken at dawn, shivering and wet, lying on the grass in Soho Square. It's raining. I notice I don't have my briefcase. I get to my feet and find, in my rear trouser pocket, my travelcard. With it is the laminated bar token. No credit card. I hope it's still behind the bar in the pub. I wander through Soho to take the Tube to Bank, from where, warmed by the Tube ride, I enjoy a leisurely walk to the broom cupboard where, of course, I don't have my key. It's in my jacket, which is also still in the pub. I hope. It's 7am, so I lie down for a kip on the hallway carpet.

Tracey wakes me up as she arrives for work just after 9am. I hurry off for a slash, then return to the now-unlocked broom cupboard.

Tortuous morning: paperwork, with a fiendish hangover. At noon, I take the Tube back across town to collect my stuff from the pub. It's all still there. I pay up and thank Tom, the landlord, apologising for the trouble I've caused.

"I've known worse, Curly," he says, smiling.

On my way back to the broom cupboard I pick up the early edition of *Penile Dementia*. The paper faithfully reports that, for a mere £2 a week, you can insure against impregnation by God Himself.

Time for another SPOOKSAFE story with a twist. First thing after lunch, I call Raymond, the news editor of Doug's local newspaper, the *Tower Hamlets Knee Trembler*, to tell him that Doug has taken out poltergeist insurance after witnessing strange paranormal activity at his home. Raymond is delighted with the exclusive and promptly sends a photographer to Doug's flat in Bethnal Green Road.

Just as we're about to finish work for the day, Tracey asks if the wording of NOB's policies ought to be dumbed down in order to make them more accessible.

I think about it for a moment, then reply, "That's an interesting idea, but unfortunately accessibility in my experience means the cynical oversimplification of information."

"Thanks, I get it," says Tracey.

"That's okay," I say, "but you must remember that in the UK, ignorance and stupidity are celebrated by the media and by politicians. The average reading age in London is ten years and most of the f*ckwits in the UK are totally incapable of differentiating between the truth and total bollocks. This is why there are so many scams and why fraud is so rife!"

Just then, I take a call from Genghis. He sounds quite distressed.

"What's the matter?" I ask.

"I've just been scammed out of my pocket money by the Windsors," he replies. "Purple Rain by Prince Philip was abysmal!" he says, before bursting out laughing.

SOME OF THE CANDLES IN HIS FLAT
HAD ALSO BENT "LIKE SOMETHING
DONE BY URI GELLER"

Friday 20 September 1996
Psychic News was first published in 1932

I'm full of ideas on how to make NOB a global brand as I arrive at work to find a polite email from Chuck, the news editor for US broadcaster Backstage Pass, thanking me for my telephone interview which, he informs me, was broadcast all the way from one end of America to the other by more than 60 radio stations during their main evening news shows.

That says global brand to me.

I have to make a flying visit to the Potteries this evening. Family business. Local news greets me with the *Stoke Rigid Digit* quoting the Bishop of Tunstall, who uncannily suggests insurance against spoofs would come in handy.

Driving back to London again, I decide to spread word of SPOOKSAFE. I call my psychic friend Leon, editor of *Psychic Insight*. This is refreshingly the only media outlet I know where the receptionist will never ask, "Does he know what it's concerning?" As the editor of *Psychic Insight*, he obviously already knows.

Saturday 21 September 1996
Sky News was founded in 1989

Among the latest press cuttings is a story in the *Catholic Popaazogalou*, storming that VIRGINSAFE is no act of God. It quotes Maria, a spokeswoman from the Christian Media Office, who suggests the insurance policy comes across as a gimmick and is in bad taste. The *Wrexham Moody Cow* and the *Newport Hair Trigger* meanwhile boldly go with the simplest of headlines: *God Almighty!*

The *Highly Polished Knob* today prints without scrutiny my claim that, as we move towards the 21st century, paranormal insurance will become as common as car or household insurance.

A lot of the coverage NOB is getting is presented ingeniously and, more often than not, this is down to the sub-editors. Subs have the huge and invaluable job of checking anything in need of verification, correcting spelling and grammar, working with the production team under impossibly tight deadlines and making sure the headlines grab the reader's attention. They also need to take care when checking details once the page has been laid out, looking out for image positioning and loads more besides.

This evening, I'm meeting Ralph for drinks at Tess Tickle's, a new pub he's discovered in Tilbury of all places. I decide to drive, as there are no trains after 8pm

Driving back home at around 90mph along the deserted A13, I'm stopped by the flashing lights of a police car behind me. As I pull over, a policewoman steps out of her vehicle in front of mine and walks straight towards me. I open the door and step quickly away from the car, which reeks of booze.

On seeing me, her demeanour suddenly changes. "Curly Watts!" she exclaims.

I can't help lying. "Yes!" I reply.

"Ooh, it's lovely to meet you," she says. "I *love* you on Corrie! Can I have your autograph?"

"Certainly!" I reply. "What's your name?"

"Shirley!" she says. I take her notebook and write, To Shirley, love Curly xxx

Shirley is delighted. She lets me off with a caution.

Tuesday 24 September 1996
Pathé News was founded in 1910

A pleasing combination of messages of gratitude and invitations for press, radio and TV interviews greets me as I walk into the broom cupboard this morning. One of these is a note faxed over from Xander, the producer of New York's Bell End TV, thanking me for being a part of the show yesterday, as well as for the complimentary ETSAFE policy that they were able to give away during the programme.

I do wonder if it'd be worth setting up a US office, given that NOB's in the press there so often. US periodical *Harlem Spoon's* features editor, Selena, runs a report on a new type of protection: impregnation by an alien. The story concludes, "Just prove that your offspring's other parent is not of this Earth and get $153,000 from NOB. (Conversion rate, week of 16 Sept 1996.)" I chuckle at Selena's determination to demonstrate her dedication to the pursuit of accuracy, in this instance pinpointing the date of the quoted GBP:USD exchange rate in a story that's complete bollocks.

NOB's also featured in the *Seattle Pink Steel*, the *Indianapolis Loose Lips*, the *San Antonio Park and Ride* and the *Madison Evangelical Nutjob*.

At noon, Tracey and I head out to an unpronounceable Italian restaurant in Soho to meet Max Clifford. I'm focused on ordering the priciest wine on offer at his expense.

Mr Clifford unfortunately turns out to be a complete wanker, but a free lunch is a free lunch. The self-proclaimed PR guru does most of the talking, which amounts to him telling us how fantastic he is and how lucky his clients are to have him.

"I can have any woman in the world!" he boasts as he bites into his focaccia. "People just want to be famous," he continues, his mouth by this time full.

"Well, you did a fantastic job for Myra Hindley," I tell him. "She's really famous and I'm sure it's all down to you."

Hardly listening, he genuinely takes that put-down as a compliment. "If you're as rich and famous as me, you can get away with absolutely anything," he says. "I'm untouchable!"

"I'm sure you are," I reply.

"The British newspapers and TV channels just love me and my stories," he says.

Soon Tracey and I are unable to stand any more of his bullshit and we voluntarily leave the restaurant sooner than planned. As we hail a cab, I ask Tracey, "What happened to the girl from Braintree who became an Avon lady?" I pause, not expecting her to answer, before saying, "Max Factor!"

"Not f*cking likely!" she says.

As we arrive back at work, I see an interesting flyer from Ipswich Insurance, advertising the company's erection all-risks cover for the construction industry. This gives me an idea. I write a NOBSAFE press release and email it to Jeremy with details of the pretty stiff demand we expect for NOB's new endowment policy.

Friday 27 September 1996
The Times published the first Court Circular in 1803

At lunchtime, I head out for a pie and a pint. Well, a few pints.

Back in the broom cupboard, Tracey passes me a call from Sheila, a freelance London correspondent for Australia Global News Network, asking if I have any NOBSAFE policyholders that she can interview for a story she's filming.

Just one, I say off the top of my head. His name is Doug Jones and he lives in the East End. Sheila takes a note of Doug's address and promptly tells me she'll be in the area on 8 October and that she'll film him for a news bulletin to be broadcast Down Under.

I reflect today on the fact that it's coming up for six months since I first began to spoof the press. With such high-profile media backlinks driving so many new customers to NOB's website, I reckon I should eventually do very well out of it, albeit at the expense of a knighthood.

I mention this to Tracey, who says, "We should both get knighthoods! We've almost single-handedly highlighted PPI mis-selling, which you tell me will become Britain's costliest consumer scandal."

"You might get one," I say, "But it's most unlikely that I will as I'm banned from visiting Buckingham Palace."

"Why are you banned?" asks Tracey.

"Well," I say, "the last time I went there was to collect my CBE from Princess Anne."

"Princess Anne's lovely," says Tracey. "She's a real credit to the Royal Family."

"She certainly is," I say, "But I unintentionally offended Her Royal Highness."

"How?" Tracey asks.

"Well," I say, "all I said was, 'Don't look so miserable, dear! Just think how I'm feeling. I came here today hoping to meet your brother.'"

"Her Royal Highness must have been appalled," says Tracey.

"She certainly was," I say. "So, I quickly said, 'No, not that one! I meant your older brother.'"

"What did she say to that?" asks Tracey.

"Nothing! Before Her Royal Highness had chance to reply, I said, 'Thanks for the free gift, but I must dash, there's a cucumber sandwich with my name on it and a free bar.' I then legged it to play drunk twister with the Queen Mother."

With that, I leave the broom cupboard early to collect my car from the garage. The MOT bill is more than my ageing Mini's worth. However, I've got my eye on a registration number plate for my rusting car. It's 12 NOB and a real bargain.

Monday 30 September 1996
Le Monde was first published in 1944

I'd completely forgotten that a TV crew was turning up from French TV channel Canal Frog this afternoon. At 5pm they appear in the doorway with bag-loads of equipment, just as I'm turning off my computer. They remind me that they're here to interview me about alien abduction cover.

I invite them in. The first thing I'm asked as they cram themselves into the broom cupboard concerns the whereabouts of the policyholder that I'd apparently promised them they could film.

Winging it, I say, "He's on his way. He won't be long." Then, in a slight panic, I step out into the corridor to call Doug's mobile. Fortunately for me, he's just crossing London Bridge on his way home from work. I ask him if he could drop by the broom cupboard. And could he please run.

While the film crew's setting up equipment in the cramped space, I offer to fetch them coffee. I head out to the one coffee shop that's still open in Leadenhall Market. Drinks brewed and paid for, in no rush, I amble back to the broom cupboard, where I hand out the hot beverages to the ungrateful French production team.

Just then, to my relief, the door flies open and there stands Doug, panting. I've no time to brief him.

"You have alien insurance cover?" asks a scrawny reporter named Pierre, clearly pushed for time as he moves his microphone in front of Doug's face.

"Er, yes," Doug says, catching his breath. I reach across the crowded broom cupboard to hand him the insurance details that I've just printed out.

"Tell me about ze policy," says Pierre.

Doug reads him the small print, as well as the various levels of compensation he can expect to receive if he's abducted, impregnated, or eaten by aliens.

Pierre immediately mocks him. "You think you can get impregnated? You're a *man!*" he exclaims. Beaming with French light entertainment, he presents Doug with a felt tip pen and a blank sheet of paper, on which he tells him to draw his insured offspring.

I lean forward and whisper to Doug, "Mr Spock," and he proceeds to draw, with childlike imprecision, a two-legged figure standing upright, with no arms and with over-sized ears. It takes four attempts for him to draw an alien without bursting into fits of giggles.

The crew might have suspected a spoof at this point, but by now, as well as having had enough of me and Doug, they've enough of a story to persuade their producer that they've done their job, so they pack up their equipment and leave.

Tuesday 1 October 1996
The San Francisco Chronicle was first published in 1865

A courier delivers a VHS recording of yesterday's interview, which is scheduled to be broadcast in France tomorrow. I give it to Tracey, who takes it to the floor below to a French-speaking friend of hers named Janine, whose office is equipped with a VHS player.

Some 20 minutes later, Tracey comes back with a big smile on her face. She explains the French prime time news broadcast is simply an excuse to take the piss out of Doug, mocking him with an effeminate voiceover and a "you stu-peed Een-glish" tone of derision.

Doug won't care. The French TV news show clearly had an agenda: to take the mickey out of the Brits. That's fine, because they gave NOB a free backlink and we had the last laugh anyway, given their report was complete bollocks.

Tracey passes me a call from Yoshi asking for an interview on Japanese Radio for the Morning Buzz breakfast show. I bullshit for a few minutes about an enormously high number of Japanese citizens who are abducted by aliens every year before hanging up, slightly dazed.

All of a sudden, my afternoon takes on a rosier hue as the legendary scribe Auberon Waugh telephones me directly to ask if there's any chance that I can meet him for a drink at his Mayfair club at 6pm this evening. He says he's proposing to write something about NOB in his next newspaper column.

The club seems quiet when I arrive. Even my distinguished host Auberon – Bron, as he likes to be called – remarks on it. After a few minutes of talking about the various media stories he's read about NOB, he asks, "Do you actually *sell* any of these polices?"

"Oh yes," I say. "*Thousands.*"

"Really?"

I pause for effect. "Well, what do *you* think?" I ask him, with an expression reflecting the fact an idiot could work out that I don't.

This brings a big smile to his face. I come clean. As I run through my spoofs so far, he seems most amused. "You must never underestimate the stupidity of the British public," I conclude.

I tell him a little more about the kind of things I've been up to and I suggest I'll try to have my diary published one day.

"I think you should!" he says.

"I've started it," I say. I hand it to him and apologise, as I have to rush off to the lavatory.

Five minutes later, I return and see that Bron's laughing as he reads. "This is riotously funny!" he says. "Really, it makes the Hitler Diaries look like a schoolboy prank!"

We chat for a bit longer until he appears to have enough material for his column, when I ask him if he'd like to come to the Khyber Pass, my favourite East End pub.

"Well, I was supposed to be seeing my dratted solicitor at eight, but the bugger seems to have cancelled, so why not?"

We collect our coats and head out into Mayfair, where I hail a black cab. "Top end of Norton Folgate," I say.

"Khyber's, yeah?" says the driver.

"That's the one," I say. Bron's impressed with the driver's knowledge.

We arrive and I usher my companion into the smoke-filled pub. Immediately a young lady presents us with her pint jar, into which I drop in a 20p piece. Then I nod to the bar on my left and ask Bron what he'd like to drink. He doesn't hear at first: his eyes are following the moves of a naked woman dancing raunchily from punter to punter.

Eventually, I carry a tray with six large whiskies and I lead him through to my usual spot, a table at the far end of the bar, beside the pool table. The naked woman gravitates towards us and deftly swipes Bron's spectacles. She then leans back across the table, interrupting a game of pool. In time to the raunchy, pounding music, she sticks one leg high in the air and rubs the lenses over her fanny, before dancing back to us and dropping the soiled specs into Bron's glass.

I panic for a moment, thinking he'll be upset. Far from it. He wipes his spectacles, puts them back on and takes a swig from his glass. Class.

Just then another young lady comes to our table and asks if we want a private dance. I shake my head, but Bron asks her, "What's the cost?"

At that moment, I rush to the loo for a slash, before returning to an empty table. Bron's coat is still on his chair, so I assume he's gone for a private viewing. A few minutes later, Bron returns, a big smile animating his face. "Well well well!" he says, rubbing his hands with glee as he sits down. "That was Meghan. Not bad for a fiver! I've put my name down for Jonelle, but I gather there's a wait."

Quite a few 20p dances later, I really have to leave. "Coming, Bron?" I ask.

He pulls his gaze from the stage, focuses briefly on me and says, "Think I'll stay a while longer, old boy."

I stand to put on my coat. "Great to meet you, Bron," I say. "Get in touch if you've any questions."

"Thanks for introducing me to this fine establishment!" he says as he too stands up and we shake hands, before Jonelle takes his other hand and leads him off for yet another private session.

The old devil.

I PANIC FOR A MOMENT THINKING
BRON WILL BE UPSET

Sunday 6 October 1996
The Sunday Telegraph was first published in 1961

Proud day today. I'm quoted in the opening line of Bron's weekly column! Kindly making out that he isn't in on the joke, he begins with one of my favourite catchphrases, "You must never underestimate the stupidity of the British public," after revealing that NOB is selling insurance to protect women against virgin birth by act of God. He goes on to say that we've already banked £300,000 in the first six weeks.

I genuinely cherish that one. Like most of the rest of the press, Bron sees the value of the story, bullshit as it is. Furthermore, like so many members of the Fourth Estate, he finds no harm in having fun and presenting the odd bit of fiction as fact – much like his own published diary columns, which fulfil the function of providing entertainment to the reader.

Reading the latest press cuttings, I see that NOB has made the front page of the *Docklands Canary Dwarf*, where it's reported that 300 British women have taken out VIRGINSAFE. In return for an annual premium of £100 each, these ladies can expect a £1 million payout in the event they find themselves in the family way without evidence of – the journalist hesitates here – breaking and entering.

I bet that raised a smile on the subs' desk.

Monday 7 October 1996
Fox News is founded today

A fax lands on my desk assuring me now that Hungary's back this side of the Iron Curtain, it's waking up to the commercial opportunities that lie in the West. Adojan from the *Budapest Brainsnooze* writes:

> "We've read interesting articles about NOB. One article said that you insure virgins against getting pregnant without sexual intercourse. We'd like to make a telephone interview about it for next Sunday's edition of my newspaper."

Happy to oblige. But first to the Grapes for a skinful.

Eventually back in the broom cupboard, I'm pleased to see that the front-page lead story of the *Algiers Anal Announcement* is about ETSAFE and the importance of buying cover in advance of uninvited aliens paying a visit. I check online and see the same story's in the *Dar es Salaam Doorstepper*, the *Kigali Chequebook Journalist* and the *Harare Death Knock*.

Tracey takes a call from Mrs Mainwaring, who appears to be enquiring about NOBSAFE for one of her customers.

"Is his name Bobbitt?" asks Tracey.

"No, it's Harry Balzac," she replies.

"Then he's probably going to be okay and would be better off simply saving his money," Tracey suggests.

"Thank you dear. I'll tell him," I hear Mrs Mainwaring say, before she rings off.

Wednesday 9 October 1996
London Weekend Television was founded in 1968

At noon, I set off to meet Doug for a drink in the Black Dog. I find him sitting in his usual spot, at a table halfway between the bar and the gents. I buy us both a pint and join him. I ask him how the interview went with Australia Global News yesterday.

"The one you didn't tell me about?" he asks.

"Yes, that's the one! Sorry about that," I reply, passing him a fat brown envelope. "Here's a little something to cover your expenses."

"F*cking NOBSAFE!" he says as he pockets his stash. "I wasn't expecting it."

"I know," I say. "What happened?"

"I slept in late as I'd taken a day's holiday and woke up to the sound of the doorbell. It was a whole bloody TV crew," he says. "The reporter was a young woman called Sheila. She told me she'd been informed that I was willing to do an interview."

"Apologies. I should have mentioned it."

Methodically, Doug takes a swig of Guinness, lights a cigarette, takes a long drag and puts his fag down in the ashtray before he continues. "I assumed they were filming me for an interview about alien abduction insurance. They looked despairingly around my filthy flat for somewhere to film me. To distract them, I began to explain why I'd bought the policy." Taking another swig and after drawing again on his cigarette, he says, "I began to tell her about my concerns about being impregnated by aliens, when Sheila interrupted me. 'Curly Cradock told me you'd bought *erection all-risks* insurance from him. Is that not right?' she said."

"F*ck!" I exclaim. "What did you do?"

"Well, I had no choice but to think on my feet and bluff my way out of it," he says. "I began by blaming my confusion on a heavy night, just as it occurred to me that I'd never actually given an interview on NOBSAFE and that I'd have to think fast what to say."

"So, what did she ask you?"

"Well, nothing at first," says Doug. "This was a TV news report, not a newspaper, so they needed to get all the props ready to bullshit the viewer. I mean entertain their audience."

"That sounds really good!" I say.

Doug continues. "I asked Alison, who also had the day off, to come to the Black Dog with us, where she'd pose as a local girl whom I'd pretend to chat up on camera."

I'm intrigued. "So, what happened?"

"Well, we wandered down the road to the pub. On the way, Alison called in at the newsagent to buy a copy of *The Anilingus* as a prop that Sheila paid for. Then I walked into the pub and asked Maureen, the barmaid, if it was okay for me to be filmed there and interviewed about knob insurance. She agreed to allow the film crew to set up their lighting system – it was only about 11am and there were still only a handful of punters in that morning."

Doug then tells me that he sat at the bar with a pint of Guinness, but deprived of a cigarette, for according to Sheila the appearance of people smoking on the TV networks is banned in Australia. As he lights a cigarette and throws the match in the ashtray he continues, "I explained that my wife is a Scottish Presbyterian, with strong views on the violation of wedding vows. Her job, I said, takes her abroad for long stretches at a time, during which I find myself unable to resist playing the field."

We're distracted by a fight starting in the far corner of the bar between two East End locals. John the landlord jumps over the bar and promptly throws two punters out onto the street to continue their hostilities.

Doug continues the story. "I told Sheila that the story of Wayne Bobbitt, the guy whose wife cut his knob off, had formed a strong impression on my wife. I said I was worried she'd do the same to me if she were ever to discover I'd been unfaithful," he says. "So I told her I'd bought a NOBSAFE policy to ensure I could afford to pay a private surgeon to sew it back on."

"Did she believe you?" I ask.

"I think so," Doug replies as he takes a long drag on his cigarette. "She asked if my wife might ever find out. I replied by telling her that I don't leave copies of the insurance policy lying around at home for her to see, but I said that she might get suspicious by the two bags of frozen peas in the freezer. 'My wife only cooks fresh vegetables,' I explained. I was quite proud of that!"

"Quick thinking!" I say.

"Well, she then asked me what the policy covers me for. I did a quick mental calculation and said, 'It's £40,000 per centimetre, so at 25 centimetres I'm covered for £1 million.'"

"Excellent! So, what did Alison do?" I ask.

"Right. Well, we planted her in the far corner of the pub, where she'd pose as a stranger sitting down quietly reading the paper she'd just bought," he says. "They filmed me pretending to identify her as a target, before adjusting my balls and approaching her."

"So it all went smoothly?" I ask.

"Yeah, I think so," says Doug, stubbing out his fag. "Half an hour later, when the cameraman and Sheila had left, Maureen overhears me telling a fellow drinker what we'd just done and about the knob insurance spoof. At this moment she interrupts me and exclaims, 'I thought you said you was insuring your *job!*'"

Friday 11 October 1996
The Carlisle Mosquito was first published in 1972

Just back from lunch at the Grapes when Doug calls. He tells me that insurer Northern Star is hosting a big press party tonight that clashes with a far more enticing event being held by General Insurance. The latter is taking journalists on a flight to Scotland for a tour of a whisky distillery. By contrast, Northern Star is just offering drinks at its London offices. No contest, really. "Poor Rosemary," he says sadly.

"Who's Rosemary?" I ask.

"She's head of media at Northern Star," Doug replies. "None of the insurance press will be there tonight unless, like me, they don't like flying. They'll all be in Scotland." Then he says, "We'll be doing Rosemary a great favour if you and Tracey can turn up. If you do, just remember to get her to bring her fake reporter business cards."

Inevitably unable to resist the temptation of free booze, at 5pm Tracey and I leave the broom cupboard to take a stroll to Northern Star's offices on the other side of Leadenhall Market. Worried that Tracey might get out of control with the booze, I tell her to watch me and to behave just as I do.

We go up in the lift to the third floor, where we're greeted by Rosemary, who has a desperately anxious expression on her face. Beyond her is an empty room, tables spread generously with booze and sandwiches for the press, none of whom have turned up, just as Doug predicted. Signs of her despair intensify when she notices Tracey's business card, presenting her as an insurance reporter for *Prison Gazette*. As Rosemary adds our names to the list on her clipboard, the lift behind us pings again and out steps Doug.

"Tracey! Good to see you!" he exclaims. "Saw your latest issue – great piece you wrote on the perils of inadequate motor insurance!"

Boy, can he bullshit. Rosemary suddenly starts to look less tense. She leads us through to the boardroom, which is empty but for three gentlemen in suits standing in a line ready to greet us. Doug walks ahead of me and Tracey and he shakes the chairman's hand.

"Terrific to see you, Sir Desmond!" he says.

"Glad you could make it, Doug," he replies. "We can have a chat about your feature on home insurance tonight if you like."

Doug smiles and nods, before heading straight for a waiter who's holding a tray of wine. I lean down and whisper to Tracey to remind her to copy what I do, before I shake hands with Sir Desmond myself, giving him an over-familiar look to confuse him and simply saying, "Hi. I'm Curly. Good to meet you." Tracey obediently does the same.

As we follow Doug's lead to take a glass of wine, I overhear a baffled Sir Desmond say to Rosemary, "They're *both* called Curly?"

[The rest of this diary entry is illegible. It's just a wine stain and I can't even read what I wrote by holding it up to the light. I do seem to recall being turfed out by the chairman, covered in puke.]

Monday 14 October 1996
The Pennsylvania Gazette published the first newspaper cartoon in 1754

Doug leaves a message on the answerphone this morning, telling me that NOB has made it into adult comic, JIZZ. I make a few business phone calls, before strolling through Leadenhall Market to the news stand to buy a copy.

I flick through the comic, chuckling, before I suddenly spot what Doug's referring to. In the *Willie Wanker* cartoon strip, the character himself proposes to buy himself a bookies' shop with the single aim of burning it down and submitting an insurance claim, so he rings his insurance broker. The cartoon frame shows the broker on the phone, sitting in his office. Prominent beside him on his desk is a calendar and the image of the month is a naked model on the steps of Lloyd's.

Very pleased with that, I photocopy the frame in question and send it to Sir David with my compliments. Meanwhile, meeting an urgent need to fill the news pages, there's an article by staff writer, Sonny, in today's *Back Door Boogie*, detailing Britain's rudest place names. They include Wetwang, Penistone, Brown Willy, Shitterton, Twatt, Cockermouth and Fannyfield. I read them out to Tracey, who responds, "They've missed out Scunthorpe and Felching."

"I don't think that there's such a place as Felching," I say. "Felching is the sucking of semen out of someone's anus. It's practised by homosexual men who engage in unprotected anal sex. There's actually an article about it in the National Library of Medicine."

"F*cking gross!" she exclaims. "I suppose though that it's better than a visit to Scunthorpe."

After lunch, I take a call from Nick, a researcher from the Big Bristols Morning programme whom I've now spoken with quite a few times. He's hoping to interview three ETSAFE policyholders. I promise to help him out in return for a backlink. I then call Doug, Joe and Tracey in turn, who all say they're happy to go to Nick's studio this afternoon. I ring Nick back to give him their phone numbers.

I thought it was the Germans who were sticklers for detail, but a letter arrives this morning from Lars at Finnish National News XTV-69 regarding our internationally acclaimed alien abduction insurance and requesting an interview "of 1 minute 30 seconds".

Just before I leave work, I take a call out of the blue from newspaper columnist AA Gill. I'd genuinely love to meet this master-scribe and national treasure! We fix lunch on Monday. *Very* excited!

Monday 21 October 1996
The Hollywood Reporter was first published in 1930

To Mayfair for lunch with AA Gill, or Adrian as he asks me to call him. It's only when he's having a post-lunch cigar that I let the news slip that NOB doesn't actually sell virgin birth insurance to girls called Mary. Adrian looks decidedly happy and, more importantly, pays the bill.

As we leave the restaurant, I manage to persuade him to join me in a black cab to neighbouring Soho.

As we head up Wardour Street, I tap the glass panel and pay the cab fare, then steer my mildly paralytic new literary friend onto the pavement leading to one of my old haunts. We walk towards Berwick Street, unmistakable from the market stalls that we, or at least I, can see on our approach. The destination I have in mind is Tuna Town, a studio on the third floor on the corner of the market street.

Sure enough, the chalky sign tells us Doreen is up for a bit of ogling and more. At the top of the bare, wooden staircase there's a hatch to our left and a doorway ahead of us. I step forward, to be greeted by an old woman in a leotard whom I've not met before. Maybe there's been a change of management. Both Adrian and I are wide-eyed with dismay.

"You two wanna drink?" asks Doreen in a baritone voice.

Adrian and I exchange glances. "I'll have a half," he says.

"Me too," I say.

"Want to buy me one?" she asks.

"No," I say.

The unwisely clad Doreen looks at me with obvious contempt. "Want to buy *me* one?" she asks again.

I assume it'll be just a third half-pint, so I nod.

"Seamus!" she calls to the man behind the sticky-looking bar stained with drink and bodily fluids. "Get us a Mai Tai and two half-Skols."

I assume Mai Tai is an Asian brand of bottled beer but a couple of minutes later, Seamus brings over a dramatically over-sized Del Boy-style cocktail and two half-pints of lager on a silver tray.

"How much is this going to cost?" asks a concerned Adrian.

There's a long pause. "One hundred and eighty-four quid," replies Seamus.

No more drinks for us, then.

With Seamus standing at the doorway, we both shade our eyes non-plussed as Doreen strips.

Adrian kindly foots the bill, waits for a scrawled-out receipt then hails a cab back round the corner on Wardour Street. As he boards the taxi, I thank him and, despite our recent dismal experience, he tells me he's definitely going to write about NOB in his weekly column. Result!

Friday 25 October 1996
The Daily Herald published the first newspaper competition in 1912

I've decided to take the bus into work this morning, popping into the newsagents on the way to buy a copy of the *Pimlico Slap & Tickle*, my local newspaper. I always read it cover to cover.

As I reach page five, I see a most interesting advertisement for this year's Pimlico Women's Institution's sexual innuendo competition. I'm not a huge fan of innuendos, but there's no harm in slipping one in occasionally. I might even enter Mavis, unless of course someone else would like to fill her slot.

I've just a couple of hours in the broom this morning before my appointment with Patrick, my optician. After clearing a backlog of paperwork, I spot an unopened envelope from the cuttings agency. Top of the pile is a story from French daily *Le Grand Sulk* about NOBSAFE – the giveaway being an image of a chap in a pin-striped suit and bowler hat with a baby carrot superimposed over his open flies. Very clever.

The cuttings agency on this occasion has failed to provide me with a translation and to be honest I can't even be bothered to reach for my French to English dictionary to put in the effort to translate what'll be ever-predictable childish ridicule of the stu-peed Een-glish.

With just the same level of xenophobia, the *Brisbane Bimboid* reports a surge in the number of Poms that can't get it up. Millicent, the editor, clearly hasn't even read the press release. No matter, for I'm fairly sure she'll have given NOB a backlink in her online version of the story and that's what counts.

After lunch, I leave the broom cupboard again to catch a train to a meeting in St. Albans with Tony, the editor of the *Hertfordshire Missing Link*. After two full bottles of wine from the buffet car and a nap, I'm woken up by a guard in Edinburgh station. Takes me a full day to get home. Still, it gives me a chance to read about a London insurer offering alien abduction insurance in today's *Highlands Standfirst*.

Saturday 26 October 1996
Independent Radio News (IRN) was founded in 1973

A couple of high-strength aspirin, a glass of water and a long bath are needed before I can tackle the papers.

A proud day. After having treated me to a tax-deductible afternoon of fun and adventure in Soho, Adrian has devoted his entire column today to NOB's antics!

After examining the conundrums that could arise in the case of any claims, Adrian then cites the mind-boggling 'fact' that there are 300 girls who believe in God but who don't believe he's to be trusted.

Like so many of his colleagues in the media, Adrian knows it's all a spoof.

Monday 28 October 1996
The Canadian Broadcasting Corporation was founded in 1936

At midday, Tracey invites me across the road for beers with her and Del. I tell her I'll join them in a few minutes. When at last I arrive, Tracey has her arm supportively around Del and I notice he's looking distinctly unhappy.

"What's wrong?" I ask him.

"It's one of my new employees," he replies. "He's a ginger called Rory who doesn't pull his weight at work. His colleagues keep complaining to me they've to do his work as well as their own."

I ask him to explain.

"Well, for a start Rory just sits around for much of the day on the phone to his mates."

"Simple. Fire the f*cker!" I tell him.

"Try telling that to the Diversity, Equality and Inclusion Inspectorate!" he cries. "I was going to give him a final written warning, but I've been told by my lawyers to avoid criticising him and now Rory has gone back to smarming at his untouchability."

"F*cking *unbelievable!*" I cry.

"Yeah, well in the print industry, we're obliged to employ a certain percentage of ginger people," says Del as he lights a cigarette. "If we don't do it then we're branded as racists and can be fined an unlimited amount."

I'm horrified and exclaim, "Applying quotas simply based on hair colour is unambiguously racist!"

Del shrugs. "They call it positive discrimination," he says.

"No discrimination is positive!" I exclaim. "*Ever!*"

"Well, what's worse is Rory's over-inflated sense of entitlement. He doesn't see anything wrong with his conduct. He genuinely believes that, because he's ginger, he's simply getting what he deserves," he says.

I think for a moment. "Well," I say, "I readily admit that the Highland clearances should never have happened. The appalling treatment of gingers was truly unacceptable. From 1750 to 1860, approximately a third of the entire population of the Highlands and Islands of Scotland were forcibly removed from their homes and transported across the Atlantic in overcrowded ships."

Del looks at me, startled. "Is that true?" he asks.

"Yes," I reply. "What's even worse is that unlike the African slaves, the gingers had no jobs to go to."

Del pauses for thought. "Forcing them to live in North America was obviously very cruel," he says, before exclaiming, "But for f*ck's sake! That was nearly 250 years ago!"

Friday 1 November 1996
Al Jazeera is founded today

Ramesh from Qatar National Radio calls to check if it's okay for him to ask me a few questions about virgin pregnancy by aliens. Sure, I reply, adding that I have one of my virgin policyholders with me.

"May I speak to her?" he asks.

"I'll put you through now," I say, passing the phone to Tracey. Listeners in Qatar are then treated to Tracey's guide to best practice when it comes to fitting a condom.

When I return to the broom cupboard after lunch, Tracey's trying to finish a crossword she started a few weeks ago. I mention to her that today's the 21st anniversary of the murder of the Yorkshire Ripper's first victim.

"That f*cker should die in prison," she replies.

"Not really," I say. "Sutcliffe is criminally insane and therefore should be locked up in a secure mental hospital for the rest of his life, rather than in prison."

"I don't understand," she says, frowning.

"Don't worry," I say. "Insanity is a complicated area of the law. We're just very lucky in the UK to have the finest judiciary in the world! That said, according to my psychic friend Leon, in the future the Lord Chief Justice will call for more ginger judges, in preference, one assumes, to better qualified and more deserving non-ginger candidates. With blatantly racist comments like that, the sooner the judiciary is replaced by superintelligent machines, the better the justice system will be!"

Monday 4 November 1996
The New York World published the first newspaper crossword in 1913

I get to work early this morning. Stacks of paperwork to catch up on. Tracey makes me an Irish coffee before getting back to her crossword.

Ten minutes later, she's still struggling with her crossword and sighing. I intervene to ask her what the problem is.

"Is there one word that contains a Q, a Y and all the vowels?" asks Tracey.

"Unquestionably!" I reply.

As I'm working my way through the paperwork, a headline at the top of the latest cuttings file catches my eye. It's from last Monday's *Limerick Pikey*. Breaking news: *The Rise of Penis Insurance!* I switch on my computer to go online, where I see the same headline used on the websites of the *Solihull Dog's Cock*, the *West Bromwich Cockless Pair*, the *Walsall Churnalist* and the *Cannock Paparazzi*.

After lunch I'm reading the papers when Tracey arrives back at her desk.

"Can you believe it!" I exclaim. "It's five years today since Robert Maxwell threw himself off his luxury yacht, the Lady Ghislaine."

"Wasn't he the tw*t who stole everyone's pension?" asks Tracey.

"Yes, but he wasn't all bad," I reply. "Mr Maxwell was the only person apart from my parents to have made a financial contribution to my legal studies."

"Really?" she asks. "How?"

"I won the Robert Maxwell prize at university for Best Examination Performance," I reply. "I really don't like the way that the press is vilifying him. Anyone would think that he was a convicted child sex trafficker."

"Was he?"

"No, of course not. Anyway, what does Robert Maxwell have in common with a girl from Braintree?"

"Tell me," she says.

"They both go down in Tenerife."

I'm about to leave work when an exciting fax arrives from John Walters, the producer of national TV show Beer Goggles, thanking me for the alien abduction policy that I sent him. John also happens to be the producer of DJ John Peel's national offbeat music show and has promised NOB a backlink and to buy me a beer when he's next in London.

Wednesday 20 November 1996
The Daily Telegraph was first published in 1855

I arrive at work early this morning to catch up on the latest cuttings. Tuesday's edition of the *Bangladesh Three Sheets to the Wind* came with a page three report that the man who brought the world alien abduction insurance, virgin birth insurance and erection all-risks insurance is worried that people may be buying insurance unnecessarily. NOB's so concerned, writes reporter Ali, that it's now planning to launch It's Not Going to Happen to You insurance.

Utter nonsense, but a backlink from the paper's news website is not to be scoffed at.

One of dozens of faxes from the media today is from cable TV's Going Commando Channel, Factual (sic) Programmes Division, outlining the debate that's going to air this Friday evening and which I've agreed to participate in, covering UFOs, aliens and alien abductions.

"There'll be a heated debate between people who have had some form of alien encounter and those who are sceptical towards the existence of aliens," explains Laura, the producer.

Sounds great fun.

A momentous afternoon, touring TV and radio studios with Joe, starting with a pre-Christmas interview on Falkirk's Radio Krankie which is investigating bizarre insurance policies. This is followed by a live TV debate at the London studios of KYTV, which gets the name NOB out to half a million viewers and a most valuable backlink too.

This evening, as the ever-dutiful godson, I pay a visit to my godmother, Sarah, at her care-home in Woking. To my great surprise, I find her watching the Big Bristols Channel. I greet her and immediately she apologies, saying, "Forgive me. I don't normally watch this garbage, but since my stroke, I've been unable to reach the TV off-button."

I step forward, reach up and press it myself and suddenly a calm descends on the room.

"How are you getting on?" I ask.

"Life's not too bad," she replies. "This morning, I woke up to a blowjob."

"Lucky you!" I exclaim.

"I know!" replies Sarah. "I'm going to fall asleep with my mouth open more often."

Saturday 23 November 1996
The Cable News Network (CNN) was founded in 1980

At noon, I make my way to the Bomb Bay Bedbath in Stratford for lunchtime drinks with Jeff and his identical twin brother, Geoff, a claims broker for one of the large American brokers at Lloyd's.

"I *love* insurance," says Geoff as we stand at the bar. I'm worried at first that he really means it, but he continues, "I now know the price of absolutely everything and the value of nothing."

"You're spot on!" I exclaim. Then, keen to illustrate that insurance wasn't my first career choice, I ask, "Did you know that my first job was as an intern working in TV?"

"Really?" asks Geoff.

"Yes," I reply. "I worked during my university holidays for a chap called Dmitri, who was the producer for a cable channel quiz show for morbidly obese contestants."

"Wow!" he exclaims. "What was it called?"

"Fact Hunt," I reply. "It was enormous fun, largely because the questions were made deliberately difficult. This was to ensure that Dmitri would never have to pay out a penny in prize money."

"Really? That seems unfair," says Geoff. "Can you remember any of the questions?"

I think for a moment. "One question was, 'What's a lettuce?' Another was, 'What's portion control?'"

"Those are hardly difficult!" he exclaims.

"They are if you're a fat c*nt," I reply. "Unfortunately, just as I was expecting to make a career out of it, Dmitri was accused of thinphobia and the show was axed after only one episode."

"What the f*ck is thinphobia?" Geoff asks.

"It refers to the active exclusion of those who eat healthily and take regular exercise," I reply. "Fact Hunt was deemed to be explicitly biased in favour of overweight people."

"That's a real shame!" exclaims Geoff. He pensively adds, "I've always wondered about the best way to get a fat girl into bed."

"That's easy," I say. "It's a piece of cake."

Having listened attentively to this two-way exchange, Jeff at this moment puts his face in his hands.

Tuesday 26 November 1996
BBC Newsnight was first broadcast in 1980

Joe and I meet in the broom cupboard, from where we're collected and driven to the Ballsdeep News studio for a show presented by the esteemed radio and TV presenter Mickey Candle. As we crawl our way through Northwest London traffic, Joe has a brainwave. He suggests we offer Mickey an exclusive. He'll claim to have been successfully awarded a £1 million pay-out for alien abduction by NOB.

We spend the rest of the journey plotting the details.

Shaking off the rain after the walk from the car to the building, I approach Gavin the producer and tell him I have an exclusive for the show and that Joe is NOB's first alien abduction claimant.

"F*ckin' hell!" he exclaims. "I'll go and tell Mickey and arrange for more airtime!"

Mickey then introduces himself and discusses the format for the show. Everything's going to plan as we neck as many drinks as we can in the green room. Joe seems to be very pissed and a little unsteady on his feet.

Five minutes later, Gavin calls us and the rest of the show's participants to go into the theatre. Joe and I make our way in and sit down.

A comedian warms up the audience and the two of us look at each other, telepathically asking the question, 'Where did they get *him* from?'

Lights go red for Live and as the camera pans out over the audience and passes us, Joe brushes back his hair and nods to the lens.

Two guests are just getting into a heated discussion about whether aliens exist or not, when suddenly Mickey moves over to me and Joe. He introduces me to the audience as "an insurance man" who covers people against alien abduction. The audience titters so I give a description of the cover, explaining that our objective is simply to part the feeble-minded from their cash.

The audience laughs loudly and I pause quite seriously, causing the crowd to quieten down. When they do so, I explain that NOB has provided thousands of people with alien abduction insurance and that we've just been notified of a claim.

The camera hones in on Joe, who's grinning like a Cheshire cat. Mickey asks him if space aliens really abducted him.

"Oh yeah," says Joe, clearly pissed, before listing the time and date of his abduction and the fact he was able to provide DNA samples and camcorder footage to prove his claim.

Then it's back to the green room for drinks while Joe snoozes in his chair.

On leaving the studio, I've to return to the broom cupboard, to email Jeremy with the spoof details of NOB's £1 million payment to Joseph Carpenter, who we state provided irrefutable camcorder footage and DNA samples of his abduction by aliens.

Sunday 1 December 1996
The Sunday Times published the first colour supplement in 1962

The latest press cuttings arrive. A story in the Tel Aviv *Wallet Moth* quotes Joe. "My friends think I'm insane," he tells the paper, explaining that he's looking forward to spending the money and proving all the sceptics wrong. The same quote is also featured in the *Lima Fish Supper* and, in Somalia, in the *Mogadishu Melon Farmer*.

As I make my way through the huge pile of cuttings, I see the entire front page of the *Zagreb Chamber of Horrors'* colour supplement features a huge picture of my face, complete with Mr Spock ears, which flags a multi-page spread topped with the headline: *Joking While Broking!*

Just as I'm preparing beans on toast for lunch, I take a call from Barnie, the presenter of the Big Bristols Drive-Time show. He wants to pre-record an interview and asks me what NOB's most unusual insurance policy has been. I describe how once I insured the Archbishop of Canterbury's genitals against injury and consequent infertility by act of God. Barnie laughs and promises NOB a backlink.

A dull afternoon is enlivened when I decide to email The X-Files star, Dana Skully, to invite her to present the million-quid payout to Joseph Carpenter to compensate him for having been abducted by aliens.

Wednesday 4 December 1996
The Swindon Advertiser was first published in 1854

I've been invited to appear with Joe on Big Bristols' Two Large Breakfasts show next Wednesday. And to top all the fun, Tracey alerts me to the fact that NOB made it into the December issue of *Rascal Sacks*, in an article headlined *Virgin on Silly*.

Of the 300 virgins who have bought immaculate conception cover, most are nuns, I'm quoted as saying – adding, "I think."

Meanwhile, I'm amused when I see that Alice, a spokeswoman for the Corporation of UK Underwriters, has responded to a press enquiry from the *Swindon Banana Hammock*. She says, "If Swindon's an area of paranormal activity, it must be due to those magic roundabouts."

Friday 6 December 1996
The Nanfang Daily was first published in 1949

I'm woken up at 5am by a phone call from the US. It's Geoff, who's over there on business. He's pissed, but he tells me he's just seen Dana Skully on the late-night Jay Lino chat show. She must have got my email because Geoff tells me that she said on air that she's due to fly over to London shortly to present a £1 million cheque to Joseph Carpenter, the world's first successful alien abduction insurance claimant.

It's worth being awakened at such an ungodly hour to hear that!

When I get to the broom cupboard, I email the broadcaster, requesting an urgent VHS copy of Jay's show, making it clear that I'm happy to be interviewed if they need me.

Meanwhile, over in Italy, numerous publications champion the fact that Joe, a young man of Italian descent, has become a lira billionaire by providing camcorder footage and DNA samples of him being abducted by aliens.

After work, I need to make my way to the Broadcasting Wank Hut. I'm being interviewed with Joe on Big Bristols Science Inaction.

Joe tells the presenter, Tariq, how an intense beam of light had just hit him and he passed out. When he awoke, he says, he was in a craft and could feel the presence of someone around me. He says he turned around and could see two large black almond eyes. "At this point, I passed out once again," he says.

Tariq then says to camera that when Joe opened his eyes, he'd been returned to his fellow earthlings, with the video evidence and DNA samples.

Then it's my turn to speak. I simply parrot, "For a very modest premium, Mr Carpenter insured himself for £1 million against alien abduction, impregnation by aliens and being eaten by aliens."

Tariq winds up the session by saying to camera that no one other than NOB has seen the alleged video footage and DNA evidence, but it must be compelling for an insurance company to pay out £1 million.

Light entertainment. You can't beat it.

Monday 9 December 1996
The Jewish Chronicle was first published in 1841

Waiting for me as I arrive at the broom cupboard this morning is an airmail package from America. I open it and give Tracey the VHS of Jay's show to watch and transcribe with her friend, Janine, in her office on the floor below.

Tracey's back an hour later. According to the transcript, Jay asks Dana if it's true that she's really going to London next week to hand over the £1 million cheque to someone by the name of Joseph Carpenter. She confirms that this is indeed true. Straight from the horse's mouth!

Off to lunch today with Sven, the fresh-faced London correspondent of the *Stockholm Neglect of Nuance*. We meet in Filthy Fannies, where I introduce him to Tracey. Sven buys us a round of drinks and pays for them with his Access card.

"Is that a company card?" I ask him.

"You've got to be kidding!" he cries.

"Really?" I ask.

"God yes," he replies. "Journalists get paid f*ck all less 10 and we still have to foot the bill for any expenses before we can claim it back. If you ever have kids, don't let them go into journalism. There's no money in it!"

Wow! I didn't realise it was *that* bad.

After a few minutes, I suggest we drink up and go to a livelier bar. I'm paying, I tell Sven. We head up Shoreditch High Street, past the boarded-up and burnt-out warehouses, towards Old Street. Apart from the occasional bus, the traffic's silent. The odd blade of grass can be spotted growing out of the surface of the side streets. It's incredible what a difference a hundred yards can make.

Our first stop is the Amazing Dancing Bare. Tracey has been paid today and NOB's bank account's taken a hit of the best part of £500. Budgeting doesn't appear to be one of Tracey's strong points, for she seems to have drawn out a wad of £5 notes for private table dances.

I drop 20p into a glass pint jug that a large-breasted, pink sequin-clad stripper named Danielle holds in front of my face. She sneers at my faux generosity and turns to Tracey, asking if she's here for the strips.

Tracey winks at her, pulls out a fiver and hands it to the well-endowed woman, who peers above the crowds to note the private room is vacant. The two of them disappear for a good 20 minutes.

Just as I'm telling Sven how I managed to strip chronic illness exclusions from NOB's PPI policies, his face lights up as he sees Tracey returning to the table. He stands straight up to greet her, blushing and quite clearly with an erection.

As I rise to go to the loo, Danielle beckons Tracey and Sven to the private viewing room. I buy another drink, then another.

The two of them have been gone for over an hour before I grab my coat and leave for home.

Tuesday 10 December 1996
The Spooner Advocate was first published in 1901

Tracey arrives at the broom cupboard at 10.30am, flustered but alive. She briefly updates me on some of the events of the evening before. It turns out Danielle had keys to the upstairs flat and that the three of them made use of the spare bedroom.

My spirits buoyed, I set off by Tube to Joe's house for a photoshoot this afternoon for the *Ho Chi Minh City Dangle Berry*. A diminutive young photographer named Pip turns up lugging several unfeasibly large cases of equipment. Joe suggests putting the classic Alien Beam Me Up picture in the background. Then Pip takes a few shots of me and Joe shaking hands and exchanging a super-sized £1 million cheque.

Joe suggests he wear my spectacles as a piss-take before yet more pictures are taken. He puts the cheque under his nose to copy the famous 'What no man?' just before saying under his breath to me, "What – no real cheque?"

Off to STD TV's North London studio with Joe. I'm not even sure what the show's called.

Lucifer the presenter says "fiction became fact" when aliens abducted him.

Joe recalls the experience of his abduction. "An intense beam of light just hit me and I passed out," he says to camera. "When I awoke, I was in a spacecraft and I saw two large black almond eyes. At this point I passed out once again."

Addressing the camera, Lucifer soberly concludes, "Despite substantial video and DNA evidence to the contrary, Joseph's story probably isn't quite enough to persuade some sceptics that he was actually abducted by aliens."

No kidding.

I forgot to bring in my phone charger with me, on a day when every TV channel, radio and regional newspaper in the UK seems to want a piece of the alien abduction action.

Finally, just before last orders, Chike, a producer at Bat-in-a-Cave Radio, calls from Sucre in Bolivia to confirm my late-night alien abduction interview before my phone battery dies.

Time to go for a pint in the Rainbow Yawn and to see if I can charge my phone.

Monday 16 December 1996
The Sydney Morning Herald was first published in 1831

Bitterly cold in the wind heading into work early this morning to help Tracey put up Christmas decorations. It's probably going to snow this afternoon.

First, though, I head to Leadenhall Market to buy NOB a Christmas tree from one of the stalls. It's a tall f*cker. As Silas the stall owner hands me my change, he asks if I'll be putting it up myself.

"No, it's for the broom cupboard," I reply. Silas looks puzzled as I turn to drag the six-foot brute behind me the hundred or so yards to work.

After collecting the post, I return to my desk. The first envelope I open is a Christmas card that promises lots of anal next year. I f*cking hate prison!

A limo picks me and Joe up after a long lunchtime session to take us to Nutgraf Productions, a German TV company with a studio in the West End. They claim their specialisation is unusual feature films.

We're led into the studio. Joe and I are both quite pissed by this time.

Everyone knows the accepted description of an alien: they all have almond-eyed, triangular heads, with olive, dolphin-like skin. But there's a problem. Fritz, the researcher, hasn't done his homework, and each of the aliens resembles an actual dolphin. Suddenly, the place is besieged by dolphin-shaped aliens walking clumsily around the set.

Joe's introduced to Wolfgang, the actor who's set to play him in the reconstruction. He's been told he resembles him, but when they're introduced, Joe looks startled. The two of them don't look anything like each other. For a start, Wolfgang is balding with grey hair, while Joe boasts a thick dark brown thatch.

Medwig, the presenter, asks, "What do you think, Joe?"

"He's my doppelgänger!"

He's a quick thinker, our Joe.

The interview begins. At great length and with fine detail, Joe tells his story of being abducted by aliens. Filming then drags on for about three hours, before the crew leaves for Alexandra Palace for a reconstruction using triangular-light special effects and to film a Robert Maxwell lookalike as the media baron who, I'd falsely told them, had agreed to pay NOB two million quid for Joe's camcorder footage and DNA samples.

Tuesday 17 December 1996
The Boston Globe was first published in 1872

Today's *Cairo Beef Bayonet* reports that Joe's alien insurance has paid off, suggesting it could be the perfect case for agents Mulder and Scully. A similar story also appears under the byline of Dang Lin Wang in the *Hong Kong Ugly Sister*. It reports that on the evening of Mr Carpenter's abduction, he was caught in an intense beam of light "like a police helicopter". The anti-gravity force within it lifted him above the ground before, he claimed, he passed out. By an amazing stroke of luck, he was able to produce "compelling evidence" of his ordeal, including camcorder footage and DNA samples taken from the scene.

The story goes on to quote me and yet more of my on-the-spot bullshit. "The work on the DNA sample was carried out by a research fellow at Braintree University. I can't give you her name due to reasons of confidentiality. But the work proved conclusively that the sample was something which was not of this Earth," I told Dang, while struggling to keep my composure.

Today's edition of the *Brixton Mugger* has a rather fetching picture of me and Joe. Clarence, the editor, has published it in response to a reader's letter that I sent in myself under the name of I.P. Freely a few days ago, asking to see detailed proof of the alien abduction and for an image of Dana Skully presenting the cheque.

At the end, the story has an editor's note: "As requested, here is a photo of the cheque presentation. Dana Skully was investigating another X-File and couldn't make it."

Strange and not altogether true.

Meanwhile, a Malaysian TV news bulletin from Kuala Lumpur has been posted on YouBend. It alerts the world to the festive news that NOB has paid £1 million to Joseph Carpenter. The screen fills with the photos taken at Joe's the other day, before showing earlier footage of Joe himself hunting UFOs.

Cut to Injian, the reporter, who asks Joe what it was like being a millionaire.

"It hasn't really sunk in yet," he says. "After all, I can hardly believe I've been paid a million quid for being abducted by aliens."

Thursday 19 December 1996
The Baltimore Sun was first published in 1837

Up early after a heavy night's festive drinking, I clamber into an awaiting limo to take me to the Big Bristols' flagship morning news show. As we approach the 7am pips, Sue, the presenter, asks me directly if NOB has paid a million quid to a Joseph Carpenter, who claims he was abducted by a star-shaped object approaching from the East, which was witnessed by a Mr Wiseman and his two brothers.

As I reply in the affirmative, Sue winks at me and newsreader Charlotte laughs so much that I rather fear she'll wet her knickers.

I say goodbye to the two wonderful ladies before making my way home. My spirits sink when I see the story in today's *Bridlington Beef Wellington*, which suggests the million-quid alien abduction claim could be a *spoof!* Shocker! The article suggests it may be more than a coincidence that in Christmas week, the alien abductee was named as Joseph Carpenter, adding my comment that he's not available for interview because he's on holiday on Mars.

I'm on the phone to Genghis, who tells me he has made a new friend called Rhys.

"He loves golf," says Genghis, "but he's not very good."

"What's his handicap?" I ask.

"He's blind!" my brother replies, before giggling uncontrollably down the phone.

The afternoon progresses well, with the *Lambeth Saggy Bottom* reporting the claim I made up a few days ago that NOB has made its money back already by selling the evidence of Joe's abduction to a media conglomerate for £2 million. However, citing industry sources, the *County Tyrone Tarred & Feathered* flags caution, suggesting the payout could simply be an "out of this world" publicity stunt.

Christmas is fast approaching, so it's time that NOB did some festive spoofing. Naff Christmas present insurance, anyone? We'll find out. I quickly draft a NAFFSAFE press release and email it to Jeremy, with additional information that there are no exclusions for socks or aftershave, or if family members are Jehovah's Witnesses.

Monday 23 December 1996
Harlech Television was founded in 1958

There's decent international coverage in this week's press cuttings. I particularly like the story in the *Georgia Giggling Stick*, which has the headline *Strange but true!* above a page-four lead story about NAFFSAFE.

The online version of the NAFFSAFE story in the *Ankara Arseovoir* kindly gives readers a link to NOB's website, as do the *Buenos Aires Spanky Hanky* and the *Bombay Raspberry Tart*.

In Christmas season-spirit, Poppy Cockburn, news editor of *The Braintree Genius* suggests taking out a Santa Clause. Geddit? Just £25 will cover you against receiving a naff gift, the story says. If your Christmas present fails a test of good taste by a panel of expert elves, then you could receive £100 in compensation with this insurance policy. Meanwhile the page-three headline in the *Made-Up Bollocks* reads: *Naff Xmas presents cover excludes socks and aftershave!* This is the opposite of what we said in the press release, but at least they've given NOB a backlink.

With only two days to go, I'm still at a loss to decide what to buy for Tracey. I obviously don't wish to buy her a naff Christmas present. I ask her if she likes Chanel No. Five.

"Nah, I usually only watch Sky None," she replies.

To my great surprise, a Christmas card arrives at the broom cupboard addressed to me from the chairman of Lloyd's. It simply says, "I still think you're a wanker, Curly. Merry Christmas, Sir David." Well, at least it's a nice card.

There's also a card from his Holiness the Pope to wish me a very happy Christmas but regretfully declining my invitation to present a cheque for £1 million to Mary Christmas, the world's second virgin birth claimant.

Thursday 26 December 1996
La Presse Canadienne was founded in 1917

A sleepy Boxing Day afternoon is interrupted by the phone. I don't reach it in time and listen instead to the voicemail. It's an ill-mannered French-Canadian reporter called André from the *Quebec Quantum Dick*, who's becoming something of a serial pest. He tells me he's flying to Paris next week and from there, he says, he wants to come over to the UK to meet Joseph Carpenter.

I call him back and I give him a spoof address in Bonnybridge, Scotland, where I claim Joe lives. I do hope André falls for it.

I pour myself a large whisky and reflect on the year. All that investment in NOB's website is finally paying off. We're now number one in Yahoo! A fast-growing number of people are now buying NOB's genuinely ethical PPI directly from the web.

My Christmas holiday is livened up immensely with a bit of NAFFSAFE coverage in the *Boston Strangler*, complete with a backlink on its website. It's one of several news stories to begin today with the headline *Get yourself a Santa Clause!* Cordelia, the news editor, reports that readers who're sick of getting awful Christmas presents from Uncle Jim and Auntie Dot can now do something about it by taking out insurance. Just £25 will buy cover against receiving a naff gift. If your appalling present fails a "good taste" test by a panel of expert elves, then you could receive £100 cash.

The Christmas present story is so popular with The *Trumpton Tower's* newsdesk that it runs another article on the same subject a few pages later in the same edition, beginning with the line, All I got for Christmas was a kettle-descaler kit. Reporter Holly writes that every Christmas morning, people open presents that are real turkeys. Namechecking NOB, she tells her readers that 210,840 people in the UK have taken out an insurance policy to protect them from receiving a naff gift.

This evening I'm meeting Doug at the Black Dog. I buy the first round before Doug turns to me and says, "Curly, you're the James T. Kirk of insurance. You boldly go where no insurance man has gone before."

I smile but correct him. "I'm the Doctor Whom of insurance. Saintly, virtuous and trapped in the wrong body. Incidentally," I add, "my friend Leon told me recently that in the future, Dr Whom will have tits!"

"Get away!" says Doug.

"No, really!" I reply. "I told him he was talking through his arse. 'Doctor Whom comes from Gallifrey, not Brighton,' I said. But he simply laughed and retorted, 'You'll see!'"

Monday 30 December 1996
Ashgabat Altyn Asyr Television was founded in 1959

First day back in the broom cupboard and the very first call of the day is from dear old Mrs Mainwaring, ringing to thank us for the Christmas hamper we sent her in return for recommending NOB to the customers in her shop.

"I cried with joy," she tells Tracey. "It was such a lovely gift and most thoughtful and generous of you to think of me."

There's something that clearly distinguishes both the correspondence and the coverage that NOB's getting in the UK from that of mainland European media. It's amazing the lengths some of the foreign media will go to secure an interview. For instance, today I've received a fax from Rejep at *Cloven Hoof*:

> Dear Mr Cradock,
>
> I am the London correspondent for *Cloven Hoof*, Turkmenistan's most popular daily newspaper with a two million daily circulation. I read the story of the payment of £1 million made by NOB to policyholder, Joseph Carpenter, on the grounds of his being kidnapped by aliens. I am sure that it's not a publicity stunt for your company and I do not have any doubt that the story is fully true. I therefore would like to contact Mr Carpenter in order to write an article for my newspaper.
>
> Would you please send by fax his address and phone number along with a copy of your payment order to Mr Carpenter, that I'm certain you keep in your files.
>
> I look forward to hearing from you.
>
> Yours sincerely
> Rejep

I quickly provide Rejep with the information he required. Then, after a dreary day of paperwork, with the only entertainment coming in the form of a voicemail from André from the *Quebec Quantum Dick* saying he's in Bonnybridge and can't find Joe's house, I set off for post-Christmas drinks with Jacob.

I greet him warmly and we walk into his new local in Romford, the Buckle Bunny. "I'm sick of Christmas!" Jacob complains. "All year long, I work my fingers to the bone to buy all the presents that Esther asked for. And what happens on Christmas morning? The fat f*cker with a beard gets all the credit!" After a moment's thought, he adds, "I suppose it was my fault for marrying Hannah in the first place."

Tuesday 31 December 1996
The West Ireland Telegraph was first published in 1926

In the post are the last press cuttings of the year. The photo of me, Joe, the £1 million cheque and the Alien Beam Me Up image are reproduced in dozens of newspapers and magazines around the world, including the *Houston Barely Credible*, the *Tokyo Quick Slash*, the *Istanbul Turkish Two-step*, the *Maryland Six-toed Hillbilly* and the *Mexico City Skidmarks*.

I sigh with relief when a fax arrives mid-afternoon from Sheila at Australia's Global News, requesting an interview with me and Joe for a prime-time nightly current affairs show amusingly called A Current Affair. I take it that Doug's cock-up with her the other day about erection all risk insurance for his 25cm penis hasn't blown my relationship with the Aussie broadcaster.

A quiet New Year's Eve. Just me, some Scotch and a dozen or so cans of Heineken. As I listen to Big Bristols Radio, I'm both delighted and surprised to hear that NOB is featured on Pick of This Year. I'm even more delighted to hear the sound of Charlie, the presenter, corpsing over the 'housewives having the willies put up them' story that was widely featured in the media earlier in the year.

The Heineken must be reaching the parts that other beers cannot reach, I think, when it suddenly dawns on me that NOB should protect the toon-army of supporters of Geordie United Football Club against trauma arising from the recent loss of their manager.

I hastily write a TOONSAFE press release and email it exclusively to Jeremy, along with my good wishes. I bet he didn't receive any naff Christmas presents.

Thursday 2 January 1997
ABC World News Tonight was first broadcast in 1953

My new year's resolution was to be less sarcastic and profane. So far, I'm off to a f*cking brilliant start.

I call Parminder on the off chance he's free for a technology catch-up. He is, and he invites me over for a coffee. As I approach his studio, I see that he's been busy. The neighbouring shop, Pen Island, now advertises its own website on their front door: www.penisland.com.

It all makes so much more sense now.

Parminder looks more depressed today than his usual up-beat self and I ask if he's okay.

"It's my father," he says. "I could never believe that he was stealing from his job as a traffic management coordinator, but every day, when I get home, all the signs are there."

He keeps his sombre composure for a moment longer, then bursts out laughing.

Back in the broom cupboard, Joe emails me the transcript of his interview with legendary radio DJ Simeon Bites on Chudleighs FM that was broadcast the week before Christmas. There have been literally dozens of radio and TV interviews from across the media, all dying to report this amusing but unlikely news fodder.

In this interview, Joe explains to Mr Bites that he was transported onto a huge green spaceship where he passed out, but not before gathering the evidence necessary to make his million-pound insurance claim.

As the interview draws to a close, he says, "Joe Carpenter was abducted by space aliens, just outside Swindon. He was then attacked by one of them but managed to smash its lights out before collecting some DNA samples and taking footage with his camcorder. More on that story as it comes in," he says before bursting into uncontrolled laughter.

A golden hour.

Friday 3 January 1997
Frankfurter Allgemeine Zeitung was first published in 1949

It's ten years since the first Red Nose Day. On the bus into work, I sit facing my elderly neighbours, Doris and Gladys, who're knitting and chatting. It's interesting to listen to them and their mature take on life.

"Ooh, I don't think I told you," crows Doris, looking up. "I caught Neville my grandson wanking and had a small stroke."

Gladys looks horrified.

"Yes, he couldn't believe how soft my hands were!" Doris exclaims.

Her elderly companion thinks for a moment then says, "My 15-year-old grandson Jamal's getting to be a right little b*stard, hanging about in a gang, taking drugs and never coming to visit me."

Doris sighs. "Well, I guess I'm lucky in that respect," she says. "Neville loves his old granny. He snuggles up on the sofa with me to watch TV, always gives me a kiss and hug whenever he comes to see me and we even do paintings together at weekends."

Gladys now sighs. "Sometimes I wish Jamal had Down syndrome too."

I ring the bell. It's my stop.

Before I go off to make my Irish coffee this morning, Mavis stands at the door and asks me whether I saw the interview with the trans-mother of two daughters on breakfast TV this morning.

"No, I'm afraid not," I reply.

"Well, when she was asked how they were all getting on, she replied that every day was like winning the Lottery."

"Well, that's nice," I venture, generously.

"Yes," replies Mavis. "When they get undressed, they've six matching balls."

Just then a fax arrives inviting me and Joe to appear on Italy's Giuseppe Ravioli Show. I get straight on the phone to Joe, whom I catch just as he's preparing for his interview with Bakari from Silvery Moon, Kenya TV's weekly astronomy programme. Giuseppe's offering all expenses, business class flights to Rome and a stay in the Ritzio, I tell him.

Needless to say, Joe's happy to join me.

Monday 6 January 1997
The Australian Broadcasting Corporation (ABC) was founded in 1932

The year has started full-on, both with new PPI business and with seemingly non-stop media interviews, as radio shows and TV appearances across Europe stack up.

I open the latest press cuttings envelope to read a report in the *Kampala Leg-Over*, which smugly reports that the UFO claim has backfired. Joseph Carpenter, says the article, has discovered that the appearance of riches doesn't always bring benefits. After receiving more than 300 calls from the media around the world about his claim, the report says, he has had to go ex-directory.

Things liven up when, at 3pm, Sheila and Gerry, her Australian cameraman, show up at the broom cupboard to interview Joe about his alien abduction experience. I give a quick interview, before they take Joe up the road to film him outside the Lloyd's building, where Sheila asks him what he'd actually seen on the spaceship.

Joe's in his element. He replies, "Literally hundreds of blonde women, Pamela Anderson-lookalikes. It was just like being in heaven."

Neither Sheila nor Gerry can keep a straight face. Sheila blurts out: "So what did they say?"

"Take me Joe, I'm yours," he replies deadpan to camera.

Filming stops. It's ten minutes before they're composed enough to do a retake.

TAKE ME JOE, I'M YOURS

Wednesday 8 January 1997
La Stampa was first published in 1867

To Heathrow for an Alitalia flight to Rome to appear on the Giuseppe Ravioli Show, a show said to be even more popular in Italy today than *Wogan* ever was in the UK.

Two separate limousines pick up Joe and me to take us to Heathrow Airport, me from Pimlico and Joe from his home in Enfield. We meet up in the business lounge, where we share two complimentary bottles of Chianti before boarding the plane. Once seated, we do our best to drink the plane dry.

On arrival at the five-star Ritzio Hotel, we stagger towards the desk to check in. The receptionist hands us each a room key and tells us that when we order anything, we should mention Giuseppe and all our costs will be covered.

I'm impressed by my room. For a start, it has a fridge laden with booze. But after a minute, Joe knocks on the door and says he's hungry, so I go with him down to the restaurant. I mention the name Giuseppe to the head waiter, Luigi, who promptly leads us through to a table with a stunning view of Rome through the window.

I order lobster *fra diavolo*, while Joe goes for the Burger Italiano.

"What drinks would you like, sirs?" asks Luigi.

"I fancy a coke," says Joe.

"Sod the Coke," I say. "Can we have your wine list, please?"

Luigi presents me with a long, elegantly bound list of fine wines.

"What do you recommend?" I ask Luigi.

He holds up his hands and pulls a face that suggests, "No, it's up to you. Leave me out of this."

I give Luigi two fingers and say, "As we're in Rome, we'll have five bottles of your finest Chianti, please."

After dinner, a limo picks us up and delivers us to the studio, where we're soon introduced to the translator, the producer, the director and finally to the legend himself, Giuseppe Ravioli. We stand at the makeshift studio bar and sample some more of Italy's finest wines.

Joe and I are both in an extremely merry mood when suddenly a gorgeous blonde walks by to talk to the producer. "Look at the tits on that!" Joe exclaims. "She must be the Marilyn Monroe of Italy!"

The buxom young lady smiles and, to our surprise, stops to speak to us. "Are you appearing on the show as well?" she asks in a sexy Italian American accent.

"Yes!" we reply in unison. I explain why we're here and I introduce Joe to her as my client, who I explain has been paid £1 million compensation for having been abducted by aliens.

She turns to Joe and says, "I've heard of your story here in Italy and in Los Angeles. What an amazing story! Is it true?"

Joe's buzzing. After 48 hours awake, including a four-hour flight, having drunk four-and-a-half bottles of wine, he could talk the hind legs off a donkey. He proceeds to tell her his 'amazing story'.

A minute or two later, I'm placed on the front row in the studio, while Joe's put on an armchair behind the stage in front of a huge red curtain, beside his translator.

The opening music then starts to play as the credits roll in front of the TV ahead of us on the floor. Suddenly the curtains start to draw back.

A thousand faces look on and clap. I sit with a huge Cheshire-cat grin. I point at Joe, wink, pull funny faces and do my best to make him laugh. Joe manages to keep a half-straight face.

Giuseppe introduces his guests one by one. When it's Joe's turn to be introduced, Giuseppe reveals, "Yes, it's true! Italians do get about: Joseph Carpenter's real name is Joseph Rossi!" His researchers have clearly been busy.

Joe proceeds to tell his story, insisting he'd not been "drinking or smoking any funny stuff" when he was abducted by aliens. Also, after describing to the film footage that he provided as evidence to NOB, he adds, "I doubt even Steven Spielberg could pull that one off." All very spontaneous.

Just at this point, the spotlight turns to me. "We've the manager of the insurance company here with us. Let's see what he has to say," says Giuseppe as the cameras turn to focus sharply onto me.

I'm now going to play the straight man of the double act.

"Good evening, Mr Cradock. Is this a stunt?" he asks. "After all you've been flown from England to a hotel, eaten well and appeared on national TV."

I wonder if he's seen our bar bill. I begin my reply in a deeply sincere tone. "The evidence Joseph has provided is extremely compelling," I say. "As you may be aware, insurance companies don't pay out unless there's sufficient reason to do so. The DNA samples and camcorder footage in question have been examined by a research fellow at Braintree University, who confirmed their authenticity."

"Can we see the evidence?" asks Giuseppe. "After all..."

I interrupt him. "Apologies, we no longer have the evidence. It's been sold to a large media conglomerate for £2 million. However, we've been assured that it'll be released this summer for all to see. Meanwhile, we've an audience at the Vatican with his Holiness the Pope at 10am tomorrow."

The rest of the audience listens in stunned silence. I fend off a couple of awkward questions before the cameras turn to another guest, whereupon I fall into a drunken stupor.

Joe tells me later that the camera zoomed in on me a few minutes later and Giuseppe joked, "It's all too much for the audience to take – even Mr Cradock has fallen asleep!"

The show ends, the curtains draw to a close and the audience claps as Joe shakes me awake, before we're driven back to the Ritzio for refreshments.

Friday 10 January 1997
The Kuwait News Agency was founded in 1956

TOONSAFE is starting to take off. *Stripe Me!* is the headline in the *Tripoli Slapped Arse*. NOB, an insurance company with a policy against abduction by aliens, the story explains, is ready to offer Geordie United fans cover for post-traumatic stress, after Colin Kerrigan recently resigned as club manager.

After lunch, Alastair, a WCTV producer, faxes me a request for my help in putting together one of the shows for the next series of Strange and Untrue. I email him back, agreeing to help provided they give me a backlink on their website, before heading off to the Grapes for a rare drink with Imelda.

I buy the first round, but Imelda has clearly not come along for the camaraderie. She's one of those people who insist they're right, regardless of evidence that she patently isn't. Finally, I wrong-foot her and point out the widely known regulatory failures of Rhino, telling her that Rhino is short-sighted, thick-skinned and that it over-charges. We get into a heated argument, before the barman throws her out for swearing.

I glance at the bar and see she's left her mobile phone. I pick it up and promptly redirect all her incoming calls to a sex line in Malaysia that I keep in my pocket diary for just such occasions, before handing it to the barman.

I finish my pint, gather my belongings and leave.

As I cross the road, I notice Imelda waddling back as hurriedly as she can to collect her phone.

I call Jeremy from my mobile to inform him that Joe's £1m alien abduction claim was a Christmas spoof, but also to assure him that he's the first to get this news. I'm expecting him to be angry, but he's completely relaxed. He sounds genuinely delighted to be given this exclusive. Craven Moorhead, editor at *UFO Tomorrow*, on the other hand was furious when I called to ask her for a quote. She told me that it was a conspiracy to deny the existence of alien life.

Sunday 12 January 1997
The Sunday People was first published in 1881

Today's *Sunday Bingo Wings'* front-page story reveals that NOB's alien abduction claim was bogus. Maurice the reporter has a bit of fun himself, reasoning that the truth is out there, but for a man supposedly paid £1 million for being abducted by aliens, the truth is, in fact, an embarrassing down-to-earth spoof.

The story describes a giant-sized cheque that was said to have been drawn on a branch of Berkleys in London's Pimlico. But Maurice has done his homework. The bank, he reports, knows nothing about it!

Far from feeling upset, I'm ecstatic. NOB's name is once again in one of the UK's most influential and respected newspapers, complete with a backlink on its website.

I cheer up further still when I start to read the trade press. I see that my friend Mike's words get top spot as Quote of the Week in a lifestyle interview in *Insurance Now!* Asked about his taste in food and referring to my own apparent penchant for what some in the Church of England see as tasteless policies, Mike replies: "I like savoury. He likes unsavoury."

Tuesday 14 January 1997
The Soho Weekly News was first published in 1973

Tracey appears to have voluntarily taken on a business development role. She's arranged a 10am meeting for me in Trafalgar Square with a woman named Araminta from the British Hookers Association. Araminta has an insurance query and she'd like to seek my advice.

I collect Ralph from his office at the Bank of England. He's treating me to lunch at Bootickles, a bijoux French restaurant in Soho. I tell him that first we're going to meet a hooker at the National Gallery Café.

"You can take a horticulture, but you can't make her think!" he says, smiling and impersonating the voice of Dorothy from the Wizard of Oz.

"Surely that's a quote from Dorothy Parker," I say.

"I know," Ralph replies, "but I can't do a Dorothy Parker voice."

We meet Araminta at the café, where I'm somewhat taken aback by the fact that she's black, beautiful and urbane. It's immediately clear that she's also a woman of remarkably high intelligence.

Ralph wanders off to buy the coffee, while Araminta and I get down to the business in hand. It takes less than half an hour to complete our insurance discussion. I'm just gathering my papers and returning them to my briefcase when Ralph returns with more coffees. The three of us turn to the subject of the arts and literature.

"Who's your favourite author?" asks Ralph.

"Ah, I hate to admit it," says Araminta. "It's Dickens."

"Mine too!" I exclaim. "Unfortunately, I've never been invited to one, even though I've got a 12 NOB."

"Really?" asks Araminta in disbelief.

"Yes!" says Ralph, nodding.

As Araminta turns to me, I explain that 12 NOB is the registration plate on my car. She's great company. Without checking first with Ralph, I invite her for lunch in another environment where she'll fit in well. I belatedly turn to Ralph, who smiles. That's a yes.

The table's not booked 'till 1pm, so there's time for a pint in the Beerwolf.

"Shit, we're late!" Ralph says, looking at his watch after a second round. We leave and follow him as he hastily cuts his way through Soho to the restaurant where, fortunately, our table is still free. As we sit down, speaking with some authority I say to the other two, "I recommend the veal."

We wash our meal down with two bottles of 1985 Bordeaux before taking a pre-pudding break. Ralph asks for the wine list again. "Let's push the boat out!" he says, excitedly. Handing the wine list back to the waiter, he orders us each a bottle of 1986 Château Latour. My jaw drops. They aren't going to come to much less than a grand.

Before leaving to get the wine, the waiter takes our pudding orders. I order Black Forest gâteau, Ralph goes for cheese, while Araminta plumps for sherry trifle.

Pudding arrives, by which time we're all seriously pissed. Araminta begins her trifle, before slowing down dramatically and making a deep, groaning noise. Then she turns to me and, all of a sudden, projectile vomit splatters onto my jacket and shirt. I'm so pissed that I can only roar with laughter as Araminta hurriedly apologises, wiping her mouth with her napkin.

"That's...fine!" I say, but I don't recall what happened after that.

Wednesday 15 January 1997
The Tundra Drums was first published in 1974

I wake up at 5am in St Dunstan's churchyard, a layer of ice on my jacket coating Araminta's sick. I stumble, shivering, along Eastcheap, from where I hail a cab to Totally Banjoed in Smithfield Market. I'm sure that a bit of vomit won't bar me from entry.

I'm right: it doesn't. I take a seat and order their largest breakfast and, with it, four triple gins and tonics. The drinks arrive first. As I down them one after the other, some feeling begins to return to my fingers and toes.

"F*ck it!" I say aloud and I proceed to order myself four pints of Bass.

Life is good. I'm feeling very much better as I leave the pub. At that moment Rob, a Smithfield porter I know, shouts at me, "You've puked down your suit, Curly!" In reply, I mumble sarcastically, "Cheers Rob, I wouldn't have noticed if you hadn't told me!"

It's approaching 8am. Just time for me to go for morning prayers at the Charterhouse. "Dear God," I say, "please save me from myself and Araminta."

"Piss off Curly!" says God, before I make my way to Lime Street to start my day.

I MAKE MY WAY TO LIME STREET
TO START THE DAY

Thursday 16 January 1997
The Jerusalem Post was first published in 1932

Despite the press release detailing the fact that NOB's alien abduction payout claim was a spoof, the *Burslem Chocolate Teapot* runs a story implying that worried Earthlings can take out an insurance policy that will pay out if they're eaten by aliens. The online version even includes a backlink.

Drinks tonight at the Pearly Queen in the Old Kent Road with Tracey and Danielle, a stripper friend of hers whom I met during a recent lunch with Sven, the London correspondent of a Swedish newspaper. Come 11.30pm, I realise I've no chance of catching the last train home. Danielle kindly offers to let me stay along with Tracey at her flat in New Cross. We take a cab to London Bridge, then run towards the platform for the last overland southbound train of the day out of central London.

After a few moments, I look up and suddenly I recognise the guy half asleep sitting opposite me. I haven't seen him since we were at university.

"Rick!" I cry.

Rick looks up, removes his glasses and rubs his lenses, focuses on me and then exclaims in surprise, "Curly, you drunken old b*stard!"

"How are you? What've you been up to?" I ask.

"Well, I just got married!" he says proudly.

"Really? Congratulations!" I drunkenly exclaim. "Who to?"

"Sue!" he says. "A girl I met a couple of years ago in the woods."

"The woods!" I exclaim. "What on Earth were you doing in the woods? *Dogging*?"

Silence descends upon the carriage and the train pulls into New Cross.

I open the door and call out, "Bye Rick!"

He doesn't reply.

Saturday 18 January 1997
The Johannesburg Daily Rapport was first published in 1970

On another bender tonight, this time with Genevieve. Several drinks in, she suddenly says, "I remember you once telling me that Africa is the birthplace of humanity."

"That's right," I say. "Everyone's ancestors come from Africa. Did I also tell you about the time I met President Mandela, at the studios of South African TV? He's a wonderful gentleman," I say.

"President Mandela! That must have been an incredible experience!" says Genevieve, standing to buy the next round.

"It certainly was!" I say. "That is until he told me how greatly honoured he was to meet his hero, Ken Barlow."

"You look nothing like Ken Barlow," says Genevieve.

"I know," I say, "but I suppose we must all look the same to him, so I just nodded politely and said it was lovely to meet him too."

"It was very kind of you not to make a fuss."

"That's very good of you to say so," I reply. "But I haven't finished the story. When I returned home to Pimlico, there was a lovely note from President Mandela, apologising for teasing me and to say that he knew it was me all along. Amazingly, he also mentioned that he considered me to be a jolly good fellow and a comic genius."

Monday 20 January 1997
The Memphis Press-Scimitar was first published in 1926

Off to Chelsea for drinks with Araminta and Genevieve this evening at the Inman's Twitch, so I've ironed my shirt and pressed my suit.

I get to the pub early just as Araminta's approaching from the other direction. Genevieve hasn't yet arrived, so we share a bottle of shiraz and she tells me about some of her new clients from the senior ranks of the clergy.

Around 20 minutes later, the larger-than-life figure of Genevieve bursts into the pub. "Sorry I'm late, darlings!" she cries, before giving me a peck on the cheek. Hanging her coat on the back of a chair, somewhat breathlessly she says, "I had to go to a last-minute press conference at Lloyd's. They've just launched a diversity and inclusion programme."

This makes me snap. "For f*ck's sake!" I exclaim. "Next, you'll be telling me that Lloyd's is going to apologise for insuring slave ships!"

Araminta looks at me, puzzled. "I doubt it," she says. "There's no one left to apologise *to*! They're all *dead*!"

"Apologising is all well and good," I say, "but it'd be better if organisations just behaved justly in the first place."

"Justly? What do you mean by justly?" asks Genevieve.

"Well," I reply, "my Auntie Phyllis used to clean Lord Denning's house. His Lordship was one of England's most eminent judges and a fantastic gentleman too. He once told me that he considered justice, in its widest sense, to mean fairness and that everyone should only receive that which they deserve."

"That's quite a mouthful!" she says. "Do you mean that's irrespective of race, creed, gender or religion?

"Of course!" I reply. "Justice is unambiguously blind."

After a brief pause, Araminta nods her head in agreement.

Thursday 23 January 1997
La Repubblica was first published in 1976

This morning, I have a meeting with Parminder to seek his advice on how it may be possible to get even more backlinks.

"You could always send letters of apology to famous people with a polite request for a backlink," he suggests. "Loads of organisations apologise these days for historic misdemeanours. None of them are sincere. They do it cynically, to manipulate public perception."

"That really is genius!" I exclaim. "I'll make up a bogus story that my Viking ancestors killed St. Edmund and then I'll email his Holiness the Pope to apologise as soon as I return to the broom cupboard."

Email: pope@vaticano.com
Subject: My sincere apologies
Message: Dear Pope John Paul II,

Please forgive me for corresponding with you directly, but it's extremely remiss of me not to have yet apologised for the wholly unacceptable conduct of my Viking ancestors who, on 20 November 869 AD, murdered St. Edmund, King and martyr, in the village of Hoxne in Suffolk, England.

I unreservedly apologise to both you and to St. Edmund's family.

I am truly very sorry for your loss and for the unnecessary distress that my ancestors have caused.

Wishing you all every blessing and kindest regards,

Curly Cradock

PS It'd be most helpful if you'd please arrange for your colleagues to provide a backlink on your most informative website to: www. nob.co.uk.

PPS If you also might graciously consider a home-page backlink as well, I'd be delighted to apologise unreservedly for the death of Thomas Becket too.

PPPS Please forgive me again. Sorry about Thomas.

Friday 24 January 1997
BBC Newsround was first broadcast in 1972

I fire up my computer in the hope that the Pope has agreed to provide the backlink I requested. Obviously a very busy man, the Pontiff has simply written:

> Email: curly@nob.co.uk
> Subject: For the attention of Curly Cradock
> Message: Wkurz się Curly!

We're on a roll. I assume that 'Wkurz się Curly!' is Polish for 'Of course, Curly!' so now I'll email Her Majesty Queen Elizabeth II to apologise for the execution of Charles I, to Bill Clinton to apologise for the assassination of Abraham Lincoln, to Jacques Chirac for the distress caused to Joan of Arc and anyone else who might be gullible enough to provide NOB with a backlink in exchange for an apology.

After lunch I get a call from Mum. She sounds really weary.

"What's the matter, Mum?" I ask, concerned.

"It's Genghis," she replies.

I'd guessed as much. "What wrong?" I ask her.

"He's up every night playing the same Lionel Richie song over and over again," she says. "I wouldn't normally mind, but it's all night long."

"Very funny," I say, before Mum tells me that Dad wants a quick word.

"Hi Curly, I've got some good news and some bad news," he says. "The good news is that I've been studying genealogy at night school and I've discovered that George Washington is one of our ancestors. The bad news is that he was a slave-owner."

I think for a moment. "It could be worse," I say. "If he'd have been a traitor and a terrorist then the US Federal Reserve wouldn't have put his image on US bank notes."

"That's a very valid point," says Dad and we chat a little longer before hanging up.

After a quick few pints in the Grapes, I decide that if I really am directly related to George Washington then I ought to write a truly sincere and genuine letter of apology.

After a bit of deliberation, I decide to email Tonto Big Bollocks, chief executive of Pow Wow County Council.

Email: <u>tonto@bigbollocks.com</u>
Subject: My sincere apologies
Message: Dear Mr Big Bollocks,

Greetings from London, I hope that my email finds you and your tribe well.

Sorry to trouble you, but I found out recently that my American ancestor kept slaves.

I wish to apologise unreservedly for his shameful conduct! Populating your land with lazy degenerate parasites was totally unacceptable! You and all other indigenous peoples deserve much better.

God bless America!
With all good wishes,
Curly Cradock

In the Grapes after work, I mention my email to Ralph, who suggests that I send a copy to Carl XVI Gustaf, the King of Sweden. "Your email will definitely have advanced fraternity between nations and you could be in line for the Nobel Peace Prize!" he says.

"Ralph, you're a genius!" I exclaim. "With my prize from Robert Maxwell, that'd make me a multi-prize winner. I'll send His Majesty a copy immediately, along with a polite request for a backlink from the website of the Swedish Royal Family."

Monday 10 February 1997
The Daily Mirror was first published in 1903

I have an early appointment today in a part of London I've never visited before, Kensal Green.

Meeting concluded, I'm out on the streets again by 9.30am. Dying for a piss, I turn into the local cemetery to look for somewhere to take a leak.

Mid-stream, from the corner of my eye, I can make out an elderly lady that looks like Gladys of all people squatting behind a gravestone.

"Mourning?" I say, once I've zipped up my flies.

It really is Gladys! "Hi Curly. No, I just needed a quick piss," she replies. "I just called the Incontinence Hotline and some wanker answering told me to 'hold on' but I just couldn't."

"I know what you mean," I tell her. "Only last week, during an important business meeting, I knew I wouldn't make it to the lavatory in time, so I pissed my pants and put them in my briefcase."

"You poor thing!" says Gladys.

"Thanks," I say. "But only past the point of no return did I realise that I hadn't brought my briefcase with me."

Darren from Double Dee TV calls to ask if NOB knows of any case studies for their show Down on your Luck presented by Lord Lucan – which "aims to make winners out of those who are down on their luck."

I tell them I know of one lady who's particularly down on her luck. "Her name's Tracey," I say. "She has the misfortune of having been reared in Braintree."

As I pass the phone to her, she protests, "No one's reared me there!"

I doubt that's true.

The existence of Dolly the cloned sheep has been announced this month. I'd like to say I've long suspected it. The story has now been featured in every national paper and on all UK radio and TV news channels, so obviously I must consider providing insurance cover to anyone who discovers that he or she has a clone. In any normal circumstances, the insurance industry doesn't offer a buy-one-get-one-free policy, but I've been looking for an opportunity to provide one and this one's just landed in my lap.

I quickly knock out two identical CLONESAFE press releases and email them both to Jeremy.

Friday 14 February 1997
BBC Radio Wales was founded in 1978

Late today into work, I find my computer screen decorated by a mosaic of colourful Post-it notes, all in Tracey's handwriting. Two of them catch my eye, both from Meat and Two Vag Productions. They want to film an interview with me about NOB's new clone insurance and, if possible, to speak with both a CLONESAFE policyholder and a clone.

After an hour of paperwork, I leave the broom cupboard to meet Geoff and Jeff in the Lamb. As identical twins they'll be perfect and, in return for a couple of pints, they both agree to pose as clone insurance policyholders for the show.

"Will we be your first false policyholders?" asks Geoff.

I raise my eyebrows. "You and half the people in my address book," I reply.

I reach down to my bag and pull out two blow-up sheep that I bought yesterday from a sex shop in Soho. "These are NOB's new mascots," I explain, before inflating them. Holding them up each in turn, I say, "The original – and the clone!"

We finish our pints and we step out of the pub and head down the road to the base of the Lloyd's building where a liveried waiter is standing.

"Good afternoon, sir!" I say. "My colleagues and I would like to invite you to help us to raise money for the Rhyl Animal Hospice. I wonder if you'd be kind enough to hold these two sheep for me to take a photograph."

The smartly uniformed gentleman promptly complies. I whip out my Instamatic and take a few shots of him posing proudly with an inflated sex toy under each arm. Then I head to Quick Snaps on Fenchurch Street to get the film developed, where I'm told the prints will be ready on Monday.

Now back to the Lamb for another pint. The pub's crowded, so I set about consolidating my belongings into one bag.

"You've really let us down!" say the sheep.

As I fold the deflated sex toys, an excited chap with a Welsh accent beside me in the bar asks me where I got them from.

"A sex shop in Soho," I reply, before showing him the box they came in. On its base are the words *Made in Wales*. "I'm sure you'll have no problem finding some when you get home," I assure him.

Just then, as I notice the picture of Genevieve pulling a pint behind the bar next to that of the Queen Mother, I suddenly worry about my unpaid bill. But at that moment, Sid the landlord suddenly comes over to me and says, "Thank you so much for the prompt payment of your bill. I received the cheque from the Big Bristols Channel the very same week. Please have a drink on the house."

"That's most kind," I say magnanimously. "I'll have a quadruple whisky please."

Sid duly obliges.

BUY ONE, GET ONE FREE

Saturday 15 February 1997
The Keswick Reminder was first published in 1896

My brother's staying with me this weekend and Tracey has kindly volunteered to come round to help look after him.

"Today's the 433rd birthday of Galileo Galilei," says Genghis, looking up from his book of famous historical scientists, a Christmas gift from Auntie Phyllis. He's completely absorbed by it.

"Who's Galileo?" asks Tracey.

"He's just a poor boy from a poor family," replies Genghis, shaking with laughter, "who created the theory of heliocentric orbits!"

Not wishing to correct him by telling him that it was Nicolaus Copernicus who created the heliocentric orbit theory, particularly when my brother's new medication is working so well, I say instead, "Looking at stars all night gets you nowhere. Or that's what the Roman Catholic Inquisition said to Galileo before they put him under house arrest."

Monday 17 February 1997
PBS News Hour was first broadcast in 1975

I call Mum and mention that Genghis got on admirably well at the weekend and to say that his new medication seems to be working well.

"It really does, doesn't it?" Mum replies, sounding both happy and relieved. "Your brother seems to be doing incredibly well. When I asked him to stop singing Wonderwall in the shower last week, he called out, 'Maybe.' Then all I could hear from the bathroom was the sound of laughter."

As I'm standing at the bottom of Lime Street waiting for Christian, the London correspondent for the *Prague Ancient Mariner* for whom I'm buying lunch, I remove my glasses to rub them clean on my shirt. As I do so, I come almost face to face with Imelda. She doesn't see me as she's walking, looking down and scowling.

"Hi Imelda!" I say. "I must say you look great without glasses."

She looks up. "Piss off Curly!" she snaps. "I don't *wear* glasses."

"Yeah, but I do," I reply, still wiping my lenses.

When I get back to the broom cupboard, I notice the press cuttings have arrived. The headline in the *Runcorn Blobstrop* brings a smile: *Clone again and again!*

Friday 21 February 1997
Scottish Television was founded in 1957

I've arranged lunch with Isla, the personal finance editor of the *Edinburgh Nosh-off*, to thank her for all the backlinks and coverage she's given NOB over the past few months. First, though, I have a meeting in the morning at the Roslin Institute, where the day turns into something of a disaster. How was I to know that there are two identical Roslin Institutes at different locations?

I'm late for lunch, but Isla is relaxed and when I finally arrive, she asks me, "Did you see Dolly?"

"I did, but I don't know which one," I reply, "I also saw the monument to Sir Walter Scott. It's magnificent – much more impressive than the Albert Memorial. Strange really, when Sir Walter named one of his most famous books after the f*cking train station!"

Isla raises her eyebrows in an ironic gesture, prompting me to ask, "What does Las Vegas have in common with Paisley?"

She shrugs.

I pause. "In both places, you can pay for sex with chips."

Monday 24 February 1997
The Gateshead Post was first published in 1937

The *Blaydon Racist* today reports that NOB has launched a policy to protect potential beneficiaries of wills should they become involved in a legal dispute with their clone. My first phone call today is from Elliott, a member of the public with a genuine enquiry about the cost of CLONESAFE.

As usual with such enquiries, I advise Elliott not to waste his money.

He thanks me and hangs up. I look up at Tracey and lament, "I seem to spend my whole life talking to retards!"

"You cheeky tw*t!" she says.

"No, not you," I say. "I mean the morons we're doing our best to help. Other than Mrs Mainwaring, when was the last time we talked to someone sensible enough to be considered at the very least a half-wit?"

"F*cking never," says Tracey, handing me a pile of post. The top-facing envelope brings a smile to my face. I open it expectantly. Sure enough, inside is a cheque from Mikhail, a very rich Russian client, for the best part of four grand.

Feeling flush, but in dire need of stimulating conversation, I ring Araminta and invite her to lunch at the Quick Quim Trim in Mayfair.

We both arrive at the same time, me by bus from the City, Araminta on foot from a meeting in New Bond Street. I'm suddenly conscious that I'm somewhat under-dressed as I look up to see Araminta approach, beaming elegantly in a Versace off-the-shoulder dress.

I'm in heaven: copious amounts of classic vintage red in me and the company of a beautiful and highly intelligent woman.

The waiter clears our plates before our conversation drifts back to work. "You may be surprised to learn that most of my clients from the clergy prefer to give it to me up the arse," Araminta tells me before taking a swig of wine.

"F*cking painful," I say. "But I can do one better than that. When I was at university, I was so pissed when climbing a metal fence that I fell and impaled myself on a spike."

Araminta winces. "Ouch!" she exclaims. "Did it hurt?"

"Yes, it hurt like f*ck!" I reply, resisting the urge to say it was an anus horribilis. I add instead, "Luckily, it hurt considerably less than it would've done had I not been anally raped as a child."

"Really?" asks Araminta, suddenly looking shocked.

"Well, yes," I reply. "After the incident with the spike, I was fortunate only to have to spend three weeks in hospital in Gateshead and to have just a temporary colostomy."

"You poor thing!" she says with genuine sympathy. "Fancy having to spend three weeks in Gateshead!"

Tuesday 25 February 1997
Televisión de El Salvador (TVES) was founded in 1964

After a lunchtime meeting with Mike in the Grapes, I've an idea for another bogus press story. This one's about a PPI policy for smokers. As it happens, NOB's never charged smokers any additional premium, but this spoof will provide further publicity and, with any luck, backlinks too.

Without further ado, I write a SMOKERSAFE press release and email it to Jeremy, complete with the assurance that smokers won't be required to cough up any additional premium.

Friday 28 February 1997
The Tombstone Epitaph was first published in 1880

A day to celebrate another appearance in *Spit Roast Daily*. The story quotes me saying, "When you lose your job or become disabled, it's not the time to give up smoking. With SMOKERSAFE, you can continue to enjoy life's little pleasures while still contributing to the government."

Meanwhile, *Spend Your Wad* magazine understands what NOB has done. Douglas, the reporter, quotes my suggestion that losing your job or becoming disabled is stressful enough without giving up smoking too.

To the Lamb for a few pints at lunchtime before I head off to an interview with Andy, a senior reporter at Phlegm Brûlée, a Scottish press agency with an office in Bvsh House, from where it sells its stories to regional UK radio and TV channels. They're hoping to cash in by giving me the opportunity to air my views about why I consider it to be unfair for smokers to be penalised by the insurance industry.

As I'm about to leave, I see none other than Jimmy f*cking Savile.

"Hi Jimmy," I say. "What are you doing here?"

"Just some charity work, Curly," he says in his unmistakably creepy voice.

As I head for the Tube, I reflect that while Jimmy may be a competent DJ, I certainly wouldn't want the f*cker to babysit.

Saturday 1 March 1997
Pretoria News was first published in 1898

At noon, I meet Ralph in Bethnal Green at the Forth Bridger, his new local, which is just around the corner from Doug's flat. He brings me a pint of Guinness just as Pink Floyd's "Brain Damage" comes on the juke box.

"You know this album?" I ask him. He certainly does, he says. So, I mention to him that Dark Side of the Moon was released on this day 24 years ago. "It's instantly recognisable from its cover," I say. "It has the Newtonian prism image that splits a ray of light into a rainbow."

"Isaac Newton was a genius for inventing homosexuality," says Ralph, nodding. "But did you know that the album's cover image itself has only six colours? It's missing indigo."

"You're right about Newton," I say. "But did you know that students at the University of Southern Africa have asked their science faculty to consider scrapping physics altogether? They claim that the laws of physics are racist because black people have contributed nothing whatsoever that advances scientific knowledge in any meaningful way."

Ralph shakes his head.

"According to them," I say, "Voodoo is more valid than Isaac Newton's theory of gravity or James Clerk Maxwell's theory of electromagnetism, because both of these gentlemen were white."

"Then they're obviously c*nts!" exclaims Ralph.

I nod and respond, "Denying the existence of gravity and electromagnetism is what you get when you have a so-called Rainbow Nation with only six colours. It's like the proverbial picnic missing a sandwich."

"Obviously not a sandwich on white bread," notes Ralph.

Sunday 2 March 1997
Wales on Sunday was first published in 1989

Under pressure from the blow-up sheep, who are keen to return to Wales, I've arranged a weekend appointment with Gawain, money editor of *Blue-Veined Piccolo* in the picturesque seaside town of Colwyn Bay.

It's love at first sight. Gawain is absolutely besotted by the sheep and they're delighted.

"NOB is a leader in its field," I begin, but Gawain isn't paying attention – until, that is, I suggest that I allow him to keep the sheep in return for a home-page backlink.

"Deal!" he replies, picking up his coat as he leaves with the sheep. None of them says goodbye.

Meeting over, I spot the front-page story in the *Swansea Sidebar of Shame*. Scientists at the elite University of Upper Wales, it says, have discovered two revolutionary new uses for sheep: meat and wool.

Monday 3 March 1997
TV-am was founded in 1983

Tracey brings me a sheaf of faxes, where I note that news doesn't always travel fast. Hans, a reporter from Jetz TV in Germany writes, "I'd like to make a report about insurance for vergins (sic) who get pregnant by God."

I outsource this task to Tracey. "Can you give this guy Hans a call? Your name is Mary from NOB. You're a virgin birth policyholder," I say as I pass her the fax, which she reads before calling him.

Just then my mobile phone rings. It's Doug. I put my Nokia on speakerphone, just so he doesn't miss the chance to hear why 'Mary' has chosen to buy VIRGINSAFE. I finally ring off as Tracey stands up to put on her coat. "Off to meet Hans for lunch," she says as she hurries out through the door.

The highlight of the day comes when I ask her how she got on at lunch. "Met Hans and his mates. Many Hans make light work!" she cries, laughing more coarsely than usual.

This afternoon I'm driving to a meeting with Anthony, one of the reporters at the *Uxbridge Anonymous Authority*, I see a sign for Brunel College of Higher Education, which proudly promises "an Uxbridge education". I ask Anthony how long he's been a journalist.

"About five years," he says. "Before that I prepared meals for drug addicts and alcoholics."

"You worked for the Salvation Army?"

"No," he says. "I was a chef at the Broadcasting Wank Hut canteen."

Interview over, I head back to the car. To the best of my knowledge, Isambard Kingdom Brunel never visited Uxbridge, but it's the birthplace of world-famous showgirl Christine Keeler.

Thursday 13 March 1997
The National Broadcasting Company (NBC) was founded in 1926

Mercifully, a quiet day in the broom cupboard today. Tracey's still trying to finish the same crossword she started in November. She asks me, "What's got four letters and is a short skirt that extends out?"

"Tutu."

"Cheers Curly, I should've known that," she says.

"Did you know that Archbishop Tutu's official title is primate of the Anglican Church of South Africa?" I ask.

"Primate!" Tracey exclaims. "Is that why I get confused between archbishops and monkeys?" she asks.

"It must be," I reply. "I can't think of any other reason."

Flicking through a copy of *Global Geographic*, I say to Tracey, "They've discovered Homo Erectus on the beach near Brighton."

"F*cking waste!"

"Did I hear someone say Homo Erectus?" asks Ralph, walking through the door.

"Sorry to disappoint you. I was only joking," I say, just as the phone rings. It's Candice from Arkansas Radio calling to arrange a pre-recorded interview about SMOKERSAFE for that morning's breakfast show. Arkansas is six hours behind us, so I reckon I've plenty of time for a pint with Ralph.

Walking through Leadenhall Market on our way to the Lamb, we pass the greengrocers. I stop to look, then say to Melanie, the stall owner, "Madam, may I please compliment you on your fantastic melons?"

She looks up and says, "Piss off Curly!"

FANTASTIC MELONS, MADAM

Monday 17 March 1997
The Boston Newsletter published the first newspaper classified advertisement in 1704

The other day it was raining, so I borrowed a military jacket from Geoff, who's in the territorial army. Then I made the mistake of wearing it while out on the lash with Araminta, so I've just picked it up from the dry cleaners.

I'm late for a live radio interview with Good Morning Vietnam. As I reach the broom cupboard, a paraplegic heading in the opposite direction swerves his wheelchair deliberately into me. Shaken but still in a rush, I find the jacket has gone from my bag.

Fuming! I ring the *Stepney Aris'* classifieds editor and place the following ad:

> To the wanker in the wheelchair that stole my camouflage jacket: You can hide, but you cannot run! Curly Cradock.

Arriving back at the broom cupboard after lunch, I mention to Tracey that I've just met Sir Dick, the Lord Mayor outside Mansion House.

"He told me that I was the Einstein of the City of London!"

"That was nice of him," she says.

"Yes," I say. "But I think he meant Frank rather than Albert."

Wednesday 26 March 1997
The Telford Gazette was first published in 1920

Up early to drive to Telford this morning for a breakfast meeting with Sebastian, the NOB-friendly editor of the *Shropshire Brain Donor*, who's been very generous with coverage and backlinks. If anyone ever tells you that journalists don't appreciate a bottle of Scotch in return for a backlink, don't believe them.

Sebastian's a lovely chap. Before we get down to business, I tell him how impressed I am by Telford's Ironbridge. "Telford is the birthplace of the industrial revolution," I say. "What's its major industry today?"

"We're making enormous strides in child-sex tourism," Sebastian says proudly. "Ten years ago, we were nowhere in the league tables, but today we can hold our heads high against Cleveland, Rochdale and Rotherham. The dynamism and hard work of our local child-sex tourist board is really paying off. We're now internationally recognised as a go-to destination. Our community can be proud," he adds, beaming.

Just as I arrive at work a fax arrives from Becca, the producer of Big Bristols' Zoey Batt show, asking for an interview at 1.15pm to be played on air at 1.15pm tomorrow. I cannily deduce this means it's a live interview.

This evening, I've a meeting with Doug at the Black Dog. Just as I'm reading the cuttings, I see a disturbing report from Florida in the *Miami Middle Finger*, which reveals that members of religious cult, Majestic Wardrobe, in California have all topped themselves. Just then Doug turns up and reads the headline of the report in front of me.

"Curly, look what you've done!" he exclaims jokingly, pointing to the article, before he picks up the Guinness that I've bought him.

I look at the story, think for a moment, then reach for my phone to ring Jeremy to tell him I've got a story for him that's been sitting under my nose for days.

"You've heard of Majestic Wardrobe?" I ask.

He replies in the affirmative.

"Well, they're NOB's clients," I tell him, brazenly lying. For good measure, I add that NOB has withdrawn ETSAFE, out of respect for the suicide victims.

I promise to email him the Majestic Wardrobe press release exclusively, as soon as I'm back at work in the morning. It's just a pity, I think, that no one from Majestic Wardrobe is left alive and available for me to attribute a spoof comment, but at least no one's around to contradict me.

" NOB TODAY CONFIRMED IT HAD WITHDRAWN ETSAFE "

Sunday 30 March 1997
Channel 5 is founded today

I make myself a holiday-strength Irish coffee and open the press cuttings envelope, where I note that NOB has made the *Chicago Back Passage* and the *San Francisco Rectal Prolapse*, both seemingly part of the same news group. The lead story in each reports that a British company is abandoning its alien insurance cover. They both directly quote in full my own made-up bollocks about the US suicides: "I'm deeply shocked and saddened by the Majestic Wardrobe deaths. NOB is now withdrawing from the alien abduction market in order to avoid a repetition."

I take a call from Vladislav, the news editor of the *Kyiv Budgie Smuggler*. After the interview, I ask him how far Chernobyl is from Kyiv.

"About 500 kilometres," he replies.

"Have you ever visited Chernobyl?" I ask.

"Yes!" replies Vladislav. "I can count on one hand how many times I've been to Chernobyl. It's fourteen."

Ah, the famous Ukrainian wit.

I make another Irish coffee and turn again to the cuttings. Pretty much the same nonsense about NOB abandoning alien abduction insurance dominates several UK regional papers, including the *Cockermouth Gobble*, the *Brixham Phishing Gazette* and the *Feltham Boobs*.

Tuesday 1 April 1997
The Guardian first published the spoof travel guide to the island of San Serif in 1977

At 6am a car picks me up to drive me in comfort for a fun interview with Bung Hole News. I don't normally suffer from motion sickness, but I've been up all night drinking magnums of pan-European pink plonk and, as we approach the studios, I throw it back up on the rear passenger seat. Vomit everywhere. Fortunately it's a silent puke. The blacked-out partition between me and the driver is closed, so I don't think he notices.

I'll send them flowers or something.

Meanwhile the *Addis Ababa Yabba Dabbas'* website today kindly provides NOB with a platform from which to announce the following: "We're now withdrawing from alien abduction insurances. We don't want to endanger any more innocent lives."

Oh well, it gets NOB's name out, as well as giving us another backlink – in this instance in a highly respected paper with a circulation of more than a million readers.

As an April Fool's joke, I announce to the world's media that I've been abducted by aliens and don't expect to return to Earth until early next year. The fact that forged banknotes with my fingerprints on them have been discovered in the London Borough of Newham is simply a coincidence. Furthermore, for the avoidance of doubt, I'll only be popping into the Old Bailey tomorrow for a quick piss and for no other reason.

Thursday 1 January 1998
The Mongolian National Broadcaster was founded in 1931

Not unusually, I enter the new year with a hangover. Its effects are exacerbated by my phone, which alerts me to a long series of missed calls and a dozen or so barely intelligible messages. Puzzles such as this, before I've even had my first drink, tend to put a downer on the rest of the day. There really should be insurance against this kind of thing.

An empty wine bottle falls over beside my bed as I fumble to grab my mobile to dial voicemail. The first message is in broken English from Khulan, a reporter at Tajikistan TV in Dushanbe. He says he wants to record an interview for tomorrow morning's news show to talk about which type of NAFFSAFE claims that NOB's received so far in the past year.

I take a couple of high-strength painkillers and give them time to work before reaching for my phone to call Khulan just as it rings again. Reporter Batjargal from *The Mongol* in Ulaanbaatar sounds excited to speak to me, but the phone cuts out after just a few seconds. Ten minutes later it rings again, but this time it's not from abroad. Where the hell's 01978? My focus is on brewing my Irish coffee, so I just let it ring.

Cautiously sipping my Bells-Brasilia brew a few minutes later, I listen to the voicemail. It's Ifan, a reporter from Wingnut TV in Wrexham, working on a programme called Weird Wales. "The immaculate conception woman in Bangor is of particular interest," says Ifan, who adds, "Anything with a Welsh slant would be good."

I call him back and tell him I'm happy to help once he confirms there'll be a backlink in it for NOB.

Friday 2 January 1998
The Rochdale Observer was first published in 1856

Giulia, a researcher from the Giuseppe Ravioli Show, calls to say that she wants to send a film crew to interview me in London. Giulia clearly hasn't done her homework. I'm banned for life by Giuseppe after I ran up a bill of several thousand pounds on drinks and fell into a drunken stupor while being interviewed during his show.

As I get dressed, I turn on the radio. Just catching the last of the 8am pips, my phone rings again. This time it's Harriet, a Big Bristols researcher, asking if I'm available for an interview this afternoon with presenter, Barbara, which will be recorded for broadcast in Saturday's Thunderbox programme.

"I'd like to speak to some of your policyholders," she says. "Are any of the 24 Anglican virgins from Inverness available for a phone interview?"

Not again! "I'm really sorry, but under data protection regulations I can't reveal my clients' identity," I say. The media always fall for that one.

Just as I hang up, *Sunday Shocker* reporter, Jasper, calls. He just wants a quote about erection all-risks insurance. "Get a stiffy or your money back!" should give them the lift needed to start the new year.

At work today, it's the usual routine: I spend the morning selling ethical, good-value PPI insurance, before spending the rest of the day spoofing the media about non-existent insurance policies in the hope of acquiring yet more backlinks.

I haven't had a drop of booze all day, for this morning I forgot my wallet. Strong coffee without whisky is like a sandwich without any filling. I take two sips before pouring the rest of the hot drink down the drain.

After a cheese sandwich from Benjy's, bought using petty cash, I arrange a trip to Rochdale to see Fenton, a lively and engaging freelance reporter for the *Rochdale Carnival Knowledge*.

Tuesday 6 January 1998
The Oldham Evening Chronicle was first published in 1854

Realistically, other than visiting Fenton, there's only one good reason to visit Rochdale. That's to pay a visit to the strangely named Elizabethan manor house named F*ck Hall. It's featured in Fullbright's Architectural Guide, which suggests it was named after all the desirable qualities of the town.

To make my trip more worthwhile, I've arranged an evening meeting with Ahmed, the editor of the *Oldham Gazoo*. I doubt there's any chance of drinks with him.

Oldham, like Rochdale, is another place greatly admired by the paedophiles of Britain and Pakistan. It does, however, have a fantastic local newspaper and a team of highly dedicated but under-resourced journalists who're doing their very best to mitigate the damage being done to their community.

It takes a lot for me to admit that I've over-indulged, but I definitely drank too much during my meeting with Ahmed. He laughed out loud at a joke I told him about the little Muslim kid who loses his mum in a busy supermarket. "What does she look like?" asks the manager. "I don't know," replies the kid. "I've only ever seen her eyes."

With another backlink secured, I make my way to the train station.

I spend the first part of the train journey back home with my head pounding. I brave the trip to the buffet carriage for the hair of the dog. After ordering a bottle of wine, I reach in my back pocket for my wallet. It's not there.

I stagger angrily back to the seat, thirsty and empty-handed and wondering quite where in Oldham I was robbed. It's one of those towns where Station Road refers to the police station. Its motto should be BEWARE OF PICKPOCKETS.

Thursday 8 January 1998
ITV World in Action was first broadcast in 1955

To the Strand with Tracey to meet Ralph for lunch. For some reason, Tracey's wheeling a suitcase behind her. As we pass the Royal Courts of Justice, she suddenly says, "I've run out of bog paper! I need to nick some from in there!"

"Why there? Why not wait till we get to the pub?" I ask.

"I know where their store cupboard is. And it's top-quality bog paper," she explains, before she makes a dash for the huge, arched entrance.

"Ok, I'll meet you in the Coal Hole," I call out, curious about her apparent acquaintance with the Royal Courts of Justice.

I cross the road at the lights and wander a short way further down the Strand into the pub, where I order myself a pint. Ralph rocks up as I'm at the bar, so I buy him his trademark Malibu and coke.

We're onto our third round before Tracey arrives, wiping mayonnaise from her face with loo roll.

"What took you so long?" I ask.

"I was caught nicking the bog paper by the Master of the Bog Rolls," she says. "He warned me, 'You'll go down for that!' So I did."

"YOU'LL GO DOWN FOR THAT," SAID
THE JUDGE, "SO I DID"

Friday 9 January 1998
The Newcastle Journal was first published in 1832

"What's the matter?" I ask Tracey when she hangs up the phone.

"That was my grandmother's doctor, ringing to tell me that Granny's died."

"I'm very sorry to hear that," I say.

"Thanks," she says wiping her eyes as she leaves the broom cupboard for the lavatory.

On her return, I suggest we take an early break for lunch. I take her to the Grapes for a drink and to talk about her late grandmother. Returning from the bar with the second round of drinks, I say to her, "That was really kind of the doctor to take the trouble to call you. That level of care for the wider family seems most unusual. You should drop him a note to thank him," I say, before asking, "Did you get his name?"

"Yes," she replies. "It was a Dr Harold Shipman."

Tuesday 13 January 1998
The Singapore Straits Times was first published in 1845

I'm in the broom cupboard skimming through the latest cuttings. On the reverse side of a story about NOB in the *Belfast Biffer*, I read that the Big Bristols Channel has abandoned a plan to produce a new TV series about Sherlock Holmes.

I look up and mention this to Holmes fan, Tracey, who exclaims, "Shit, no Sherlock!"

It's a quiet afternoon. Tracey's listening to Big Bristols Radio, which is broadcasting a programme dedicated to 1970s punk music.

I look up and ask, "Have you ever heard of John Lydon?"

"No, I don't think so," she replies.

"He was the front man of the Sex Pistols," I tell her.

"You mean Johnny Rotten?"

"Yes, him," I say, nodding. "I used to insure the band when I was at Lloyd's. Lydon claims he was banned for life by the Big Bristols Channel for trying to stop paedophiles from indecently assaulting some of the young girls who appeared on the channel's weekly music chart show."

"I don't believe it!" says Tracey. "Did you know that they recently called for action on the sexual abuse of teenagers?"

"Was that after calling, 'Lights, camera...'" I muse.

For some unknown reason there's also a sudden show of interest in the media about clone insurance. I see a story from the *North Pole Chilly Willy*, which has the headline: *"Here Today, Clone Tomorrow!"* The subs must still be recovering from Christmas.

Tracey mentions that she met Del's grandparents Winston and Dionne for the first time yesterday.

"How did it go?" I ask her.

"Well," she says, "when I asked Winston what he did for a living, Dionne replied, 'I'm a ventriloquist.'"

Thursday 5 February 1998
The Royston Crow was first published in 1855

Starting the day with a quick coffee in Dinky Doos, my *favourite* Leadenhall Market café, I overhear a sweet, endearing conversation between a mother and her young daughter at the next table.

They're talking about illness and vaccination, when I hear the daughter ask, "Mum, why didn't you vaccinate me?"

The mother replies, "I didn't want you to get autism, dear."

"Thanks, Mum," says her daughter. "I wouldn't have been able to cope with autism as *well* as polio."

Just as I arrive at the broom cupboard, I notice a formal-looking envelope with a Chepstow postmark. I open it excitedly, hoping someone has left me something in their will. But no. It merely says:

> Dear Mr Cradock,
>
> I'd like to remind you that BBC is an acronym for Big Bristols Channel and not a genre of ethnic pornography that focuses on black men with large penises. Please desist from your unlawful use of our trademark immediately.
>
> Yours Faithfully,
> Idi Amin
> General Counsel
> Big Bristols Channel

Later that evening I'm having a quick pint with Ralph in the Grapes, where I mention the letter that I received today from the Big Bristols Channel. "They're total wankers!" I say.

"I agree," says Ralph. "I've heard that someone working for the Channel has been raping his dogs and is considered to be the world's worst animal abuser."

"Not Sir Dennis Attleborough I hope," I say.

"No!" says Ralph. "Of course not, but I've also heard that there's another one of the c*nts at the Channel who possesses images of children being sexually abused."

"If that's true then the Big Bristols Channel is morally bankrupt!" I exclaim. I pause before adding, "Having said that, I'm sure they'll be able to scrape together enough money to give the two f*ckers a massive pay-rise."

Monday 9 February 1998
CBS 60 Minutes was first broadcast in 1968

As I make my way to the Lloyd's building's and pass through the revolving doors, I'm approached by Rupert, an old underwriting colleague of mine, who invites me into his office for a mug of coffee.

He brings the drinks to the table and sits opposite me. Then, as I top up my drink with a bottle of whisky, he discreetly asks me whether I'd be interested in joining a secret society.

I reflect for a second. My grandfather was a 32nd-degree freemason but, given that freemasonry has no female representation and that it entails ritual embracing, I suspect that the whole movement might just be cover for repressed homosexuality. I mention this to Rupert, who looks concerned, before explaining that he was inviting me to join AA.

I politely decline Rupert's kind offer and tell him that I already have roadside assistance for my 12 NOB.

I arrive in the broom cupboard to see a fax coming out of the machine from *Canberra Nine Bob Note*. Franco the reporter there is asking for more detail on NOB's announcement several months ago that it's withdrawing alien abduction cover. The fax is dated today.

I know Australia's a long way away, but this seems ridiculous. It's not as though I sent the press release there by ship. If I had done, maybe it could have at least had the excuse of having been held up at one of the country's perpetual dockers' strikes.

I need to get away from work for a few hours. Fortunately, I've arranged what promises to be a highly enjoyable lunch with the formidable radio presenter Jamie Dodger. I've agreed to insure his tongue for £1 million and he seems quite excited.

I AM GOING TO INSURE HIS TONGUE
FOR A MILLION QUID, AND HE SEEMS
QUITE EXCITED

Wednesday 11 March 1998
The Wakefield Gazette was first published in 1854

After a boozy lunch in the Grapes, I return to the broom cupboard to collect my briefcase and I announce to Tracey, "Right, I'm off to meet Matilda, a journalist from the *Maldon Four-Letter Words* in Tolleshunt D'Arcy this afternoon."

"That sounds lovely!" she replies.

"You'd think so from its poetic name," I reply. "However, it's the village where Jeremy Bamber reportedly killed his step parents, his step sister and her two six-year-old twins."

"What a b*stard!"

"You're right. He is!" I say. "His mother was an unmarried vicar's daughter from Leicester."

"Fancy having the bad luck to adopt a f*cker like him!" she exclaims.

"He's now serving a whole-life sentence in Wakefield Prison," I tell her.

Her whole complexion changes. "He doesn't deserve *that*," she says. "No *one* should be forced to live in *Wakefield*," she adds.

This evening a car takes me – very pissed – to the Broadcasting Wank Hut, where I make my way to the Big Bristols World Tomorrow studio to be interviewed by a highly respected Scottish journalist named Isabel. She wants to know more about Jamie's tongue insurance.

When I'm introduced to her, Isabel clocks how drunk I am and she doesn't look happy. She even refuses to shake my hand. Matters take a turn for the worse when I tell her that the ugliest people in the UK come from her hometown of Aberdeen. "It's all those sea monsters," I explain with a shrug, abandoning my plan to ask her for a backlink. Finally, when I leave, Isabel doesn't even say goodbye.

I soon cheer up, however, for on my way out I've the honour of being bumped into by Pierre, the channel's legendary disability correspondent. Jokingly I say, "Hi Pierre, aren't you the bloke who said, 'I don't mind being blind, I'm just glad I'm not ugly'?"

He laughs and steps forward to feel my face, before saying, "Piss off Curly!"

Monday 23 March 1998
The Wirral Globe was first published in 1973

I've got to drive to the Wirral peninsular today for a meeting with Penelope, the editor of the *Birkenhead Goo Gargle*. It's a hell of a journey, but the lobscouse for lunch across the Mersey should make it worthwhile. Provided the f*cking tunnel's open, of course.

It is. Over a prawn cocktail starter, I ask Penelope, "Why do so many women in Wirral wear gold shoes?"

"You mean like these ones?" she asks, sticking one of her gold stilettos out from beneath the table.

I quickly change the subject. "What's it like living in Wirral?" I ask her.

"Brilliant!" she replies. "The sunsets are wonderful and there are many delightful beach walks. Mind you, you can't really walk anywhere barefoot because of all the dog shit and syringes."

To cheer her up, I ask Penelope if she'd heard that earlier today, police had cordoned off Birkenhead town centre when a suspicious object was discovered in a car. It later turned out to be a tax disc, I tell her.

Wednesday 1 April 1998
BBC News first broadcast the Smell-O-Vision spoof in 1965

I'm in the broom cupboard early this morning to find Tracey already at her desk. As I hang my jacket next to hers, she says, "Can I ask a question?"

"Isn't that an oxymoron?"

"What the f*ck's an oxymoron?" she says.

"It's a self-contradicting word or series of words," I reply. "'Awfully good' is one example, or 'free is only worth what you paid for it' is another. Or 'a verbal contract isn't worth the paper it's written on'. This is why I'm always telling you to appear sincere when you're talking to a customer."

"Even when I don't mean it?" she asks.

"*Especially* then!"

"Clever!" she says. "Do you know any more of those oxy-things?"

"Yes," I reply. "Columnist Victor Lewis-Smith recently suggested 'airline food'. And I pay you far too much, but you're definitely worth it," I add.

"Cheeky tw*t."

I see that the *Bogota Buttmuncher*, the *Jakarta Shitgibbon* and the *Honolulu Public Convenience* all report that leaked intelligence reports warn that Iraq is planning to unleash a deadly anthrax attack in the West. Sounds pretty unlikely, but if NOB is to support its false claims that it provides a policy for every paranoia then we must jump on this bandwagon too. Besides, we could do with the backlinks.

Two years ago, NOB became the only PPI provider in the UK to cover acts of terrorism. Needless to say, this initiative received no publicity. Our ANTHRAXSAFE press release, on the other hand, will be emailed to Jeremy, in the spirit of April Fools, so fingers crossed!

Friday 3 April 1998
The Western Mail was first published in 1869

Doug calls me on my mobile to say that he took a surprise call this morning from Liam, a mate of his from university who's now living in Tehran. Liam mentioned that NOB's anthrax story has been featured on Iranian state radio. I'm tickled by that. Just like Monty Python's Man with Three Buttocks, I can now say that I've been on Persian radio and the Forces Network.

It feels very much as though I'm acting against my better judgement, but today I'm driving to Cardiff to meet Rhodri, the editor of the *South Wales Willie Welly*. I refuse to pay to cross the Severn Bridge to get into Wales, so I'm going via Gloucester and Saundersfoot. It was in the village of Saundersfoot where, some eight years before the Wright Brothers took to the air, aviation enthusiast Harold Frost flew for 500 yards in an aircraft that he'd designed himself. Unfortunately, Mr Frost never received any recognition and there's no memorial to him, although I did see the tree that he flew into.

Rhodri is a delightful young man who kindly tells me some interesting facts about the fine city of Cardiff. He tells me that only ten percent of the population speak Welsh and that it has more green space per person than any other city in the UK.

"Is that for the sheep?" I ask.

"Absolutely not!" he replies. "It's a myth that in Wales the men are men and the sheep are nervous."

"Please forgive me," I say. "Any other interesting facts?"

"Cardiff has the world's oldest record shop. And TV news presenter Huw Edwards graduated with first-class honours from University College Cardiff in 1983," he says, still apparently smarting from my sheep comment, despite my apology.

I take a tour of the city centre, where I'm taken aback by how clean the place is. I pass a newsagent with several Welsh regional papers on the stand outside, among them the *Llanfairpwllgwyngyll Sheep Shagger*, which has the front-page headline: *Anthrax panic relief!*

Monday 6 April 1998
The Daily Express was first published in 1900

The website of the *Memphis Masthead* reports today that NOB has cashed in with a vengeance on the latest panic sweeping Britain and has sold 25,000 policies at £100 each for cover against death or injury from anthrax. According to the article, actuaries reckon the odds are about the same as the chance of asteroid collision. I'm quoted legitimising the story by suggesting that these bugs are freely available to Saddam Hussein and that we're therefore providing insurance against something that could really happen.

The *Sefton Exposé* also runs the story with a clever headline saying that NOB has launched the *Mother of All Policies*! Drily, it quotes my prediction that we'll be accused of ambulance-chasing, which of course is exactly what we're doing – or rather would be, if any of these spoof insurance policies actually existed.

Returning from lunch at the Grapes, I find Tracey on the phone to Mrs Mainwaring, this time evidently trying to reassure her that Saddam Hussain is not going to drop anthrax onto Croydon.

"Don't panic Mrs Mainwaring," she says. "It's just the media issuing scare stories to sell more newspapers and to get more viewers and listeners. You're going to be fine and you really don't need to buy anthrax insurance."

When Tracey finishes her call, I tell her, "Leon told me that if Saddam Hussein is ever found guilty of his crimes against humanity, he'll only receive a suspended sentence."

Enjoyable afternoon reading the press cuttings. Several German daily papers, including the *Frankfurt Cum Bucket*, the *Dresden Soapy Titwank* and the *Berlin Shirtlifter*, report that NOB is offering anthrax insurance. And Bingo! Each story includes a backlink! A quick calculation suggests the three mainland European titles' circulation alone adds up to more than a million copies.

On the phone to a client, Tracey's getting irate and close to losing her patience. When she hangs up, she looks across at me and exclaims, "That f*cker was a real spazz."

"Tracey, you shouldn't use the word spazz," I say. "It's what you call someone who has cerebral palsy. In future, please just use the word *retard* when referring to someone who possesses the intellectual depth of a hairdresser. It's very important that you don't cause unintentional offence."

This evening, Ralph invited us as his guests to a function that he's attending in the 16th-century Merchant's Hall off Cheapside. It's a pretty uneventful occasion. When we leave, I lead Ralph and Tracey onto the strangely renamed Gropec*nt Lane where, in the heat of the moment, Tracey lifts her skirt and boldly says to Ralph, "Are you sure I can't tempt you?"

"Ooh you are *awful*...But I like you!" he replies, doing a poor impression of seventies comedian, Dick Emery.

Thursday 9 April 1998
The Barnsley Chronicle was first published in 1858

An email arrives from Georgina, London correspondent at the *Sodom and Gomorrah Apocalypse* – famous for being one the largest political magazines in the Middle East, with a circulation of over four million – inviting me to a phone interview to discuss ANTHRAXSAFE.

I hesitate before asking Tracey to arrange it. She once said, "So what if I don't know what Armageddon means? It's not like it's the end of the world."

I'm supposed to go on a long drive tomorrow to meet Gwyneth, the personal finance correspondent of the *Chocolate Sandwich* in Rhyl. I've never been to Rhyl and I always like to do a bit of research before any such excursion.

The first bit of detail I find comes in the form of a recent news article by Ezra, the news editor on Gwyneth's paper, who describes his town as a sprawling concrete jungle, with a horrible town centre, few if any bars worth visiting and nowhere decent to eat.

I make my excuses to Gwyneth. A backlink is useful, but not at any cost. Besides, I've the delights of Barnsley and Preston to look forward to tomorrow.

Friday 1 May 1998
The Lancashire Post was first published in 1886

I'm up at 4am and soon I'm on the M1 to drive north to meet Roy, the editor of the *Barnsley Chubblies*. I like visiting Yorkshire. The people are more friendly than I find them to be down south and Roy comes across as a decent and considerate gentleman.

After our meeting I ask him what it's like living in Barnsley.

"To be honest, life's really miserable and stressful here," he says. "There's no escape. Nobody has any fun and there's nothing to do. That's why we have tidal waves of unmarried mothers."

"I'm sorry to hear that," I reply. "I've got a lunch meeting with Alf, editor of the *Preston Puff Piece*. Do you know him?"

"Yes," he replies. "He's a fantastic journalist and a lovely man. Please pass on my best wishes."

After asking Roy for a backlink, I bid him farewell and drive off to a café on the outskirts of Preston to meet Alf.

He's on good form. I pass on Roy's best wishes and I treat him to a bacon balm cake and a disposable cup of coffee, before setting off to see the world's most famous bus station.

To my dismay, as I near my destination the smell of urine and excrement are overpoweringly awful. I conclude that the disgusting place should be avoided at all costs.

Just then, I spot the bus station. I'm impressed! It's immaculately clean and the staff are most helpful and friendly.

Just as I arrive back at the broom cupboard after a five-hour drive on the motorway, I take a call from Lance. The first thing he starts talking about is the World Cup, a subject in which I'd have thought by now he'd understand I've absolutely no interest. On the other hand, I *do* want to get more backlinks for NOB and, like the TOONSAFE story last year, a World Cup story might help, so I half-listen to him.

I hang up and scribble down some notes before passing them over to Tracey for her to write up a CUPSAFE press release and email it to Jeremy. I tell her to add that in Scotland, CUPSAFE is aimed at compensating Scottish fans against trauma arising from an England victory.

Monday 4 May 1998
The Boston Gazette published the first newspaper sports report in 1733

___

The Big Bristols Channel has taken the bait. Giving NOB a backlink, it reports that a football fan will get damages of £1 million if England are knocked out of the World Cup early and he suffers trauma.

Lance Lyde from Ipswich, Suffolk, the report says, has taken out insurance that has cost him £100 plus £5 tax.

It quotes him saying that he took out the policy following years of disappointment when England failed to progress to the final stages of a competition and the agony of watching them lose through penalty shoot outs.

If England are knocked out, NOB will turn to five sports commentators to judge if their exit's premature. Mr Lyde will then have to provide medical evidence showing he has suffered severe psychological trauma to get his seven-figure pay-out, the report concludes.

Yet more evidence of the great value the citizens of Britain are getting from their free monthly subscription to the Big Bristols Channel.

After lunch, I make my way from Farringdon back to the broom cupboard following a highly successful meeting with Aziz, the business editor of the *Karachi Kiddy Fiddler*, who's on a rare visit to London. I'm walking through Leadenhall Market, towards the Lamb, when I see Imelda and her equally fugly finance director, Cynthia.

"Where's Cinderella?" I ask them jovially.

"Piss off Curly!" they both reply.

Friday 8 May 1998
The Clerkenwell Dial was first published in 1862

End of the week. Tracey leaves and I lock up just before 5pm, then set out to enjoy a few drinks to start the weekend at the Wank Puffin in Clerkenwell with Leon.

As he thanks me for his pint, Leon says, "Did you know, Curly, in a couple of decades from now there'll be a football World Cup and a second one, too, where only women are eligible to play?"

"That's outrageously sexist!" I exclaim. "There is only one Earth and there should only be one World Cup, where men, women and the freaks of nature with tits and bollocks are all eligible to play, based purely on their ability on the pitch."

Leon laughs. "Women'll *never* agree to that!" he says. "In 20 years time, they'll be demanding equal pay, even though there won't be a single woman alive who's capable of earning a place in any Premier Division club where men are allowed to play."

"What about the women footballers with bollocks?" I ask.

"Apologies," says Leon. "I was obviously referring to women footballers without bollocks, but that reminds me. Did I tell you that Declan, my news editor, is shagging twins from his local ladies' football team who both like it up the arse?"

"How does he tell them apart?" I ask.

"That's easy," says Leon. "Lesley's got massive tits and a shaved pussy and Ashley has a moustache and big hairy bollocks."

Wednesday 13 May 1998
The Ruhr Nachrichten was first published in 1949

Lunchtime drinks at the Dickweasel with Ralph. He tells me that next week is the fifth anniversary of the day he started work at the Bank of England. In reply, I tell him that today it's exactly 55 years since the Dambusters' raid.

"What was that all about?" he asks.

"I can't believe you don't know!" I exclaim in surprise. "That was when Wing Commander Guy Gibson led 617 Squadron of the Royal Air Force on an audacious bombing raid to destroy three dams in the Ruhr valley."

Ralph tilts his head slightly in thought.

I continue, "He was only 24 at the time and he received the Victoria Cross for his bravery. He was killed in action some 16 months later."

"I remember now!" exclaims Ralph. "Is it true that Wing Commander Gibson had a Labrador called Ginger?"

I nod. "Did I tell you what Leon told me about the RAF?" I ask.

Ralph shakes his head.

"I can quote him more or less verbatim," I say, somewhat boastfully. "He told me that in future the RAF will not be recruiting on merit but instead will focus on increasing diversity across all minority groups including race, religion and beliefs, age, disability, gender and sexual orientation."

"Whoah!" exclaims Ralph, alarmed.

Pretending to defend the RAF, I reply, "As an animal lover, I unreservedly applaud this move. The people of Britain will be far safer with more Gingers and fewer Guy Gibsons."

Monday 18 May 1998
The Manchester Weekly Journal was first published in 1724

Tracey leaves for home straight after work today to meet Del, so I call Genevieve to see if she's up for a pint at the Bronx Cheers in Soho. She is indeed. She's in Regent Street and in need of a drink. I reach the pub to find a vacant table and I put my bag down on the floor beside it. Moments later, just as I'm struggling to hang my coat over the back of a chair, in walks Genevieve, wearing her Princess Di wig. I greet her, before going up to the bar and asking to run a tab. Tom the landlord hands me a laminated beige token bearing the number seven. After necking a double whisky, I return to the table, where I place two bottles of red wine and two wine glasses.

Genevieve and I are chatting when, out of the blue, my old friend Tony Wilson walks up to the table and casually greets me. "Hi Curly – and is this who I think it is?" he asks.

Genevieve looks up smiling. She reaches out and shakes his hand. "Lovely to meet you!" says Tony, bowing.

"Please, come and join us!" I say. He immediately crosses to the other end of the bar, gathers his belongings and returns to sit with us. Opening his briefcase, he hands me a small brown padded envelope.

"Are these what I think they are?" I ask.

"They certainly are," says Tony.

Once I open the envelope, I see two cassettes. One is labelled Unknown Pleasures and the other Closer. "Both are signed by Ian Curtis," says Tony, shedding a small tear. "It's really ironic because Ian told me just before he died that committing suicide would be the last thing he'd ever do."

I am more than just a little touched to receive such a wonderful gift. After a brief moment of silent contemplation, the three of us proceed to get utterly pissed. Before we know it, it's time for Tony to catch the last train to Manchester.

Wednesday 20 May 1998
The Oxford Mail was first published in 1928

I'm in Oxford today to drop off a bottle of Champagne for Abigail, senior reporter for *Oxford Chuftie Plug*.

After the meeting, we pass an apparently paralytic Thalidomide gentleman sitting on a park bench. Genghis looks up at me and asks, "What do you call a drunk Thalidomide victim?"

"Do tell me," I say.

It turns out it's a genuine question, not a joke, for my brother frowns and replies pensively, "Well, you obviously can't call him legless! That would be rude."

Friday 22 May 1998
The Sacramento Bee was first published in 1857

When I arrived at work this morning, Tracey looks up and exclaims, "You look absolutely *knackered* Curly! Are you okay?"

"I'm fine," I say, "I've been up all night working as a volunteer for a new suicide helpline called The Philistines."

"That's really good of you," she says. "How did you get on?"

"I think I did really well," I reply. "Clara, the manager, told me that it's essential to ensure that people who call in don't kill themselves, no matter what!"

"That's obviously most important," agrees Tracey, nodding.

"It most certainly is," I say. "My first and only call was from a gentleman called Forbes, who sounded really depressed. He said that he was going to kill himself because Daisy, his wife, was divorcing him and taking the kids. Apparently, it's because he accidentally 'put it in the wrong hole.'"

"What a poor sod!" says Tracey, "So, what did you tell him?"

"Well, I thought she had a point really, as it was her sister's," I say, "But then I reminded myself of what Clara had ordered me to do. I spent a few moments desperately thinking it through, before suggesting to Forbes that it'd make much more sense for him to kill Daisy instead.

"That seemed to do the trick and he rang off much happier."

After Tracey makes us both some coffee, I make sure that she's off the phone and quiet ahead of my Big Bristols Radio phone interview with Chris Heavens. I dial in and wait. A moment later, Tracey complains that the silence annoys her.

I snap, "Sshh! I'm just waiting for that ginger c*n...oh hello, Chris!"

I ring off after speaking to him for a few minutes, switch the radio back on and turn the dial to my listening station of choice, Radio 9, just in time to catch a harrowing story about a bear that's crossed the border into Bavaria. The creature is a cherished symbol of the south-eastern German state. Yet the cross-border bear in question is suddenly under threat of execution by the Bavarian authorities.

With urgent action required, I'm immediately compelled to help save the poor creature's life by providing it with liability insurance.

A quick call to my old Lloyd's boss, Robin, and the bear is insured. Next, and without a moment to spare, I call Julia, the editor of the *Newcastle Thunderballs*, to tell her about the insurance, before hastily drafting a BEARSAFE press release and emailing it to Jeremy, as well as to Jürgen at *German News* and Günter at *Austria Press*.

Monday 25 May 1998
The Cambodian Press Agency was founded in 1978

The cuttings agency faxes me a batch of the latest stories out today. The *Phnom Penh Scoop* editor, Akara, reveals that I'm miffed, to say the least, at the threat to the endangered alpine bear. The report explains that I'd heard on the radio yesterday that the German authorities had asked hunters to shoot the bear after it killed a dozen sheep and numerous chickens. Accordingly, Akara says, I rushed to insure the animal for a tidy £1 million for any damage the bear might cause, in the hope of persuading the authorities to delay its execution until a "more humane" alternative can be found.

This evening, I learn from the home page of the *Münich Vaj* of the shocking news that instead of saving the bear, the German authorities have shot it dead by firing squad.

They could simply have stunned it and returned it to its home across the border. The bear-murdering b*stards.

Wednesday 27 May 1998
CBS Evening News was first broadcast in 1941

Tracey calls me while I'm in the pub. A German film crew from Uber Alles TV has turned up to film me. I neck my pint and cross back over the road to meet them at the main entrance of Lloyd's.

They ask to do a few B-roll shots, which they explain they'll use to fill in around the interview itself. For this, they ask me to walk along Lime Street and into shot. It never occurred to me how difficult goose-stepping could be while pissed.

Thursday 28 May 1998
The Seattle Times was first published in 1891

I get to the broom cupboard and Bingo! Rod calls to tell me there's a black-tie do tomorrow at the German Embassy and that he's been invited. But I think about it for a moment. "Um, why have they invited you and Emu to such a diplomatically significant international event?" I ask.

"Well," says Rod, "the City of Hull is in the Hanseatic league and has particularly strong ties to Germany."

"And?"

"Hanseatic League representatives are often among the throng at these events," says Rod.

Perhaps he's right. Maybe one of the hapless wankers at the German Embassy has invited Rod Hull, instead of the mayor of Kingston-upon-Hull.

Who cares? I'm cleaning my dress shirt and pressing my DJ when I get home tonight.

I ask Tracey if she fancies a go at crashing tomorrow night's event. "Free booze if nothing else," I tell her.

The *Nairobi Ringpiece* has more coverage on the scandalous murder of the Bavarian bear. It reports that I was involved in a bear market – geddit? – when I insured the bruin at risk.

Friday 29 May 1998
Deutschlandfunk Radio was founded in 1962

I close the broom cupboard before Tracey and I set out to take the Circle Line from Monument to Sloane Square. We're in no hurry as we take a leisurely stroll to Belgravia. Ahead, I spot Rod and Emu getting out of a cab across the road from the embassy in Belgrave Square.

We're the best part of an hour early for the event, so we adjourn to one of my favourite Mayfair pubs, the Atomic Mutton. It's a bit of a walk, but we've got time. I step up to the bar to order a round.

"That's...Emu!" stammers the barman in apparent amazement.

"Indeed," I reply. "Now, the bird quite fancies some Champagne."

I take a bottle of Dom Pérignon and three Champagne flutes on a tray to where Rod and Tracey are sitting with Emu. We toast the extinct bear. The fizz goes down extraordinarily quickly, so I order another bottle.

The elegant pub fills up quickly. Before long there are queues at the bar, so we finish our Champagne and set off on our way to the German Embassy. I goose-step up the stairs to the entrance of the grand Regency building, where I'm met by a uniformed doorman named Rudolf. I give him a Nazi salute then turn round, just as Rod carries Emu up the stairs. Rudolf pulls a sour face at Tracey, for whom Rod gentlemanly steps aside to allow her to walk in first. She's closely followed by Emu, who gooses the doorman on the way through the entrance, bringing a brief smile to the face of the sour Kraut.

Despite our best efforts, Tracey and I are to be deprived of dinner. Instead, she steams around necking abandoned Champagne flutes as diners are called to take their seats, while I chuck schooners of Bavarian beer down my throat at the bar. I'm assured that it'll remain open throughout the evening.

A waiter with a tray of fizz offers me a glass, explaining when I ask that it's a type of German sparkling wine called Sekt. I neck two glasses that he swiftly replaces before manoeuvring his way to fetch another tray.

Rod and Emu are seated next to the ambassador himself, who complains there must have been a mistake. However, what truly f*cks up his day is when Rod necks one too many glasses of Sekt with his Black Forest gâteau and chunders straight down the ambassador's three-piece dinner suit.

I wish I'd seen it. Tracey catches a glimpse and says the ambassador doesn't look happy. Having committed a Sekts offence, Rod and Emu hurry out of the dining hall. I take this as a cue for us to leave and we all jump into one of the black cabs waiting in front of the embassy.

I think we made our point quite effectively. Bear-murdering b*stards.

Saturday 30 May 1998
The Dallas Morning News was first published in 1885

Bliss! The weekend! Bugger all to do today apart from meeting up with Tracey and Del for drinks this evening.

I climb out of bed to go to the bathroom, where I clock myself in the mirror. I look like Bigfoot! I resolve to try Sweeney's, the new barbers that's just opened down the road. For just a fiver a trim, it's definitely worth a go.

Nursing a mid-scale hangover, I brew myself an Irish coffee, which I neck before heading out.

Shelly, the hairdresser, appears to be in a bad mood. She says nothing to me when I take my seat, which I quietly note is so much better than having to hear the banalities uttered by most hairdressers.

I say to Shelly, "Make me look sexy."

At this, she puts down her scissors beside the washbasin, reaches into the cupboard below and opens herself a bottle of Jack Daniels.

After a couple of minutes of glugging, she gives me a curious look and asks me, "Are you Curly Cradock?"

"I am!" I reply proudly, adjusting my tie.

"I thought so!" says Shelly. "I've heard that you once claimed that hairdressers have the intellectual depth of retards."

"No, of course I didn't!" I say, catching sight of the eye-wateringly sharp scissors beside the sink.

Shelly smiles for just a moment, then gets to work. In silence, I'm happy to say.

Some 20 minutes later she finishes with a flourish and a smile. I pay and leave the premises unscathed.

Three hours later, I take a shower and set out to meet Tracey and Del in Soho. I greet them then head to the bar to buy a round. Just as I do, Tracey shrieks, "Curly, someone's shaved 'tw*t' in the back of your head!"

"F*ck – really?" I say. I wondered why Shelley hadn't shown me the mirror.

"Don't worry, Curly," says Tracey. "It'll grow on you."

"Very funny!" I say.

"Listen, Curly, don't worry," says Del. "I once went to a Jamaican hairdresser. It was dreadful."

After a few more rounds I say goodbye to Tracey and Del, for I have to drive to Pontefract tomorrow for a Sunday lunch meeting with Sabrina, editor of the *Yorkshire Whippet Keeper.*

Monday 1 June 1998
NBC Camel News Caravan was first broadcast in 1949

As soon as I arrive at the broom cupboard, Tracey asks, "How was Pontefract?"

"I'll just say one word: 'liquorice'. If you get it, great. If you don't, that's fine too. But you should probably read more."

Just then, a fax arrives from the cuttings agency. It's a copy of an early edition of the *Manila Ladyboy*, reporting today their time – seven hours ahead of London – that NOB has launched THE DOGS' BOLLOCKS, a policy to pay up to three months' salary if the policyholder has to take time off work to care for a sick pet.

I'd forgotten about that – I was very pissed at the time. The Patent Office is still considering the application, according to the report, which concludes that a nation waits with bated breath.

Before I leave work, via a GAYSAFE press release that I send to Jeremy, I announce to the world that NOB is to target the pink pound. This is at best a bogus story rather than a spoof one, as NOB was the first PPI provider in the world to provide all customers with protection from HIV/AIDS. This includes gay men, who are treated just the same as everyone else, as you'd expect.

Thursday 4 June 1998
Movietone News was founded in 1928

Choke Ondik, a reporter on *The Braintree Genius*, suggests that NOB deserves a Queen's Award for launching a PPI policy aimed at gay men and women that isn't loaded with heavy premiums and doesn't require a medical examination.

The report quotes me saying it has been suggested that offering HIV/AIDS cover to everyone is financial suicide, but that in fact if you carve away the prejudice, the risk is minimal and can be absorbed within NOB's standard rate. Potent stuff!

The *Pink Cumbeard*, however, reports that a leading national insurer – NOB, obviously – is launching a product that *increases* the cost of premiums for gays, lesbians or policyholders who are HIV-positive. Er, that's the opposite of what we're doing, but thanks anyway, guys.

Oh well, you can't win 'em all. But the backlink on their website will be useful.

The *Hove Pink Flamingo* takes the issue of minority injustices seriously, in a column that focuses on homosexuals paying the price of being gay. Gay men, it says, may now have the same age of consent as their heterosexual peers, but, with the exception of NOB, they're still not being treated fairly, as they've to pay an additional premium on the grounds of their sexuality alone.

Drinks after work with Tracey and Del in Old Compton Street. A rainbow flag is on display prominently above the pub door. A designer with an eye for detail and a pint in his hand, Del studies it. After a few moments he says, "All the colours on that flag are straight!"

Friday 19 June 1998

The Edinburgh Evening News was first published in 1873

Tracey arrives bright and early to the broom cupboard this morning. She tells me that Del has an unusual print order. "He says he's been asked to print invitations for a Cocks in Frocks event that's being organised by Shitforbrains Insurance in September."

"You've got to be kidding!" I cry. "What the f*ck are they doing that for?"

"Well, I for one would like to go!" she says, defensively.

"You're not allowed!" I say. "And I'd never go to an event like this. It's grossly discriminatory to women! Besides, I wouldn't want to be in the company of any f*cking flaggots."

"What's a flaggot?" asks Tracey.

I pause to think. "A flaggot is a person whose sexual interests are atypical," I tell her. "This can include sexual attraction to prepubescent children, the consumption of gender fluids such as menstrual blood, or sexual arousal from urination, vomit or flatulence. The medical profession believes that there are at least 500 other similarly gross activities, including sex with fruit," I add.

"Really?" she says.

"Yes, really," I say, "When I split up with Vicky, she went f*cking bananas."

"I've seen lots of strange people when the funfair comes to Braintree," says Tracey. "It's great fun and I always wondered what the flag with 500 colours stood for!"

"I thought that funfairs no longer had freak shows," I say. "Where's Marie Stopes when England needs her?"

"Who's Marie Stopes?" asks Tracey.

"She was a famous abortionist from Edinburgh," I reply.

"Edinburgh?" she asks.

"Yes," I say. "Marie Stopes was much more effective at killing the English than Robert the Bruce, but that's probably because Robert was born in Writtle in Essex, rather than in Scotland."

Pints tonight with Isaac, editor of the *Stamford Hill Gang Bang*.

I buy the first round. I put the drinks on the table then, as obsessed with anniversaries as ever, I mention that today is the birthday of Anne Frank.

Isaac puts his glass straight back on the table and says keenly, "She showed a level of cunning and resolve of which all Jews should be very proud," he says.

"Of course," I reply with a reflective tone of measured solemnity.

"Yup," says Isaac. "Anne managed two years' rent-free."

Tuesday 23 June 1998
Paris Match was first published in 1949

Evening drinks with Ralph and he seems excited to see me. He sits down opposite me and tells me about a short film that he saw for the first time yesterday evening.

"It's called Gaygingers from Outer Space," he says.

"You've got to be f*cking kidding!" I reply.

"No!" Ralph says, "Straight up! And it's actually an amazing film."

"What's it about?" I ask.

"Well, it was made in the Netherlands about six years ago and follows a group of intergalactic homosexual ginger men from the planet Anus," he says. "They discover the presence of female creatures on planet Earth and then, using ray-guns, they eliminate them one by one, much to the relief of the hitherto oppressed male population.

"Really? Feminists will be delighted," I say, quickly adding, "if there are any left."

Monday 29 June 1998
The Illustrated London News published the first newspaper gossip column in 1850

It's a chilly morning for late June as I set out for the Tube. At the station, I pick up a discarded copy of *Minge* from a bin at the far end of the platform to read on my way in to work. The whole magazine seems to be exclusively dedicated to celebrity gossip and adverts.

I arrive to find Tracey and Mavis chatting in the broom cupboard. I ask them, "Have either of you heard of pegging? It's mentioned several times in this magazine."

"Duh!" they both say, simultaneously rolling their eyes.

"Of course," says Tracey.

"What is it, then?" I ask.

"Pegging is where a woman performs anal sex on someone else, using a strap-on dildo," she says.

"F*cking gross!" I reply. "They'll soon be touching cloth."

"What's touching cloth?" asks Mavis.

"According to the Uxbridge English Dictionary, touching cloth means that you need to shit so badly that it has made some contact with your underwear. Touching socks on the other hand means that you've already shat yourself."

"Even more gross!" Tracey says.

"Apparently, it's quite a common occurrence for anyone who regularly has a strap-on dildo stuffed up their arse," I say, adding, "and also for anyone who's impaled himself on a spike."

"Fucking painfully!" adds Mavis.

"It was," I say. "But not as painful as a Walford, which my dictionary describes as 'a severe attack of pancreatitis, which can only be relieved by being sucked off in a layby.'"

Thursday 2 July 1998
El Mundo was first published in 1989

After lunch today, I take a call from the US. It's Harvey, the agent of international superstar Michael Jackson. He tells me he'll be in London next week and says he'd like to meet up with me, after reading about NOB in the *Nashville Ball-Buster*.

This gives me an idea. I make a quick call to Joaquin, the proprietor of Elizabeth's lookalike agency, to arrange a Michael Jackson lookalike for NOB. It'll be top-notch publicity to have him photographed with the I LOVE NOB placard that Tracey used a couple of years ago when she stripped naked on the steps of Lloyd's.

For the sake of what Parminder calls 'link juice', I'm delighted to receive a call from Olga, the London bureau chief of Russia's largest daily paper, *Komsomolskaya Stalina*.

Her first question is a matter of due diligence as she asks whether I'm the same Curly Cradock who beat Boris Yeltsin in a drinking competition.

"Yes, I am," I say proudly.

"Excellent!" says Olga. "And my second question is this: does NOB *really* insure hookers against alien abduction and contracting mad cow disease?"

"It certainly does, Olga," I solemnly reply. We conclude the call with a few niceties before I hang up.

Sunday 5 July 1998
The News of the World was first published in 1843

To Bishopsgate – Filthy Fannies to be precise – to meet NOB's very own Michael Jackson. While waiting, I buy myself a pint. I've downed half of it before my phone rings. I answer the call and hear, "It's Michael. I'm outside!" Whoever's calling does a great impersonation of that creepy voice.

I neck the rest of my pint and step outside. It's a peaceful Sunday evening, so there aren't the usual bucketloads of Essex spilling out of Liverpool Street station and I make my way easily to the limo parked across the street.

Wow! As I sit next to Michael and slam closed the door, I truly feel as though I'm actually face-to-face with one of the world's most famous pop stars. I introduce myself and I say to Ronnie the driver, "Fulham. Browns please."

The long vehicle – a white one, obviously – reverses and then holds up the weekend traffic in every direction as it performs a clumsy seven-point turn before making its way across town to SW10. As we drive, Michael tells me how honoured he is to be working for NOB.

Eventually we reach the strippers pub. Michael steps onto the narrow pavement with an effeminate swagger, turns to face me and says, "F*ck Browns. Let's go to Whites!" before bursting out laughing.

I take a full roll of 24 photos of him holding the I LOVE NOB placard, before we go inside to get shit-faced. Before we know it, they're calling last orders, so we neck our drinks, before climbing back in the limo.

"Home?" asks Michael.

"F*ck that," I reply. Never one to let the opportunity of an after-hours drinking session pass me by, I ask Ronnie to drive us the half a mile or so to the Bird & Dog in Chelsea Harbour. That place never closes until the last person leaves.

I ring the bell on the pub's side door. A minute later, Clive, the landlord, opens the door a crack in case it's the Old Bill. Then he sees me, flings it wide open and says, "Orright Curly? Nice to see you! Busy, yeah?" We meander our way into the pub, where there are perhaps half a dozen punters. Clive politely makes no comment on my companion.

The hours slip by and I admire Clive's apparently unwavering devotion to keeping his pub open until the last punter leaves. At about 4am, however, it's just starting to get light when even he gives up. Michael is fast asleep on the bench when Clive crosses from the bar to ask if I'd mind leaving.

"What about Michael?" I say, pointing at the snoring form on the bench opposite.

Clive looks across at Michael's sleeping form, then says, "You can leave him. I'll be back here about eleven, yeah?"

FUCK BROWNS, LET'S GO
TO WHITES

Thursday 9 July 1998
The Kansas City Star was first published in 1880

When I reach work, Blart Attack Radio News brings word that the US President has admitted that he *did* have a sexual relationship with former intern Monica Lewinsky.

Rising to the challenge, I send a complimentary NOBSAFE policy to President Clinton and a press release to Jeremy that includes a spoof comment from White House spokesman, Eaton Beaver, who believes that President Clinton will be thrilled to receive such a generous gift.

Friday 10 July 1998
ITV News at Ten was first broadcast in 1967

As I start to open the post, I see that NOB is featured in this week's *Washington Coffin-Dodger*, the *Dallas Armchair Revolutionary* and the *New Orleans Party Pooper*. This prompts me to ask Tracey, "What have Joseph of Nazareth and Bill Clinton got in common?"

"Both have a wife called Hillary?" she suggests.

"Very funny, but no," I reply. "Both said, 'I did not have sexual relations with that woman.'"

I sent last yesterday's NOBSAFE press release out in haste, so today I'm issuing a more carefully crafted version for Jeremy's Transatlantic competitor US-based Global News Distribution, adding the further spoof that the policy received by Mr Clinton was in fact a gift from an unnamed Republican Party member. Yes, really!

I managed to make time yesterday for phone calls to reporters from no fewer than twelve French regional newspapers enquiring about NOBSAFE. Do I detect a bit of penis envy *français*? I suppose, though, that they do have a point, as demand for erection insurance is on the rise.

By the time I got round to speaking to Adam, news editor for the *Gravesend Embalmer*, I'd clearly got a bit carried away, telling him that sales of the policy were heavily concentrated in Kent. This was later picked up by the *Crayford Cocoa Sombrero* and the *Dartford Numpty*.

Press cuttings today make it clear that the USA has received and understood the message that NOB's selling a product its citizens need, with the *Utah Gynecolumnist*, the *Nashville Shit Licker* and the *Columbus Knobber* all reporting that thousands of men are taking out insurance in case they become impotent, so they can afford to pay for the 'wonder drug' Viagra.

Meanwhile, the *Rhode Island Retard* reports that insurers have spotted a rising trend. Oo-err!

Friday 17 July 1998
The Miami Herald was first published in 1903

I'm in the broom cupboard with Tracey, discussing how best to promote NOBSAFE. Mavis is outside polishing the floor, so I call her in to seek her advice.

"You should get Roger Moore to help you," suggests Mavis.

"Roger Moore!" I exclaim. "You're an absolute genius, Mavis."

In order to find Roger's telephone number, I decide to become a cowboy and to give Yahoo! a try. I type in 'Roger Moore', but all I get are adverts for erectile dysfunction treatment. However, eventually I find his number and when I call him, I discover that he's a real gentleman: courteous, helpful and spontaneously kind.

"I regret that I am fully engaged at the moment," Roger says. "But very best of luck and thank you so much for kindly thinking of me."

I'm so overwhelmed that I make a note to remind myself that the next time I speak with his Holiness the Pope, I must suggest to him that he consider making Roger a saint.

Onwards and upwards. Annabelle, news editor for the *Port Vale Urinal*, writes today that for an insurance salesman, there are no lengths to which Curly Cradock will not go, no bandwagon he'll not clamber aboard. Having already offered policies against virgin birth and alien abduction, she writes, I've now turned my gaze towards that most booming of professions, the male stripper. This policy is "the full Monty," as Annabelle inevitably puts it.

Pretty much the same story appears under the byline of Kerry Oki on the *Yokohama Made-Up Bollocks* website and by Jenny Tayla on the *Alcatraz Great Escape*.

At 3pm, just as Tracey and I return from a moderately boozy lunch, the phone rings. Tracey takes the call. "Good afternoon, Mrs Mainwaring, it's lovely to hear from you. How may I help you today?"

After a minute Tracey says, "I'll find out for you. Please hold on Mrs Mainwaring." She holds her phone to her chest and says to me, "One of Mrs Mainwaring's customers, a lady called Laffmy Titsoff, wants to know if NOB's policies cover elective surgery."

"They certainly do!" I reply. "In fact, please tell Mrs Mainwaring that NOB's the only PPI provider in the country to do so. And can you ask her what type of surgery it is?"

Tracey asks Mrs Mainwaring the same question, then puts her on hold again and tells me, "Laffmy's considering a sex-change and having five penises, so she can buy knickers that fit like a glove."

"Well then, advise Mrs Mainwaring to tell Laffmy that she needs to think very carefully before committing to such major surgery," I reply. "Having five penises will certainly have its ups and downs."

Wednesday 29 July 1998
The Female Tatler published the first newspaper agony column for women in 1709

I'm very upset. I've just broken the last of my special-edition Charles and Di mugs, which were made to commemorate the couple's wedding in July 1981. I bought six of them at half price when they formally separated in 1992, along with half a dozen Mel & Kim mugs. Now I need some more.

At lunchtime, rather than going to the pub, I head out to Woolworths in Leadenhall Market. The cheapest mugs I can find there are all plain white, but they'll do. I carry them back to the broom cupboard.

On my desk is a new ruling from the Diversity, Equality and Inclusion Inspectorate, which is actively putting pressure on employers to become more diverse and inclusive. Without further ado, I return to Woolworths, where I admire the colourful crockery on display. Basket in hand, I buy a brown mug to represent the coprophiles, a pink mug to the paedophiles and a black mug to represent the necrophiles.

As I head to the till, I spot a lovely green mug, which I realise will be perfect to represent sheep-shaggers. Sorted! With my mug in the kitchen with the missing handle representing those who have chosen to have their genitals or tits chopped off, my mugs are now fully compliant with the proposed new standards.

I almost forgot! For anyone who thinks that my new white mugs are racist, I've the perfect mug for them too. It simply says WANKER! – a thoughtful gift I received last Christmas from Sir David.

After a restrained lunch at the Grapes, I return relatively sober to the broom cupboard, where Tracey tells me she's writing a letter to Deirdre, *Water Sports'* agony aunt.

When she finishes, Tracey asks me, "How does this sound?" She clears her throat then reads aloud, "Dear Deirdre, my boyfriend Del told me that the best cure for constipation was anal sex. I didn't believe him at first, but he insisted and so the other night I let him stick his big fat nob up my bum. He's just rung me this morning to say that he wants to try it again as he's still constipated. What should I do? Signed Tracey."

"That's great, but it might be best to ask Mavis," I suggest. "After all, you aren't a sad person with no one else to talk to."

Wednesday 5 August 1998
The Manchester Guardian was first published in 1821

I wake up today on the broom cupboard floor in my creased suit. Grabbing firmly onto the lavatory pan that doubles as my seat, I heave myself to my feet and go for a slash, before checking my diary to see what meetings I have to look forward to today.

Bollocks. I have to be in Manchester for 5pm I vaguely recall agreeing to appear on Tomorrow with Trevor McCampbell.

At noon, I head out to take the Tube to Euston for the northward journey. The train is crowded and I can't see any free non-reserved seats. In the second carriage down past first class I see an empty seat that's only reserved from Manchester up to Glasgow. Perfect.

I've just got myself settled when, a couple of minutes later, an inspector comes through.

I produce my ticket. "Where are you off to, Curly?" he asks.

"Manchester," I say. "To appear on Tomorrow with Trevor McCampbell," I add, somewhat boastfully.

"With a face like yours, you'd be better off on the radio!" he says, laughing.

Under my breath I say, "That was so funny I've just pissed myself."

Not quietly enough. The inspector turns back to me and says, "Piss off Curly!"

Cheeky sod.

Time for lunch. I walk through the train to the buffet car, where I stock up with eight miniature bottles of plonk. I return to my seat, where I open and neck them one after the other, before taking a nap.

I wake up being jabbed sharply by an elderly woman with a walking stick. "You're in my seat!" she crows.

"This seat is free as far as Manchester!" I say, outraged.

"We've just *left* Manchester!" she retorts.

Bugger! The next stop is half an hour away. I shuffle down the carriage for a bit more room in which to stand. It's a bugger of a journey, although I'm briefly entertained by a copy of the *Nelson Columnist* on the table beside me, which has on the front page a story about NOBSAFE.

After standing for the last part of the journey, I get off at f*cking Lancaster and hail a cab back to Manchester. Laurie, the producer, did say they'd pay my expenses.

When the cab finally drops me off at the studios, Hassan, the driver, says, "Good luck, Curly!"

"Cheers!" I say, pocketing my receipt as I make my way inside.

Arriving far later than planned, I meet Laurie, who hastily introduces me to the great Trevor McCampbell. This is a great privilege. He's every bit as courteous and polite in real life as his TV persona.

When the interview is finished and I'm preparing to leave the studio, I bump into the real-life Curly Watts.

"F*ck me! I really must give up the booze," we say in unison. Unfortunately, I don't have the chance to discuss clone insurance with Curly, as I have to hurry to catch the train back to London.

Thursday 6 August 1998
BBC World Service was founded in 1932

Business is finally going well. NOB can now afford to pay for a proper if very modest HQ. I hear through the grapevine that there's a small office available to rent on the floor below. I make a quick call to George, the landlord, to introduce myself and we're in business.

For sentimental reasons, I shall refer to the new office as the broom cupboard. Though small, it's significantly more spacious than the last one and now we'll have proper chairs rather than lavatory units.

NOB's performing better on the web than I'd ever hoped, with more than a hundred online PPI sales per day. I'll soon be able to repay Sambo properly for his wise counsel.

As it happens, unbeknown to him, I've sent a CV that I composed for him to every elite university in the world, along with forged testimonials that detail his intellectual depth, professional experience and moral character. I'm particularly proud of the reference I forged for him from Prime Minister Tony Brown.

Sambo spent several years behind bars, but he's a wise and virtuous man who has done much to contribute to society. I've therefore commissioned Del to produce a fake Royal Pardon and Elizabeth has agreed to be photographed with Sambo holding it when he's released from jail.

Monday 10 August 1998
The Medway News was first published in 1855

I'm looking forward to evening drinks with Troy, the editor of the *Medway Corned Beef Cudgel*, not least because of the curious name of the pub he's suggested, the Seaman Stains, which is located near to the historic dockyard in Chatham.

I take the train and disembark in what's renowned for being the most depraved area of Kent, as well as the most deprived. More broken furniture, bags of rubbish and fridges adorn the street corners than signposts. I suppose it's to be expected from a town whose motto I'm told is, 'Screaming, Shouting, Fighting!'

The filthy air follows me into the pub, where I decline the offer of a knock-off Armani track suit. I spot Troy. He's the oldest hack I know and well past conventional retirement age. We shake hands before I step up to the bar, where I try to attract the barman's attention. He soon sees me, notices I'm wearing a suit rather than designer chav clothing and shouts at me angrily, "What are *you* looking at?"

It must be quiz night.

Eventually I get served. I carry the drinks to the table, where I ask Troy why on Earth he's chosen to live in Chatham.

"God only knows!" he replies. "It's such a violent town. At weekends these days, there are literally hundreds of young people fighting late into the night. My front porch sometimes doubles as an A&E room."

"Really? That bad?" I ask, horrified.

"Curly, as a young man I fought in the war," he says. "I felt safer on Omaha Beach than I do going out for a takeaway in Chatham on a Friday night."

Troy's sombre mood doesn't change through much of the evening, although he smiles as I tell him about some of the coverage NOB has had from NOBSAFE.

In an effort to try to cheer him up, as I'm about to leave the pub for the train station, I ask him, "What do you call a man from Braintree with big ears and a crooked dick?"

"Tell me," he says.

"F*cks Funny!" I say.

He laughs, just as we both duck a flying bottle.

Tuesday 11 August 1998
The Malaysian National News Agency was founded in 1968

Off to meet Ralph today. I've proposed a summer pub crawl, starting at lunchtime at the Barbados Pissbucket. We down a dozen or so half-pints of strong lager before walking on to the Lamb & Chicken. This particular pub dates from Charles II and is situated on Watling Street, one of the Romans' most famous straight roads – sorry, Ralph – where we move onto pints of Bass.

Ralph often gets morose when he's pissed. Today's one such occasion. He's onto about his twelfth pint before he suddenly starts crying into his beer.

"What's the matter now?" I ask him.

"I think that I'm a disappointment to my parents," he says.

"In what way?" I ask.

"It started on my 18th birthday," he says. "I met my dad in the pub and I told him that I'd just had my first blowjob. He congratulated me and he offered to buy me a large whisky to celebrate. When I told him a single one would be enough to take away the taste, Dad wasn't impressed," Ralph adds, quite unnecessarily.

In an effort to cheer Ralph up, I ask him if he's booked his summer holiday yet. That does the trick.

"I'm off next week," he says. "Holiday cottaging in the Cotswolds."

Wednesday 12 August 1998
The Hull Daily Mail was first published in 1885

I'm still pissed from last night when I wake up at dawn on the broom cupboard floor and I remember that I've got to drive to Kingston-upon-Hull of all places today to meet Hector, the editor of the *Hull Clusterf*ck*, to give him a bottle of whisky to thank him for his support.

I'm taking Doug with me, as he's got nothing else on and he tells me that one of the things he loves most about his job as a journalist is being able to choose to do whatever the f*ck he wants within reason, just so long as he delivers a scoop from time to time and meets his news deadlines.

I brave an early morning Tube home for a shower and to put on clean clothes, before calling Doug to check he's still up for the trip. He sounds remarkably bubbly. I drive to his house in Bethnal Green to pick him up, before setting out on the long journey north. On the way, Doug enlightens me with information about Hull from a guidebook he purchased yesterday.

"Hull is both a cultural wasteland and a sporting desert," he says. "The inhabitants are apparently so hideous that the city council are planning to build a giant aquarium called The Deep to display the ugly f*ckers!"

After a successful meeting with Hector, we head back to the car and drive south across the Humber Bridge. "Ah!" says Doug, "You must now have what I guess must be the best possible view of Hull."

"What do you mean?" I ask

"Look in your rear-view mirror!" he chuckles.

At that moment, my mobile phone rings. It's Florence, a researcher from Big Bristols Radio's Tomorrow programme. She wants to know how many ANTHRAXSAFE policies NOB has sold since we first started to offer the cover. The answer's obviously zero.

I ask Florence if she'll give NOB a backlink on the Big Bristols website. She agrees.

"Thirty-one thousand, two hundred and seventeen," I reply.

Monday 17 August 1998
The Dallas Times Herald was first published in 1888

Fantastic news! Sambo has written from Belmarsh to tell me that the Texas Institute of Advanced Computing has offered him a very senior position, without even subjecting him to an interview. I know they've been looking for some time to appoint someone of his calibre. This is a position that he can take up immediately he's released from prison, or, as I've led them to believe, once he's freed from his non-compete agreement.

More invaluable free publicity today. In the business section of the *Salem Weekly Warlock*, reporter Chloe comically refers in the first paragraph of her lead story to NOB's insurance cover for sex, drugs and the dog that bit the gasman. The *Derby Angle*, the *Macclesfield Filler* and the *Newbury Cub Reporter* all have the same story on their website. And they're not even part of the same publishing group!

I make it out of work in time to meet Ralph in the Grapes for a swift one or two, before heading off to a fancy-dress party that's being hosted by the English Insurance Agents Association.

When I return from the bar I ask Ralph, "What would you call a bloke who chooses to have his genitals surgically removed and later regrets it?"

"Obviously not a wanker," says Ralph. "What about a c*nt?"

"That works," I reply. "But I must say that having your bollocks chopped off certainly takes balls."

Tuesday 18 August 1998
DD Punjabi TV is founded today

I get into work late with a bloody awful hangover.

"Jesus, your face is sweating!" Tracey exclaims as I sit down. "Are you okay, Curly?"

"My head feels like a Punjabi sewer," I reply, before making myself a large hair-of-the-dog Irish coffee.

A little too loudly for my liking, Tracey asks me how it went at the fancy-dress party yesterday evening.

"Really good," I say. "The only costume the fancy dress shop had left in my size was a gingerbread man. So, with my hair dyed ginger and with some fake-tan I borrowed from Mavis, I certainly looked the part."

"Did you meet anyone interesting?" asks Tracey.

"Yes, I met a chap called Basil," I say, "He's one of the senior recruitment guys from Big Bristols Channel, who was dressed as a llama. We got chatting and he told me his employers are looking to recruit more gingers. He then offered me a job presenting a series on unusual insurance."

Tracey looks impressed. "Brilliant! You'd make a fantastic TV presenter, Curly."

I shrug and say, "I do hope so, because having my bollocks dyed ginger will be a small price to pay for a regular spot on national television."

Luckily, I'm feeling very much better after a few pints at lunchtime in the Grapes. I've booked a cab for 4pm as I'm off to the Broadcasting Wank Hut for a late afternoon interview on PPI mis-selling by banks for Money Chest, set to be broadcast on Saturday morning. Philip, the presenter, is a well-respected old-school journalist, who kindly invites me for a beer after the interview.

Bringing me a pint, he says, "In the seventies we called it 'picking up fag-ends.' Today it's called 'serious journalism'. The garbage we're asked to produce today would never have been broadcast when I began my career 25 years ago. Everyone in the media now is trying to reach the lowest common denominator, as intelligent reporting is now considered elitist."

"That's a great shame," I say. "Thanks for the beer. I'm afraid I'll have to leave at six to go to my night school class."

"What are you studying?" asks Philip.

"Poetry!" I reply. "I'm really enjoying this course. When I first started a couple of months ago, they suggested that owing to my dyslexia I wouldn't be any good."

"I assume you've proved them wrong," says Philip generously.

"Indeed, I have!" I reply. "So far, I've made a lovely pair of jugs and a very fetching vase."

Friday 21 August 1998
The Tasmanian News was first published in 1883

At 11am Tracey makes some coffee and reads the *Cyprus Manoeuvre*. After a couple of minutes, she looks up and says, "Can you believe that it's six years since the topless photograph of the Duchess of Scunthorpe was published by the red tops?"

"Really? Six years? I remember that well," I reply. "She was sucking the toes of her bald financial adviser whilst holidaying in St Tropez."

"That's right," says Tracey. "Her Grace is such a credit to the nobility."

"Indeed," I reply. "That disgraceful gutter-press coverage was a gross infringement of her privacy."

After lunch, I hear on Radio Gobshite that there's been a reported sighting of the fearsome Tasmanian Tiger. It's time for a bit of tiger-related PR, even though I never saw any of the beasts when I lived in Tasmania. With tongue in cheek, I write a TIGERSAFE press release, which Tracey emails to Jeremy with a spoof comment from Pearl Necklass of the Tasmanian Cats Protection League, who allegedly told me that the tigers are now in very safe hands and that they've been greatly relieved of their cash.

Thursday 27 August 1998
The Manchester Evening News was first published in 1868

I wake up with a start at 5am. I've got a crashing headache that isn't helped by a mysterious sense of panic. I vaguely remember being out last night on a bender with Donald and Dylan from the *Friends of Dorothy*. Boy those guys can drink!

I look over the edge of my bed and see that my jacket and briefcase made it home. It must just have been something I said or did that's unsettling me.

For the second time this month, I've no choice but to visit Manchester. I've decided to drive and Ralph has asked to come along for the ride. He says he loves the place. My own affection for the city is underpinned by the fact that the city's journalists have long been great supporters of NOB.

Ralph's attraction to Manchester becomes apparent when, after my meeting, he leads me to one of its openly gay districts. There he tells me he's popping indoors for a bit. A bit of quite *what* he doesn't say. I sit on a canal-side bench to lap up the view of the man-made waterway and its surrounds, where I notice the occasional suited businessman mince along the towpath, apparently in the hope of meeting other like-minded gentlemen.

From a few yards' distance, I notice a colourfully dressed young man approach a chap in a black duffel coat who's standing half-hidden in the bushes. The young man hands him a wad of cash. At first, I assume that there must be a local pay-up-front policy with regard to anal sex. But then the chap in the dark coat hands him a small envelope and the buyer scuttles off. So presumably it's drugs he's selling, not his arse.

I look at my watch. It's been over half an hour and Ralph is still not back. To my left, I see a sign crying out for attention. I open my briefcase again, take out a new bottle of Tippex and cross the canal path, where I meticulously white out the C in Canal Street.

Just as I'm screwing back the lid Ralph comes trotting down the steps, looking very pleased with himself.

It's just over two years since the city was devastated by its biggest bomb since World War Two. But resilient Manchester is a fine city, particularly if you discount the paedophile gangs, the muggers and the drugs trade. If you do pay a visit, the chances are you'll be offered a brew with a smile, have your teeth removed with pliers, or be cordially invited to commit an act of gross indecency. Or quite possibly all three.

Friday 28 August 1998
Euronews was founded in 1993

When I arrive at the broom cupboard I receive a phone call from Farez, editor of the *Beirut Starfish trooper*, who says he's writing an article about TIGERSAFE. When Ali suggests that you're no more likely to bump into a Tasmanian Tiger than you are to meet Bigfoot, I tell him that I agree and he's so shocked by my honesty (sic) that he kindly agrees to provide NOB with a backlink.

Mid-morning, I hear Tracey say on the phone, "Don't panic Mrs Mainwaring!" There's a long pause before she says persuasively, "The Tasmanian tiger is very unlikely to come to Croydon. I really don't think you need to waste your money on TIGERSAFE."

I'm preparing for a telephone interview with Radio Austria on the subject of unusual insurance and it'll be useful to know the distance between Vienna and Hobart (9,940 miles, if you're asking) as the Tasmanian tiger is a very good swimmer, or at least it would be if it weren't extinct.

Monday 31 August 1998
The Daily Star was first published in 1978

Today's a bank holiday and I'm off to meet Genevieve in the Arse Goblin, to drink a toast to the memory of the wonderful Princess Di, the People's Princess, who died a year ago today.

We're both subdued as we observe five minutes of silent contemplation. Genevieve is the first to break the peace when she asks, "What does 'up the Gary' mean?"

Taken aback, I tell her, "It's Cockney rhyming slang for Gary f*cking Glitter, or up the shitter, a reference to anal sex. Why do you ask?"

"Gabriel, my new boyfriend, asked if I'd like it 'up the Gary' and I didn't know what he meant," she says.

"Well, Lady Chatterley seemed to like it. Perhaps you should ask Mavis about it," I suggest.

"Good idea. I shall," says Genevieve. "By the way, did you know that Gary won an Ivor Marshmallow Award in recognition of his excellence in music writing?"

"No, I wasn't aware of that," I reply.

"Yes," says Genevieve. "Previous winners included Marc Bolan, David Bowie and George Harrison but I'm not sure if they all liked it 'up the Gary.'"

Tuesday 1 September 1998
The New Zealand Herald was first published in 1863

I'm just reading through cuttings when I see the *Wormwood Scrubber* has run a double-page spread looking at unusual policies and where to find them. There's a common theme here: all roads lead to NOB.

Even further afield, the *Guantanamo Bay Danger Wank*'s website today reports that while scientific evidence says the Tasmanian tiger has been extinct for more than 60 years, Tasmania's tourist board is not so sure. Tourism chiefs, it says, have taken out a A$1 million policy with a firm of London underwriters to insure against the reappearance of the tan-and-black-striped thylacine.

The post arrives and among the letters is one from Sambo, writing to let me know that he's due to be set free on Friday. That's just three days from now. I'm so chuffed for him!

I get straight on the phone to Belmarsh to ask them to let my former cellmate know that I'll be there to collect him, before I open the rest of the day's post.

Friday 4 September 1998
Channel 4 News was first broadcast in 1982

Sambo is being released from prison today. I take the fake Royal pardon out of my drawer simply to admire it. Del has done a fantastic job, producing a formidable, detailed and elegant scroll that resembles something that you'd expect to see hanging on the wall of an ecclesiastical building.

I pick up Elizabeth at 8am and set off for Belmarsh for the last time. I hope.

At around 9am, the late summer sun is shining as Sambo walks through the security gates a free man. He's in high spirits, although he looks a little bewildered to see the Queen, who smiles and presents him with the forged Royal pardon. Instamatic at the ready, I take a few shots of this auspicious event, before we walk together to the car park.

I've booked a table for lunch at 1.30pm at Saunders on the Strand, near the hotel where I've booked him in for his first night of freedom. Elizabeth can't join us for lunch as she has a prior engagement. We drop her off on London Bridge, leaving plenty of time to buy Sambo some new clothes. The suit he wore when he arrived at Belmarsh is now far too large for his girth, which has shrunk considerably during his long period of incarceration.

I drive the pair of us to on the West End and park in a multi-storey not far from Jermyn Street for the perfect wardrobe shop: Turnbull & Asser for half a dozen shirts, John Lobb for shoes – buy one, get one free today – bingo! Crombie for an overcoat, Harvie & Hudson for two suits and, finally, Gieves & Hawkes for cufflinks, socks, underwear and everything else that he may need.

He walks out looking every bit the refined gentleman that he is.

"F*ck! Luggage!" I exclaim suddenly. We should have bought that first. Sambo follows as I hastily cut through to Piccadilly where, in Fortnum & Mason, I buy him a set of leather cases on wheels. As we leave the posh department store it's still only 12.30pm, which means there's just time for swift quart at the Tutti Frutti in Brewer Street. Sambo just asks for an orange juice. In the pub, we pack all the clothes he isn't wearing into the suitcase, neck our drinks and jump on a bus to Saunders.

Sambo is amazing. He's just spent an unspeakably long stretch of time behind bars, yet after barely four hours he strides confidently into this high-class restaurant with the air of someone who dines there regularly.

We take our seats as a waiter promptly hands us each a menu. Before we order any food, I scan the wine list.

"Red or white?" I ask Sambo.

"Oh, you choose," he replies.

I order an Australian Riesling, then excuse myself to pay a visit to the lavatory. On my return the waiter turns up with the wine and we both order two courses for lunch. We then get down to talking about the arrangements for his exciting academic post in Texas. Sambo explains he has some money stashed away, but that he doesn't know how quickly he can get hold of it.

At this moment, I reach into my jacket and present him with a thousand non-forged US dollars in cash and a ticket for tomorrow on Concorde to New York and one for a connecting flight to Dallas Fort Worth International. He studies the documents and smiles, then looks up and says to me, "You lose perspective a bit, being in a cell for such a long time. I think I am hugely indebted to you."

"Quite the reverse," I say, filling his glass before passing him a forged Jamaican passport.

Still in something of a daze, Sambo drinks very cautiously, knowing how booze can corrupt the mind – especially, as he puts it, a blank canvas. "I'd forgotten what alcohol tastes like," he says, before taking another sip. He tips his head slightly and, with a broad smile, exclaims, "Nectar!"

Even though he carefully paces himself, he's pretty inebriated by 6.30pm. I pay the bill and support him as he staggers apologetically out to the street and, with the luggage in tow, I escort him to his hotel.

I've thought this through. Sambo is going to be no one's poor relation and, without him noticing – quite easily, in the circumstances – before I leave, I slip an envelope with another $25,000 into one of his suitcases, along with a note to express my gratitude and friendship. I'm going to miss him.

We shake hands, before he's escorted to his room. As I leave, I arrange a wake-up call for Sambo at 8.30am tomorrow and I hand the concierge a wad of cash and ask him to book him a limo to take him to Heathrow after he's had his breakfast.

COMPARED TO FORGING BANK NOTES
FORGING A ROYAL PARDON IS A
PIECE OF PISS

Saturday 5 September 1998
The Liverpool Echo was first published in 1879

I awaken to the sound of the phone. It's Sambo, ringing from a Heathrow callbox to thank me and to say he'll be in touch soon. Just before he rings off, he states the obvious: that this is the first hangover he's had in years. "It's like bumping into an old enemy for the first time in years and noticing that he's every bit as much of a fiend as when you last knew him," he adds, thoughtfully.

The mystery surrounding my uneasy feeling the other day at having said or done something I couldn't recall is solved as the latest issue of the *Friends of Dorothy* lands on my desk, along with the rest of the post. I tear open the magazine's polythene wrapper, to find to my great relief that I was worrying unnecessarily. They've simply run a story about NOB's broom cupboard upgrade.

Headlined *New City HQ!* it reports on our move to new, tiny business premises as 'Global insurer moves to prestigious Lime Street office complex.'

Tobias, a senior reporter from the *Liverpool Devil's Handshake*, calls to invite me to meet him for lunch in his home city on Friday. I'm quite fond of my hubcaps and so, keen to avoid the sticky-fingered folk of Liverpool, I try to decline the offer but I'm unsuccessful. However, by way of consolation, it occurs to me that while I'm there, I may get the chance to meet with my old friend Cilla, for a long-overdue cream tea.

Liverpool, to quote LibDem leader Paddy Ashdown, is 'poor, neglected and overwhelmed by crime'. But it has a magnificent waterfront and I wonder to myself if Liverpool is a World Heritage Site. If it isn't one already, it bloody well ought to be. I'll write to UNESCO to nominate Liverpool. I'll also mention the massive contribution black people made to the city's fantastic civic buildings.

Thursday 17 September 1998
The Hexham Courant was first published in 1864

A stupidly early start this morning. I'm driving to Hexham to meet Jane, a reporter on the *Northumberland Dash for Gash*. Sometimes the lengths I go to for a backlink don't seem to make any sense at all, but Hexham has a fine Norman abbey, and I'm looking forward to a ham and pease pudding stottie cake for breakfast.

I reach the paper's offices, where I'm annoyed to be told that Jane is in fact waiting for me at Housesteads on Hadrian's Wall, which is another half-hour's drive away.

When I finally get there, I find a young woman slumped over the wall with an empty vodka bottle in her hand. I assume this is what's meant by a borderline alcoholic.

Just as I get back to the car, I discover a producer at The Stars at Night named Maggie has finally caught up with all the fuss about aliens from a couple of years ago and I'm thrilled to find myself invited to be interviewed tomorrow by astronomer, Patrick Moore, at the Jodrell Bank Observatory in Cheshire.

Friday 18 September 1998
The Southend Echo was first published in 1969

Patrick's a living legend. I grab at the opportunity to discuss with him the probabilistic argument used to estimate the number of active, communicative extra-terrestrial civilisations in the Milky Way.

The accomplished TV presenter has alarming and forthright views on the existence of aliens. This causes me to reflect that if ETSAFE actually existed, I'd be putting up the premiums right now.

After the interview I ask him, "What's the difference between Braintree and a crop circle?"

Patrick thinks for a moment. "A Crop Circle might just contain signs of intelligence," he ventures.

Straight in the front of the net!

When I get back to the broom cupboard, Tracey asks me, "How did you get on with Patrick this morning?"

"I think we got on really well," I reply. "He's a formidable chap. He even explained to me, in terms that I'd understand, how most stars die."

"How's that?" asks Tracey.

"Usually from an overdose," I reply.

She thinks for a moment, before asking, "Did he say anything else?"

"Yes," I say. "He told me that black holes matter."

She goes off to make coffee. When she returns, Tracey says, "Del drove me to Southend last night."

"F*cking Southend! Why the f*ck did he do that?" I ask, appalled, adding, "I caught crabs the last time I went there. The place is a complete shithole."

"I've no idea," says Tracey. "All I said was that I wanted him to kiss me somewhere that's wet, warm and smelly."

I ASKED HIM TO KISS ME SOMEWHERE WET, WARM AND SMELLY AND SO HE DROVE ME TO SOUTHEND

Saturday 26 September 1998
The Burton Daily Mail was first published in 1898

As I'm driving home to the Potteries to see Genghis, I decide to take the scenic route along the A50, which takes me through the centre of Burton-on-Trent.

I park at the Lovely Jugglies and dash in for a piss. The loo doesn't look as though it's been cleaned since I was last in here. Dead flies decorate the dirty tiles beneath the filthy frosted windowpanes. I wash my hands and walk through to the lounge. I smile at the well-endowed woman behind the bar and place my order for two quart jugs of Bass. As she passes me the drinks across the bar. I complement her with, "Fantastic jugs, madam!"

"Piss off Curly!" she says with a smile.

Tuesday 29 September 1998
NBC Meet the Press was first broadcast in 1947

Following a call last week to send a female NOB representative to be interviewed live on Fluffy Bunny TV, I dispatch Tracey this morning to the studio. This turns out not to have been my greatest-ever idea, for when Saffron, the presenter, asks for her thoughts on Roe vs. Wade, Tracey replies, "It depends how deep the water is."

When she returns to the broom cupboard, I mention that today is Yom Kippur, the holiest day of the Jewish year, which encourages fasting, prayer, abstention from physical pleasures and refraining from work.

"My friend Ariel's just converted to Judaism!" she exclaims.

"Really?" I say.

"Yeah, though he's not very happy about it after he opted for a discount circumcision," says Tracey. "He told me it was a rip-off."

Genghis is on new medication and he's handling it well. So well, in fact, that I tell him I'm treating him to tea this evening. Mum's a terrible cook, but my brother never complains.

"Where are we going?" he asks excitedly.

"You choose," I say. "Anywhere you fancy."

"In that case I'd like to go to the Golden Shower takeaway," he asks. "My friend Bilguun says it's the best!"

Bilguun sounds like a mong too, but although I've never tried this place, I agree to get tea from there. In all fairness, when we arrive the food smells delicious, so I order beef in black bean sauce, egg fried rice and Singapore noodles. Genghis orders sweet and sour chicken, chow mein, curry sauce and large chips to share.

Just as I'm paying, Lance calls. I greet him and ask him how he's doing. After five minutes, I say goodbye and Genghis says to me, "Lance isn't a very common name these days, but in the Middle Ages parents called their children Lance a lot."

I sometimes suspect my brother's a comic genius on the quiet. His new meds are working well.

Back home, I lay the table. Just as I sit down with Genghis to eat, my phone rings again. It's Dave. "Don't wait for me, tuck in," I tell Genghis before moving into the living room to answer the call.

When I hang up ten minutes later, I return to find that Genghis has only left me the chow mein and half the chips.

"You've eaten my tea!" I exclaim.

Genghis looks genuinely mortified. "Sorry, Curly!" he says. "All Chinese look the same to me."

Smiling, I tuck into what's left of the takeaway.

Tuesday 6 October 1998
Newmarket Journal was first published in 1872

After a most enjoyable lunch in Suffolk with Lester, the editor of the *Newmarket Saddle*, I sidle cheerfully back to the broom cupboard to see what the cuttings have brought. As I hang up my jacket, Tracey asks me, "How was Newmarket?"

"Too many iron hoofs for my liking," I reply.

"I thought you *liked* horses," she says.

"They're okay," I reply. "To be honest, I don't really like French food. Give me roast beef any day."

"F*cking French!" exclaims Tracey. "Do they really eat horses?"

"They certainly do," I say. "Anyway, it reminded me of that wanker from Braintree who shoved nine plastic horses up his rectum. When he went to hospital, he was told that his condition was stable."

Just as I'm about to leave work, Genghis calls my mobile. "Hi, Curly," he says. "Lorraine, my girlfriend, has just broken up with me for quoting Elvis Presley lyrics and I'm all shook up!"

"Very funny," I say. "Are you okay?"

"I'm fine," says Genghis. "Her much prettier sister wants to go out with me and so I can see Clare-Lee now Lorraine has gone."

Tuesday 13 October 1998
Capital Radio was founded in 1973

On my way home, feeling flush, I pop into Waitrose for a bottle of their own-label champagne. The ladies here are always cheerful. On my way to pay, I pass the customer service desk and clock the name badge on the lapel of the lady who's standing waiting to answer any enquiries.

"Judy!" I say. "How cute! What did you name the other one?"

"Piss off Curly!" Judy snaps.

Not *always* cheerful, then.

Wednesday 14 October 1998
The Glasgow Evening Times was first published in 1876

Ralph and I are flying to Glasgow for a meeting I've arranged with Hamish, one of NOB's most lucrative clients. We're taking the plane from Gatwick, because I've got to be back in London for a meeting with Fred this evening.

When we reach our destination, the receptionist brings us each a cup of coffee and Hamish comes out of his office to greet us and to tell me that he wants to buy insurance for 80 female employees at his Glasgow warehouse.

Suddenly Ralph interjects, saying, "It'll be hard to find anyone who's prepared to cover such a risk."

"Why on Earth is that?" asks Hamish.

"An unspeakably high proportion of Glasgow women are morbidly obese," Ralph explains. "They're more concerned with deep-fried Mars bars than they are with healthy eating."

Worried that Ralph's succeeded in losing me a client, I promise Hamish I'll come back to him with some competitive quotes for the insurance he's after.

Relieved when the business meeting's over, I remark that there's time for a spot of lunch. "My treat," I say. "What do you fancy?"

"Well, there's a nice seafood restaurant not too far from here," Hamish suggests.

"If you don't mind, I'll pass on that one," says Ralph. "I avoid seafood in Glasgow."

"Really?" asks Hamish. "Why's that?"

"I'm put off by the thought of eating a Glasgow oyster," Ralph replies.

"What's a Glasgow oyster?" asks Hamish.

"It's a substantial gobbit of phlegm," I tell him.

He still looks confused. Ralph explains, "The taste is indistinguishable from an ordinary oyster, but they're slightly greener in colour and they lack the same aphrodisiac qualities as a result of the projectile vomiting that usually follows their consumption."

We decide to skip lunch and head straight back to the airport. On the way, we notice a sign that's clearly been defaced. It says: "Welcome to Glasgow, birthplace of Moors Murderer Ian Brady."

Monday 19 October 1998
Anglia Television was founded in 1959

This afternoon, I'm travelling to Norwich to meet Edmund, the editor of the *Goggle-Eyed Whore*. I decide to take the train and I wake up just as it's pulling into my station. It soon becomes apparent that when visiting Norwich, 'awake' is not a desirable state in which to be. Edmund, however, is an amusing chap who, after kindly agreeing to give NOB a backlink, mentions that Keith his news editor can count all his sexual relationships on one hand: three cousins, two aunties and his mum.

"Very funny," I reply. "But I suppose that does make sense. After all, Anne Boleyn was born in Norfolk and she had six fingers too."

"She did," says Edmund, "and according to the *Windsor Squid Marks*, Anne was an accomplished player of both her brother's pink oboe and the harpsichord."

On the train home, I'm touching cloth. I walk from one end of the train to the other but can't find a single lavatory that's in working order. I don't have a choice. I just have to sit there and hold it.

After a few minutes the woman sitting opposite looks up. Frowning and in a crescendo of disgust, she asks, "Is that *poo* you're holding?"

Friday 30 October 1998
The Leicester Mercury was first published in 1874

A nice plug for NOB and a backlink from Deepak, a reporter on the *Leicester F*ckover*. For those who don't know Leicester, it's a fine city. It may be famous for wife-beating, animal cruelty and for the sexual exploitation of children, but it has an outstanding cathedral and other wonderful historic buildings. Famous residents have included Simon de Montfort and John Merrick, the Elephant Man. Richard III is also believed to be buried there too – minus his bollocks, of course, which were cut off at Bosworth Field.

I'm sitting at my desk reading a travel agent's holiday brochure, dreaming of a seaside break, when Mavis pops by, looking pissed off.

"How're you, Mavis?" I bravely ask her.

"F*cking annoyed!" she snaps. "I've just visited Spangles, the new sex shop in Leadenhall Market, to treat myself to a new vibrator."

She's standing before me, hands on hips, looking very cross, but I can't for the life of me tell why she should be so upset.

"The manager said I could choose any from their range on the wall," she explains, "but when I told him 'I'll take the big red one on the right,' the f*cker told me, 'That's our fire extinguisher.'"

Friday 6 November 1998
The Ghana News Agency was founded in 1957

The weather was so shit this morning that I decided to drive to work. After a four-hour lunchtime session in the Grapes with Ralph, I don't bother going back to the broom cupboard to sober up and instead go straight to my car to drive home.

I don't get far. I am stopped by Bob, an off-duty policeman whom I recognise as a regular from the Grapes. "Good evening, Curly. Where do we intend to drive to tonight?" asks Bob.

"Nowhere that need concern you, Bob," I reply.

"Next time you see me, Curly, I'll be in uniform," he warns me.

"Unlikely, wanker," I slur. "I don't eat at Big Max. Although I did once falsely claim to insure their entire workforce against contracting CJD."

Bad move. He beckons over a colleague, who promptly arrests me. I am then driven in a panda car to Bishopsgate nick, where I'm led in handcuffs to be photographed and breathalysed, before being led to a cell.

Half an hour later, my tea is brought to me on a plastic tray by Bob. He's now wearing uniform. As he passes the food through, he says, "Fries with that?"

I am allowed to make one call, so I ring Fred, who's in surprisingly good spirits. He agrees to come to see me. "Bonus," he says. "Overtime!"

Two more hours pass before the cell door is unlocked and in walks Fred. He looks less sternly at me than I'd have expected in the circumstances. "As you're already on probation, you're looking at three years and a lifetime driving ban," he says. A shudder passes through my entire body as this sinks in.

"Unless..." he begins.

I love hearing that word and I'll embrace it, whatever it entails.

"Unless we take the alternative route."

I try to interject. "Belt up and listen!" he snaps, before telling me that Tracey and Del are both under surveillance. Del is allegedly dealing in large quantities of dangerously low-quality cocaine and the City of London Police want to discover the identity of the criminal mastermind behind it. Neither Del nor Tracey can be relied on to grass up whoever it is, so my co-operation is needed in exchange for more lenient charges against me.

"Whatever it takes," I say.

"Right," says Fred. "See you again on Sunday." Then he stands up and summons Bob to open the cell door.

Sunday 8 November 1998
The Mail on Sunday was first published in 1982

Things get worse before – I hope – they're going to get better. After eating an over-salty scrambled egg with dog meat, I mean sausage, I'm handcuffed and driven to the familiar surroundings of Belmarsh.

"Can I have my usual cell?" I ask Stavros the prison warder leading me inside.

"Piss off Curly!" he says. But I'm at least given a cell to myself for a change.

It's mid-afternoon before Fred arrives. He gives me back my mobile, which I handed over when I was arrested, along with my diary from my briefcase and my fountain pen. Then he tells me to ring Tracey. There's no answer, so I leave a message asking her to call me urgently.

Fred stands and turns to face me again. "The ball's in your court," he says. As the cell door is locked, I look down at my mobile, willing Tracey to call.

I spend an agonising evening incarcerated with no news from Tracey.

Overnight, kept awake by the endless din outside, I run through various scenarios, mentally terrorised by the grim prospect of staying banged up again for years.

Wednesday 11 November 1998
The Albanian Telegraphic Agency was founded in 1912

Still no news from Tracey. My head is spinning. I can't even eat the food and I could really do with a proper drink.

I had about 20 minutes' sleep last night. I was kept awake by worrying about a long prison sentence, all the while trying to formulate a cast-iron plan to get myself out of this mess.

F*ck it. I resolve simply to make up some totally unbelievable bullshit that Fred will think is true.

Breakfast is passed through the cell door on a plastic tray. I'm slowly jabbing at my scrambled egg with a spoon, when suddenly my mobile rings.

"Hi Curly, it's Tracey," comes the welcome voice over the phone. "Had you forgotten I'm on holiday with Del in Canvey Island? What's up? Where are you?"

"Tracey!" I exclaim. "I need you to listen. If Fred mentions Mother Teresa, I want you and Del to look shocked that he has found her out."

"Mother Teresa...is she the woman from Live Aid?"

"Yes, that's right," I say.

"OK. Mother Teresa. Both look shocked," she says, processing the instruction, before asking, "When are you coming back to the broom cupboard?"

"I'm not sure," I say. "Soon, I hope." I then hang up, before calling Fred to grass up the world's most famous Roman Catholic nun as Del's dodgy coke supplier.

He picks up straight away. "Wow!" he says when I tell him. "We've been keeping an eye on her for some years now! We've always wondered why she had so much money in her Vatican bank account. Leave it with me."

"Clueless c*nt," I say aloud as I hang up. Sighing with relief, I settle down for a well-earned nap.

Tuesday 17 November 1998
The Iranian Global News Agency was founded in 1963

Six days of radio silence have gone by when, at noon, I take another call on my mobile. It's Fred. He tells me that all charges against me have been dropped and that I'll be released this evening. The *relief!* I ring Tracey to let her know the good news.

Freedom at last! I'm led out of jail by Eddie, a warder who looks the spitting image of Dickie Davies.

"Ever see World of Sport?" I ask him.

"Piss off Curly!" he replies.

Out of jail in plenty of time for Christmas parties, I head straight to the City. I push open the broom cupboard door to see that Tracey's decorated it for Christmas. On my desk is a pile of embossed corporate invitations.

"Welcome back!" she says. Beaming as she hands me a Christmas card and a very large Scotch, she says, "'Tis the season to gatecrash as many jolly events as possible!"

"Any calls from Uncle Fred?" I ask.

I'm delighted to hear that there have been none.

HMP BELMARSH

CNVT

Wednesday 18 November 1998
The Daily Courant published the first newspaper lonely hearts advertisement in 1702

Mavis is down in the dumps as she's not had a single response to the lonely-hearts advertisement she placed last week in the *Whitechapel Write-Off*. To cheer her up I offer to take her to the Elephant for a quick drink. As we approach the pub I ask her, "What would you like?"

"I'm not really sure," she says.

"How about a double entendre?" I suggest. "I'm sure the barman will give you one."

"That'd be nice, but could I please have a gin & tonic?" asks Mavis.

We arrive at the pub, where she suddenly says to me, "I've changed my mind. Can you please ask that handsome barman to put his fat cock inside me?"

"Certainly," I say and I make my way to the bar.

Friday 20 November 1998

Good Morning Television was founded in 1993

Just as I arrive at the broom cupboard, the phone rings. Tracey answers and after a few minutes she looks up and asks, "Curly, do NOB's PPI policies cover injuries sustained in an explosion?"

"Of course," I reply.

"I think we may have another claim then," says Tracey. "There's been an explosion at the paint factory where this woman's husband works. He's currently missing, presumed red."

"Very funny," I say. "Did you know I once failed a health & safety course? The examiner asked me what steps I'd take in the event of an explosion. 'F*cking large ones' apparently wasn't an acceptable answer."

After a tedious morning of paperwork, I tell Tracey that six years ago this week, Windsor Castle famously caught fire. Ben, my journalist friend from the *Eton Double Adapter*, was sent to Windsor when it happened.

There was huge pressure from just about every newspaper and every broadcaster around the world to get the first picture of the fire itself. Ben was on a written warning at the time, so he knew he had to deliver a worthy story.

The problem, he said, was that nobody could get inside the castle walls except the fire brigade. The fancy dress shop was closed by this time so he couldn't do a Mr Benn. So instead, he went with a camera into the pub opposite the castle, stood in the hearth and zoomed in on a burning log. He developed the film that evening and took it straight to his editor.

Exclusive: Picture of burning rafter at Windsor Castle! was the headline of the front-page story the next day.

Ben kept his job.

Wednesday 25 November 1998
The Pennsylvania Packet and Daily Advertiser was first published in 1784

Getting back into a routine after my autumn break at Her Majesty's pleasure, when the phone rings. Tracey takes the call. A few moments later she asks, "Does NOB cover dwarfs?"

"Of course!" I reply. "We treat everyone equally."

Tracey conveys this to the potential client on the phone, listens for a few moments, then says to me, "He wants to know, if he signs up today, when he'll get his policy documents."

"Tell him not long – they'll be with him shortly."

A minute later, Tracey puts the phone down, confident NOB has a new client. She asks me, "What's the difference between a dwarf and a midget?"

"Very little," I reply, adding, "Did you hear about the midget that got pick-pocketed? I can't believe someone could stoop so low."

Normality has resumed. In the Grapes this evening with Ralph, I tell him that today's Dennis Nilsen's birthday.

"Really?" Ralph says. "I actually once went on a date with Dennis. I was very pissed and don't remember much about it, other than a funny smell in his flat. In the circumstances, I think I was very lucky indeed to wake-up with just a sore bum."

"You certainly were lucky! Anyway, what's the difference between a tyrannosaurus and a megasorearse?" I ask him.

"Do tell!" he replies.

"About 65 million years."

Thursday 26 November 1998
The Mvskoke News was first published in 1970

Walking up Ludgate Hill this morning on my way to meet Aiyana, the London correspondent of the *Upper Shit-Creek Wigwam*, I see a crowd of indigenous Americans filing out of St Paul's Cathedral. I approach one of them, whom I take to be the chief, to ask him what's going on.

"Today's Thanksgiving and we've all been invited here for a service to celebrate," he tells me. "Can you believe it? We were all given one of these wonderful blankets by the US Government!"

"That was most kind and thoughtful of them," I reply, nodding.

I mention my meeting to Tracey when I reach the broom cupboard. "This morning, I met a most interesting gentleman. Did you know that there are more Jews in America than there are indigenous Americans? It just goes to prove that genocide is just one more thing that Americans are better at than the Germans."

Monday 30 November 1998
The Yorkshire Post was first published in 1754

Up ridiculously early this morning to drive north for a meeting in York with Siobhan, the finance editor of the *Yorkshire Duck Smuggler*. York's a fine city, but I'd suggest that you arrange a mortgage first if you want to visit York Minster.

When I meet Siobhan, I find her enchanting. She has a broad Yorkshire accent, she drinks like a fish and she pays for lunch. It's a fallacy that Yorkshire people are tight-fisted. They're not. They're just canny and don't like to be taken for fools.

A couple of hours later as I'm on my way back out of the city, I see a fantastic Christmas gift for Imelda in one of the city's many independent shops. It's a green T-shirt illustrated with a big, pink circle and a pack of hounds chasing a fox. Beneath this are the words, 'York Hunt is the Biggest in England'. Imelda likes fox hunting, so I buy her one. In size XXXL.

Then, leaving York and in no hurry to get back to London, I take a detour to visit the far superior Beverley Minster, a gothic masterpiece. It's only 30 miles down the A1079 and there's no charge to enter.

Tuesday 1 December 1998
The China News Service was founded in 1952

Heading out for lunchtime drinks at the Grapes with Ralph. I carry a tray to a round table in the corner of the pub, next to a large group of Chinese businessmen in Western-style suits.

"This may not be a popular view, but I believe that the Chinese nation is going to be the *saviour* of humanity," I venture. "They're incredibly hard-working people who want to advance their prospects. They also ensure that their children are literate, numerate and capable of employment."

"I think you're right," says Ralph. "Incidentally, did I tell you what Del's Chinese dodgy coke supplier Feng once asked me?"

"No, what?" I ask.

"'Do you like my cocaine?' he asked. 'I certainly do,' I told him. "Get Carter is one of my favourite films.'"

What larks.

Getting ready for another black-tie event tonight, this time the Lord Mayor's Banquet in the City of London's ancient Guildhall. I was unable to find my cufflinks, so I've brought a couple of sandwich bag ties from my kitchen drawer. Taking my dress shirt out of my bag, I note that it only has wine stains back and front, but crucially not on the upper-middle chest area – the only part of the article not concealed by the tux.

All set, I wander down past the Bank of England to the Guildhall. Eventually taking my seat in the dining hall, I note a cluster of wine bottles in the middle of the table – enough red and white to be reached by each guest and, furthermore, replaced when empty by watchful waiters. I neck a bottle of red and then notice the woman to my right isn't drinking white, so I down two bottles of that. Very refreshing.

Mid-way through the dinner, I disappear for a slash. Emerging from the lavatory, I see Mildred, the attendant. I compliment her, saying they're the most elegant and well-kept lavatories I've ever seen. "I've never been to a lavatory where the urinals have taps," I tell her.

Mildred looks at me appalled and says, "Piss off Curly, you've used the ladies. Those were *sinks!*"

"Oh, I'm terribly sorry," I say. "If you take a look, you'll see someone's switched the ladies and gents signs over." As she gets up to check, I quickly dash off back to the dining hall. As every man here is wearing a tux, I can't see her easily picking me out in an identity parade.

I'VE NEVER SEEN A URINAL
WITH TAPS BEFORE

Tuesday 8 December 1998
The Whitby Gazette was first published in 1854

I drive all the way to Whitby this morning, just to meet Hazel, the editor of the *Whitby Enamel Bucket*. I notice the residents of Whitby aren't half miserable.

I ask Hazel why the locals seem so depressed.

"I've no idea," she replies. "They should count their blessings and try to find good things in a bad situation."

"I couldn't agree more," I say. "My Auntie Phyllis recently bought a brand-new trampoline for my brother, Genghis. All he wanted to do was sit all day in his wheelchair and cry."

After securing another backlink from Hazel, I'm walking down the High Street and I spot a perfect Christmas gift for Mavis.

"How much is the Goth dildo in the window?" I ask the shopkeeper.

She replies, "Piss off Curly, that's a cactus!"

When I eventually get back to the broom cupboard, Tracey's on the phone. Across the desk, I see her expression light up. A minute later as she rings off, she excitedly tells me I've won high praise from the Lord Mayor. I look at her, puzzled. Holding up her notepad, she exclaims, "After your performance in the Guildhall last Wednesday, he says he's given you a Latin title!"

I read what she has written. It says, Persona non grata.

"What's it mean?" she asks.

"Essentially, it means, 'Piss off Curly!'" I reply. "Please remind me to ask Del to add the inscription to my next set of business cards."

Wednesday 16 December 1998
The New York Times was first published in 1851

There's a Christmas card on my desk when I get to work. It's from Mavis, signed with lots of kisses and hearts. I tell Tracey I'm trying to think of a good gift to buy Mavis.

"How about a BBC?" she suggests.

"Good call!" I reply as I decide to buy Mavis a big box of chocolates.

Only joking. I know what BBC means, even if the wankers at the Big Bristols Channel don't.

When I return from the loo, the post has arrived and there's a card addressed to me with a Belmarsh postmark. I quickly open it and it's from Mother Teresa. It reads:

> Dearest Curly,
>
> You are a very naughty boy for stitching me up as a dodgy coke supplier. I'll have you know that I only supply coke of the highest quality! However, in the circumstances your stitch-up was understandable and I forgive you unreservedly.
> Wishing you a very happy Christmas.
>
> With lots of love,
> Mother Teresa x
>
> PS If you help me to escape, then as soon as I'm free, I'll arrange for loads of backlink to NOB from my friends on the dark web.

I show the lovely card to Tracey and decide to visit Mother Teresa at the earliest opportunity with a big box of chocolates containing a hidden file and hacksaw so that she can escape to arrange the backlinks she promised.

Evening drinks with Tracey and Ralph in the Blind Bugger, a well-preserved Tudor pub on the North side of Mile End Road. After putting a couple of glasses of mulled wine on the table, I pull out a fax from my briefcase and unfold it. "I've been honoured with a profile by *Mortgage Refusal*," I say. "Robert the editor has sent me a questionnaire in advance of the interview," showing Tracey the fax.

She takes it from me and starts to read it. "The first question is, what are your hobbies?" she says.

"I want a clever way of saying that I keep a diary and that I've a fascination with tits." I pause to reflect. "I've got it! Let's go with 'word-botching'!"

"Okay, next question," she says. "Who's your hero?"

"That's easy!" I say. "It's Bill Tutte. In 1942, whilst working at Bletchley Park, he broke the Lorenz cipher using only a pen and paper."

"I've never heard of him," says Tracey.

"Don't worry, he should be really famous, with his image on our banknotes, but his considerable achievements have been lost to history. Next time I print some, I'll make sure that it is."

"Okay then, what about Top Cat?" asks Tracey.

"Brilliant!" I reply. "A pussy with a penis is a vote for gender equality."

She reads nearly a dozen other questions before reaching the last one.

"Final question. Why did you go into insurance?" she asks.

I reply, "I was destined for a brilliant career at the bar, but being a bit of a spastic I confused barrister with barista and got a job with the Lloyd's of London coffee house."

"Shall I put, 'Because I'm a spastic' then?"

"That'll do perfectly," I say.

Monday 21 December 1998
The Boulder Daily Camera was first published in 1890

The broom cupboard is unusually bright today with the Christmas lights Tracey's put up around the walls. When she comes in from lunch with a Pound Mart bag of goodies for her family, she seems unusually excited.

"When I was eight years old, my mum told me Father Christmas doesn't exist," she says, placing her shopping on the desk. "Well, I had the last laugh," she says. "Guess who I saw in the shopping centre today!"

A quick drink after work in the Grapes with Geoff and Jeff. The bar's inevitably packed with Christmas crowds. I make my way to buy the first round and take the drinks to the corner of the pub, where there's just enough space to place them.

"When we were six, Santa gave us coal for Christmas," Jeff says just as Slade starts to blare out from the juke box. He raises his voice, "We weren't very happy, so the following year we decided to get him back by poisoning his cookies!" he shouts. "Can you believe it? The b*stard found out and killed our dad!"

Monday 28 December 1998
The Falmouth Packet was first published in 1829

That was a short break, but if we close the broom cupboard for any longer the backlog of paperwork will become too much for Tracey to handle.

"How was your Christmas?" I ask her as she arrives for work.

"I was f*cking burgled by six dwarfs! Not Happy," she replies.

"I'm very sorry to hear that," I say. "David the news editor of the *Aztec Two-step* was a victim of ID theft. Now we just call him Dav. Also, I've just heard on the news that there's a gang systematically shoplifting clothes in order of size. Police say they're still at large."

I'm getting ready to leave at around lunchtime when Genghis calls my mobile. "My friend, Connor, said he was sad because he didn't know the lyrics to YMCA. I told him, 'Young man, there's no need to feel down'," he says, before bursting into laughter.

"Okay," I say. "What happened when the newspaper editor met the chief of the cannibals? He became the editor-in-chief."

Christmas crackers. You can't beat them.

Friday 1 January 1999
Die Welt was first published in 1946

It's a Bank Holiday but I'm celebrating New Year's Day with Tracey at a pub in Clacton-on-Sea called the Essex Low Life. It's amazing to look back on the last 32 months or so and to see how much her work has improved. I've decided to double her salary again when she has her next annual review in April.

"Can you believe it – it's four years to the day since Fred West topped himself!" I tell her when I bring the first drinks to the table.

"Really?" she says.

"Yes," I reply. "And I can tell you a true story about Fred West. When my Auntie Phyllis lived in Gloucester, Fred did some building work for her. She told me that he was really nice and did an excellent job. He also gave her one of his promotional mugs to thank her for the work."

"Did it have 'Patios a speciality'?" she asks.

"No, I don't think so," I reply. "I'll tell you what, though, I often wonder whether it's me or Auntie Phyllis who has the darker sense of humour. For Christmas, she bought Genghis a book entitled Self Defence Tactics for the Wheelchair-Bound."

"Well, that's not very nice!" she says, frowning.

"No – he really likes it!" I reply. "He told me, 'If you're attacked by a mob of clowns, go for the juggler.'"

Monday 4 January 1999
TV Globo Brasília was founded in 1971

Up early to go through last week's press nuggets from the cuttings agency. I notice there seems to be a sudden burst of interest in alien abduction insurance in South America. After a series of UFO sightings in the city of Varginha – Brazil's equivalent of Roswell – a flurry of reports mentioning NOB have appeared in the Brazilian press, including the *São Paolo Exit Wound*, the *Rio Faecal Touch* and the *Manaus Daily Fannicure.*

Two and a half years after launching spoof virgin birth insurance onto an unsuspecting media corps, I receive a fax from Virgil, a reporter from the London bureau of *Filthy Sanchez*, asking for "a quick word about the insurance policies against virgin birth."

The global magazine sells around four million copies every month, so it's worth responding.

"Take as long as you want," I reply. And he does. I only hope doesn't take as long to give NOB a backlink.

Tuesday 5 January 1999
The South Wales Evening Post was first published in 1893

Tracey and I leave the broom cupboard and walk to Cannon Street to catch a bus to meet Ralph.

"I fancy some decent nosh," he says as he hails a black cab that takes us to a grubby-looking Mediterranean kebab restaurant called Mustafa's across the road from Paddington Station. Ralph knows his eateries, so I assume they must serve really good food.

"I'll have a bottle of red," I say as we sit down.

"I don't think they have a booze licence," says Tracey, frowning.

"Leave it with me," says Ralph, who's clearly familiar with the place. He disappears into the kitchen with Mustafa, the owner, then returns a couple of minutes later with two aluminium water jugs filled with cheap red wine, from which he pours us each a plastic tumbler full. It's truly disgusting, but it's redeemed by the reassuring aroma of alcohol. I neck my first cup, then pour a second, before we order food.

My battery's dead, so I ask to borrow Ralph's phone. "Hello, Araminta?" I say when she finally answers. "Where are you?"

She tells me she's just leaving for home after a meeting in Edgware Road, so I invite her to join us in Paddington. "We're five minutes away from you, literally," I plead. She agrees to meet us, prompting me to order four more jugs of the red liquid.

I don't remember anything else. I slowly wake up in the dark, on a train, in a railway siding, with the strong, familiar aroma of Araminta's puke. My head is throbbing. No idea how I got here. My phone battery is of course still dead. But miraculously I've my briefcase with me. I pull myself up off the carriage floor and as I do so I lunge forward and out of the half-open door, promptly falling about three feet to the ground, pulled down by the weight of my briefcase.

Picking myself up again, I look around. All I can see around me in every direction are parked trains. I walk by the side of the one I was on, hoping I'll come to a station. At the end of my train ("*my*" train!) is the start of another ageing, two-tone blue, eight-carriage brute. I turn to look for a clue as to where I am and, on the front, it says Swansea.

F*ck! That's half a day's travel back to London.

I follow the next two trains until I see that ahead, around a bend in the track, there's nothing. Just moonlit industrial wasteland and fields. I take a long leak onto the railway track, then decide there's only one thing for me to do: turn around and go back.

I'm walking back in the other direction, passing carriage after carriage, until I see lights and people ahead of me. In the distance I hear an echoey announcement with a Welsh accent declaring that the 2.04am to Paddington will depart from platform four. With two minutes to spare I break into a run, reach the station concourse and dash in the direction of platforms 2, 3 and 4. I stagger onto the platform, where I see the last train to London is slowly starting to move.

Bollocks to that. My briefcase in my left hand, I grab hold of the door handle of the rear carriage and, ignoring the furious guard blowing his whistle from the platform, I jump onto the wooden ledge, pull down the handle and swing myself through the door, slamming it closed again behind me. I even manage to do the Vs to the guard while he can still see me.

I take a seat in the half-empty carriage and fall back asleep, awakening again only as passengers clamber over me to disembark at Paddington.

Desperate for a piss again and to wash Araminta's foul-smelling sick off me, I walk round the corner of the street to Big Dick's Halfway Inn, the first hotel I see. I ask to use their lavatory. Bladder emptied, I return to the reception and request a room for the night.

Dawn, the receptionist, asks for a credit card. Instead, I hand her a spoof business card and say, "Send it to Accounts Payable at the Big Bristols Channel." She smiles. Piece of piss.

In my room, I remove my suit and take a shower, before putting on a white robe that's hanging in the ensuite. Then, I run the towel under the hot tap and wipe down my jacket and trousers, removing most of the vomit. I hang the wet clothes on the radiator and plug in my phone.

I need some painkillers for my headache. I order them on room service, before I open my briefcase. I *knew* there must have been a reason it felt heavier than usual: It's filled with copies of *Privates*, *Girls on Top*, *Spunky Birthday* and *Readers Wives*, as well as Benito's favourite, *Tits & Fannies*.

Not an entirely wasted trip, then, wherever the f*ck it was that I went.

I TURN TO LOOK FOR A CLUE AS TO WHERE I AM AND THE FRONT OF THE TRAIN IT SAYS "SWANSEA"

Wednesday 6 January 1999
The Wolverhampton Express & Star was first published in 1874

I wake up at 7am to find the suit has dried nicely, although the room still reeks of vomit. I dress and take the fire exit down to the ground floor. I then stealthily swing round the corner to take the Circle Line to Monument.

As I'm approaching the broom cupboard, Rod rings to tell me excitedly that tomorrow he's been invited to open a new exhibition of giant crabs at the Wolverhampton Sea Life Centre.

"Would Genghis like to come as my assistant?" asks Rod.

"I'm sure he would!" I say. After thanking him, I ring my parents to get it arranged.

Thursday 7 January 1999
BBC Breakfast News was first broadcast in 1989

Genghis meets Rod and Emu in his Sunday best outside the Sea Life Centre. On walking into the arena via the VIP entrance, the three of them are greeted with wild cries of excitement from crowds of children and their parents, delighted to see Emu and thrilled at the prospect of seeing the giant crabs.

I stand away to the side of the arena with Genghis's wheelchair in case he should need it. I look out into the audience. I glance at Emu, praying that he refrain from his usual vulgarities. To my relief, he's on his best behaviour and delights the crowd when he performs, using Genghis as a prop.

Genghis is clearly having a wonderful time, delighted to see the sharks, the rays, the seahorses and, most importantly of all, the giant crabs. The staff excel themselves. A few of them of student age ask for Emu's claw-print and Genghis is granted lifetime free entry.

At the end of the day, exhausted, Genghis enthusiastically tells our parents all about his experience, leaving them in no doubt as to what a wonderful time he had and how kind so many people were to him.

"They gave me a free shark!" he says.

"Is it called Gnasher?" asks Dad.

"No," says Genghis, "It's called Feargal. Rod told me that Feargal is the scariest of all the sharks and this shark is really scary."

"Really?" he says. "And what about the crabs?"

"They were brill and really scary too," Genghis replies. "One of them was the size of a car."

"The size of a car? Surely not!" says Dad. "Do you think it could eat a whole child?"

"*Easy!*" says Genghis.

Rod, Emu and I wave good-bye and head back to London down the M6. We eventually walk into the Grapes to meet Tracey. Rod, scratching his bollocks, says, "F*ck, I should've asked while I was there for the best way to get rid of crabs."

Fishing in her handbag, Tracey produces a tube of cream. "Try this," she says.

Rod takes it from her and asks, "Where's this from?"

"The STD clinic," she replies. "Mavis gave it to me."

"A friend of mine once did work experience in one of those clinics," he says. "She was the only person in the whole place who could correctly spell gonorrhoea and syphilis."

"Sy-phi-lis," I say, articulating the syllables. "I'd better make certain that I spell Phyllis correctly when I next write my auntie's birthday card, or she'll have my bollocks."

My round.

Friday 8 January 1999
The Ipswich Star was first published in 1885

Genghis was such a success at the Sea Life Centre that Rod invites him to join him and Emu for an event at Ipswich Zoo on Sunday. "Genghis will love it," I assure him.

"Great," says Rod. "I'm standing in at the last minute for David Bellamy, who's got the shits."

I make a quick call to my parents to work out the logistics of getting Genghis from the Potteries to Ipswich. We all arrange to meet at the main entrance at 9.30am, half an hour before Emu's performance.

"Remember," I warn Rod, "wild animals are very dangerous, even at a zoo. Last year, when I met Stephanie, the editor of the *Suffolk Five-Pinter*, I was mauled by a moose."

"Mauled by a *moose*?" says Rod.

"Oh yes," I reply. "You've got to be especially careful when you're approached by any moose with tattooed legs and an ankle bracelet. The one I met fondled my bollocks and said, 'Give me your number, sexy!' When I asked if she had a pen, she told me she had, so I told her to get back in it pronto before her keeper noticed she was missing."

Sunday 10 January 1999
The Sunday Sport was first published in 1986

We arrive promptly at the zoo, where Genghis struggles to contain his excitement on being informed that Rod has wangled a VIP golden ticket for him.

"Remember the moose," I say to Rod as I take up my position as wheelchair monitor. Moments later, Rod, Emu and Genghis walk on stage.

By noon, Genghis looks very tired, so I take him his wheelchair and he waves goodbye as I manoeuvre him from the stage. The crowd sees him off with a huge round of applause, before Emu and Rod carry on together for the next hour or so.

We're back home in the Potteries by 7pm. Genghis is carrying an enormous toy lion. "The keepers gave me this for feeding the lions," he tells Dad.

"Did you give them finch, chimps and mushy bees?" Dad asks.

Genghis looks at me strangely for a few moments then says, "No, I gave them meat!"

"He's acquired some new material," I say with a wink. This prompts Genghis to turn and ask Dad, "What's brown and sticky?"

"I don't know," he says. "What *is* brown and sticky?"

"A stick insect!" says Genghis, laughing. Not Freddie Mercury's ring finger, then.

And there's more. "What's orange and sounds like a parrot?" asks Genghis.

I shrug.

"A carrot!" says Genghis.

"Did you have a camel ride?" Dad asks.

"No, it had the hump!" says Genghis.

Wholesome family entertainment. Now it's time for some tits and fannies.

Thursday 14 January 1999
The TASS news agency was founded in 1904

I'm only in the broom cupboard for a minute before the phone rings. It's Jacob. "How was your Christmas?" I ask.

"Christmas is like any other day for me, sitting at the dinner table looking at a big fat bird who no longer gobbles," he replies.

When we finish our conversation, I take a call from Parminder for the first time in ages. Immediately he asks me a question that alarms me. "Have you heard of Google?"

"It sounds serious, but your GP should be able to get rid of it with a strong course of antibiotics," I reply.

"No, it's nothing like that," he tells me, "It's basically an updated Yahoo! that's better at finding URLs."

I think for a moment. "What, you mean a sort of uniform resource locator locator?"

"More or less," Parminder replies. "But they describe themselves as a search engine."

"Interesting," I say. "That's a stupid name, though. No one's ever going to use a term like search engine."

"Well maybe not, but it is interesting, because right now Google's robot is as smart as an ox. Not only can I get it to rank NOB number one, but if you get me to produce multiple websites for you, I can get them all to rank on Google's front page."

I think for a moment. "Let's go for it!" I reply.

When I return to the broom cupboard Tracey passes me a call from Norris, the owner of Himalayan expedition company Far & Wide. He tells me that Arthur Fishcake, leader of the National Union of Steelworkers, has recommended NOB as a specialist in unusual insurances. It's clearly now time for Yeti attack insurance.

I quickly compose a YETISAFE press release and email it to Jeremy.

Wednesday 20 January 1999
The South China Morning Post was first published in 1903

It's taken just one email to the UK Press Distribution Network for the stories to start coming in. The first I see is in the *Bergen-Belsen Demise*, which laments that in these days of "'elf'n'safety hysteria", mountaineering trip leader, Norris, couldn't allow clients anywhere near Everest without adequate insurance and he's therefore consulted NOB.

The *Orlando Dirt Box* names Norris as a fervent believer in the half-ape, half-man creature, while in Skegness the *Bollock Brain* goes large on the story, with a half-page piece featuring a picture of him, alongside an artist's impression of the Yeti. It quotes me saying that when it comes to paying claims, the insurance industry has an *abominable* reputation.

"Do Yetis buy insurance?" asks Tracey as she brings me my first Irish coffee of the day.

Wow! What's the difference between a Yeti and a girl from Braintree with a high IQ? There've been reported sightings of the Yeti.

Other big circulation papers are rising to the occasion. The headline in the *Bloxwich Stonker* describes YETISAFE as *Snow Joke!* As, coincidentally, does the *Kidderminster Love Puff*.

Daz, a news reporter from Boogie FM, calls my mobile to record an interview about YETISAFE for the station's morning show tomorrow. Once I'm off the phone, I ask Tracey whether she's heard the rumour that a Yeti has an unfeasibly large penis. Her eyes glaze over as I go out to buy us each a sandwich for lunch.

On my return to the broom cupboard, I find her on the phone to Norris, enquiring whether there are any spaces left on his next Yeti-hunting trip.

Tuesday 26 January 1999
The Jakarta Post was first published in 1983

I've just finished a call with Almo, features editor on the *Helsinki Spotted Dick*, when Tracey asks, "What does LGBTQ stand for?"

"I've no f*cking idea!" I reply. "Whenever I've asked that question myself, I've never received a straight answer." I think for a moment, then say, "It's one of those terms used by people who look at life through a prism."

"Okay then, what does gender fluid mean?" she asks.

"Sorry, I've no idea about that either," I say. "Please pass me my copy of the Uxbridge English Dictionary."

Tracey hands me the book and I soon tell her that gender fluid has three alternative definitions. Glancing down at the dictionary, I explain, "The first is a gender identity that's not fixed and can change over time, depending on the situation. The second is the climax of sex or masturbation, while the third is what attention-seeking, exhibitionist non-entities sometimes call themselves."

Before Tracey has the chance to respond, the phone rings and I receive some wonderful news: Parminder and his team have completed their work far sooner than expected. NOB is now the owner of nine new websites. They're all interlinked while different enough from each other to fool Google's robot. Fingers crossed!

Wednesday 27 January 1999
The Independent was first published in 1986

After several hours of preparing forms, signing cheques and taking calls, I finally make it out for a pint with Ralph. I mention to him that some of today's papers report that on this day in 1945, Soviet troops liberated the few remaining prisoners at Auschwitz-Birkenau. "Of the 1.3 million sent there, 1.1 million were killed," I tell him. "This equates to a mortality rate of around 85%."

"That's terrible!" says Ralph.

"It certainly is," I reply, "and very much worse than the mortality rate of around 18% for the twelve million African slaves who were kidnapped for transportation across the Atlantic."

"We're increasingly being told that the American slave trade was history's worst crime against humanity," muses Ralph.

"It was certainly horrific," I say. "But it wasn't the worst, by far. During the Rape of Nanjing, more than 12.5 million Chinese civilians were slaughtered by Japanese forces."

"I suppose slavery gets undue prominence in the West because of the increasing tendency among black people to re-write the history of colonialism," says Ralph.

"Sadly yes." I say. "Leon tells me that in the next few decades the descendants of the black Africans who rounded up their own people and sold them into slavery will attempt to whitewash the wrongdoing of their ancestors by shifting the entire blame onto white people. They'll even accuse westerners of genocide, despite the fact that the vast majority of those kidnapped died whilst being held captive by black Africans."

"American slavery wasn't genocide," says Ralph. "It's an appalling thing to say, but slaves were a valuable commodity and were worth much more alive than dead."

"You're absolutely right," I say. "The only American genocide that I'm aware of was the extermination of the indigenous peoples of America between 1492 and 1900. During this time, they suffered a 96% drop in population and a 98% loss of their ancestral homelands."

"That's shocking!" says Ralph. "This must be why black people are always banging on about the suffering of the indigenous Americans and trying to obtain compensation for them."

"It must be." I reply. "But as they're all dead, their efforts might be better spent in seeking compensation for the many hundreds of children alive today who have been sexually abused by members of the clergy."

"You're right," I say. "It would, but you've got to admire their kindness and decency. If they were greedy and selfish, they'd be seeking compensation for themselves instead!"

Monday 1 February 1999
Inter Press Service was founded in 1964

Hungover today after going on a bender last night with Ralph. Tracey brings me a warm mug of Irish coffee that I gratefully sup before, belatedly, looking through last week's press cuttings. Overwhelmingly, they're YETISAFE stories and they come from all over the world. The Falkland Islands' *Daily Albatros* stirs up local concerns about the abominable snowman, while the *Hollywood Stretched Quimousine* is pretty dour and judgemental. Its headline is: *Pigs Might Fly!*

This afternoon, I've a meeting on the other side of Leadenhall Market for a meeting with Eric, a venture capitalist who's after a business such as NOB to offer ethical PPI to his clients.

Feeling flush and good-humoured after signing a potentially lucrative deal, I saunter back to work.

"Don't panic Mrs Mainwaring," I hear Tracey say as I walk into the broom cupboard. "A Yeti is very unlikely to come to Croydon. I really do not think you need to waste your money on YETISAFE."

When Tracey hangs up, I tell her, "Bigfoot is sometimes confused with Sasquatch, Yeti never complains."

I seem to spend a considerable amount of my working life driving to the arse-end of the country on NOB's quest simply to acquire bloody backlinks. Journalists from numerous regional newspapers are forever asking me to meet them in person. Today's invite is from Reginald, the personal finance editor of the *Egg-White Cannon*, in the famous GM-crop town of Taunton.

I manage to persuade him to conduct the interview by phone. Some 20 minutes later, I cross the road for a lunchtime pint at the Grapes.

When I return to the broom cupboard, I take a call from Parminder. He sounds quite excited.

"Guess what, Curly!" he exclaims. "NOB now holds all ten front-page listings on Google for all your search terms!" He goes on to explain, somewhat more calmly, "It's all about the power of those backlinks that you're getting from the media. As long as you keep getting them then I'll be able to keep NOB at the top of the first page of both Yahoo! and Google. No one will be able to come close to you!"

I promise there and then to make sure I carry on getting whatever press coverage I can. "Just show me a bandwagon and I'll jump on it," I assure him.

Wednesday 10 February 1999
Trinidad and Tobago Television was founded in 1962

Freezing cold day. I'm incognito in a woollen hat and dark glasses, just as a silver Mercedes pulls up on the road outside the broom cupboard to take me to the Big Bristols breakfast show studios in East London. It's a pre-recorded interview where I'm going to talk to the studio audience about NOB's Valentine's Day impotency cover, a variation of NOBSAFE.

Les, the driver, tells me we're actually riding today in presenter Jill Dando's car. I ask if he's driven anyone else that's famous.

"We get loads of superstars," says Les. "I once picked up Princess Di with Curly Watts. Curly kept asking me to stop the car so that he could buy vodka. He was so pissed when I dropped him off that Princess Di had to help me to carry him into his house in Pimlico."

In the studio an hour or so later, I'm miked up and suddenly faced with the show's co-presenter, Frank Bough, who asks me first of all how insurance claims need to be proved in order for a payout for impotence to be made.

I explain to him that loss assessors would ask the claimant some pretty stiff questions. That gets a laugh. Meanwhile, my support act today is Anglo-Canadian girl band, the All Sinners.

Saturday 13 February 1999
National Broadcasting Services of Thailand (NBT) was founded in 1930

It's Joe's stag-do tonight. He tells me he wants a calm night, as he's flying out to Bangkok tomorrow to get married to Aranya, his Thai fiancé.

"I don't want anything dramatic," he says. "I really don't want to end up in the *Guided Muscle*."

"Trust me," I say reassuringly. "It'll be calm."

This is going to be something of a challenge. I'm confident, though.

After a fine evening of shockingly funny comedy at a pub in Islington, a couple of dozen of us take a hired bus to a pub up the road from Joe's flat called the Fondleberries. It just so happens that three members of girl band, The Magnificent Babes, are there.

One of them is a former stripper. Say no more.

On my way home, I drop by Euston station to pick up the early editions of a few of tomorrow's papers. The speed of the press will never cease to amaze me. Just a couple of hours after Joe's stag party, a double-page spread appears in the early edition of the *Guided Muscle*, two-thirds of it featuring a picture of Joe staring at a stark-naked young lady's breasts as she performs a dance for him.

I wonder if Aranya will buy a newspaper to read on the plane. It'll make their honeymoon that much more interesting if she reads what Joe's been up to.

Monday 15 February 1999
The Slough Observer was first published in 1883

A long drive this afternoon to Slough just for a quick drink with Aanya, news editor of the *Slough Chocolate Log*. This also provides me with a rare excuse to indulge myself at my favourite eatery, Weston's Bakery. Standing in the doorway is the familiar figure of Wendy, the manager.

"Fantastic baps, madam!" I remark.

"Piss off Curly!" Wendy replies.

Wednesday 17 February 1999
The Ethiopian Broadcasting Corporation was founded in 1935

Mid-morning in the broom cupboard and just before Tracey goes off to make coffee, I tell her about a disgusting advert I saw on TV last night for a money-grabbing African charity.

Zebo, a half-blind, five-year-old orphan, has to ride a seven-mile journey to school every day with only one leg on a bicycle with buckled wheels and no brakes.

It concludes, "Please give just a small donation of ten pounds and we'll send you the video. It's f*cking hilarious!"

Meanwhile Ron, the owner of the Fox pub in the Essex village of Finchingfield, has a chicken named Violet, whose life has come under threat from some of the local war veterans. This calls for intervention. I can't stand cruelty to animals, so I've approached Ron to award him a free £1 million insurance policy against the chicken being killed by any member of Finchingfield War Veterans Association.

This morning, I quickly concoct a CHICKENSAFE press release and email it to Jeremy.

I then figure that there can't have been many chickens insured for £1 million, so I also call Guinness World Records.

Thursday 18 February 1999
The Black Country Bugle was first published in 1972

Off to Birmingham this morning to appear on Killjoy for a live interview with Ron and Violet. Bit awkward, travelling on a train with a live chicken. Reminds me of taking public transport in France.

Great TV interview – great wine, anyway. As the broadcaster's paying my expenses, back in London, I stagger off the train and jump into a black cab home.

An hour later, I'm about to fall asleep on the sofa when I get a call from Ron. He tells me he got so pissed at the studios that he left Violet on the train. He had to go back and collect her from the left luggage facility at King's Cross.

Friday 19 February 1999
Newsweek was first published in 1933

Ron calls this morning with news of a letter from Guinness World Records informing him that Violet is now the world's most valuable bird. "They've sent me a certificate!" he proudly tells me.

To hold such a record is a major achievement, particularly since I fondly remember growing up watching Ross and Norris McWhirter and Roy Castle present Record Beaters on television, when I'd observe with fascination the way they'd carefully scrutinise the legitimacy of any claim to the title of Guinness World Record.

With just one persuasive phone call, I've managed to blow away the prestigious awards' extensive control mechanism with a spoof!

Monday 22 February 1999
Channel Four was founded in 1982

There's a message from a very distressed Ron on the answerphone informing me that Violet's been killed. I get straight on the blower to Jeremy to let him know about Violet and to see if he's free for a drink at lunchtime.

Word spreads fast. *The Toxteth Riot* today asks who killed the £1 million chicken. The story reveals that NOB will look into the circumstances surrounding Violet's untimely end and it reports that Essex police have been asked to investigate.

The *Thaxted Geezerbird* also considers the chicken's mysterious sudden demise, with owner Ron admitting that despite Violet's violent end, he doesn't expect to become a millionaire.

Fortifying the spoof, I remark that NOB would require evidence to substantiate a claim – adding that it's often the most ludicrous claims that get paid out quickest.

Meanwhile, the Bulldykes newswire in Limerick runs the news story with the headline: *Britons Cry Fowl!*

It's the *Mortgage Refusal* awards tonight. I've brought my tux in specially. NOB's up for an award and, on this occasion, I'm going alone because Tracey's going out for dinner with Del this evening.

At 4pm, I'm changing into my DJ. Just as I'm wrestling with braces in the corner of the broom cupboard, Tracey calls out to me, "Ron's on the phone! He says he wants to make a claim under Violet's policy!"

"Then tell him to get stuffed!" I reply, tucking in my shirt. "I'm off to the Savoy to collect an Excellence in Customer Service award."

Friday 26 February 1999
The Macclesfield Express was first published in 1981

Friday visit to the Stockport to meet Nellie, news editor of the *Greater Manchester Femtex*. I notice it's not just property that's cheap here. Everything seems a bargain compared with the prices charged in London. I've got an hour to fill before my next meeting in Macclesfield, so I decide to do a bit of shopping. It's Tracey's birthday in a few weeks. Approaching the perfume store, I pass a shop called LIZA'S KNOCKERS and I notice a woman that I take to be Liza standing in the doorway, smiling.

"Fantastic knockers, madam," I observe.

"Piss off Curly!" she replies, smiling.

Making my way back to the train station I take a call on my mobile from Lance's sister, Nancy. Small talk done with, she tells me that she's hugely jealous at all the publicity Lance has been getting, before adding, "I'd *love* to be on TV! Can I be one of NOB's spoof clients?"

"Sure you can!" I reply. "Leave it with me."

FANTASTIC KNOCKERS MADAM

Tuesday 2 March 1999
The Jefferson Jimplecute was first published in 1848

"I love these black-tie events," I say to Tracey as I tuck in my shirt.

"You need to hurry up," she replies. "You're going to be late for Violet's funeral!"

Just as I'm tying a full Windsor, Tracey asks, "Is Ron going for the smoking or non-smoking option?"

"Non-smoking," I reply. "Unless my mother's cooking, chickens are usually roasted rather than cremated, but Ron's arranged to have Violet buried at Westminster Abbey, next to Colonel Sanders."

This evening in the car heading on the M4 to Slough, I hear on the radio the sad news that Dusty Springfield's died. She was only 59 years old.

My mission today is to help Wendy from the bakers fill out an unemployment claim form. I've also been able to arrange a curry this evening with Aanya from the *Slough Chocolate Log* to thank her for the backlink she gave to NOB after we met a couple of weeks ago.

I meet Wendy in a café up the road from her bakery.

"I'm really sorry to hear you lost your job," I say.

"Thank you," she replies. "When the bakery burnt down, the business was toast." So, no sense of humour failure then, despite the grim circumstances.

In the space of less than half an hour, we complete all necessary paperwork – and I've still got time to get to the restaurant to meet Aanya.

I'm tucking into my jalfrezi when Ashok the waiter comes to our table. He stands with his hands behind his back and asks, "Curry okay?"

Before I get chance to reply, Aanya says, "If you must, just one song, then piss off."

Ashok smiles and approaches the next table.

I consider this to be an important reminder, not that it was needed, of how smart and witty the average journalist happens to be.

Wednesday 3 March 1999
The Milwaukee Journal Sentinel was first published in 1837

Nothing interesting's happening in the world of insurance today. The only thing of note occurs when I take a call from Jacob, who tells me he's having marital problems.

"All I said to Hannah was that I thought she'd look sexier with her hair back," he tells me.

"Well, what do you expect?" I ask him. "That's really not a very kind thing to say to a woman having chemotherapy."

Just then, I receive a call from Rod. He sounds annoyed. Says he's having TV problems. "I can't get WCTV," he says. "Gotta fix that bloody aerial!"

I'm just about to leave work when Luke the manager at the Wolverhampton Sea Life Centre calls. He's concerned that the giant crabs are so scary that they're putting off potential visitors. He says he wants to be able to advertise the fact that any visitors are comprehensively covered by the centre's insurance.

Both standing and thinking on my feet, I offer him a complimentary CRABSAFE policy. After all, Luke and his team were fantastic with Genghis when he visited and this will give NOB more free publicity and backlinks.

The only way to top that would be to offer moose cover to Ipswich Zoo, but I decide to save that one for later. I quickly draft a CRABSAFE press release and email it to Jeremy.

Wednesday 10 March 1999
Paramount News was founded in 1927

I'm about to leave the broom cupboard when I get another call from Rod. He still sounds angry about his TV reception.

"Played around with the aerial and now all I can get now is the Big bloody Bristols Channel," he complains.

"Well, if you climb on the roof, remember not to take Emu with you!" I quip.

We set a date to meet up a week on Friday in London, before I head off to the Elephant with today's papers.

An image of giant crabs features in the *Port-au-Prince Shitizen*, with a caption explaining that the Wolverhampton Sea Life Centre has insured the aggressive marine beasts for £1 million against injury to the public.

News of the aquatic cover also appears in today's *Copenhagen Gingle*, where I'm quoted explaining that the insurance rate was decided after our actuaries had calculated the chance of an attack was highly likely. Meanwhile, *Claw Blimey!* is the creative headline in nearly two dozen national and regional papers in the UK.

I have to work late. Half an hour after Tracey leaves for home, Ralph drops by, complaining about a sore wrist. For the past week he's been printing out and packaging a quarter of a million Bank of England strategy documents and he claims it's given him a repetitive strain injury.

"Better than a sore arse," I say with mock sympathy.

"Piss off Curly," he says, "It really hurts."

"It's all that wanking," I tell him. "You're going to have to give it up."

"It doesn't hurt *that* much," he says.

Mavis is dusting outside the broom cupboard and she pops her head around the door. "I'll do it for you, dear," she says.

"Thanks very kind," says Ralph, "But there is one problem. Well two, really."

"And what's that?" asks Mavis.

"You've got tits," says Ralph.

"Good point," she replies. "Come with me. I'll introduce you to Henry."

I wonder who the f*ck Henry is as Ralph follows Mavis back out of the broom cupboard.

Tuesday 16 March 1999
Metro's first issue is published today

I bring my tuxedo in with me to work today, as I plan to gatecrash tonight's Ipswich Insurance awards event. No sign of Tracey. The answerphone informs me that she's off sick.

Endless calls to and from Dave. There's a £4.47 difference preventing NOB's accounts from balancing.

After a few hours of toil, I make my way to the Grapes, where I take a call on my mobile from Doug, bringing me the sudden, tragic news that Rod was on his roof trying to adjust his TV aerial when he fell and has died.

Grief-stricken and with tears in my eyes, I decide to give the awards event a miss and instead go to the bar for a quadruple Chivas Regal.

It's what Rod would have wanted.

Monday 22 March 1999
The Daily Express published its first newspaper horoscope in 1930

Ralph drops by the broom cupboard for an Irish coffee and a moment of silence and reflection in memory of Rod.

Just after I bid Ralph an emotional farewell, I take a call from Martha, a reporter on the *Jersey Goalmouth Scramble*, who sounds very pleased to tell me that the Jersey government has discovered a revolutionary new use for Jersey's children's homes. "They're going to use them to house the island's orphans and to keep them safe," she says.

"Really?" I reply. "About time!"

Knight of the realm, child rapist and Liberal MP for Rochdale Cyril f*cking Smith was a frequent visitor to Jersey. He once said, "No one should be persecuted because of whom they love." Whenever I hear the media say that it always reminds me of that odious, fat c*nt.

The afternoon gets off to a shaky start involving spilled whisky - a terrible waste - and missing invoices that we're finally able to trace.

• Around 4pm, Tracey finishes a call with Mrs Mainwaring and says, "I succeeded in putting her off buying CRABSAFE."

"That's good," I say.

"Yes, when she told me that her star sign was Capricorn rather than Cancer, she agreed with me that she was probably going to be fine without the cover," says Tracey.

I chuckle, then say, "Did I tell you about Finbar? Yesterday he walked into our local fishmongers carrying a crab. He asked Marina the piscatrix, 'Do you sell crab cakes?' She replied, 'Yes we do.' 'Great,' said Finbar, 'because today's his birthday.'"

Wednesday 24 March 1999

The Turkish Radio and Television Corporation (TRT) was founded in 1964

To the Potteries for a couple of days. I show Genghis the World Record certificate and he's most impressed! He loves the Guinness Book of Records and every Christmas I give him a new one, a remainder on discount from the previous year. He never notices.

"You'll be in it this year!" he cries excitedly.

"Well, next year," I say. Then I suddenly recall that I taped a few episodes of Record Beaters from several years ago. I go upstairs, pull down the loft ladder and climb up to the attic, where I eventually locate a box with dozens of video cassettes and, alongside them, our old Betamax recorder.

In two loads, I carefully carry them down before carefully plugging the machine into the TV in the corner of the living room. After dusting down the top of the cassettes, I look through the labels. The third one I come to has six episodes of the show taped back-to-back. As I finally play the first tape, I call Genghis in from the kitchen. He's immediately glued to the screen.

Two hours later, I return to see him waving excitedly at the TV. Just as the last episode of Record Beaters ends, he starts to sing: "De-dication's what you need!" He's almost in tune too, which is most unusual.

Friday 26 March 1999
The Naples Daily News was founded in 1923

After going through numerous files and receipts, I make a call to Dave, telling him that I've found the £4.47 that was missing. Dave's a creative chap who once told me that there are three types of accountants: The ones that can count and the other ones that can't.

It's Rod's funeral at 4pm today. Tracey and I are in a sombre mood. We pay our respects by having a minute of silence before our taxi arrives to take us to the crematorium.

Thursday 1 April 1999
The MIT Technology Review first published the return of the Woolly Mammoth spoof in 1984

I take a call this morning from Dougal, a reporter on the *Inverness Gob Job*, asking if I've any news. In the spirit of April Fools, I think for a moment, then offer him a Royal exclusive.

An hour later, I'm in the broom cupboard when Mavis pops in for a quick chat.

"Hi Mavis. How're you?"

"Orright," Mavis replies. "I wanna ask a favour."

"Of course," I reply.

"I don't want to shake hands with men in the workplace anymore, in line with my religious beliefs on modesty," she says.

"Of course. I'll fully respect your wishes."

"April fool!" she exclaims, laughing.

"Okay, do you fancy playing the rape game?"

"Oh no!"

"That's the spirit!" I say. "April fool!"

I'm about to leave work when I take a call from Araminta. "Sorry not to have asked before now, but I've been away. How was Rod's funeral?" she says.

"Very sad," I say, solemnly. "But the reception was great!"

Monday 5 April 1999
Sky One was founded in 1982

After a shit weekend, much of it spent thinking about Rod, I arrive at work just after 9am. I'm surprised to be greeted by Ralph. He's just returned from his cruising holiday in San Francisco and he's in a very good mood.

"Holidays are lovely, but the security and immigration checks are a real pain," I say. "When I last visited Tasmania, I only had my Pimlico passport with me and the immigration officer asked me if I had a criminal record."

"Really?" says Ralph, taken aback. "What did you say?"

"Well, I thought about telling him that I didn't think you still needed one. But instead, I told him that numerous ancestors had been penally transported to Tasmania and that was an important lesson learnt."

"What did he say to that?" asks Ralph.

"Piss off Curly!"

After a most enjoyable lunch with Leon, my head's spinning over his predictions for life 20 years from now. When I reach work, I pour myself a mug of Irish whisky without the coffee and mention Leon's remarks on gender to Mavis. "According to Leon, in future, everyone will be allowed to choose to be referred to as he, she, they, or something else," I tell her.

"What the f*ck is something else?" asks Mavis.

"I haven't a clue," I reply. "Seriously though, you've got to feel very sorry for the parents of a 'something else'. It'd be a proper bad-heir-day!"

"It certainly would," says Mavis.

"Leon also mentioned that in the future, urinals will be banned."

"Why would anyone try to get urinals banned?" asks Mavis. "I'm always having to clean piss off the seats in the bogs here."

"Don't look at me!" I plead. "According to Tracey, I just piss in the sink. However, you do make a very valid point, Mavis. Both men and women with penises should always be able to use a urinal."

Meanwhile, my new friend, Dougal, at the *Inverness Gobjob* has risen to the bait, exclusively revealing that 300 members of the Royal household, who assist the monarch in her official duties, are covered by a new PPI policy from NOB.

Just as I'm about to leave work, I receive a call from Juliette, Her Majesty's private secretary. She's not happy and demands that I issue an immediate apology and a retraction. Instead, I hang up, before emailing her an insurance certificate for a fictional Mr & Mrs Royle of Lower High Road, Ilford. That should do the trick.

Thursday 15 April 1999
BBC Panorama was first broadcast in 1953

As I arrive at the broom cupboard today, I mention to Tracey that I saw Stan, my dwarf neighbour, at the bus stop.

"'Jump in, Stan, I'll give you a lift home,' I said. 'Piss off Curly!' he replied."

"What an ungrateful little sod!" says Tracey.

"That's just what I thought!" I reply. "I just zipped my rucksack back up and carried on walking."

But as Tracey disappears to make some coffee, I do feel some sympathy for my diminutive neighbour, as I reflect on the fact that statistically six out of seven dwarfs aren't Happy.

I'm meeting Parminder for lunch today. He's suggested we meet at Naan Better, a vegetarian curry house in Stepney. I arrive in the vicinity of the restaurant sooner than planned. As I look around me, I begin to wonder why God decided to place the arsehole of the universe – known locally as Tower Hamlets – directly on the Greenwich Meridian.

I take the opportunity to ask what else NOB can do to improve the optimisation, as Parminder calls it, of its websites.

"Google loves video," he replies. "If you can produce one that becomes popular on YouBend and other video-sharing websites, with links back to NOB, then that'll be very worthwhile indeed."

"How do I make a video that's popular?" I ask.

"Sexual acts with kittens is one way, but I know that you can't stand animal cruelty. So just do something that's controversial, something that gets hypersensitive f*ckwits foaming at the mouth," he says.

A waiter takes our order, then Parminder looks across the table at me and explains, "It's all about getting likes and about going viral."

On my return to the broom cupboard, I'm determined to pursue Parminder's ingenious suggestion of using videos to add potency to NOB's websites, so I put in a call to Ralph, who once told me he's an amateur videographer. He kindly agrees to shoot NOB's first video.

Some months ago, I tell him, I made a referral to the Diversity, Equality & Inclusion Inspectorate in respect of genetic discrimination and the disgraceful fact that hundreds of thousands of people in the UK are being denied access to essential financial products. I add, "It soon became obvious that the inspectorate employs the same calibre of useless c*nt as every other Government quango when a spokeswoman responded, 'The issue of genetic discrimination is outside our remit.'"

Straight after lunch, I set about writing the script.

Monday 19 April 1999
Universal Newsreel was founded in 1929

Whist wondering how best to make our video controversial, I ask Tracey, "Do you think that Del would dress up to be filmed as a g*lly, if it was for an ethical cause?"

Tracey looks shocked.

I hastily say, "I fully understand that he might not want to do so. A g*lly is a grotesque symbol of anti-black imagery. He might however consider that if a goal is morally important enough, then any method of getting it is acceptable."

She thinks for a moment, then says, "Well, what if you explain to him *why* you're doing it?"

I get onto the phone to Del. To my surprise he agrees to my proposal without hesitation. "Count me in!" he says. "My dad died of cancer in his thirties and, because of this, I haven't been able to buy life insurance myself. It's a f*cking disgrace!"

"It is indeed," I say. "There's a government-backed flood insurance scheme for f*ckwits who buy houses built on flood-plains, but none that offers life cover to anyone at risk of an inherited disease."

I call Genevieve to see if she still has her Princess Di wig and, if so, whether she'd be willing, in a very good cause, to become her *doppelgänger* once again.

"Love to, darling! Then we can go for lunch."

"On me and your choice," I reply. "See you in Westminster on St George's Day at 10am."

Drinks tonight with Ralph. I say to him, "French newspapers are reporting that today's the anniversary of the death of Thierry Paulin."

"Wasn't he the one known as the Monster of Montmartre, the gay, mixed-race serial killer – the one who murdered 21 elderly French women?" asks Ralph.

"That's the f*cker!" I reply. "I was pleased when he died from AIDS in prison."

"Oi!" says Ralph. "You really shouldn't go around half-casting aspersions."

Friday 23 April 1999
BBC Today was first broadcast in 1957

Lights, camera, action!

Del, Genevieve, Ralph and I make our way to one of Westminster's most prestigious addresses this morning. We're going to make NOB's video outside the luxurious offices of the Diversity, Equality & Inclusion Inspectorate.

Del and Genevieve have learnt their lines and are good to go. Del is wearing his g*lly suit, while Genevieve is wearing her Princess Di wig.

As Ralph films, Del walks into shot, crying.

Genevieve: "Why so sad, G*lly? Please don't cry."

Del: "I've just been turned down for life insurance and I can't get a mortgage. They say that because my dad died of cancer in his thirties, I'm at much greater risk and therefore uninsurable."

Genevieve: "That's absolutely disgraceful, G*lly. You're not being treated fairly! If I were you, I'd f*ck-off back to G*llyland. Genetic discrimination has been illegal there for a quarter of a century."

Del: "Thank you so much. I don't think that I've any other option, if I wish to own my own home."

Genevieve: "Good luck, G*lly!"

"That's a wrap!" I say. "Let's go and get pissed."

I buy the first round and, as I bring the drinks to the table, Del suggests, "With any luck, in future scientists will be able to ensure that babies are no longer born with inherited diseases."

"Let's hope so," I reply. "But I'm surprised that you're a supporter of eugenics. Some people think that it's science's greatest scandal."

"Only people who've never visited Braintree would think that eugenics is a bad thing!" says Del, laughing.

Monday 26 April 1999
The Irish News was first published in 1891

First thing this morning, I'm in the broom cupboard enjoying a quick sharpener with Mavis when she tells me that her friend, Sandra, now identifies as ambigender.

"What the f*ck's ambigender?" I ask.

"Sandra tells me that it includes anyone who experiences two genders simultaneously, with no fluidity or shifting," says Mavis.

"Isn't that just another way of saying Sandra enjoys a cock in all holes?" I ask.

"I've no idea," says Mavis. "But, if it is, I'll definitely think about it for myself."

"According to Professor Heinz of the Harvard College of Further Education, there are 57 recorded genders," I tell her. "If I were you, I wouldn't restrict yourself to just two."

"That's a very good point, Curly," says Mavis, "Two just isn't enough!"

"Think about it carefully though," I say. "When Ralph came out of the closet, he was ridiculed, insulted, and thrown out."

Mavis looks appalled.

"Mind you," I add, "he really shouldn't have had that wank at British Home Stores."

Tuesday 27 April 1999
The Eastern Daily Press was first published in 1872

I'm in the broom cupboard, giving an interview with Fabia, the news editor for *Repartee Weekly*, when she asks me for my advice on how best to respond when someone is being rude or offensive.

"Two fingers and a f*ck-off has worked well since the battle of Crécy in 1346," I tell her. "It works even better with people from Norfolk, as they tend to have more fingers to choose from."

"Piss off Curly!" snaps Fabia. "I'm from Thetford!"

"That works well too!" I exclaim, but Fabia has already rung off.

Puzzled, Tracey then asks me what the initials CII stand for.

"That's a very good question," I say. "The organisation responsible for education in the insurance industry is the Confederated Insurance Inspectorate, or the CII. Unofficially, however, these letters are widely recognised in the City of London as standing for C*nts In Insurance."

"Why's that?" she asks.

"Any excuse for profanity," I reply. "But I do have a letter from one of the c*nts in insurance, advising that a master's degree in ethics from the University of London did not match the current CII exam learning outcomes."

"Surely ethics is fundamental to insurance!" she pleads.

"It most certainly is," I reply. "Princess Di was the Patron of the CII, but I just can't help thinking that there's another member of the Royal Family who's much more ethically aligned to them than she was."

"You mean like the one who's friends with Jimmy f*cking Savile?" asks Tracey.

"Yes!" I reply. "But in fact, I think that several of them are Jimmy's friends."

This evening, I make it out for evening drinks in Hampshire with Oscar, editor of the *Aldershot Dishonourable Discharge*. Not much to report, but he does make me laugh when he tells me, "I wasn't close to my brother when he died, which is lucky really."

"Why's that?" I ask.

"He stepped on a landmine," says Oscar.

Sunday 9 May 1999
The Observer was first published in 1791

Mother's Day. I'm up early to catch the train to visit Mum and to treat her to a cream tea at Trentham Gardens.

Just as I turn into Mum's Road, I recognise a familiar figure walking in my direction. It's Caleb, an old friend from school.

"How are you?" I ask.

"Great thanks, Curly," he replies. "I'm just off to the pub to celebrate. Yesterday, I opened three birthday cards and I'm over £100 to the good."

"I thought your birthday was in *November*," I say.

"It is," he replies. "But I've just got a new job as a postman."

On the train back to London, Television North researcher, Louise, calls my mobile to invite me to the broadcaster's Leeds Bradford TV studio, to appear on Up & Over, where she'd like me to deliver the notion that *everyone* should take out insurance against alien abduction and impregnation.

No sane person would ever voluntarily choose to visit Leeds Bradford. However, since I need to meet up with Stanley, a senior reporter on the *Yorkshire Daily Jamboree*, I reluctantly agree to turn up to be filmed.

I skim through the latest cuttings and chuckle when I come across a story about CUPSAFE. It strikes me that now would be the ideal time to fulfil my promise to Nancy and to try to get her as much publicity as we got for Lance, so I call *White Trash* and offer them an exclusive. I explain that for £210, NOB has insured the good looks of 26-year-old mum, Nancy Jones, for £100,000, as she's concerned that her husband Ronald will leave her if her attractiveness fades.

I take a taxi from Euston to the broom cupboard and, once I've told Nancy what I'm doing, I hastily draft a FACESAFE press release and email it to the magazine with a spoof comment from me that cover is widely available for anyone who fears that they may fail the wolf-whistle test and be declared unattractive by a panel of ten builders.

Wednesday 12 May 1999
The Toledo Blade was first published in 1835

Tracey and I are both bright and early in the broom cupboard today. I ask her, "Did you know that each year the Uxbridge English Dictionary adds new words?"

"Do they?" she asks.

"Oh yes," I reply. "This year's words are emoji, blog, social-networking and jullible."

"I've never heard of jullible," says Tracey. "What's it mean?"

"It means 'easily persuaded to believe something credulous.'"

"Oh, really?"

"Yes," I reply. "You know, Professor Stephen Hawking once said to me: 'Girls from Braintree have a remarkably high intellect.'"

"That was very kind of him," she says.

"It certainly was. He must have been thinking about the girl from Braintree who got fired from her job at the bank after an old lady came in to check her balance and she pushed her over."

"Very funny," says Tracey. "If I was given 50p for every time you made a crap joke about the stupidity of girls from Braintree, I'd now have £17.20."

I switch on the radio. Serial killer Dennis Nilsen is dead.

In today's cuttings, a story in the World News section of the *Osaka Yellow Peril* today has a photo of Nancy standing next to Ronald who, according to the spoof story, fell for her "stunning figure and tanned legs" when they met eight years ago. It says she took the policy out as a birthday present for him, as he "keeps joking he'll leave her if she becomes 'ugly'".

Meanwhile a column in the *Shetland Hand Job* cites Nancy's concern that her hubby wouldn't still love her if she weighed 15 stone.

The same news story is also featured in today's *Jarrow Jubblies*, as well as the *Thanet Stringer*, the *Grimsby Cutaway* and the *South Yorkshire Chapel*.

When I return to the broom cupboard after lunch, I find Tracey speaking with Mrs Mainwaring, this time successfully persuading her that, as a woman in her seventies, she really doesn't need to buy FACESAFE.

Just as she's finishing her call, the other phone rings. It's Genghis, ringing to tell me that he's just split-up from his girlfriend, Clare-Lee.

"She said she was leaving me due to my obsession with The Monkees pop group. I thought she was joking. Then I saw her face," he says, before bursting into fits of laughter.

Monday 17 May 1999

BBC Have I Got News for You was first broadcast in 1990

At 6am, Nancy calls me as I'm preparing to leave for Stanstead Airport for my flight to Leeds Bradford Airport. She's absolutely delighted about her appearance yesterday on There Is No News Today.

"Did you *see* it?" she asks me excitedly. "I couldn't *believe* it when I saw my photo on TV and watched the presenter Ian himself talking about me!"

If Monopoly ever decided to do a Yorkshire version of its game, Leeds Bradford would definitely be brown. In all fairness though, it isn't completely shit. It's close to the M62 and it has a splendid town hall.

Wednesday 19 May 1999
Yomiuri Shimbun was first published in 1874

Busy morning. In the broom cupboard at just before noon, Tracey takes a call. After a few moments, she puts the receiver to her chest, looks across at me and asks whether NOB's PPI policies cover diabetes.

"Yes, of course they do," I reply.

When she finishes the call, I ask her, "What's the average size of a person with diabetes in the UK?"

"I've no idea," she says.

"The same as everyone else minus two feet."

At lunchtime, I drop in for a pint at the Grapes, where I hear that Moors murderer Ian Brady has died. Not one for believing in things like Heaven or Hell, I do nonetheless hope he rots in the latter of these destinations.

I return to the broom cupboard to find Tracey and Mavis talking, not unusually, about sex.

"I can only achieve orgasm in the doggy position nowadays," complains Mavis.

"So? What's the problem?" Tracey asks.

"The dog's got bad breath," Mavis replies.

I head straight back to the pub.

Friday 21 May 1999
The Aberdeen Press and Journal was first published in 1747

In the broom cupboard this morning, Tracey's on the phone to a client. "Curly, I've got a gentleman on the phone who says his penis has fallen off due to an overdose of steroids. Can he make a claim under his PPI policy?" she asks.

"Anabolic?" I ask.

"One moment...Nah, just this dick," she says.

"Then tell him of course he can make a claim," I say.

Some people can't take a joke. I take a call this afternoon from Kirsty, a *Daily Teuchter* reader from Scotland, asking if I can insure her face. I never wish to part the feeble-minded from their cash, so I do my best to put her off. But Kirsty is insistent and starts to lose her temper.

"Okay then," I say. "What's your postcode?"

"It's AB1..."

"Can I please stop you there, Kirsty?" I say. "Our underwriters won't cover the people of Aberdeen against becoming ugly."

"Why the f*ck not?" asks a bewildered Kirsty.

"I'm afraid they say they can't possibly provide beauty insurance to residents of a city famous for its sea monsters," I explain. "Sorry about that Kirsty."

CLICK-CLICK-BRRRRRR.

I make my way to Brixton this afternoon, flush with my ticket to the 1999 Annual Political Correctness Convention. It's a pivotal event. I believe it's of utmost importance to be careful to avoid forms of expression that exclude, marginalise or insult people who're socially disadvantaged or confronted by discrimination.

As I am leaving this worthy event, an attractive brunette calls out to me, "Hi blondie!" Obviously not wishing to cause offence I reply, "Hi darkie!" At this, her jollity turns to anger. "Piss off Curly!" she shouts. Without responding, I continue on my way.

Having a drink with Tracey and Del after work, I mention my encounter this afternoon. Del is shocked. "That's outrageous, Curly!" he exclaims. "Everyone knows that you're whiter than white when it comes to darkies."

Monday 31 May 1999
The Minnesota Star Tribune was first published in 1867

Midway through a hectic morning in the broom cupboard, I receive a call out of the blue from Jacob.

"Curly, I need your help!" he pleads, a true sense of urgency in his voice.

I nod to Tracey to finish my pile from the envelope-stuffing we'd been doing together.

"Go ahead, Jacob," I say.

"Thanks. Do you remember that I used the legacy I got from my grandmother to buy an off licence?" he asks.

"I certainly do," I reply. "I remember being f*cking delighted!"

"Well, business has been really poor recently," he says. "I don't want the hassle of claiming on my PPI policy. Is there any chance you can help me get more customers?"

"It'd be my pleasure to help you in any way that I can," I say. "Let me have a think. I'll call you back this afternoon."

I resume giving Tracey a hand with the mail-out before allowing myself just 20 minutes in which to down a large whisky and a couple of quick pints in the Grapes. Then, as I make my way back to work, I bump into Rupert, who once suggested that I join Alcoholics Anonymous. Bingo! He's given me an idea for Jacob.

Back at my desk, I'm happy to see Tracey has made great headway. The mailing will be finished in time to catch this evening's post. I call Jacob and suggest that he place an advert in his local paper that says, "If you think you're an alcoholic, call [the number of your off licence]."

"Curly, you're a f*cking genius," he says.

"Good luck," I say. "Incidentally," I add, "did I tell you about the two burglars who were robbing an off licence? One turns to the other and asks, 'Is this whisky?' The other replies, 'Yeah, but not as wisky as wobbing a bank.'"

Wednesday 2 June 1999
The Bristol Post was first published in 1932

In Bristol to buy breakfast for Roddie, a senior reporter on the venerable *Bristol Spittoon*. Bristol these days seems to be plagued with vandalism, drugs and teenage pregnancy. The civic buildings may not be as fine as those in Liverpool, but the graffiti is far more accomplished.

As I'm walking past the collegiate church of All Saints in Corn Street, with its famous Rysbrack memorial to Edward Colston, I observe a film crew shooting a commercial for Flush, my favourite brand of loo-roll, because of its catchy 'love at first shite' advertising slogan.

As the boom operator swings the mike, he knocks a large stack of rolls onto me. Clueless c*nt! Fortunately, I suffer just soft tissue damage and I continue my journey to the car park.

My efforts to publicise the fact that NOB's PPI policies treat all customers fairly are starting to pay off. Doug's photo appears today in the *Lipstick Lesbian*, alongside a story in which he's posing as a self-employed computer programmer who's has just made a successful claim on his PAYMENTSAFE policy.

The paper, which must sell close to a million copies every day, has even published NOB's phone number and included a backlink alongside the story on its website. Ker-ching!

A rewarding day of back-to-back phone calls from self-employed computer programmers applying for PAYMENTSAFE promise a great holiday for me this summer – and a well-earned bonus for Tracey.

After a few pints at the Grapes, I carefully create, print and then post a bogus insurance certificate to William Wallace of the Aberdeen Cock Mess Monster Appreciation Society. The policy purports to insure him for £1 million in respect of death or serious injury occasioned by the Cock Mess Monster.

I then quickly type a MESSIESAFE press release and email it to Jeremy.

Friday 18 June 1999
Gazette de France published the first newspaper readers' letter in 1631

I drop by the newsagent on the way to work, where I note that the *Freetown Love Sausage* has run the news story that William Wallace is insured for £1 million in case Messie eats him. It cites bookies' odds of 500/1 against the over-sized creature being found. Along with my admission that while I don't believe in Messie, NOB never turns down a risk.

The *Maputo Leg-Over* is less kind. The news story on its website is backed up by an opinion piece, which suggests there's one born every minute. It concludes that there's more chance of a lottery win than a Messie attack.

They're not wrong.

I've a long wait for my optician appointment with Patrick this afternoon, so I fill the time penning a letter in the name of Mrs Norma Snockers of Chelmsford to Anita Wyderbox, the guest economist at the *Wembley No Score Drawers*, asking whether insurance policies against being attacked by the Cock Mess Monster are actually worth buying. I seal and address the envelope and drop it into the receptionist's franking tray.

When I return to work, I notice that Mr Wallace's local paper of choice, the *Sweaty Sock*, has swallowed the bait and spread the news of his delight on receiving his new MESSIESAFE policy. Reports reveal that he now feels it's safe to go fishing because, should anything happen to him, his family will be well-looked after. He adds that he knows Messie hasn't attacked anyone since 565 AD, but he's more concerned that the monster may come up to the surface and accidentally knock him out of his boat.

He concludes with the maxim, 'It's better to be safe than sorry.' My thoughts exactly, William.

Friday 25 June 1999
The Northampton Chronicle & Echo was first published in 1880

My parents drop Genghis off at the broom cupboard early, as they're going away for a long weekend. They share my love of religious architecture and they're travelling to Ghent to see the 15th-century polyptych altarpiece in St Bavo's Cathedral by Hubert and Jan van Eyck.

Tracey arrives while I'm taking a call from Gus, one of the reporters for the *Northampton Jiggery Pokery*. He says he wants to meet me urgently, to discuss a new feature he's writing on PPI. An article and a backlink on the website of such a prestigious newspaper can only help NOB's publicity campaign.

I hang up and explain my dilemma to Tracey when, just as I'm wondering both how to get me and Genghis to Northamptonshire and quite what I am going to do to keep him amused when I get there, she kindly offers to take Genghis to the Tower of London while I travel north by myself.

It's a beautiful morning when I finally arrive a few minutes early for my meeting. The sun is shining and the birds are singing. I see a sweet-looking. middle-aged woman in her front garden watering plants beneath a chorus of singing birds and I cheerfully say to her, "You've got great tits!"

She looks up at me. "Piss off Curly!" she replies.

Two hours later, meeting with Gus over, I head back to London by train before finally arriving at the broom cupboard just before 5pm, where Genghis excitedly tells me about the day the two of them have had. "We saw the ravens, the Beefeaters and the Crown Jewels," he says. Before telling me how they both enjoyed a slap-up lunch, had two ice-creams from Tracey's school friend, Mr Whippy and this brilliant toy bird from the shop.

"How much do I owe you?" I ask.

"Not a f*ckin' penny!" she says, laughing. "We got free ice-cream, we were treated to lunch and we were given the toy for free. Oh, and they didn't charge us for entry!"

"All free? Really?"

"Yes!" says Tracey. "And I'm just going back there this evening for a spit-roast with two real Beefeaters, followed by an all-you-can-eat Beefeater dinner."

"Slapper!" I say laughing.

She leaves, saying farewell to Genghis and giving him a kiss.

I look at the toy raven and say, "Is that a blackbird?"

"No, mong!" exclaims Genghis. "It's a raven and I really love it!"

I am overwhelmed by Tracey's kindness. My brother's smiling as he holds the bird close to his chest and sings quietly to it, "Dedication's what you need."

YOU'VE GOT GREAT TITS

Friday 2 July 1999
The Times of India was first published in 1838

Just as I arrive at the broom cupboard, the phone rings. It's Jacob.

"Hi Curly," he says, "I've got some fantastic news to share with you. I mentioned a few months ago that Hannah was suffering from agoraphobia. Well, yesterday she was really brave and we went out for a coffee together."

"That's really fantastic news," I say. "Please pass on my congratulations and good wishes to Hannah."

At lunchtime, I'm in a queue at the Post Office, thinking to myself that I've never met anyone suffering from agoraphobia, when I spot a perfect greetings card for Hannah. It features a lovely rainbow and says, 'Well done you for being so brave and coming out.'

How thoughtful of them to do this. I'll email Imelda's friend, Paula, who works there installing a new computer system, to tell her what a fantastic job the Post Office is doing.

When I get back to the broom cupboard, I see that the *Wembley No Score Drawers* has not only published Mrs Snockers' letter, but has also kindly responded to it in some considerable detail, concluding that if you can find an insurance company willing to cover you against being attacked by Messie, you should take up the offer, particularly if you live in Aberdeen.

Just as we are about to leave for the day, a call comes in from Rex, a Big Bristols researcher. He tells me a special edition of Jim'll Risk It is set to be filmed at the end of the month to commemorate five years since the last episode of the show was screened and they're inviting Genghis to appear! He'll be chuffed to bits.

Friday 9 July 1999
El País was first published in 1976

I arrive at the broom cupboard just as Tracey's finishing a call.

"That was Mrs Mainwaring," she says as she hangs up. "She was concerned about the Cock Mess Monster. But don't worry, I was able to reassure her that Messie has never been spotted in Croydon."

"That's great," I say. "Thank you. By the way, what's got two hundred teeth and holds back a monster?"

"I don't know. Tell me," she says.

"My zip!" I reply.

"That's not what Vicky said," she says as she gets up to make some coffee.

Just then a fax arrives from New York. It's from Helen, a researcher for Brokenwind TV's Millennium Domes, proposing to send a film crew to the UK to interview me, William Wallace and the Cock Mess Monster, if a date can be found when we're all available. I *love* that show and I assure Helen I'll check on Messie's availability straight away.

Doug calls to suggest we try out a new strip pub that's just opened in bleak and rundown Shoreditch called The Boobie Trap. Tracey and I are just about finished for the day, so we close the broom cupboard and grab a cab to meet Doug.

We march through the grim, neglected streets, keeping an eye out for muggers on the quest for easy money. As we finally make our way into the pub, Tracey waves across the bar to someone she knows. Mandy, a stripper holding a pint jug, promptly comes over to us and anxiously tells my assistant that she's the only performer who's made it to work today. Tracey promptly puts her beer on the bar counter and follows her acquaintance to a doorway at the rear of the pub.

A minute later, Mandy reappears and jumps onto a small stage and starts to dance naked around a pole. Another minute passes by before Tracey appears in a silk bikini, carrying a pint jug of her own. Punters drop in small change as she makes her way through the bar towards us.

"Really?" I say, putting a fiver into her pint glass.

"It's all hands on deck!" she replies with a shrug as she puts her jug behind the bar, before skipping gaily on stage to release jugs of her own.

After her dance, she returns to pick up her donations from the punters.

I smile at her and nod. "Impressive," I say.

"Thanks," she says, before taking a swig of beer. I down the rest of my pint and Doug and I make our way out into the daylight.

Tuesday 20 July 1999
The Cape Canaveral Cocoa Tribune was first published in 1917

I'm in the broom cupboard and mention to Tracey that today is the anniversary of the most momentous event in human history.

"Really?" says Tracey. "What was that?"

"Forty years ago today," I say, "Rosa Parks became the first woman in human history to travel to the dark side of the moon."

"I was unaware of that," says Tracey.

"Yes," I say. "Supremacists in the media suppressed the information and concentrated instead on the much later spaceflight to the Moon by Neil Armstrong, Buzz Aldrin and Michael Collins."

"That's disgraceful!" says Tracey.

"It is!" I say. "But thankfully, Ms Parks' considerable achievements will be recognised by poet and songwriter Phil Snott-Heron. According to Leon, Mr Snott-Heron's song, "Darkie on the Moon," will not only become a number-one hit in over a hundred countries, but in 2030 will become the most popular song of all time."

"Well, at least she'll get the recognition she deserves," says Tracey.

"Yes!" I say, "Definitely better late than never, but did you know that her spaceflight was almost cancelled?"

"Really?" Says Tracey.

"Yes, really!" I say. "Ms Parks fell asleep on her bus to Cape Canaveral and nearly missed her stop."

Just as I reflect on this, I take a call from Genghis, who asks me to listen to a Dean Martin song he's just learned.

"When the moon hits your knees, and you mispronounce trees, sycamore!" he sings, before bursting into laughter.

"That's more Dean Martian," I suggest.

I say goodbye and hang up the phone. I wonder if there is in fact a moon-related spoof that'd get NOB more backlinks. I'm sure there is one that wouldn't involve having my trousers around my ankles.

Thursday 22 July 1999
BBC PM was first broadcast in 1970

I'm late leaving the broom cupboard this evening and I bump into Mavis, who's finished work for the day herself. I invite her for a pint over the road, where she tells me that 35 years ago to the day, she was in the audience of Pick of the Pops.

"That must have been amazing!" I say.

"It was absolutely brilliant!" says Mavis. "I saw The Beatles, who performed A Hard Day's Night, The Rolling Stones who performed It's All Over Now and The Beach Boys who performed I Get Around. John Lennon gave me his autograph. It was easily the best day of my life!"

"How old were you?" I ask.

"I was twelve," says Mavis.

"How did you manage to get tickets?" I ask.

"Jimmy came to our children's home and told me that if I sucked his cock, he'd take me to the show in his Rolls Royce."

"That's f*cking disgraceful!" I exclaim.

"I don't think so, not really," she says. "Jimmy and his friends were really kind to us girls. They brought us drinks, makeup and cigarettes." She pauses, then says, "I thought it was a bit strange that he wanted me to fix it for him by putting my finger up his bum and saying, 'Clunk Click', but he told me that if I did it, then the children's home would get a free colour TV licence. We didn't have a TV, but it made Jimmy happy."

"For f*cks' sake!" I exclaim, horrified. I pause. "It reminds me of the story about the rapist, the paedophile and the DJ who walked into a bar. The barman asked, 'What are you drinking, Jimmy?'"

"Jimmy's nice and you shouldn't make fun of him!" Mavis exclaims. "He also got me tickets to It's a Kickabout at the Pebble Beach studios in Birmingham, where I also had a really lovely day. I drank a whole bottle of Champagne to myself and passed out. I only wish I'd known beforehand that Champagne gives you a terrible hangover and a sore fanny."

Friday 23 July 1999
The News Agency of Nigeria was founded in 1976

As I arrive at work today, I'm taken aback by a large, beautifully wrapped parcel tied with a big red bow that's been placed on the floor beside the broom cupboard door. I bend down to pick up the package and pull out a card that's wedged behind the ribbon. It's addressed to me.

Just as I'm eagerly fishing for my keys, Tracey arrives. She unlocks the door and we both enter, keen to discover what's in the parcel. I keenly tear open the wrapping to reveal a wonderfully detailed crystal globe on a silver plinth inscribed with the words Global Ethics Awards. I look up and proudly say, "NOB is now officially the world's most ethical insurance provider!"

"What a fantastic achievement!" Tracey replies, somewhat spellbound. "It's brilliant to have our hard work and dedication acknowledged. Who's it from?" she asks.

I pull out the printed material from inside the wrapping paper I've just discarded and read the text aloud: "Each year, Abimbola, publisher of the *Lagos Scamwich*, brings together a panel of leading scientists, academics and innovators for a lunch in Lagos to determine the most ethical company in a number of categories, ranging from financial services, to arms-dealing and to people-trafficking."

"Wow!" Tracey says. "Does this mean we'll be going to Africa?"

"Sadly not," I reply. "However, we'll certainly be able to put the logo onto our letterhead and email footer."

"Del will be happy with the extra work," she says.

"That's good," I reply. "Now, along with the Excellence in Customer Service award we received in February from Mikey and Benni at *My Mortgage Weekly*, NOB's a multi-award-winning company."

"That's great!" says Tracey. "And it doesn't matter about Africa. Del and all my friends and family are going to be very impressed that I work at the most ethical insurance provider in the world!"

"Go ahead and tell them for sure," I say. "You do realise, though, don't you, that the vast majority of awards are a total scam?"

She looks at me, puzzled, so I explain, "I paid Abimbola two thousand dollars in cash for the ethics award. This is why all those banks who sell shit PPI go on to win loads of awards."

Tracey frowns, but I continue. "They may not actually be as blatant as me by paying cash for their awards, but they do pay large sums of money to the organisations who create the awards for tables at their award ceremonies. Then, award in hand, they seduce those same organisations with advertisements from their hefty marketing budgets."

"That's f*cking disgusting!"

"Indeed it is," I say, "But don't look so sad. I've got something here that'll cheer you up." Opening my desk drawer, I reach in and produce a shiny gold star that came from the top of last year's Christmas tree. "Here you go. You're NOB's employee of the month!"

"Really?" she replies, once again looking spellbound. "Thank you so much, Curly! I'm really thrilled!"

As I close my desk drawer, I glance across for acknowledgement of the rich irony but I neither see nor hear a trace. Everything I just told her about awards seems to have gone in one ear and straight out of the other.

Middle Finger Productions, a cable TV production company based in Maidstone, has identified NOB as a purveyor of unusual insurance policies. Paul, the producer, calls to say he read about NOB in the *Maidstone Belter* and says he'd like to invite me to appear on a TV show called Total Bollocks. He tells me he'd like me to explain to the audience that I work for an insurance company that sells virgin birth cover, to find out whether they find the claim convincing or "total bollocks". I tell him I'll be happy to go.

A fax soon arrives with the details. "We're delighted that you've agreed to appear on Total Bollocks presented by a Sion Miow. The idea of the show is to fool the audience. You insure people for the most bizarre things, including cover for virgins against the risk of immaculate conception. This is exactly what we're looking for and I'd be very grateful if you could spare the time to tell me about this most interesting and unusual insurance."

On second thoughts, I don't really want to hike all the way to Maidstone just for this. I reach for my phone. "Doug?"

"Hi Curly. Can't speak long – I'm on deadline."

"Fancy a trip to Maidstone?"

"No," he says.

"Expenses paid," I say.

"Maybe," he says.

Of course he does. I call Paul to say that I can't make it, but that I'll send NOB's senior underwriter, Doug Jones, in my place.

Thursday 29 July 1999
The Hastings & St. Leonards Observer was first published in 1859

I leave Tracey in charge of the broom cupboard for a couple of days as I drive off for a lunch meeting in Bournemouth with Denis, a reporter on the *Dorset Muck Spreader*. I've then got to drive to Hastings for evening drinks with Norman, the personal finance editor of the *Ham Shank*, before I can enjoy a relaxing weekend break in Brighton.

Norman is in good form when I meet him, but he clearly laments the demise of his town in recent years. "Hastings tries to market itself to tourists as a glass of Champagne," he says. "But when they arrive, they soon discover that it's more like a bucket of piss."

To cheer him up, I say, "You know what they call an arrow that fails to hit its target? Projectile dysfunction."

It's an exciting day for Genghis too. Rex is collecting him in Jimmy's Rolls Royce to take him to Brand's Hatch, to drive a Sinclair C5 around the main racing track for the Jim'll Risk It special. It's a shame I can't go myself.

Tuesday 3 August 1999
The Brighton Argus was first published in 1880

When I arrive at the broom cupboard, Tracey asks me how my trip went.

"Well, Hastings is like a turd sprinkled with glitter," I say. "And in Brighton they ran out of glitter, but it does have a lovely seabird sanctuary."

Wednesday 4 August 1999
The Tampa Bay Times was first published in 1884

The Jim'll Risk It studio show is being filmed this evening, but work has piled up while I've been away, so I've no choice but to stay and work late. Tracey's kindly volunteered to escort Genghis to the studio by train and to carry his medication. I promise to join them at the studio later.

There's so much paperwork to get through that I don't arrive until the final credits are rolling and the last guests are leaving the studio. Just as I'm looking around for my brother, ahead of me in the darkness, I hear Tracey exclaim in a shocked voice, "Put that away Jimmy, you sick tw*t!"

When we're back in the car, Tracey looks at me and says, "I forgot to tell you what Jimmy said to me when I challenged him."

"Please tell me!" I say.

"'A little bit of who you fancy does you good.'"

"What a c*nt!" I say.

"I really regret not kicking the f*cker in his child-size bollocks," replies Tracey.

From the front passenger seat, Genghis turns his head and says to us both, "Jimmy said you should take a girl before she bleeds, but I don't know where you're supposed to take her."

"Well!" I say after taking a deep breath, "Jimmy is a member of a religious cult whose members worship the number zero. They're called nonces and believe that it's morally acceptable to have sex with girls before they turn into women. There are other religious groups who also do this, but most decent people consider that it's not possible for a young girl to properly consent to having sex with a much older man."

"That's awful," says Genghis, sounding outraged.

"What about in Scotland?" asks Tracey.

"Forgive me, you're quite right," I reply. "In Scotland, taking a girl before she bleeds means before taking her to hospital to have her tits cut off and pumping her so full of drugs that she grows a beard."

"That's gross!" says Genghis. "Really gross!"

"It is," I say. "Later, when these mutilated girls realise that they aren't men after all, they sue the hospitals that performed their surgery for millions of pounds, leaving them with no money to buy essential personal protection equipment for their staff."

Genghis seems shocked. "Surely that cannot be true!" he exclaims.

"Sorry, Genghis," I say, "I was only pulling your leg."

"Sometimes, Curly, you can be quite sick," he retorts.

"Sorry, Genghis and sorry, Tracey," I say winking to Tracey in the rear-view mirror.

PUT THAT AWAY JIMMY, YOU
SICK TW*T!

Sunday 8 August 1999
The oldest surviving newspaper, Wiener Zeitung, was first published in 1703

Today I'm standing outside 160 Abbott Road in Poplar, the birthplace of Tommy Flowers, designer of Colossus; the world's first programmable electronic computer. Colossus was used extensively at Station X in Bletchley and also at GCHQ in Cheltenham, where it was instrumental in preventing a Cold War nuclear apocalypse. Unfortunately for Tommy he didn't have tits, and as a white, working-class heterosexual, he was not brown, posh or gay enough for his considerable achievements to be officially recognised. There's no blue plaque for Tommy either, but only a short walk away there is one in Powis Road, dedicated to an Indian rapist and paedophile who visited Poplar in 1931.

On the lash this evening with Doug at his local, the Black Dog. I end up crashing at his flat, where he plays me the video of the Total Bollocks show that he appeared on in Maidstone.

I'm impressed! His presentation is impeccably delivered. With a straight face and without so much as a smile, he walks on stage and explains that he's the senior underwriter for NOB, a London-based insurer that specialises in unusual risks, such as virgin birth.

"Anything else?" Sion the presenter asks him.

"We also have a policy for the partially sighted," Doug replies.

"Sounds interesting," he says. "What's that entail?"

"The print's very small," Doug replies, deadpan.

This gets the biggest laugh, upsetting Sion, a professional comedian who clearly doesn't like being upstaged.

The studio audience verdict: A guy claiming to be being responsible for making Madame Tussauds models' genitals was talking total bollocks and the insurance guy – Doug – was telling the truth.

There's irony in there somewhere.

Tuesday 10 August 1999
The New Statesman was first published in 1913

This morning I'm driving to the Potteries to collect Genghis again, to look after him this evening in London.

The City of London's summer party season is in full swing. Tonight, it's a tarts-and-vicars party, hosted by Clyde, a friend of Araminta's from Act of God Insurance. She assures me this one will be an easy event for us to gatecrash.

Genghis is coming with us in his wheelchair, dressed as a choirboy. I'm going as a priest, in a crimson cassock and white surplice. Tracey's going as herself.

We lock up the broom cupboard at 4pm and cross the road for some pre-party libation in the Grapes. I go to the bar, while Tracey takes care of Genghis. I'm about to pay when Araminta shows up beside me looking elegant, but dressed as a vicar.

I order her a glass of wine and we carry the drinks to our table. Genghis looks up at Araminta and says shyly, "You're very beautiful."

She smiles warmly at him.

"She is," I say to my brother, placing the drinks on the table. "But it's what's in here that counts," I stress, raising my right hand and holding it to my chest.

"Her tits, you mean?" asks Genghis.

Trying not to laugh, I say, "No, mong, her *heart.*"

We take a black cab across town to the party, where we encounter an impressive bunch of tart and vicars. Suddenly I bump into my old friend, Justin, who, like Tracey, has come dressed as a tart.

"Hi Justin!" I say. "How the devil *are* you?"

"F*cking great!" he replies.

"Did I hear correctly that you're hoping to become ordained?"

"That's right," he says.

"What the f*ck do you want to do that for?" I ask him.

"Free wine!" he replies. "And if I play my cards right and become the head of the UK's biggest paedophile gang, I'll get to live at Lambeth Palace," he adds.

"That makes sense," I say. "Very best of luck."

"You too, Curly," he says.

Sitting with Genghis, I know that you don't need to be a rocket scientist to make a positive contribution to humanity. "It's what's in there that counts: tits!"

Talking of tits, across the room I spot Natalie, Tracey's well-endowed flatmate who's just shown up. "You're *The Braintree Genius'* Page 3 model, aren't you?" I say to Natalie.

"Yes!" she replies with a broad smile.

She then looks me straight in the eye, places a hand beneath each huge breast, lifting them both up and asks, "Are these worth insuring?"

I reply without hesitation, "Natalie, those fantastic breasts need to be insured as soon as possible. They're national as well as natural assets. Let's get them covered for the benefit of mankind. Shall I undertake a risk assessment?"

"Curly, you can hold my breasts anytime you like!" Natalie exclaims. "But in return I want to see your 12 NOB!"

Saturday 14 August 1999
The Braintree & Witham Times was first published in 1929

Tonight, I'm risking a trip to Braintree. Taking the train from Liverpool Street into deepest Essex, I'm puzzled when I observe that much of the train is occupied by shifty-looking middle-aged men clad in raincoats of various shades of fawn, all of which could do with a clean.

"Excuse me," I say to the gentleman in the raincoat opposite me, "why are there so many men on the train wearing filthy raincoats?"

"If you watched breakfast TV this morning, you'd know that Braintree is the filthiest town in England," he replies.

"Really?" I say. "I thought that by 'filthy', they were referring to the litter."

Through the window, I note the sight of used condoms, empty cigarette packets, beer cans, fast-food wrappers and other general litter that reassuringly greets arrivals to Braintree.

I step off the train, as do dozens of filthy raincoat-clad gentlemen.

"Tickets!" snaps the moose at the barrier, before she wipes dripping snot from her nose onto the sleeve of her uniform. This is not an invitation to participate in conversation. However, I'm unable to resist saying, "It's always a privilege madam to meet someone who's as lovely as you!"

As I cross the ticket hall to leave the station, she shouts after me, "Piss off Curly!"

Smiling, I make my way up the hill, skirting my way around the vomit of the night before and the litter that decorates much of the pavement.

It crosses my mind that Braintree may have been the inspiration for Gin Lane by William Hogarth. But then again, perhaps not. This shithole is much worse, with far more litter.

Tuesday 17 August 1999
Société de radio et de télévision du Bénin was founded in 1972

I've got a lunchtime meeting today with Zendaya from Benin Bongo Bongo Broadcasting. Specifically, she wants to know if the Cock Mess Monster poses a threat to residents near to Lake Nokoué. It obviously does, so I've brought along a spoof policy for her to give to them. In return, she might give NOB a backlink, which would be highly worthwhile from such a prestigious African Broadcaster.

When I return to the broom cupboard, I discover that just one brief call last Friday to the busy newsdesk of *The Braintree Genius* has paid off. A front page splash by senior reporter Penny Tration informs readers that Natalie, the paper's Page 3 model, has insured her assets with NOB for £10 million. The story comes complete with a picture of her manually supporting her boobs. Or, as we in the insurance industry prefer to call it, protecting her assets.

Also, there's a treat in store for Tracey today. Due to the rising popularity of the Huw Jardons, a world-famous group of male strippers, Buddy, their manager, has contacted NOB to insure each member's member for £2 million. I ask Tracey to type up a new NOBSAFE press release and to email it to Jeremy.

Monday 30 August 1999
The Uganda Broadcasting Corporation (UBC) was founded in 1963

I ring-fence a couple of hours for lunch with the press and head to Fleet Street to meet Lucy, a reporter from the *Redbridge Pantymonium*. I'm just rising to get a second round when she stops me. It's barely been 45 minutes, yet she tells me she has to get back to the office. I look at her in disbelief.

But it's true! Journalists' resources seem to be getting much tighter now. With so much of their reporters' work done via the Internet these days, newspaper proprietors are cashing in by slashing staff numbers. Lucy has to leave!

Oh, well. Much sooner than I'd planned, I saunter back to the broom cupboard, where I hear on the radio that a famous tea company is making all its TV monkeys redundant. This is outrageous. If an infinite number of monkeys, with an infinite amount of time, can eventually produce the works of Shakespeare, getting them to sell PPI will be a piece of piss. I ask Tracey to contact Angela their agent immediately, before crossing the road for another couple of pints.

On my return, I ask her how she got on.

"We're too late," she says. "The tea monkeys have all been offered jobs by the Big Bristols Channel, for a new production of the Life of Thomas Cromwell. Apparently, one was also chosen to host Masterbrain and a tea monkey is going to be the new Doctor Whom." I think about it for a moment before I reply, "Never mind, at least they've still got jobs, so NOB won't have to pay their unemployment claims."

"Have you insured any other famous TV animals?" asks Tracey, just as Del turns up with some newly printed stationery.

"Only Tony the Tiger and Charlie the Cheetah," I reply. "Oh, and all of the lions at Uganda's State Zoo, during its annual Pride Festival. Afternoon, Del," I say.

"Afternoon, Curly," he replies. "You mention insuring Charlie the Cheetah. Did I ever tell you the story that my friend Azibo told me? She's a primary school teacher in Brixton who said to her class, 'I've two words. The first is cheetah and the second is dandelion. Can anybody use these in a single sentence?' One student, Thabo raised his hand and said, 'The cheetah is faster dandelion.'"

Thursday 2 September 1999
The Nottingham Post was first published in 1878

Lovely coverage today in my favourite paper of record, the *Portsmouth Handy Shandy*. The headline *Penis insurance with knobs on!* draws readers into a report suggesting that NOB is now insuring each member of the Huw Jardons for £2 million against impotence in the event that they get the 'dreaded dangly' and things go limp.

I'm back in the broom cupboard at 3pm Noah, a junior reporter from the *Nottingham Glittering Generality*, rings to ask whether NOB has sold a penis insurance policy to anyone in Nottingham. Only two, I reply: one to the mayor and one to the chief constable.

This evening, Dave drives me to an evening seminar for accountants and their clients at the headquarters of the Royal Bank of Staffordshire. Over the course of the first hour of the event, I discover there really is a trade even more dull than insurance. Finally, the presentation entitled Self-Assessment Tax Returns: An Opportunity for Banks comes to an end and there's a 30-minute break.

I'm the first in line at the refreshment table. I turn and wave to an imaginary group of delegates across the room and call out, "You all want red?" before shamelessly loading a tray with six glasses of wine that I take back to my seat to neck while flicking through my notes and chatting with a few of the others around the table about the mind-numbingly dull subject matter of the evening so far.

A few minutes later, I return to the refreshments table to swipe, greedily and unchallenged, the last four glasses of wine, then once again I take my seat, ready to take on the bankers.

The next speaker at the podium begins by telling delegates that not only do banks offer fantastic PPI policies, but that in future they'll be able to assist clients with the planned new self-assessment tax-filing.

I've had enough. I leap from my chair and shout, "That's f*cking ridiculous! What do *you* lot know about tax-filing? Next, you'll be selling pissing fish and chips! Thanks for the wine!"

In rapid succession, I slug down the contents of the remaining glasses in front of me, before announcing, "We're leaving!" to no one in particular.

A puzzled Dave joins me as I abandon a stunned audience and an even more stunned speaker and we head back to his car, where I promptly fall asleep.

Monday 6 September 1999
Private Eye was first published in 1961

I'm driving North today to meet Guy, the personal finance editor of the *Sunderland Snatch*. I set off at 4:55am and turn on the radio. Five minutes later, it brings news of the sudden death of Kensington & Chelsea MP Alan Clark.

I pull into a petrol station on the A1, buy a pasty and a tank of petrol and set off straight back to London. Hands-free, I ring Guy to cancel my meeting. A couple of minutes later I ring Hugo, a UK-based freelancer for the *Kensington Misleading Analogy*, who's a sucker for a bit of bullshit.

"Hi, Curly! How are you?" he asks.

I reply, "Great, now that I've heard the news about Alan Clark!"

"What do you mean?"

"There's going to be a by-election and I'm going to stand as a candidate," I lie.

"Okay..."

"I'm going to run on an insurance ticket," I say, making up the story as I speak. "Sensible policies for a happier Britain."

As I finish the call, I decide that the time has come to try to achieve the impossible with an attempt to spoof *Public Eye*. Nearly every newspaper, TV station and radio channel in the world has fallen for NOB's spoofs, but there remains that one jewel in the crown.

Tuesday 7 September 1999
De Telegraaf was first published in 1893

I wake up still fixated with that trophy of trophies. It can't be done frivolously. *Public Eye* will be aware that the only reliable fact underpinning the coverage NOB receives is my insatiable appetite for backlinks. They'll certainly be doing their job and looking out to trip me up.

Tracey passes me a fax from Anneke, the personal finance editor of the *Rotterdam Moon Cricket*, asking me if I could write an article on PPI.

NOB doesn't provide PPI to anyone outside the UK, but Anneke's promised a backlink, so it's worth doing. I call Doug to ask if he'd be interested in writing the article for me in return for £50.

Of course he would. "I'll feature Hans Brinker in it," he says.

"Who the f*ck's Hans Brinker?"

"He was the little Dutch boy who put his finger in the dyke," he explains. He promises to send the copy before lunch.

Doug's article is in my email box by the time I return from lunch. I send it to Anneke, before heading down the corridor to make myself an Irish coffee. By the time I'm back at my desk, she's left me a message saying how unimpressed she is with my offensive use of the word 'dyke'.

I ring her directly to apologise, but she remains obstinately unimpressed. Obviously a dike.

Monday 13 September 1999
Hearst Metrotone News was founded in 1914

Chatting last week with Adam, a reporter from the *Cromer Crabs*, I mentioned my not-so-new number plate. He faxes over the published story today, which reports that my 12 NOB numberplate stops traffic. Described as a 39-year-old joker, I'm quoted telling the paper that I just love the reaction that it gets from other motorists: "Women drive past shouting, 'You wish!' – but I jokingly shout back, 'So do you!'"

The power of the press. You can't beat it.

It's approaching lunchtime, so it's time to go in for the kill. I phone *Public Eye* and speak to the receptionist. I explain the nature of my call before she puts me straight through to the editorial desk.

An hour later, lugging with me NOB's huge press-cuttings file, I take a Tube into London to meet Doug at Oxford Circus, from where we walk to *Public Eye*'s nearby offices.

Reporter Claire introduces herself in the reception on the ground floor, before leading us into a small, cluttered office. I cut to the chase and explain to her why, when her paper had so carefully and completely avoided printing the spoofs that NOB would put out to the press, on this occasion we could be trusted. I tell her that I am standing as a candidate in the Kensington & Chelsea by-election as a representative of the Sensible Insurance Policies party.

Thursday 16 September 1999
Tyne Tees Television was founded in 1959

Big day. *Public Eye* is due out today.

I meet Doug at Bank station. We head straight to the newsagent to buy the paper and bingo! The story's there, outlining what NOB has been up to, singling out a few papers that have fallen for my spoofs and implying that there's a deficit in the media when it comes to checking facts. It then goes on to reveal my spoof claim that I'm standing for election in the hope that sensible insurance policies will make for a happier Britain.

Result! I've spoofed *Public Eye*!

It's nice to see my spoof political career is also being given prominence in the *Westminster Tomfoolery* today. I've acquired household name status, too: the story mentions the name Curly Cradock but, assuming the reader will know who I am, it doesn't even bother to mention NOB. The article reveals that, following the publication of the *Public Eye* story, my party has deselected me. A similar story is featured in the *Worcester Tosspot*, which concludes by quoting me saying that I now have no choice but to wait for the next election.

It's taken a while, but the Huw Jardons' penis insurance is at last the focus of a comment piece in the *Cleethorpes Bottom-Feeder*. Headlined *Maestro Man!* and conveying a "View of Britain from the passenger's seat," the paper's website today reports that male strippers are insuring their knobs for £2 million each, in case an audience member decides to steal a souvenir during one of their shows.

I'm also quoted abroad in the *Montreal Maiden Aunt*, telling the reporter that I don't blame the men for insuring their willies, adding modestly that I was going to insure my own once, but was unable to find an insurance policy big enough to accommodate my 12 NOB.

I've a growing cluster of clients in Yorkshire whose people clearly recognise a good financial deal when they see one. The most lucrative of these clients is Seymour. I take a call from him this morning, during which I promise to visit. Hanging up, I say, "I've got to go to f*cking Rotherham."

Tracey looks up from her copy of the *Holloway Trouser Trumpet* and asks, "Isn't that the town where paedophiles outnumber Nobel Prize winners by 10,000 to one?"

"No, don't be silly!" I reply. "Rotherham has never produced a Nobel Prize winner." As I pour whisky into my coffee, I thoughtfully add, "I think you may be confusing Rotherham with Bingley. There, local physicist, Fred Hoyle, *should* have been awarded a Nobel prize, but it was wrongly given to his boss instead."

Thursday 23 September 1999
Yorkshire Television was founded in 1968

I'm heading to Yorkshire today to meet Seymour and to drop off a bottle of Scotch to each of the journalists in the county who have kindly provided NOB with backlinks. I set out at dawn for Staffordshire to collect Genghis on the way north. He still loves to go on these trips, and it gives a break for our parents, who're both in their sixties.

After a late morning meeting with Sasha, a freelancer for the *Halifax Procrasturbation*, we stop for a lunch of tea and teacakes. I must say that in Yorkshire there seems to be no shortage of fantastic establishments in which to fortify yourself.

As we drive out of town, in slow traffic, I notice a large sign, standing out amid a line of derelict stores. It reads, P Sutcliffe – Quality Butcher. The owner must have enlisted the same branding agency to choose his business name as the one used by the Golden Shower takeaway, Touching Cloth the dry cleaners, Hand Jobs the nail bar and, of course, the wanker who thought that 'primate' would be a good name for the head of an African church.

Monday 27 September 1999
Bloomberg News was founded in 1990

I ask Tracey if she thinks Natalie would be up for earning £50, posing as a fake SPOOKSAFE claimant. I've heard she's been looking for a way to avoid her creditors. Announcing her death by poltergeist attack is as good a way as any.

Tracey picks up the phone, dials and then speaks for a few moments, before hanging up again. She looks across at me and says, "It just so happens that on the 12th of October, Natalie will be posing outside the Bank of England to promote the www.titsandfannies.com website. She says she'll be happy to meet you to discuss your proposal straight after that."

Pleased at this news, I leave the broom cupboard for a leisurely lunch at the Gay Hussar in Soho with Morgan, a freelance journalist who writes for the *Fenny Drayton Fiend*, the *Leicester Wife-Beater* and the *Lutterworth Pompom*. I tell him about Natalie's forthcoming strip outside the Bank of England.

Friday 1 October 1999
The Salt Lake Tribune was first published in 1870

Morgan has come up trumps! All three of his papers report that Natalie, whose breasts are insured by NOB for £10 million, will soon appear stark naked at the main entrance to the Bank of England to promote a porn website. The report goes on to quote a spokesman for City of London police, saying she'll be arrested immediately.

Tracey arrives at the broom cupboard looking distinctly unhappy.

"What's the matter?" I ask.

"It's Del," she says. "He applied for a job at the Big Bristols Channel presenting the Great British Printing Press."

"Good idea. He deserves to get the job," I say. "So, what's up?"

"He was the best qualified by far," says Tracey, almost in tears, "but he was told that they've given the job to a ginger bloke called Angus, who has no formal printing qualifications and very little experience in the print industry, just because he played President Mandela as Number Six in the channel's Robben Island remake of The Prisoner."

"A ginger actor playing President Mandela is grotesque!" I reply, outraged. "It's the worst example of racebending that I've ever heard of."

"I completely agree," says Tracey. "Their casting decisions are totally biased, but at least they'll never dare to employ a ginger actress to play Snow White!"

Monday 4 October 1999
The Birmingham Mail was first published in 1870

I'm about to head out when Birmingham's favourite son, Freddie the Fox, appears at the broom cupboard door.

"Freddie! How nice to see you!" I say. Tracey gets straight to her feet to fetch refreshments for our visitor.

Downcast, Freddie doesn't hang about with niceties and gets straight to the point.

"I'm very sorry, but I may need to make an unemployment claim," he says. "I'm not as popular as I used to be and I'm not getting any work."

"Freddie, you're a national icon!" I tell him. "You put the great into Great Britain!"

"Tell the viewers that," he sullenly replies.

"F*ck PPI!" I say. "We simply need to do something to make you great again."

"What about insuring his tail for £1 million?" Tracey suggests, as she places a bowl of water and three whiskies on the table.

"Brum Brum!" says Freddie.

Brilliant. I tell her, "You write the press release while I call Why-Aye Pet Insurance in Newcastle. We'll soon get Freddie's tail covered. And Freddie – get some elocution lessons. Did you see the report in the *West Midlands Purple Pearler*? It says that regional accents can have a detrimental impact on people's employment prospects. Particularly the Brummie accent, which it says is considered to be the worst in the UK."

"Instead of Brum Brum! how about Boom Boom!" Freddie suggests, and in less than an hour, foxtastic gentleman and national superstar Freddie the Fox is insured and the FREDDIESAFE press release is ready to go to Jeremy.

"Actually, I'm not sure about Boom Boom," I say. "How about Bang Bang? I don't think a fox would ever say Boom Boom."

"Bang Bang!" says Freddie.

Wednesday 6 October 1999
The Daily Express published the first newspaper 'And Finally' news story in 1951

Freddie the Fox is front-page news for the first time in fifteen years. His story's been taken up by 35 regional UK newspapers including the *Grimsby Plonker*, the *Sandwell Tpyo*, the *Blackburn Copy Taster*, the *Luton Shelved*, the *Arun Marmalade Dropper*, the *Biddulph Dispatch*, the *East Kilbride Shoddy Journalist*, the *Dunfermline Come-on* and the *Isle of Wight Yarn*.

And still they come! In Warrington, *The Humdinger* runs with a headline decreeing Freddie the Fox to have *A rear that's dear!* Oh dear.

I open the live feed from the cuttings agency. Today's *Mickey Bliss' And Finally* piece reveals Freddie the Fox's tail has the same sum insured as only one of Jake the Peg's three legs and both of Stephen Hawking's. Meanwhile in Moscow, the *Morning Mumbas* runs a light-hearted piece reporting that, although the story about Freddie insuring his tail may be thought to be a furry tail (Bang Bang!), it's actually true.

The *Rhythm Stick* has a somewhat more cynical take, cleverly observing that the fox's tail is now insured for rather more than the few quid it originally cost to produce him. Atticus, the news editor of respected theatre magazine *Dancing Queen* goes further, suggesting that the insurance policy is just a vehicle to help promote Freddie's career. Perish the thought!

Evening drinks loom next week with Ruby, a reporter on the *Huddersfield Hefty Clefty*, who's invited me to her hometown to meet her editorial team. It's a long way to go for a backlink, but a gallon of Webster's Yorkshire Bitter will make the journey worthwhile.

Just as I finalise the details and hang up, Tracey says, "A client asked me the other day why NOB only has one insurance premium rate. Why is that?"

"Because I never like to put anyone into a category, nor do I like to label anyone," I explain. "We're all equal."

"Aren't there any exceptions?" she asks. "NOB insures some really unusual people and I'm surprised that they're all treated the same."

"That's the very nature of NOB's business!" I reply. "Everyone is indeed treated the same. Even retards!" I pause. "Can you remember that stupid f*cker from Braintree who was 'shocked' when she found out her toaster wasn't waterproof?"

"That was me!" Tracey exclaims.

"Was it? Sorry!"

Monday 11 October 1999
The Essex Chronicle was first published in 1764

After a skinful at the Black Maria, Tracey's new local, I was far too pissed to drive home. I wake up at 6am feeling absolutely dreadful. Tracey brews a jug of Nescafé, pours me a mug and then produces a carton of milk from her handbag.

"That's the last of the coffee," she says.

While I check my phone for messages, she casually pours the milk rather than the usual whisky into my mug. As she does so, I glance across and notice a yellowing chunk of whey drop like a landmine into the coffee before, in slow motion, rising to the top again, dispersing off-white fragments over the dark surface of the drink.

"It shouldn't be off," she shrugs. "I only bought it on Thursday."

Tracey and I make ourselves presentable before setting off to meet Martin, the business editor of the *Basildon Shitwreak*. Chav Town, as it's known locally, has the highest rate of teenage pregnancy in the UK, along with the highest rate of STD. I do hope that the backlink they give NOB comes without any other type of virus.

After the meeting, the car remarkably not having been stolen, we drive on to Finchingfield for lunch at Violet's, the newly renamed pub, with Dwayne, a freelance reporter who writes for several titles across East Anglia, including the *Chelmsford Chuckspreader*.

With the assurance of several backlinks, we say goodbye to Dwayne, before proceeding to get tired and emotional, raising numerous toasts to Rod and to Violet.

"Rod once told me the last time he was here, Emu pecked Violet to death," says Tracey. "He said Emu couldn't stand Violet getting all the good press."

I hope Ron doesn't find out.

"IT SHOULDN'T BE OFF. I ONLY BOUGHT IT ON THURSDAY"

Tuesday 12 October 1999
The Moskovskiye Vedomosti published the first newspaper obituary in 1757

I make my way to the Bank of England to meet Natalie after her photoshoot where, I'm delighted to see, she wasn't arrested. When I finally manage to assure her that she won't actually need to be killed by a ghost, she agrees to become NOB's fake SPOOKSAFE claimant. I offer her a quick drink to seal the deal and we head to the Grapes.

As we turn to make our way to the pub, Sir Eddie, the Bank of England governor, steps out onto Threadneedle Street to approach a waiting limo. I wave to him and shout, "Not many of those to a pound!"

Sir Eddie looks across at me, screws up his eyes for a moment and shouts, "Piss off Curly!" before being driven away at speed.

When I eventually return to the broom cupboard, I write a quick press release to advise Jeremy that NOB has paid £100,000 to the family of a young lady killed by a poltergeist. I remember to embargo it until just before Hallowe'en, to give it maximum impact.

NOT MANY OF THOSE TO A £1

Friday 15 October 1999
The London Evening Standard was first published in 1827

Following a transatlantic call to Sambo, who sounds as though he's enjoying his new job, I clear my desk of urgent work before inviting Tracey, Araminta and Ralph for drinks in the Elephant. I tell them I want to brainstorm a new idea for another corporate video.

"I'm completely open to all suggestions, but the subject matter must be provocative," I tell them as we sit down in the pub.

Ralph ventures, "What about discrimination against call-centre workers from Darlington?"

"That's an excellent suggestion," I say. "It's definitely 'discrim up-north', although those Darlington employers do have a valid point."

"You could try a different tack," Araminta says. "Live Aid was staged fourteen years ago. You could tie your video into the suffering of Africans. Do you know that today across Africa there are estimated to be over ten million men, women and children living in slavery? That's nearly as many as were captured for transportation across the Atlantic."

"GOTCHA!" I say. "You're an absolute genius, Araminta. NOB will produce a video about black African slave-owners who are keeping their slaves in debasement."

"Are there really black African slave-owners today?" asks Tracey.

"Of course, there are!" I reply. "There are tens of thousands of them, yet most black people today can't be bothered to do anything at all to stop modern African enslavement."

"That's because they're too busy seeking compensation for indigenous Americans," says Ralph. "Anyway, what about filming Kofi Annan, secretary-general of the United Nations?"

"Kofi Annan it is!" I reply. "And perhaps we can also invite Archbishop Tutu."

I buy another round, before popping back to the broom cupboard to check Google and to find the archbishop's number. Google is fantastic! I manage to get straight through to His Grace.

Back in the pub, Ralph asks, "What did he say?"

"He said, 'Piss off Curly!'" I reply. "Only joking. His Grace told me that he was unfortunately not available at such short notice, as he's currently on a worldwide tour to promote Black Beauties, his new biography of Anna Sewell's Aunt Jemima."

"What about a tea monkey instead?" Tracey suggests.

"Brilliant!" I exclaim. "We'll have a tea monkey in the anthropomorphic role of a primate asking Kofi Annan if black lives matter more than compensation."

Araminta's beginning to have second thoughts. "I really don't think that raising the subject of black African slave ownership is a good idea," she says. "It'll be deeply upsetting to many black slave-owners."

"Thanks Araminta," I say. "But as far as I'm concerned, black people should not be kept in debasement in any civilised society. Besides, a video such as this will generate *loads* of backlinks."

"Ok," she says, "but I think you may have a problem. Do you really think that Kofi Annan would be willing to be interviewed by a tea monkey?"

"Mr Annan might not notice the difference between a primate and an archbishop," I say. "But you're probably right! Tracey, please ring David Bellamy and arrange for two tea monkeys. If we've two primates, we might get a slot on Praise the Lord, particularly if Mr Shifter brings his piano.

Saturday 16 October 1999
The Houston Chronicle was first published in 1901

Off to collect Genghis to look after him as our parents are going away for the weekend. As we drive back to London, my brother reels off the names of the winners in the 1996 Olympics. He's really looking forward to next year as I've promised to take him to Sydney as a special treat to celebrate his 18th birthday.

"The Paralympics should be great fun too," I tell him.

"The *what*?" he says.

"The Olympic Games for the disabled," I reply.

"But *why*?" he exclaims. "I don't understand."

"Well, the Olympics are about the promotion and recognition of super humanism."

"I know! But watching mongs like me isn't a spec..."

He battles to articulate the term 'spectator sport. It's probably his new medication, so I help him out.

"Yeah. Grow tess," he says, bouncing angrily in his car seat. Then he closes his eyes and, as he falls asleep, I wonder what else they might come up with. Pole-vaulting for the morbidly obese, high-jumping for dwarfs, or perhaps even one-legged arse-kicking.

Sunday 17 October 1999
The Sunday Mirror was first published in 1915

This morning, Genghis asks if we can watch a film, so I push him in his wheelchair down the road to the local video library. There he points out that the films advertised on sale are cheaper to buy outright than those advertised for rent. I promptly head to the shelves in question at the back of the store to see if there are any worth watching. It normally takes ages for us to choose a film, but in a matter of seconds I notice, sandwiched between a Barbara Woodhouse dog-training VHS and an X-rated Danish Blue, is a rare Betamax video of highlights of the 1996 Atlanta Summer Paralympics. At only two quid, it's a bargain! I pay for it and push the wheelchair back to the house, to watch the Paralympics with Genghis.

To begin with, it looks as though the video is knackered. I take it out again and give it a good shake and bash it against the palm of my other hand before replacing it back in the machine. This does the trick. Genghis looks puzzled as he watches.

Soon the commentator goes barmy with excitement as a race is lost by a pallid-looking competitor. Genghis roars with laughter, singing, "Med-ication's what you need!"

Funny, but also prescient of him, for a moment later, in the excitement, he suddenly locks into a seizure. Immediately I place cushions around his head as he stares blankly into space, before I fetch and administer a dose of his anti-epilepsy medicine. The poor kid.

I switch the TV back off and after a few minutes Genghis has more or less recovered from his fit. I pack his luggage and wheelchair in the car and we eventually set off somewhat later than I'd planned.

Monday 18 October 1999
L'Osservatore Romano was first published in 1861

As I'm about to pop over to the Grapes for a glass or two for lunch, I take a call on my mobile from a very irate Pope, who's ordered me to withdraw VIRGINSAFE. "I can't just withdraw it at the last minute," I plead, but his Holiness is insistent. I reluctantly agree to his request and I email a press release to Jeremy with a spoof comment from Stella Virgin of the Scottish Nuns Alliance, who allegedly told me that no one should be forced to withdraw anything at the last moment.

Thursday 21 October 1999
The Windsor and Eton Express was first published in 1812

Odd morning. I'm reading the *Milton Keynes Hipocrocapig*, where I see that the finalists in the 1999 UK Child-Sex Tourism Awards have been announced. Every one of the sex tourist boards from Leeds Bradford, Oldham, Rochdale, Rotherham, Cleveland and Telford are hoping to win this highly prestigious award.

I mention this to Tracey, along with the fact that Romancing the Bone Capital Partners is the lead sponsor, who's promising to provide an all-expenses-paid weekend in Windsor to the lucky winner.

"Why would any promoter of sex tourism want to go to Windsor?" asks Tracey.

I shrug. "It's beyond me," I reply. "I've absolutely *no* idea."

Meanwhile the Big Bristols news website is the first to bring to public attention the VIRGINSAFE withdrawal story with the headline: *Sisters lose Second Coming Cover!* It reports that complaints have led insurers to withdraw the cover issued to a couple of dozen nuns in the event they're impregnated by the Messiah.

The story quotes me saying, "His Holiness the Pope was insistent that the cover was withdrawn and the women concerned have been informed."

Monday 25 October 1999

The Essex County Standard was first published in 1831

We've invited Ralph to the broom cupboard to help with a brainstorming session on NOB's new life insurance initiative, which is to provide decent life cover at reasonable prices, without invasive medical or family history questions.

"It needs to be a policy that appeals to all," I say to the cramped room.

"What about LIFESAFE?" Ralph suggests.

I tell him that while that sounds okay, I think we need something a little catchier – a name that reflects the low premiums.

"How about LOWLIFE?" Tracey suggests.

"F*cking perfect!" I say.

"We could launch it with a press conference in Chelmsford," she says. "It's the birthplace of radio and the home of Toad of Toad Hall."

Ralph muses, "LOWLIFE is a good suggestion, but do you really want to hold a press conference at the home of Toad of Toad Hall? Have you seen toad spawn? There'll be hundreds of the ugly f*ckers."

"What about Felsted?" asks Tracey. "That's nearby both Chelmsford and Braintree," she says, suddenly showing herself to be something of an expert on Essex geography.

"There's a famous school there where Oliver Cromwell sent his children," says Ralph.

"Wasn't he the tw*t that abolished Christmas?" asks Tracey.

"Indeed he was," I reply. "My parents were Jehovah's Witnesses and Christmas in our house was more like Hungary than f*cking Turkey. But yes, Felsted sounds good."

"Great," says Ralph. "I'll ring my friend, Charles, to see if he'll let us use the theatre."

He gets on the phone for a couple of minutes, hangs up and says, "All sorted!"

"Thanks," I say. "All we need now is a celebrity to front it."

As she fills her glass, Tracey pipes up, "What about Sinead Goody?"

"Who?" I ask.

"She's someone that I know who lives locally. She's not all that famous at the moment, but she's always saying she will be one day," Tracey replies, before taking a swig of wine.

I like her suggestion. If nothing else, she'll be a cheap hire. I take her number and call the young woman to invite her along.

"Good afternoon, Sinead," I say. "My name is Curly Cradock. A colleague of mine, Tracey, has given me your number. What I am ringing for is to propose a little PR work for you." Sinead doesn't respond, so I continue, explaining to her about LOWLIFE.

"Who the f*ck are you calling lowlife?" she snaps.

"Don't get out of your pram," I say.

"Are you calling me a paedo?" snaps Sinead.

"No, Sinead, I'm not calling you a paedo," I say in despair, "but I do have a quick question. What do you call a chav in a box?" I pause for a second. "Innit!" I say.

CLICK-CLICK-BRRRRRR.

The trials and tribulations of life insurance are all too much. NOB will stick exclusively with PPI, so we make our way to the Grapes for a very well-earned drink.

Wednesday 27 October 1999
Radiodiffusion-Télévision Ivoirienne (RTI) was founded in 1962

I'm in the broom cupboard on my own and as I put down the phone Ralph arrives.

"Sorry to interrupt you," he says.

"Don't worry," I say. "It was only Tracey. She's used up all her sick leave, so she's called in dead."

"It's Halloween on Sunday, so I suppose that's a very witty excuse for not coming into work," Ralph says.

"It certainly is," I say. "Anyway, I shouldn't complain. Tracey's been fantastic over the past three years and I really don't know what I'd have done without her."

Thursday 28 October 1999
Fortean Times was first published in 1973

Tracey's made it into work this morning and tells me she's missing Del, whom she hasn't seen for the past week. "He's really busy at work," she says. "His biggest client, Uncle Bruce's Porridge Oats, have decided to remove Uncle Bruce's picture from all their packaging."

"Really?" I say. "That's bizarre. Why?"

"They've been wanting to get rid of him for years," she says. "They believe that they'll sell more porridge without a ginger on the packaging, so they've just removed him."

"That's preposterous!" I say. "The legendary Uncle Bruce is a positive ginger icon who deserves much better."

"Well, Del says they told him that they want to make their brand more inclusive," she says.

"How does getting rid of Uncle Bruce make their brand more inclusive?" I ask her in disbelief. "If you ask me, they're cynically doing the opposite of what they're purporting to do, simply to manipulate the opinion of f*ckwits."

"Poor Uncle Bruce," says Tracey.

I start to read the latest cuttings and see a report written by Freya, a journalist on the *Nicosia Salad Dodger*. It says that NOB paid out £100,000 to a policyholder from Braintree who was killed by a ghost. Freya has also provided NOB with an ever-welcome backlink.

I say to Tracey, "This reminds me of my Auntie Phyllis who once promised to pay a poltergeist £10,000 to leave her home forever. But when she didn't pay up, it repossessed her house."

Saturday 30 October 1999
What the Papers Say was first broadcast in 1956

Saturday drinks with Leon. We start talking about ethical – and unethical – insurance policies and, somehow, we get onto the subject of Mary Whitehouse.

"I like her," Leon says assertively. "It's *amazing* how she can train those dogs."

"I think you're thinking of Barbara Woodhouse," I venture. "Mary Whitehouse was the woman who founded the National Viewers' and Listeners' Association."

"Like the DVLA only with an N!" he exclaims.

"If you like," I reply. "She used it as a platform to criticise the Big Bristols Channel for what she perceived as a lack of accountability and excessive use of bad language and portrayals of sex and violence in its programmes."

"Well, I like *her* too," says Leon.

I get up to buy a round. As I return, Leon says, "I foresee that in just a few decades from now, the Government will introduce legislation making it a hate-crime to say hurtful things about paedophiles."

"Bollocks!" I retort. "I dread to think what Mary Whitehouse would say about that."

"She'd be horrified!" says Leon. "Having said that, Jim'll Risk It was her favourite programme and in 1977, she gave Jimmy f*cking Savile an award to celebrate his wholesome family entertainment."

"I'd forgotten about that," I say with a shudder. "How different things look in hindsight!"

Sunday 31 October 1999
The Wigan Post was first published in 1950

I'm spending Halloween this year in Wigan, the scariest place I know. I'm here for a meeting with Vinny, a reporter from the *Wigan Kill Fee*.

As we finish our chat, Vinny points out of the window to my right and warns me, "Never walk past those high-rise flats alone at night."

He has a point. Wigan is a truly scary place, although it does have one redeeming feature: transvestites residing in the town can at least benefit from a Wigan address.

In my hotel room, I'm reading the latest cuttings. Yesterday's *Harrowgate Misprint* hardly disguises its disbelief in today's edition, suggesting that readers who hear things that go bump in the night should get in touch with NOB, which offers SPOOKSAFE insurance, a policy that promises pay-outs of up to £100,000 to customers who suffer at the hands of poltergeists, ghosts or phantoms.

Meanwhile I'm at last starting to make some decent money. NOB has also triggered a shakeup of the PPI market, now that the media have finally begun to grasp the magnitude of the PPI mis-selling scandal. At this rate, the Financial Regulation & Compliance Executive may even put a stop to banks selling worthless PPI insurance to vulnerable British consumers.

Watch this space!

THE NATIONAL MEDIA ARE AWAKENING
TO THE RACKET OF BANKS' PPI
MIS-SELLING

Monday 1 November 1999
Associated Television was founded in 1955

Over a quick pint after work with Ralph, I mention my conversation with Leon on Saturday and this gets us onto the subject of public information films.

"The Central Office of Information issued the first one in 1945," says Ralph. "But probably the most famous one is the Clunk Click Every Trip film that Jimmy f*cking Savile made in 1971."

"Savile's obviously a complete c*nt, but he's also an enigma," I reply. "That film must have saved the lives of a great many people."

"I agree," says Ralph. "He's certainly a charlatan, but he must be very clever."

"Well, he's a member of Mensa," I say. "In 1970 and 1975 he was interviewed on Your Life Will Soon Be Over, first by Pol Pot and then by Kim Il-Sung. In 1990, he was knighted by the Duke of York (only joking Your Grace) and was given a Papal knighthood by Pope John Paul II."

Ralph looks increasingly shocked. To change the subject from Savile, I ask him, "Have you heard about the Piltdown man?

"No, please tell me," he says.

"In 1912, there was a paleoanthropological spoof, in which bone fragments from primates were presented as fossilised remains of an early human, belonging to a group of prehistoric people called meanderthals, who wandered wherever they liked. The theory was only disproved in 1953."

"Cool! Did the Piltdown man appear on Your life Will Soon Be Over?" asks Ralph.

"He most certainly did," I lie.

Tuesday 2 November 1999
The Belfast Telegraph was first published in 1870

Out for a beer tonight with Araminta. "We're completely f*cked," I tell her as I bring over the first round. "We're living in a society where political and public figures are failing to curb racist hate speech and xenophobic rhetoric. They should bring back hanging!"

Araminta nods her head. "A number of my ancestors were lynched in Mississippi, but my Great-Uncle Benjamin was luckier than the rest," she says. "On the day he was due to be executed, they ran out of rope. He later wrote in his diary, 'No noose is good news.'"

"Very funny," I say. "But seriously, I'm also becoming increasingly concerned about racism within the ranks of the police."

"Well, racism is encouraged at government level," she replies. "The Home Office allows interest groups such as the National Ginger Police Association to proliferate, despite the fact that their sole purpose is to enhance the quality of service to ginger communities of the UK. I completely disapprove!"

"Yes, that's despicable," I say. "But at least knife crime has been eradicated. I can't remember the last time I read of a ginger citizen having been murdered by a machete-wielding child."

"Well, indeed," she replies. "But didn't Leon mention to you that it'll take another quarter of a century for the United Nations Committee for the Elimination of Racial Discrimination to recommend decisive action to eliminate racial discrimination within UK policing?"

"What do you expect?" I ask. "They're all lazy gypsy b*stards!"

"Not all gypsies are b*stards," says Araminta.

"Apologies, you're quite right," I say. "In 1975, the British Gypsy Council only made Jimmy f*cking Savile a life member because he owned a motorhome. Also, when I bought some clothes pegs from a kindly gypsy lady called Malina, she said I'd mistakenly given her too much money and then she invited me back to hers for a good time."

"Really?" asks Araminta astonished.

"Yes, really," I reply. "I went on the dodgems, the waltzers and the ghost train and I even went home with a goldfish!"

Sunday 7 November 1999
The Oxford Gazette became Britain's first newspaper in 1665

Sundays can sometimes be a drag. I call Ralph to invite him for a drink. Walking into the Toblerone Tunnel in Blackwall, I tell him, "It's 30 years since Led Zeppelin released Whole Lotta Love!"

"Really?" he replies, looking surprised. "I can't believe it."

I buy a round. On returning with the drinks, I tell Ralph that Led Zeppelin never appeared on Pick of the Pops, even though that particular song was used as the theme for many years.

"That reminds me of you," he says. "You spoofed Guinness World Records into giving you a World Record, but you'll never get one for conducting the world's biggest-ever spoof."

I smile and reply, "'That's Rock and Roll'!"

"Changing the subject," I say, "I genuinely believe that the media urgently requires a cognitive recalibration."

"That's not going to happen until they put a stop to cynical and manipulative charlatans influencing and controlling the credulous," he says.

"Well, I'm sorry," I say, "but NOB needs those backlinks."

I stand up to buy another round.

Wednesday 10 November 1999
The Northern Echo was first published in 1870

I'm courageously out for drinks with Araminta this evening.

"How do you know when a girl from Braintree is having an orgasm?" I ask her.

"I've no idea," she replies.

"She drops her corta panda!"

"What's a corta panda?" she asks, frowning.

"A large hamburger," I reply.

Araminta looks at me with a look of dramatic sympathy. "You're always telling crap jokes and taking the piss, but there seems to be an inner sadness about you that I can't put my finger on," she says.

"Well, I was conceived in the sanitary capital of England, so taking the piss is obligatory," I say. "And yes, I do tell jokes, but I think it may be a defence mechanism. I think I've mentioned to you before that I was anally raped as a child. What I didn't tell you is that it happened when I was only eight years old."

"Really? That's outrageous. You must be very angry."

"I'm beyond angry!" I exclaim. "The rapist in question was a priest at my local Catholic Church who gave every impression of being a decent, virtuous person whom you'd love to have as your friend and neighbour."

"Did you ever tell your parents or the police?" asks Araminta, looking aghast.

"No! I thought it was my fault and that I was to blame."

"Well, of course you weren't to blame!" she says.

"For years, I suffered panic attacks and felt worthless. I also self-harmed myself in ways that I really don't wish to go into," I tell her.

"My God!" she exclaims. "Have you seen a counsellor?"

"No," I reply. "I've never wanted to be labelled as a victim."

"You're probably suffering from post-traumatic stress disorder," says Araminta. "Counselling will help you to cope. What happen to the person who raped you?"

"Nothing, but about fifteen years later he was killed in a hit-and-run car accident. Thankfully, the driver was never caught and was able to get the car discreetly scrapped."

"That's probably divine justice," she says.

"It was certainly justice, but I'm not sure about the divine bit. Now tell me," I say, "What's the difference between Curly Cradock's arse and Emu?"

"I've no idea," says Araminta.

"You can only get one hand up Emu!"

She shakes her head. "That's really sick," she says.

"I know," I say. "Anyway, what do a child who's been anally raped and a chap breaking off an engagement with a girl from Braintree have in common?"

"I'm sure you're going to tell me," she says.

"Neither of them gets their ring back."

Friday 12 November 1999
The Langley Advance Times was first published in 1931

In the broom cupboard, I say to Tracey, "Araminta has suggested that I turn my diaries into a book and try to get it published. What do you think?"

"I think that that's great idea!" she replies. "But you'll need to get a well-known literary person on the front cover to recommend it."

"That's a brilliant idea," I say. "If I made up some bollocks about being the cousin of Adrian Mole aged 32½, I could send the manuscript to Constantin, the editor of the *Transylvania Literary Supplement*. I believe he's a graduate of Braintree University, so there's a good chance he'll fall for it."

"I think that most unlikely," says Tracey. "No one's going to fall for that bullshit."

"You're probably right," I concede. "Besides, when I was born, God gave me the option of choosing between the ability to finish stories or having a large penis. Obviously, I chose the latter."

"Does that mean that if you do finish your book, Vicky was right, and you do have a small one?" she asks.

"I really did prefer it when you weren't taking wise crack," I say, wounded.

"Well, it's hardly my fault that the Central Intelligence Agency are trailing cognitive enhancement drugs in Braintree," says Tracey. "Mind you, whoever it was who chose Braintree is a total wanker! The residents of Barking are much more stupid."

"They certainly are," I say. "But the CIA probably have a litter fetish."

In the Grapes for a quick pint after work, I pick up a discarded copy of the *Wembley Think Piece*, which has a news report about a super-moon that's soon to appear in the night sky. The British public is obviously going to need werewolf insurance.

Back in the broom cupboard, I swiftly compose a WOLFSAFE press release and email it to Jeremy with full details of NOB's new 'furred party' insurance policy.

Thursday 18 November 1999
The Sing Tao Daily was first published in 1938

I start the day with a scan of the latest press cuttings. Quite a few papers have picked up on WOLFSAFE. The *Muscat Eat Out* brings a smile with its headline on page seven: *Insurance that'll have you howling with laughter!*

Just as Tracey brings me my first Irish coffee of the day, I mention to her that it's nearly 25 years since the Jehovah's Witnesses stated that the first 6,000 years of human existence would come to an end.

"Did it?" asks Tracey.

"It most certainly did!" I reply. "All of their various predictions have proved to be completely accurate."

"How clever!" says Tracey.

"They most certainly are," I say. "Last year I bought a Jehovah Witness-themed advent calendar for my parents."

"Did they like it?" she asks.

"Unfortunately not," I reply. "Behind every door was someone waiting to tell them to f*ck off!"

To the Elephant for lunchtime drinks with Mike, who tells me that the Financial Regulation & Compliance Executive has branded me as an 'unhelpful maverick'.

"They say that they can't find any evidence of PPI mis-selling and that, by speaking out, you're bringing the insurance industry into disrepute," he says.

"F*ck 'em!" I reply. "It's hardly as though I'm providing Gary f*cking Glitter with travel insurance."

"True," Mike says.

"Mind you, I do know which syndicate does (only joking Lloyd's) and I suppose that providing insurance for paedophiles who travel abroad to rape children is what you get when ethics doesn't match the Confederated Insurance Inspectorate's learning outcomes."

"I agree, but even so, they'll put NOB out of business if you carry on," Mike warns me. "You're committing career suicide."

"I'm simply trying to do the right thing and put a stop to the PPI rip-off," I insist.

"Well, you're a braver man than me," he says.

When I return to the broom cupboard, Tracey observes, "We haven't heard from Mrs Mainwaring in a while. I wonder if she's okay. I'm very surprised that she hasn't called to try and buy WOLFSAFE."

"I'm sure she's okay. She's made of stern stuff," I say. "But if you don't hear from her in a couple of days, perhaps you should give her a call at the shop."

"Good idea," says Tracey, "I'll do that."

Friday 19 November 1999
Kyodo News was founded in 1945

The *Doha Sausage Grappler* today reports that as the once-in-a-lifetime super-moon approaches, Colchester housewife Krystal Methven has taken out werewolf cover with NOB, claiming she's worried that her body will become covered in hair.

In the *Tijuana Highway Robbery*, there's an article that takes up half the page with the headline *Furred party fire and theft!* together with a standfirst, which states that NOB is head and shoulders above its competitors when it comes to unusual insurance. Similar headlines are also to be found in both the *Grub Street Journo* and *The Valley of the Shadow of Death Snatchphrase*.

The phone rings just as I'm about to go to lunch. It's Mike, calling from an international insurance conference in Tokyo to tell me that Itsuki, one of his fellow speakers, showed him a story about WOLFSAFE in a Japanese daily newspaper, the name of which he can't pronounce, but which sells more than 10 million copies a day. "Itsuki and his colleagues were all talking about it," he says. "The paper's an avid follower of NOB's developments, all of which are fed to them by Yoko, one of their London correspondents."

This isn't one I'd noticed in the cuttings' files, so I promise him a pint when he gets back to the UK if he can bring me back a copy of the story.

After a few too many pints in the Grapes, I decide to call Adrian, a reporter on the *Harlow Itchy Ring*, to offer him an exclusive story. I tell him NOB's just received its first werewolf insurance claim from a middle-aged woman, Wilma Fingerdo, who lives in Harlow.

Wilma's worst nightmare came true, I told him, when she turned into a werewolf. I also add that she submitted her claim by howling down the phone.

Tuesday 23 November 1999
Guangzhou Daily was first published in 1952

Adrian's come up trumps! Both the *Harlow Itchy Ring* and its sister title the *Epping Tickle* report NOB's first £1 million werewolf claim.

I'm always impressed at the fluent crap I can come out with when I'm totally bladdered. I'm quoted explaining to Adrian that it'll take a little more than being hairy around the face to be able to make a successful claim, but obviously we'll be awaiting the results with interest. I add that it's most unlikely, but that you never know. "After all," I say, "this is Harlow we're talking about."

Wednesday 24 November 1999
United Press International was founded in 1907

I arrive late to the boom cupboard this morning to find a concerned Tracey, who says, "I called the Cat Protection shop as you suggested and spoke with Brenda, the manager. She told me that Mrs Mainwaring has not been at work for the past two weeks and she, too has become very concerned about Mrs Mainwaring's welfare. I'm going to drive to see her after work."

"You can leave now if you like," I say.

"Thanks, Curly, I will," says Tracey.

As she puts her coat on, I say, "Also, remember to let Del know if you're going to be late. He's joining us for drinks at six."

She nods and leaves and I press on with work.

At 5pm I get a call from Tracey, who sounds distressed. "The journey was a nightmare!" she says. "I called Del to let him know where I was and he told me to be careful as there were reports of a car going the wrong way on the M25. But it wasn't just one car – there were hundreds of the f*ckers!"

"Are you okay?"

"I'm fine, but I'm standing outside Mrs Mainwaring's house and there's no answer. There's also a light on in the upstairs bedroom. I'm really getting worried."

"There's nothing that you can do there now," I say. "Go straight home and I'll ring Del to tell him to meet you there. And drive safely. I'll call Croydon police station and seek their advice and let you know what they say."

I hang up and get straight on to Croydon police HQ. Bill the duty sergeant is beyond brilliant and can't have been more helpful. "We'll take a look," he says. "If we need to gain access, we'll call one of our local burglars, to avoid any damage to the property. I hope to be able to give you more information in a couple of hours."

Just over an hour later, Bill calls back and says, "I'm really sorry to have to inform you over the telephone, but we found Mrs Mainwaring dead in bed. There are no suspicious circumstances and the officers in attendance think it may have been a heart attack. She looked very peaceful."

I thank Bill and call Tracey, who's arrived safely home. Del is with her and I tell her the very sad news. She bursts in tears. I tell her not to come into work tomorrow and that I'll ring Mrs Mainwaring's colleague, Brenda, to let her know the sad news.

Friday 26 November 1999
The Economist was first published in 1843

I'm enjoying an early morning Irish coffee with Tracey and Mavis when there's an unexpected knock at the broom cupboard door. Before I get chance to greet our guest, in barges a fat, odious tw*t who, as they'd say in the Potteries, forgot to bring her manners.

"I'm from the Diversity, Equality & Inclusion Inspectorate," she storms, uninvited. "NOB is in serious breach of our regulations," she says, "You've got 14 days to become more diverse, or you're out of business!"

Rallying to my defence, Mavis says, "I'm a Jewish refugee and I came to England on the Kindertransport after my parents were executed by the Nazis."

"Irrelevant!" says the woman. "I was told by the Abbott of Hackney Abbey that Jews aren't a persecuted minority."

Tracey pipes up, "NOB has the most diverse set of mugs in the whole of the City of London. Our printer's black and our web designer's an Indian!"

"That's also totally irrelevant! I'll be back in 14 days!" she snaps, before slamming the door behind her.

"F*ck that!" I say. "I'll get some legal advice. I'll start by giving Lord Denning a call."

I manage to get through to his Lordship. After a brief conversation, I hang up.

"What did the judge say?"

"His Lordship told me to use my intelligence," I reply. "That's exactly what I'm going to do. Tracey, you can self-identify as an Aboriginal Australian Satanist who was born a woman but who's always felt that she was a food-mixer. In future, you'll be known as Ken Wood. Mavis, on Mondays, Wednesdays and Fridays you can self-identify as a toaster and will be known as Russell Hobbs. On each of the other days you can self-identify as an indigenous American Zoroastrian, who's bicurious."

"How exciting!" says Mavis. "I've always liked the name Sue."

"I think you mean Sioux," I say. "But never mind, NOB will always support your right to self-identify in any way that you want to. I myself will self-identify as a ginger, lesbian, quaker dwarf with only one leg, except at Christmas when I'll self-identify as a reindeer."

"That's ridiculous!" exclaims Mavis. "You're a six-foot four-inch, two-legged, able-bodied. blond male who doesn't have antlers and whose nose isn't red."

"It's not my fault that I'm trapped in the wrong body!" I retort. "Anyway, that should sort the f*ckers out."

Just as we're about to leave work, Tracey answers her phone. "Del says he'd like a quick word," she tells me as she passes me her mobile.

"Curly, you're a f*cking genius!" says Del. "I now self-identify as ginger myself and I've given that wanker, Rory, the sack. "Good call!" I say to Del, before handing the mobile back to Tracey.

"These f*ckers are always picking on the small guy," says Tracey, "I bet the Royal Family don't get a visit from the Diversity, Equality & Inclusion Inspectorate forcing them to become more diverse."

"Actually," I say, "according to Leon they do, but I think he was pulling my leg."

Saturday 27 November 1999
Le Figaro was first published in 1826

Saturday evening drinks with Ralph. I mention my conversation yesterday with Lord Denning. To my very great surprise, Ralph claims, "Lord Denning is England's greatest judge. He always used his considerable intellectual gifts to achieve justice."

Gobsmacked, I reply, "Are you not aware that his lordship once said, 'We must not allow this cult of homosexuality to develop in our land. We must preserve our moral and spiritual values'?"

"I am," says Ralph. "We're all entitled to express our honestly held beliefs. However, please listen. I've something very important to tell you. This morning my sister, Rona, took Felicity, my eight-year-old niece to the swimming pool. They were in the women's changing rooms when someone with a beard and a penis stripped naked in front of them and began waving his cock around. Rona immediately reported this to the swimming pool manager, who called the police."

"Quite right too!" I say.

"Yes! But then it was Rona who was arrested!" Ralph exclaims. "The wanker she reported is called Juliette Dangly-Balls who 'self-identifies' as a woman. Rona is now in very serious trouble. She was arrested at the scene, taken to her local police station and is now on bail, waiting to see if she's going to be prosecuted for a hate crime of all things!"

"F*cking unbelievable!" I cry. "Waving your cock in front of a young girl can surely never be acceptable! Well, unless you're standing outside the West London Broadcasting Wank Hut."

"We're living in a very strange world," says Ralph.

"Indeed we are," I reply. "Parminder recently came out as a trans woman and now has a boyfriend called Shane."

"Has he told his parents?" asks Ralph.

"Yes, I believe so," I say.

"How did they take it?" asks Ralph.

"They took it extremely well," I reply. "Parminder told me that they said to him that they no longer had a son and he has brought Shane to the family."

"Perhaps we should all meet up over Christmas," says Ralph. "Parminder can eat, drink and be Mary."

"Mary!" I laugh. "Ralph, you're a f*cking genius! What about if next year NOB announces that it has paid a £1 million to a trans woman who gave birth by immaculate conception? It'll be the crowning glory of NOB's media spoofing career."

"The media will certainly go absolutely crazy for the story," says Ralph. "But do you think that Parminder will play ball?"

"I don't see why not," I say, "Parminder's a lovely person, but it's a widely accepted truth that most trans people are attention-seekers with an excessive need for admiration, so he should definitely be interested. Besides, no one in the media will question the physical impossibility of a man giving birth."

"It's certainly worth a try," says Ralph. "But where'll you find a baby?"

"To quote Christopher Reeve, before he went showjumping," I say, "'that's a piece of piss!' I'll simply give Joaquin a call from the lookalike agency to arrange for a lookalike baby Christ. It'll be well worth the cost. The thousands of links that we'll get from the global media will ensure that NOB remains at the top of Google and Yahoo! forever!"

Monday 29 November 1999
NPR Morning Edition was first broadcast in 1979

Busy morning clearing my to-do list to make time for the Christmas party season. Just before noon, Araminta drops by the broom cupboard to share some good news.

"I've completed my doctorate and I've just got two job offers!" she cries. I'm so pleased for her I give her a hug, before asking what the posts are.

"The first is a junior fellowship at Cambridgeshire University," she says. "The second is at the Patent Office, as a junior examiner.

I ponder for a moment. "Cambridgeshire University is worth a punt," I say. "But personally, I'd take the one at the Patent Office. Albert Einstein worked at the one in Vienna, where he was given time off to write scientific papers." I pause to think, then add, "I also heard from Leon that in the future Cambridgeshire University is going to be offering so-called Breezy scholarships exclusively to ginger students, with the financial support of one of the biggest culprits of the PPI mis-selling scandal."

"That's institutional racism at its worst!" says Araminta. "I couldn't possibly go there. I'd be very concerned that they'd only given me a job on the basis of the colour of my skin, rather than on merit."

I quickly change the subject. "Remind me, what was the name of your thesis?"

"Will intelligent machines lead to a technological singularity?" Araminta replies.

"F*ck me!" says Tracey, suddenly opening her desk drawer. "This vibrator has ten settings. Does that make it an intelligent machine?"

"Certainly!" exclaims Araminta. Not to be outdone, she removes a sparkling 12-inch vibrator of her own from her handbag. "'A Real Bobby-dazzler' is how it's described on the box," she says.

Tracey starts to laugh uncontrollably. "I couldn't use that!" she exclaims. "It'd be like being f*cked by that tangoed tw*t from the TV!"

Araminta shrugs and drops Bobby into the wastepaper basket. I surreptitiously take it out and put it into my desk drawer before we cross the road to the Grapes to celebrate her good fortune.

When I return to the broom cupboard, I've got time to get in one last press release to announce the launch of an insurance policy that protects against a blow-out party on the big day. I quickly think of things that could prevent a great party, before returning to the broom cupboard and emailing a MILLENNIUMSAFE press release to Jeremy, with Tracey's new official name of Ken Wood.

Tuesday 30 November 1999
The Asahi Shimbun was first published in 1879

I'm proud of my ability to spin a yarn. If you overdo things during the course of the Millennium weekend, according to Latham, a personal finance reporter at the *Devil's Island Redneck*, for a mere £100 premium, NOB's policy will pay out £500 should you find yourself waking up next to a sea monster, or hospitalised by alcohol poisoning on the big night.

Yesterday, as well as spoofing Latham, I also lied to numerous employees of the Croydon Coroner's Court. This is a considerably more serious matter and one that could result in a return to Belmarsh. I told them that my name was Dickie Longfellow and that I was Mrs Mainwaring's nephew, her closest living blood relative and her next of kin.

There was no malice and I didn't wish to cause any inconvenience, but I do have a 12 NOB and simply wanted to discover both the cause of her death and the funeral arrangements.

As I suspected, it was a myocardial infarction, the medical term for a heart attack. What *did* surprise me was discovering that there was to be no funeral. Mrs Mainwaring had previously made it known that she wished to donate her body for medical research and it has already been collected by Croydon Hospital Medical School.

To the very last, the kindness and decency of this lovely lady greatly humbles me.

Wednesday 1 December 1999
The Glasgow Herald was first published in 1783

Today the *Athens Scumbag* quotes my explanation that NOB is not encouraging people to behave badly, but that we do want to make sure they've some protection if the biggest party of the millennium goes wrong for them.

The paper's Scottish cousin, the *Motherwell Tatties*, runs its own regional take on the spoof story. I explain in the report that we expect to get a disproportionately high number of Scottish people signing up to the insurance, given that Scots have a reputation as real party people.

A scan of websites shows further earnest coverage of MILLENNIUMSAFE north of the border in the *Renfrewshire Noddy*, the *Stornoway Boot Slapper* and the *Lerwick Lickalotopus*.

Thursday 2 December 1999
The Derby Telegraph was first published in 1879

Early start this morning with a drive up to the Potteries to collect Genghis for a trip to Derby, where I'm due to meet up with Albert, a senior business reporter on the *Derby Dog Catcher*. My brother's normally chatty on such outings, but this morning he falls straight to sleep in the car.

When we arrive in Derby, Genghis is still asleep and I physically have to wake him to get him out of the car. During the meeting he stays asleep in his wheelchair and he's only half-awake as I wheel him back to the car. This is a pity. I wanted to show him the lesser delights of Derby, where, to put it mildly, an alarmingly high proportion of the residents display disturbing antisocial behaviour traits. Violent crime seems to face you every way you turn in this bleak and scary city.

I lift Genghis into his car seat. He doesn't stir once all the way back to the Potteries.

Friday 3 December 1999
Radio Luxembourg was founded in 1933

This evening I'm having evening drinks with Leon at Blacks, an upmarket gentleman's club in Mayfair. His treat. He's coming to the broom cupboard at 6pm, which gives me an hour or so to finish various bits of tedious, neglected paperwork.

Punctual as ever and just as the pips are sounding, Leon arrives in a suit that looks as if it cost more than my car. We take the lift together and, as we step onto the pavement, a chauffeur-driven Rolls-Royce draws to the kerb.

"Hop in!" says Leon.

Dumbfounded, I do as he says and we make our way through heavy traffic to Mayfair.

"How did you manage to afford this?" I ask. "Did you win the Lottery?"

"I've won it for the past three Saturdays," says Leon. "And I'm going to win it tomorrow, too."

Leon clocks my expression, so by way of explanation he says, "I suspect they'll change the rules to stop psychics taking part, but journalism just isn't what it used to be. Playing the Lottery is far more lucrative and much less time-consuming."

Arriving at the club, we take a table in the drawing room and toast his good fortune with vintage Krug, before he brings up one of our previous conversations. "You mentioned a few months ago that the chief executive of the Financial Regulation & Compliance Executive told you that she could find no evidence of PPI mis-selling," he says.

"I did! Well remembered!" I exclaim. "It's a scandal of *epic* proportions."

"Yes. Well, I thought you'd be interested to know that in 2011 the total amount of compensation paid to customers who complained about the way they were sold PPI will amount to nearly £40 billion. The good news for you, however, is that NOB won't receive a single legitimate complaint and its compensation bill will be zero," says Leon.

"That doesn't surprise me in the least," I say. "I'm delighted to know the wretched banks will have their comeuppance. Compensation companies are going to have a field day."

"Um...you're right!" says Leon.

I continue, "You know, one of those f*ckers called me yesterday and asked me if I'd had an accident that wasn't my fault! I had in fact just touched socks, but rather than telling him that, I told him I'd broken my leg in three places. He sounded hugely excited and told me I could get upwards of 20 grand."

Leon looks amazed.

I nod and add, "Not bad, considering I only paid £15 for the table."

Tuesday 7 December 1999
NBC News was founded in 1940

I get to the broom cupboard early this morning to finish off urgent paperwork. After a few minutes, Mavis pops her head around the door.

"Thanks for Bobby and the flowers, Curly," she says. "How did you know that today's my birthday?"

"I just did," I reply. "Happy Birthday Mavis. Any good?"

"F*cking brilliant!" she replies, before glancing over her shoulder and whispering, "But I did chip one of my teeth!"

"Have fun," I say. "And next year, I'll arrange with Terry for you to have seamen instead of flowers."

"Cheers, Curly, that'd be lovely too!"

Ralph calls. It's the first time I've had the chance to speak to him in ages. He brings great news! "Thursday night is the bank's Christmas party at the V&A. Would you like to come as my guest? Bring a friend too if you'd like," he says, before ringing off.

Thursday 9 December 1999
The Kensington News and West London Times was first published in 1869

I'm consistently overwhelmed by the kindness and decency of Ralph. Although privileged, with a public-school background, he's always thoughtful and kind to everyone from Tracey and Del to Mavis. He's generous with drinks, he's never crass and he's comfortably self-effacing, always taking the piss both out of himself and other gay men.

Now, I can see an opportunity to help his employment prospects and I'm keen to take it. I'll invite Elizabeth as my plus-one. Having a lady who appeals to the evening's partygoers can only work to Ralph's advantage. It'll also make a nice change for Sir Eddie and his guests to have a famous celebrity in attendance.

I call Elizabeth to ask if she's free to join me this evening. As good fortune would have it, my Queen-lookalike friend plans to be in town Christmas shopping today and she says she'd be delighted to attend the event later on, as long as she can get changed in the broom cupboard beforehand.

I'm feeling pleased with myself for having had such an inspired idea. So pleased, in fact, that I feel I deserve a drink. I treat myself to a bottle of Oddballs' finest Rioja, before Elizabeth arrives and we take a cab to the V&A in South Kensington.

The first hour passes by peacefully. Everything seems to be going very well when, suddenly, my sense of ease is shaken. I clock Elizabeth deftly grabbing an open bottle of wine from behind the bar and promptly necking it. My heart sinks when I see that she doesn't even appear to care whether or not her actions have been noticed. In fact, several people standing nearby are bewildered by the sight of Her Majesty the Queen drinking straight from a bottle.

Ralph appears completely oblivious to all of this as he comes up to me to introduce me to some of his new work colleagues. However, my concern now is not with Ralph, but with Elizabeth. Her voice is slurring as I hear her speak to what looks like a senior banker. Suddenly the colour of her face starts to match that of the wine in her glass. She hiccups and her complexion changes an even deeper red as she heaves forward, showering her interlocutor in rouge-tinted, semi-masticated hors d'oeuvres.

The pong is overpowering. With my upper arm shielding my nose, I look around, alarmed, at the wider hall. Expressions of bewilderment more than awe now adorn the faces of the partygoers as Sir Eddie cautiously approaches the woman he assumes to be Her Majesty the Queen. As he nears her, she leans back and promptly projects a gallon or so of vomit on him. Removing his opaque glasses and wiping his eyes with his sleeve, the governor rushes off in the direction of the lavatory.

I courageously disappear into the night.

Friday 10 December 1999
USA Today was first published in 1982

Sir Eddie calls the bank's directors to a meeting first thing today to discuss how to address the outrageous antics of Her Royal Highness. Collectively appalled by her atrocious behaviour, they vote unanimously on three proposals. The first is to fire the employee responsible for inviting her – an easy scapegoat. The second is to close the Queen's account with the Bank. And the third is to remove her image from all future banknotes.

Ralph is summoned after lunch to the boardroom to see Sir Eddie, where he apologises profusely for the inexplicable conduct of his friend.

To no avail. He's dismissed on the spot. Sadly, he gathers his belongings from his desk in a holdall and leaves for the last time, before giving me a call to check I'm at work today and asking to drop by for a quick chat. I can guess why.

He soon knocks on the broom cupboard door and walks in nervously. Before he can speak, I tell him, "Of course your PPI policy will cover you."

Immediately he relaxes.

"And look on the bright side," I add. "At least you aren't a banker anymore."

"You're right," he says. "I'm going to set up an artists' colony, supported by my PPI claim money." He pauses, then asks, "Will there still be enough for me to live on?"

"I should think so," I reply. "Your PPI policy pays out 80% of your salary for the next two years. Also, it's tax-free so you're actually going to be better off than you were when you were still working at the bank."

Ralph beams as he fills in a claim form and, with a huge smile on his face, he joins me for a skinful in the Grapes.

"How did Rona get on with the police?" I ask after buying the first round.

"Really well, thanks for asking," he replies. "The police discovered that Juliette Dangly-Balls is a convicted paedophile, with a string of convictions for indecent exposure. Her lawyers now think that it's most unlikely that she'll receive a custodial sentence if she pleads guilty to a transphobic hate crime."

Tuesday 14 December 1999
The Wagga Wagga Daily Advertiser was first published in 1868

I've a strong sense of foreboding as I make my way to the broom cupboard this morning. I get to my desk, where I take a call from Dad. He tells me that Genghis has passed away, quietly and in his sleep.

Dad is crying, I am now crying, and, seeing this, Tracey becomes very distressed. I can hardly speak and I ask Dad if I can call him back.

"What's the matter?" asks Tracey when I hang up.

"It's Genghis," I say. "He's died."

Shocked at first and now in floods of tears, Tracey excuses herself and rushes off to the Ladies.

I compose myself again and call Dad back. "Was he unwell?" I ask.

"No, not at all," Dad replies. "He was laughing and joking as usual when he took his raven to bed at about ten," he says.

"I'll get the first train I can and come home immediately," I suggest, but Dad insists that he and Mum are okay and that there's nothing that I can do for the time being.

"Where's Genghis now?" I ask.

"He's still in bed," says Dad. "We're just waiting for the ambulance."

My eyes are streaming with tears. I promise to call back in a little while to speak to Mum.

Tracey returns, still very upset. "It's so terribly sad," she says. "Genghis was such a lovely person. I can't believe I won't see him again." She looks across the corridor, then turns to look back at me. "How are your parents doing?" she asks.

"Okay, I think," I say. "I'm just going to ring Mum."

"Let me go and get some coffee," says Tracey. As she turns to leave the broom cupboard, I see tears running down her cheeks and all her makeup is smudged.

"You look like a panda," I say and she smiles.

I call Mum. To my relief, she and Dad seem to be coping well. I arrange to go home first thing tomorrow morning.

Tracey returns with the coffee and she too appears reassured to hear that my parents are okay. "Is it okay if I come to the funeral?" she asks.

"Of course you should," I reply. "Mum would love to have you there. If you can, it'd be hugely appreciated," I add.

More tears stream down her cheeks.

"It's a funny thing, though," I say. "My parents are lapsed Jehovah's Witnesses, so f*ck knows what type of funeral it'll be."

With that, we conclude that today we should close the broom cupboard and go to drink a toast to the memory of Genghis.

The world is now a much-diminished place. In the pub, we raise our glasses more than once to Genghis.

Tuesday 28 December 1999
PBS Frontline was first broadcast in 1983

Over the past two weeks I've had neither the inclination nor the heart to commit my thoughts or feelings to my diary. Everyone's emotions are still raw and we're all saddened by our loss. I've spoken with my parents every day. I'm relieved at their decision that Genghis will have a humanist funeral. Rather than focusing on faith, the service will celebrate his life and the considerable joy he's brought to those who've known him.

The undertakers from Last-Stop Funeral Care have been most supportive and they've put my parents in contact with a wonderful lady named Jan, from the British Humanist Association. I've spoken with Jan on a few occasions already and I'm able to provide her with an insight into the joy that knowing Genghis brought to everyone.

"A most unusual name," she says, pensively.

"Not if you knew him," I reply.

When Tracey and I arrive at my parents' home, the house is crammed with flowers and cards. Neighbours from one end of the street to the other have prepared and brought along food to save Mum having to cook and they're all on-hand to do anything they can to help. Tracey and I stay for a light lunch before going to the registry office. We'll then go to the funeral parlour to say goodbye to Genghis.

It's 2pm and a rather too cheerful young man asks if we're there to "hatch, match or dispatch".

"We're here to register a death," I say solemnly.

"Forgive me," he says and we press ahead with the formalities.

The funeral parlour is a few minutes' walk away, but neither Tracey nor I are tempted into any of the pubs we pass.

As we enter the mortuary chapel, we're both taken aback. There's no coffin. Genghis is simply covered in a shroud. Neither of us can say a word. We simply sit, holding each other's hand tightly. I'm not sure how long we're there. It's probably 30 minutes before we each kiss his forehead and shower him with tears.

We thank everyone for their kindness and bid them farewell.

"I need a f*cking drink now," I say, as we make our way into the Old Blue Jug. Consumed with sadness, we sup in silence. Once again, I'm greatly impressed by Tracey's kindness and humanity. I give her a hug and thank her, both of us still crying.

Wednesday 29 December 1999
BBC Radio Stoke was founded in 1968

Tracey slept in my old bed and I lay awake in Genghis's bed for the whole of last night, before getting up at 5am to go for a long walk.

Back home again a couple of hours later, to my surprise everyone is up and resolute. This is a shit day, but we need to support each other to get through it. Mum's cooking bacon, eggs, cheese and oatcakes.

There's no hearse, nor are there any other funeral cars, as the local Crematorium is less than a five-minute walk away from my parents' house. As we're leaving, we discover that the whole street – more than 200 people – is waiting silently along our route to help carry us on our short journey.

Jan greets us as we arrive and calmly reassures us that this is simply a service of celebration for Genghis's life. Genghis is already there at the front of the chapel. We make our way slowly to the front seats. Mum is the first to cry, followed by Tracey, as soon as she sees the raven.

The chapel's packed with people wishing to pay their respects, to support us all and to say good-bye to Genghis.

I only have vague memories of what happened during the service. I don't remember the music, but I do remember the point at the end when my brother began to move backwards and the curtains closed.

As we make our way to thank everyone for coming, Mum stops and, mortified, says, "Now he's not going to see the Olympics."

Through tears, I notice some extraordinary logos are displayed on the wall adjacent to the exit. Going for a closer look, I say to Mum, "Did you know that this is a multi-award-winning crematorium?"

"Of course," says Mum, smiling for the first time today. "Apparently, it's also twinned with the crematorium in Luton and has just signed a suicide pact with the one in Crewe."

I now know where I get my sarcasm from and what should have been a very shit day was, in the end, as good as it could have been. If you ever get the opportunity to visit the Potteries, the crematorium is definitely worth a visit, but perhaps only once, after you've actually died.

DID YOU KNOW THAT THIS IS A
MULTI-AWARD-WINNING CREMATORIUM

Thursday 30 December 1999
The Labette Avenue was first published in 1882

After all the stress of yesterday, Tracey and I are both back today at work. The mood is sombre.

"Life's so much sadder now," says Tracey. "In the last month, I've lost two of my closest and most cherished friends."

She stands up from her chair and sets off to make us both some coffee and I busy myself opening the post. There are a couple of bank statements and a few bits of assorted junk mail that I put straight in the bin. My attention is then drawn by an official, formal-looking letter addressed to Tracey, in an envelope stamped STRICTLY PRIVATE & CONFIDENTIAL – ADDRESSEE ONLY. I slide it to the other side of the desk and wait for Tracey to return.

She places the two mugs on the table, then picks up and opens the letter. As she begins to read it, somewhat impatiently I ask her what it says.

"Look for yourself!" she says handing it back across the desk to me in disbelief.

I clock that it's from a firm of Lincoln's Inn Field's solicitors, whose name I immediately recognise. They're the executors of Mrs Betsy Mainwaring's last will and testament. The letter states in effect that Tracey is to receive a bequest of no less than £10 million, "to acknowledge her kindness and for being a dear friend".

"This must be a joke," says Tracey.

Reading on, I shake my head. "It isn't," I tell her. "I know this firm well. They're highly regarded."

Tracey's face is a picture of shock. I thank her for the coffee, pour in a splash of whisky and take a sip, before saying, "I'm absolutely delighted for you!" A few moments later I ask her, "What do you think you're going to do with the money?"

"I can't believe it!" she says and she sits deep in thought for a couple of minutes before replying. "If this is for real then I'll put at least half of it towards Ralph's artists' colony," she says. "It's the kind of thing I've always wanted to do and this way I can support Ralph, too."

"That's really kind of you," I tell her. "Any thoughts on what you'll do with the rest?"

"Yes," she says firmly. "I'm going to become a Name at Lloyd's! I've heard that they make huge profits and I'd like to get my hands on some of those."

The CIA's trial of cognitive enhancement in Braintree has obviously finished. In the new year, I'll suggest that Tracey seeks proper financial advice. Just not from a bank.

Friday 31 December 1999
At midnight the Millennium Bug will devastate all computer systems and the worldwide web will disappear forever

I'm spending today locked in a police cell. Last night I was driving home absolutely plastered after Christmas drinks with Ralph, when I was flashed by a police car on the North Circular. I thought they wanted a race, so I gave them one, but I had to concede it when I rolled my 12 NOB at the Hangar Lane gyratory.

Despite the obvious risk of a tsunami of unemployment claims from bar staff in the City of London, I've decided to give up the booze. This is a good thing on many levels beyond just a healthier liver.

Meanwhile, Her Majesty the Queen tries to use her bank card to buy a case of vintage Bollinger from the Balmoral branch of Queen Victoria Wine. Her card is declined and confiscated.

She immediately rings Sir Eddie to give him a bollocking, before calling NOB to claim on her MILLENNIUMSAFE policy.

About Curly Cradock
Curly Cradock was born in Hobart, Tasmania, on April Fool's Day 1960

Curly Cradock is fondly remembered as the Einstein (Frank rather than Albert) of the City of London, as a PR genius and as a provocateur who waged a one-man insurgency against financial greed and animal cruelty. With only an honorary PhD in sarcasm and a Guinness World Record, Curly became a pioneer of the early internet. He also exposed the UK's largest financial mis-selling scandal and was responsible for the most potent media hoax of the twentieth century. During his lifetime, Curly received no official recognition for his good works. He was, however, awarded a prize for ethical conduct, but as this was obtained by means of a corrupt payment, it probably doesn't count, unlike the one he got from Robert Maxwell for coming top in criminal law at university. Unfortunately, no prizes were given to Curly for beating Her Majesty the Queen Mother at drunk Twister, Boris Yeltsin at the yard of vodka, or for helping Mother Teresa escape from prison.